GENTLEST OF WILD THINGS

ALSO BY SARAH UNDERWOOD

Lies We Sing to the Sea

GENTLEST
OF
WILD
THINGS

SARAH UNDERWOOD

HARPER

An Imprint of HarperCollinsPublishers

Library of Congress Control Number: 2023943346
ISBN 978-0-06-323452-9

Typography by Corina Lupp
24 25 26 27 28 LBC 5 4 3 2 1
First Edition

for my little sister, Helen—
who makes me kinder
and who I love very much

"But the instant the light fell that way, and the mysteries of the couch were revealed, she beheld the very gentlest and sweetest of all wild creatures . . . at sight of whom the glad flame of the lamp shone doubly bright, and even the wicked knife repented of its edge."

—Apuleius, *The Story of Eros and Psyche*
Edward Carpenter, 1923

PROLOGUE

Alexandra

Alexandra hurled herself through the storeroom door and slammed it shut behind her. There was no lock, nothing to keep it closed, but she pressed the length of her body against the wood and prayed that it would be enough. There was a brass skewer in her hand, snatched from the hearthside as she'd hurtled past it and still flecked with grease and scraps of charred meat. Alexandra clutched it like a sword. Her feet were bare and filthy, the flesh of her arm torn wide open and sticky with blood. Every breath she drew was a gasp—ragged and painful. And *loud.* Too loud. She would be heard. She would be *found.*

No sooner had the thought crossed her mind than there was a sound in the room beyond, a dull, regular thudding. And beneath that, the patter of bare feet on stone. Closer and closer they came, until she could have sworn they were right beside her. Alexandra clasped both hands to her mouth so that the cold of the skewer pressed against her lips. Her throat was raw from screaming; if there was anyone left in the house, she knew by now that they would not be coming to her aid. There was nothing left to do but stay quiet and hope.

She drew in a long, slow breath, cringing as the air whistled in her throat, and strained to listen for movement on the other side of the door. Silence. Alexandra exhaled as quietly as she could and counted from one to twelve, her lips shaping the names of the gods atop Olympus. Nothing. She counted back from twelve to one, ending on Aphrodite. There was no sound now; whatever lay beyond the door was *waiting*. Or, perhaps, it was gone? Alexandra allowed herself the smallest glimmer of hope.

Without lowering her shaking hands from her mouth she turned her head, slowly, slowly, to face the door.

Ah. Not gone. The realization hit her like a blow and she froze, staring. On the other side of the door, through the gaps in the worn wood, a bloodshot golden eye stared back at her. A sob escaped the tight cage of Alexandra's fingers, and the eye narrowed, crinkling at the corners. Alexandra caught a fleeting glimpse of pale bloodless lips—pulled apart and baring teeth. Then they were gone. The eye, the lips, the teeth, all gone.

But where had they gone? *Where?*

Alexandra was not left wondering for long. With an awful rending sound, the door was ripped from its hinges and slammed into her. The skewer clattered uselessly from her fingers as she went flying back into the storeroom, crashing into the sacks that lined the wall. Her head smacked hard against the stone. The sacks were kept atop a low wooden bench to keep them from the damp of the floor and the sand that covered it in a fine layer, but they toppled readily as Alexandra hit them, following her to the ground. She lay there like a discarded doll, dizzy and panting, surrounded by lentils and seeds and grain and the first spill of blood. The door rested atop her. A dull, distant ache radiated from the wrist she'd fallen on.

She turned her head painfully to the side. Her vision spun. Beneath the bulk of the door, she could see nothing but a patch of hazy seed-scattered floor. For a moment, everything was still, then a shadow rippled across the ground, followed by the dancing glimmer of a reflection. A glint of metal like the shine of firelight off a blade. Alexandra turned her head away. What use was watching? It would only make her more afraid. She squeezed her eyes shut and waited, her pulse thrumming frantically in her ears, her throat, her belly, and the tips of her bloodied fingers.

When the door was lifted from her, it was with something like gentleness. A gasp rushed past her lips as the pressure on her chest released and she felt something warm dribbling from the corner of her mouth. Blood. The taste was overwhelming as it began to carve a path across her cheek to drip from her jaw. The dull pain of her wrist flared and hardened. Broken, she was almost sure of it.

There was a sharp ringing thud, something solid making contact with the floor so close to her face that she felt the disturbance in the soft short curls that framed her face. Alexandra whimpered.

"Shhh." A rustling of fabric as the monster knelt. A careful hand caressed Alexandra's face, wiping the blood away. Then the soothing shushing gave way to a foul wet sucking. Alexandra squeezed her eyes shut tighter. Her lips shaped the words of a prayer to Persephone, lady of flowers, goddess of a spring Alexandra would not live to see through.

The hand returned to her jaw and Alexandra leaned wearily into the cool press of fingers. Another hand cupped her opposite cheek so that her face was cradled, tenderly, between two palms. "Please," croaked Alexandra.

She was not sure what she was asking for. But the grip of fingers on her flesh tightened in response—they held her head in a sudden vise, then jerked it sideways.

Alexandra thought she felt it when her neck broke.

I

NO EARTHLY CREATURE

Eirene

Eirene regarded the basket of plums with the same distaste she would have shown the rotting corpse of a rabbit.

The individual fruits were perfect—plump, richly pigmented, unmarked, and identical. They could not have been on the doorstep for long; the morning dew was only just beginning to collect on their shining skins, and Eirene couldn't help but watch a droplet mark a slow, inviting trail downward. Despite herself, she inhaled, and the air was thick with their fragrance.

"Gods, *again*?" Phoebe materialized at her shoulder without warning, a slender, serious wraith in her ivory chiton.

Eirene started, snatching her hands back from the basket of plums. She had barely registered herself reaching for them. "I wasn't . . . ," she began guiltily.

Phoebe hardly seemed to hear her. Her brow was furrowed, and her teeth worried at her lower lip as she leaned past Eirene for a closer look. "The third basket in as many days," she observed flatly. "And they're from *him*, aren't they?"

Eirene nodded reluctantly, unable to meet her twin sister's eyes. "Who but Leandros could find plums at this time of year?" And it was not just plums. Yesterday it had been figs and the day before that pears and a cluster of golden grapes—all perfectly ripe, all impossible to find in these late spring days on Zakynthos.

Eirene had not allowed a single one over the threshold.

Perhaps she was cautious to the point of ridiculousness, but everything about Leandros frightened her. His rumored beauty, unnatural and captivating; the grand house he owned in the hills with its single looming tower; his claims that the blood of gods—of Eros and his divine mother, Aphrodite—flowed in his veins. Then there were the bottled Desires he sold to the wealthiest islanders. He claimed he had inherited the power of love itself, that he could thaw even the iciest of hearts.

Eirene had seen enough to believe it, and she wouldn't be allowing Leandros anywhere near Phoebe, or her heart. What business did Leandros have sending gifts—ones that seemed a lot like *courting* gifts if you asked Eirene—when he already had a wife at home? Round-hipped, wide-eyed Alexandra with her clever tongue and bright laugh had been admired for years and for miles and golden Leandros had won her within weeks of arriving on the island. He *had* his prize and he'd taken enough from Eirene. Neither she nor Phoebe had seen their old friend since her marriage.

"Are we going to tell Stavros?" Phoebe crouched down and picked up a single plum. She straightened, turning it over in her palms. Eirene watched her sister with a knot in her throat.

Phoebe had been plagued by a recurrent fever throughout their childhood—the same fever that had claimed their parents—and it had always been up to Eirene to nurse her sister through each terrifying bout. Over the years, she'd learned which herbs would cool Phoebe's brow or coax her into a heavy dreamless sleep. She'd mastered the art of swapping the sweat-drenched blankets out around her sister's prone form, and she'd even perfected a bone-broth stew that Phoebe could keep down when everything else made her retch.

Still, despite Eirene's best efforts, Phoebe seemed to grow

slighter with each passing winter. Shadows gathered beneath the jut of her collarbones. Over time, the warm brown of her skin had become sallow; her dark curls had lost their luster.

"Eat it," said Eirene reluctantly, nodding at the plum in Phoebe's hands. Though she wouldn't touch a single one herself, she would not—could not—stop Phoebe. They were just plums. They couldn't do her any harm. "As many as you want. But I'm throwing them in the river when you're finished. I don't want Stavros knowing about this."

"He'll find out eventually," said Phoebe reasonably. She pulled apart her plum with her fingers, plucking the stone from the shining yellow flesh with a practiced ease. She tucked one half into each cheek and spoke with her mouth full. "He might be drunk half the time, but he isn't stupid."

"I have to disagree," said Eirene.

"*And,*" said Phoebe, "the window in his bedchamber overlooks the path—one day, he'll sleep off the wine a little earlier and catch sight of whoever's delivering the fruit." She swallowed. Her next words were clear. "Or Leandros will just tell him. Whatever it is he has to tell."

"Perhaps Leandros prefers to keep his business his own."

Phoebe shrugged and ducked down for another plum. Eirene got the sense she was hiding her face. Her voice quavered on her next words. "If you say so."

"I do," said Eirene, with more confidence than she felt. "Are you done? The light's good—if you finish off that chlamys you're making I can take it with me to the market. And I can get rid of these before Stavros sees." She bent down and swung the basket of plums into her arms. Their scent hit her again, harder, and her mouth filled with saliva. She must have been hungrier than she realized.

"Let me have one more." Phoebe stretched out her hand. Her calloused fingers were sticky with juice and there were crescents of dark plum skin caught beneath the bitten-down nails. Eirene couldn't stifle the shiver of guilt that ran down her spine; weaving was a fiercely physical task and it cost Phoebe more than angry new blisters and dozens of little cuts where the rough twists of wool had been drawn across her flesh. She would work from dawn till dusk, until she physically could not go on and the relentless overwork pushed her into another spell of sickness. She needed rest—they both knew it—but no one had talent like Phoebe. They could not afford for her to stop, and Phoebe would say as much whenever Eirene begged her to take even a day of respite.

Eirene pushed two more plums into her sister's dye-stained palm. "Go on," she said gruffly. "I need to leave soon."

"Don't forget to pick the rosemary," said Phoebe. "The physician always needs more *and* he pays well for it."

"I *know*," said Eirene, who had forgotten to pick the rosemary. "Mind your own business. Is the chlamys ready?"

Phoebe rolled her eyes. "Don't harass me. You can't hurry art." Before Eirene could reply—to say that she'd better hurry if she didn't want to starve—Phoebe had whirled on one bare foot, the plums clutched to her chest, and scurried into the house. Her footsteps were light on the tiled floor. They were all but silent on the stairs.

It was an unspoken rule between the two of them, staying quiet until they knew that Stavros had awoken. Even then, they kept their voices low—their cousin was invariably in a foul temper after a night of heavy drinking and losses at the gambling tables. Last night had been one of Leandros's grand symposia, where all his guests drank for free, so Stavros would be twice as unpleasant this morning.

Eirene scowled at the thought of the symposium. If Stavros ever knew of Leandros's gifts, he'd certainly make the same assumption that Eirene had—that Leandros grew bored of his wife. That he sought a new addition to his bed. Stavros would be overjoyed at the prospect of having such a powerful ally; no matter that Phoebe would be little more than a mistress, easily discarded—Stavros would march her to Leandros's gilded bedchamber himself.

It could not be allowed to happen. Eirene squared her shoulders, propped the basket on her hip, and set off down the path toward the river. She cursed Leandros with every step.

The house that Eirene and Phoebe shared with their cousin stood alone atop a low hill outside the village. It was an unremarkable building, indistinguishable from every other in the village below: two stories of mud and wood, a handful of windows, and a wide straw-thatched roof in dire need of repair. Stavros's father had been a shepherd, and the house's position gave it a fine prospect over the now empty pastures and the river that wound around them. It also meant that its occupants had to tramp up and down the hill every time they went out, which only served to add to Eirene's foul temper as she stalked back up the path.

The remaining plums had not sunk when she'd tossed them into the river; they'd bobbed on the water's surface, mocking her even as they were swept downstream. She'd kept the basket to use for herbs—she always needed more baskets—but she'd smacked it against every tree she'd passed on her way back, swept it through the dust outside the house, and made sure to tuck it beneath the stack of others she kept by the door. Now battered and dusty, it blended in seamlessly. Phoebe was right—as much as he drank,

Stavros remained surprisingly sharp-witted. He could spot any new purchase in an instant and would spend weeks hounding Eirene over it. Once, she'd finally bought herself new sandals, two years after the old ones had first started falling apart, and he'd been so enraged he'd threatened to turn her out onto the street for wasting his money. *His* money, as if he'd earned a single coin. Even the memory of it made Eirene's cheeks hot with anger. She scowled and gave the pile of baskets another kick for good measure.

Inside, she stoked the hearth that burned low in the center of the single downstairs room before padding up the only staircase, placing her feet carefully as to make only the smallest sounds. When she reached the chamber she shared with Phoebe, for sleeping and working alike, she gave the door a gentle push. It gave way beneath her touch.

Eirene slipped inside. "Phoebe?"

Her twin was perched on her stool in a patch of dappled light by the window, the finished chlamys—woven in strands of cream and wine—clutched in her slender arms. She did not turn to face Eirene right away; it was only after another, quieter, "Phoebe?" that she did.

"Eirene," said Phoebe. She smiled and, looking like that—even with dark circles under her eyes and hollows in her cheeks and an anxious twitch in her fingers—it was easy to see why Leandros wanted her. She was not just lovely; she was thoughtful and deliberate and kinder than Eirene ever was. Eirene was quick to temper, but Phoebe always knew how to soothe her rage with a few careful words.

Phoebe cleared her throat. She shook out the chlamys: a long rectangle of pale wool, a pattern picked out on its edges in crimson. "Here."

Eirene took it. She had a sickening thought that this might be the last thing Phoebe made before she was snatched away by Leandros. No. *No.* That would not happen. Eirene would not allow it. She cleared her throat. "It's pretty."

"And?"

Eirene winced. Was she truly that easy to read? "Nothing." She scrambled for an excuse. "Well, just that the cold weather is coming to an end. Not so many people needing new cloaks."

Phoebe frowned. "You'll manage. You always do."

"Yes," Eirene agreed too hastily.

There was a long silence as the two of them gazed at one another. Phoebe chewed on her lower lip and clasped her hands together. There was blood on her teeth.

Eirene broke the quiet first. "I suppose I should get going." She turned back toward the door.

"Eirene?" Phoebe's voice was suddenly very small.

"Yes, Phoebe?"

"You'll make sure you get a good price for it, won't you? You never know how long the money might have to last."

Eirene tightened her grip on the cloak, her fingers digging into the soft wool. They wouldn't make it to the end of the summer without Phoebe. Not with Stavros gambling away every coin he could get his hands on, buying more wine than he could ever afford, and forcing Eirene to slink shamefaced into the brothel in the morning to pay off his bills. And that was just *money.* How long could Eirene bear to be parted from Phoebe? They had come into the world entwined already, born knowing one another better than anyone else ever could. Eirene wasn't sure she knew how to exist on her own. "Phoebe—" she began.

A peculiar look passed across Phoebe's face. "Don't forget the rosemary," she said.

There might have been more, but they both froze at movement in the neighboring room. There was a rustle of blankets, then the thud of unsteady feet on floorboards. Stavros had awoken. Phoebe's expression hardened. Eirene felt her own face twist. Together, they listened to Stavros lurch toward his window and throw open the shutters. A pause, then there came the distinct sound of urination, followed by an indecently loud grunt of relief. Another time, they might have grinned at each other, smothered their sniggers, but today—

"Eirene," Phoebe began, "do you ever think maybe I should—"

"No," said Eirene. The word was hard and brittle, like a broken jar in her mouth.

"You know what Leandros is. You know what he can do. Could you really stop me if I was determined to go? If I loved him?"

"You *don't* love him," snapped Eirene.

"I'm *afraid*," said Phoebe.

Eirene had swallowed the broken pieces of the jar; now they were tearing their way through her insides. "Afraid of what?"

"That I will." Phoebe spoke quietly, but each word was painfully clear. "Love him. That he'll make me, and you won't be able to stop him."

II

THE FIRST ARROW

Eirene

It was midmorning by the time Eirene arrived at the market square, laden down with baskets of fresh herbs—five bundles of that damned rosemary alongside the parsley and the fennel and the mint and the rest. Beside the herbs was a careful selection of tinctures she'd brewed and decanted into little clay jars and, finally—kept meticulously separate from the rest so as not to dirty it—Phoebe's cloak. Which she intended to sell for more than all the rest combined. She still felt sick to her stomach, Phoebe's words echoing through her ears. *I'm afraid.*

He'll make me, and you won't be able to stop him.

Eirene set the baskets down clumsily. The blanket she used as her storefront was strapped to her back. She pulled it free and knelt to spread it over the ground in her usual spot—easily identifiable by the neat row of rocks left there. She placed one at each corner of the blanket, then sat back on her heels, staring out at the square with dismay.

The market had once seemed to Eirene to be the beating heart of the village: a bustling, buzzing hive of activity full of carts and stalls and rickety tables and dozens of people shoving their way between them. Now, with half the sellers gone and fewer buyers with each passing day, it was like a graveyard.

Today, only two other stalls were manned: the shoemaker's,

which she hadn't seen sell a pair in weeks, run by a craftsman so ancient he probably remembered the Titans' reign but had forgotten that he wanted to make money; and the baker's cart, with its mountains of fresh pillowy bread. That one was tended by a tall girl with a drawn pale face. Xenia. It made Eirene's heart ache to look at her. Xenia had been a living ghost since her little sister, Clyte, had left to check the bakery ovens one morning and never returned. There were rumors they'd tracked her to the house of a merchant three villages over, and that the man had spat in their faces when they'd demanded her safe return. He'd claimed that Clyte was his wife and that her family had no rightful claim to her anymore. Now, standing alone at her cart, Xenia gazed blankly at the steaming piles of flatbread before her. Unable to stand witness to her suffering a moment longer, Eirene looked away, her eyes searching the rest of the square. It was a pitiful sight.

Though most of the unused carts had at least been dragged away, a handful remained—on their sides, with broken wheels, the wood rotting away—as if their owners had vanished into thin air. More likely, they had been recruited into Leandros's growing staff. It seemed everyone in the village served him these days.

The abandoned stalls were just as depressing. One had belonged to the village physician. He had stopped sending his apprentices out to the market with bottles of tinctures and fragrant poultices. Another had belonged to a young woman who sold bundles of flowers from her garden, baskets of dried petals, and tiny jars of rose oil. After selling a particularly beautiful tapestry of Phoebe's last summer, Eirene had bought two jars of the oil—one for Phoebe and one for her—and rationed it as if it were ambrosia, putting a single drop behind each of her ears in the morning. She'd heard no story of what had happened to the flower seller. One day, she had simply been gone, her stall deserted, her garden left to go wild.

Behind that was the goat shepherd's stand. The goat pen stood empty, the stall before it equally barren. This late in spring, with summer a matter of days away, the kidding season was long finished and even the weakest of the newborns would have been put to pasture. This was the time when the shepherd usually sent his daughters to the market with the first of the year's kids—sturdy, vocal things that would fetch a decent price and provide a great deal of amusement to the rest of the stallholders as they leaped easily from their pens and led muscular Chloe or sweet little Frona on a wild chase. But there were no braying little goats here and, even more conspicuously, no Chloe or Frona.

Eirene frowned at the abandoned stall as she began to unpack her herbs and spread them out upon the blanket. The word was that a pair of noblemen from the north of Kefalonia had become enamored with the girls on a visit to the village—more likely, on their way to one of Leandros's famed symposia, since little else drew such attendants—and had spirited them away to become their brides. The shepherd would not have let his daughters go without a fight, if it had not been for both girls declaring themselves utterly and completely in love.

Few people dared to whisper what they all thought—that it was not love at all but Desire. Desire made and offered and sold for an extraordinary sum by Leandros.

Eirene scowled, her fist tightening around the bouquet of parsley she held. It was a welcome relief when a familiar cry split the air. "Rosemary!"

Eirene looked up, already grinning, the tension falling from her limbs like water off a duck's sleek back. Damon was the physician's boy, but he was also Eirene's friend. Perhaps the only real friend she had in the village now, since the rest of them—not just Alexandra and Chloe and Frona and Clyte, but Alcestis and Elene and Ianthe too—had suddenly been plucked up and carried away to marriages in the far-off corners of Zakynthos. Eirene had waited patiently, naively, for word of some kind, an invitation to visit or just the idle gossip from their new homes. Ianthe, the last to disappear, had been married a full season and Eirene was still waiting.

"Rosemary!" Damon declared again, startling her from her thoughts as he snatched up two of the bundles that Eirene had just laid down. Eirene realized she'd been grinding her teeth and forced herself to relax her jaw. She turned her attention to Damon. Strands of his shaggy dusty-brown hair fell into his eye, catching on the leather patch that covered the remnants of the other, the eye the fever had stolen from him. He pushed the loose curls back and grinned at her, folding his skinny torso in a mocking bow. "Eirene, my rosemary queen, you have saved me once again. We're fresh out, and you know it'll be my fault if it stays that way."

Eirene laughed, sitting back on her haunches. "There're three more bunches in there for you. Does your master need anything else?"

"Mint, peony root, parsley, fennel, sideritis," Damon rattled off. His chiton hung ragged to his pale bony shins and Eirene frowned at it absently as she methodically retrieved the herbs he'd asked for. It said much of the physician that he kept his apprentice so poorly attired. Perhaps it lessened a little of her jealousy that Damon—her friend truly, but a boy without even a fraction of her skill—had been taken on while she had been turned away.

Her humiliation had been bitter. The physician always bought her herbs, had even taken her advice on the best way to brew them once or twice. But when she had finally mustered up the courage to admit to him what she wanted—to learn from him, to be a true physician herself—he had turned her away without a moment's thought.

"And saffron if you have it," added Damon hopefully.

Eirene blinked away the memory of the healer's rejection and laughed, perhaps with more scorn than her friend deserved. Her hands were full with a neat package of peony root, wrapped in a square of sackcloth. "Saffron?" she scoffed. "And where would I find saffron on Zakynthos at this time of year? They're an autumn flower. Be sensible, Damon."

He shrugged, putting his hands out for the peony. "Rumor says there's crocus patches growing on the cliffs. *Special* patches, it says."

Eirene snorted and tossed him the package, then set to work retrieving the fennel and parsley. "Sounds to me like someone's trying to thin out the competition by sending them on ridiculous expeditions. Those cliffs are treacherous."

"I'm sure someone will try it." Damon picked at the edges of the sackcloth. "Not everyone is afraid of heights."

Eirene scowled. "Do you *want* to pay double for that?"

He ignored her irritation and leaned in closer. "The whispers came from Leandros's man."

Eirene stiffened. "What?"

"Right. Some fool will get it in his head that he can trade a crocus for one of Leandros's Desires and then—"

"Leandros would hardly part with his Desires for so little." Eirene could feel the flicker of her heartbeat drumming behind her eyes. She blinked hard and busied herself with bundling sideritis. "It would take a great fool to believe that there are saffron crocuses growing on Zakynthos, let alone to think that a hundred of them could pay for one drop of Desire." She forced certainty into her voice and thrust the remaining herbs up at Damon. He balanced them atop the others with some difficulty. "Leandros is a liar and he is poisoning our home with his vile enchantments. Soon, everyone else will realize it, and then he'll depart Zakynthos just as swiftly as he came. Good riddance."

No matter that Leandros had been there nearly five years now, arriving in the desolation that had followed the fever and swiftly setting up his household to take advantage of whoever was left. Eirene clenched her fists. "How much is all this worth, then?" She changed the subject abruptly, waving her hands at the precarious piles of herbs in Damon's arms. He was avoiding eye contact, though she couldn't be sure whether that was because of her tirade or because of the question he must know she was about to ask. "Enough to pay for Phoebe's medicine?"

Damon winced. "Eirene—"

She interrupted him quickly, before his expression could become *too* pitying. She had not expected a yes. "It's fine. How much is left?"

Eirene had an unusual arrangement with the physician. He provided her with a particular tincture for Phoebe, one she had never quite managed to replicate. He claimed it had magic in it—some enchantment from his long-ago travels on the mainland—and Eirene staunchly disbelieved him. But the truth of the matter was that there was *something* about it she could never identify. And it helped Phoebe. When she had one of her worst days, shivering and nauseous and dizzy, a splash of the medicine steeped in hot water could soothe the very worst of it. She would still retch at the smell of most food, of course, and it did not eliminate the fever entirely, but it would bring it down enough that it would not be deadly. Sometimes that was all they could hope for. Eirene paid off her debt to the healer with a ready and regular supply of her herbs.

"The end of the month, he told me," said Damon.

Eirene sighed. She just had to hope the warmer spring weather kept Phoebe strong. "It'll have to do."

"I thought you said she needs it less often now."

"One good year guarantees nothing," said Eirene stubbornly.

Damon shrugged. "I suppose not." He scuffed his battered sandals against the dirt. Then his face brightened. "Still, don't you want to know what I heard about Leandros from my master?"

"I don't know. . . ." Eirene wished she did not care. But she did. The more she knew about Leandros, the better she could protect Phoebe from him.

"It's about his wife."

That settled it. Eirene gritted her teeth. "What is it?"

Damon looked about quickly, then, seemingly satisfied that no one was eavesdropping, knelt down with Eirene and leaned in surreptitiously.

Eirene leaned back from the branches of rosemary that were abruptly shoved into her face. "Damon!" she protested. "Careful."

Damon ignored her, leaning in closer again. "When Leandros's wife died, my master—"

"She *what*?" Without quite meaning to, Eirene shot to her feet, almost headbutting Damon in the process. Her vision blurred alarmingly and she swayed where she stood. Leandros's wife had died. *Alexandra* had died. Alexandra, who had been two years her senior, bold and bossy, full of joy and wit and charm. Alexandra, whose cheeks had always been round and pink, whose skin was bright and suntanned, who the fever had barely even touched. Alexandra, who was so alive.

Until, without warning, without explanation, she wasn't.

The final realization hit Eirene like a rockfall. She clutched at Damon for stability, her mind racing with sudden clarity and understanding and cold, terrifying dread. There was a new danger now, and Alexandra's death had just been the start of it.

If she was dead, then Leandros no longer had a wife. Which meant that Leandros did not want Phoebe as a lover to discard by the year's end. He wanted to *marry* her.

"Eirene?" Damon's strangled voice seemed to be coming from very far away. "*Eirene.*"

Eirene blinked, clearing some of the fog over her eyes. "Oh," she said. She'd caught Damon by the front of his chiton and seemed to be doing her best to choke him. "Sorry," she managed, and let go. She took a stumbling step backward, tripping over the edge of her blanket. Damon lunged to steady her, succeeding only in yanking on her hair as she tumbled to the ground. She sat among her herbs, her scalp smarting, her tailbone stinging, her ears ringing with the words *when Leandros's wife died*, over and over and over.

"Eirene." Damon knelt beside her. "Are you all right? I'm sorry, I didn't realize you didn't know. I'd forgotten you were friends, or I'd have never—"

"When did she die?" interrupted Eirene. She pushed her hair back from her face, suddenly hating the brush of her curls on her cheeks. Her grip, her control over the world around her, was slipping faster than she knew how to handle.

"Five days ago," said Damon. "In the evening, I think, but my master was called for first thing the next morning."

Five days. It was so few. Leandros's first gift for Phoebe had been sent just two days later.

Damon lowered his voice "And that's not all."

He leaned in. Eirene leaned back just a little; she couldn't bear anyone being so close to her right now. She was sure she was on the verge of tears and Damon seemed oblivious. His cheeks were still flushed with the thrill of his secret. "Last night, I overheard my master talking with old Otus, who digs the graves of patients who die and must have buried Alexandra, too, because they both were agreeing that it was no ordinary death. No *natural* death, I mean. They were saying that there was something terribly, awfully wrong with her."

"Something wrong with her," repeated Eirene in a whisper.

Damon nodded. "Something wrong with the *body*. As if she had been savaged by an animal, some kind of wild thing. A wolf maybe, or a bear, or a lion." He leaned in again and this time Eirene did not move away. Damon spoke in the faintest of whispers: "My master said she had been—"

"Well, I am loath to break apart this little romance," interrupted a hard, irritable voice.

Eirene sprang back from Damon, knocking into a basket of parsley and sending the herb flying everywhere. She blinked up at the newcomer and recognized with an irrepressible shiver the mint-green edges of his chiton and the shining brass brooches pinning it at his shoulders. Peiros. Leandros's manservant. The only member of the household who wasn't brought in from the village each morning to be dismissed again each evening before the sun had even set. If Leandros had secrets, Peiros surely knew them all. Peiros would know exactly what Leandros intended with Phoebe.

Peiros cleared his throat. "And yet," he continued with pointed disdain, "I must. I cannot wait around all day. A word of advice, herbalist—continue your courting *after* you've sold your wares."

Damon spluttered. "Courting? I am *not*—"

"Damon," said Eirene swiftly, before Damon could blurt out

what they had *actually* been discussing. "Your master will be expecting you." She pressed a hand to her side and tried to force herself to breathe more evenly. She could handle Peiros. He was just a man.

Damon hadn't moved. He glanced between Eirene and Peiros with wide eyes.

"*Damon*," said Eirene again.

Damon took the hint. He shot a final appraising look at Peiros, then scurried away, his arms laden with bundles of herbs and the package of peony root. *For women's pains*, recalled Eirene bitterly as she watched him go. *And for the treatment of convulsions.* She did not begrudge her friend his post, not really, not always, but— *gods*—how she longed to join him.

"Herbalist?"

With great reluctance, Eirene returned her attention to the man towering above her. She clambered to her feet, brushing every speck of dirt and greenery from her chiton before condescending to meet his eyes. She curled her lip pointedly. "What can I do for you?"

He looked over her remaining wares, raising his brows as his gaze came to rest on the mess of spilled parsley. Eirene scowled. She was the best herbalist on the whole island and she knew it. Her selection was the greatest and her plants the finest. When she could, she hounded the foreign visitors to the village with requests for seeds and bulbs and cuttings, and paid them handsomely for their troubles if they ever returned with what she asked for. It was that which meant there was dried Laconian thyme laid out before her alongside Olympus yarrow and the delicate flowers of the Acropolis.

Some folks liked to tease that she was blessed by Demeter; even Phoebe would smile and say that nothing could do anything but thrive if Eirene set her hands on it. Still, as much as Eirene made her prayers and her offerings, she could claim no godly favor. Everything she had, she had clawed from the earth with her own work-worn hands.

"Are you listening?"

Eirene blinked, yanked rudely from her thoughts. "What?" Normally, she tried to be polite to customers, but this man was *Leandros's,* so he deserved all her scorn. She didn't want his coin. She wanted nothing to do with him or his master.

Peiros gave her an oily smile. "I was asking after your sister. Pretty Phoebe."

Eirene stiffened. "What about her?"

Peiros toyed with one of his brooches. "How is her health?"

That wasn't the question Eirene had expected. *How does she feel about marrying a monster?* would have been her first guess. But her *health*? What could that matter? "Fine," she said tersely.

"But she doesn't join you at the market?" Peiros was watching her closely with unsettling, interested eyes.

"She's weaving," snapped Eirene. It was a hard walk to the village and back, and Phoebe reserved all her energy for weaving now. Eirene wished they were not so poor, that Phoebe did not feel she had to work as she did just to keep them all fed.

"Shame. I should have liked to have seen her," said Peiros idly. "But I suppose it can't be helped. I'll take everything you have here."

Eirene blinked. "What?"

"I *said* that I'll take it all." He tapped his sandaled foot impatiently on the dusty earth as he spoke. "Everything you're selling."

"What?" She needed to stop saying what. He wanted to buy everything. *Everything.* Eirene shot to her feet. "I mean, are you sure? All of it?"

"Is that a problem?"

Damn her principles to Hades and back. She would not scorn Leandros's custom if Leandros's custom was *this*. This would be enough coin for a month. More than a month if she could keep it hidden from Stavros. Enough coin that Eirene might be able to convince Phoebe to spend a few days away from her loom. Maybe they could go to the sea or at least down to the river. When was the last time they had swam together? Eirene forced herself to offer Peiros her most beatific smile. "Not at *all*." She quickly tidied the mint back into its basket and arranged the herbs and tinctures in front of him. "You can return the baskets to me tomorrow. The same spot."

He sniffed dismissively. "I'll buy the baskets, too."

"Of course." Eirene could scarcely draw breath. Oh, she'd charge him twice their value without blinking. "Do you need help carrying your purchases to your"—she cast her eyes around—"cart?"

"No cart. I can manage a handful of baskets, girl."

"Well then . . ." Eirene gave the purse tied to his belt a significant look.

Peiros was not looking at her; he was staring, frowning, at something behind her. "How much for that?" he said abruptly. "With all the rest?"

Eirene turned to follow the line of his gaze. Her heart gave a leap. Phoebe's cloak, still rolled neatly in its basket. She'd not gotten around to unpacking it, to folding it in such a way that the careful details of the trim would catch the eye of any passerby. Except this one. Not one of Leandros's men.

Peiros was still waiting for a reply.

"It's expensive," she said at last.

"Name your price."

The money wasn't worth the risk. Eirene named a price so outrageous she wondered how she did not choke on the number. Twice its true worth if not more.

Peiros hardly blinked. "Done." He opened his purse and began to count out the coins.

"Done?" echoed Eirene. "You—you're buying it?"

He did not look up from his purse. "You are a very poor peddler," he said. "One would almost think you don't want to see your wares sold."

Eirene opened her mouth to retort. Then, as he withdrew his hand from the purse and her eyes caught the glimmer of silver, she shut it.

"Here." Peiros thrust the coins at her and she had just enough time to cup her hands together before silver was spilling into them. She gazed at the money blankly. So much for a simple cloak. How could such a price ever be justified? Then slowly, stiffly, as if the movements were not her own, she turned and dropped the mess of silver into an empty rosemary basket.

When she turned back, Peiros was scooping up the baskets of herbs and roots. He jerked his head impatiently at her. "The weaving, too." And somewhere in the back of her mind she registered that he did not even know what he had bought. It could have been a blanket or a saddlecloth. Cold bars of apprehension seemed to cage her chest. She had made a mistake. What could Leandros do with his Desires and Phoebe's weaving? Could he enchant her away from her family? Force her to accept his relentless attentions? No, surely not. If Desire could work so distantly, then the whole village—the whole *island*—would be under Leandros's thumb. And it wasn't. Not quite yet. This must be another plot to woo Phoebe, a display of wealth akin to a bird's bright plumage. But Phoebe would never know of it. Eirene snatched up the cloak and wordlessly added it to the pile in Peiros's arms.

His answer was a short grunt. He turned smartly on his heels, the baskets teetering, and marched away.

III

PERILS ON WATER

Eirene

Eirene stood there for some time, her mind blank with incredulity. What had just happened? Was it a dream? But, no, there were the coins, as plain as the nose on her face. She crossed her eyes. Yes, her nose was definitely still there.

As if in a daze, she gathered up the few empty baskets from Damon's purchases. The money she stowed in the leather purse tied about her waist. She'd never seen it so full. That realization ignited the first flicker of hope in her heart—with this money she could pay off her debt to the healer, no herbs required. Perhaps she could even beg another jar of tincture that would last them well into the winter. And dyes. She could not stop herself from smiling just a little. *Dyes.* Rich, rare pigments from the mainland so that Phoebe's next work was not just skillfully rendered but woven in the brightest colors there were. Eirene could demand an even greater price for such a piece.

That was, if Leandros did not claim Phoebe first. The thought was instantly sobering.

Eirene swayed where she stood, rocking between her toes and her heels, seized with the sudden urge to run. Back to the house, back to Phoebe, if only to be certain that her sister was still there.

Of course she'll still be there. Eirene shook her head, as if that would clear it of the anxious fog that hung over her thoughts. It wasn't as though Leandros would just snatch Phoebe from her home in the middle of the day. Eirene glanced up at the sky—at the weak sun struggling to break through the clouds directly above her. That decided it; it was barely midday and there was too much risk in returning now, with her purse full and Stavros certainly still at home. Besides, Damon hadn't finished telling her about Alexandra—Peiros had cut him off—and Eirene wanted to know *everything*.

Phoebe was safe for now, and Eirene was going to do whatever she could to make sure she stayed that way.

The physician's house was a squat mud-brick building on the west side of the village. By the time Eirene slipped back out through the open door the sun had reached its peak in the sky and begun to descend.

The purse at her waist was noticeably lighter and she held a round stoppered jar—Phoebe's medicine, the old jar paid off in full. She'd bought dyes, too, rare ones that the physician had collected on his trips to the mainland—a purple she knew her sister would love, and the red she tore through like wildfire. Damon had been gone by the time she'd arrived—sent by his master on an errand to the north of the island—so she still did not know what he had been about to tell her, but the colors of the dye and the thought of Phoebe's face when she saw them had been enough to ease the weight of dread on her heart. Eirene cradled the jar against her chest and made for home.

As she neared the eastern edge of the village, Eirene slowed. Ahead loomed the walls of the brothel. A relatively recent addition to the landscape, the building was quiet and dark now, but come early evening the windows would be bright with light and laughter. There were new girls every week and they seemed to grow sweeter—and younger—each time. Leandros must be turning a pretty profit. Everyone knew it was his magic that kept them so lovely.

Eirene knew from the smell of his clothes, discarded on the stairs for her and Phoebe to collect and wash, that Stavros spent many a night here; had he had the coin for it? She set her jaw and pulled the strings of her purse tighter. Stavros could pay his own debts today.

She marched past the brothel, turning the jar over and over in her hand and trying to convince herself that she'd done the right thing. She was a good sister. She had sold Phoebe's cloak. She had bought Phoebe's medicine. She had frightened off Peiros, so that he would not steal Phoebe away. So why did she feel like she'd made a terrible mistake?

"This will last you another season. Don't leave it so late next time. My master does not like to be hurried."

Eirene stopped dead, her fingers stilling on the curve of the jar. She knew that voice. *Peiros.* Without quite realizing she was doing it, she flattened herself against the brothel wall and held her breath, listening.

"I am sure that I paid quite enough for the inconvenience." The answering voice was undoubtably one of a wealthy man. Plummy, colored with the sharpness of entitlement. "I will not be hurried through such a delicate business."

"You would do well to remember your place. My *master—*"

Eirene strained to hear more, but Peiros's voice had fallen to little more than a whisper. Well, if she could not hear him, the least she could do was *see* him. She squared her shoulders and marched around the corner. Where she walked straight into someone—someone warm and smelling faintly of roses and small enough that their collision knocked her straight to the ground, the breath tumbling from her lips in a high bewildered gasp.

Unable to stop herself in time, Eirene tripped over her, and they were reduced to a tangle of limbs and bewilderment in the dirt. She cradled the jar against her chest as she fell, careful not to let it be damaged.

"Watch where you're going, won't you?" The voice came from someone standing nearby—pompous and irritated.

"Hard to see around corners," said Eirene only a little sharply. "Why on earth were you standing there?" She sat back on her haunches and examined the girl she'd bowled over. Thin, dark hair, narrow brown arms. The girl was tiny and birdlike, even though she was a year Eirene's senior—seventeen to Eirene's sixteen.

"Ianthe!" Eirene was surprised by her own delight, by the flood of relief that went through her. She'd been so caught up in worrying about Phoebe, she'd quite forgotten that anyone else existed. But Ianthe was here; she was fine. "Sorry for smashing into you like that." She offered Ianthe her hand. "I haven't seen you for *months*! Where have you been?"

Ianthe took Eirene's proffered hand and offered her a bright, stupid smile. Her eyes were utterly blank. "Hello."

No. No, no, no. Understanding flooded Eirene in an instant. It was not like Ianthe to stare like that, as if there wasn't a thought in her head. Ianthe's father was a blacksmith, and she had kept a small stall for him at the market. It was impossible to cheat her; Eirene had always admired Ianthe's quick wits and her sharp tongue. But Desire—for what else could it be?—had stolen them.

"I'll ask that one such as yourself does not speak to my wife."

There was suddenly a hand tight about Eirene's forearm. She lost her grip on Ianthe as she was hauled unceremoniously to her feet. She found herself staring into the watery blue eyes of a man.

She recoiled from him. His skin was a translucent grayish film stretched over the stark bones of his face. His lips were narrow and dry and twisted into a cruel smile. The expression exposed teeth that were a fetching shade of brown.

"Your wife." Eirene repeated. This man was old enough to be Ianthe's father. Her *grandfather*, even. She cast a slow appraising eye over him. He was richly attired: his chlamys an expensive yellow, his chiton finely woven and trimmed with a repeating pattern in the same hue as the cloak. It was pinned at his shoulders with matching gold brooches. And behind him, watching her with shrewd narrowed eyes, was Peiros. Eirene looked between them, fear blooming like a weed in her belly.

"Yes," snapped the man. "My wife." He had made no move to retrieve Ianthe from the dirt. She sat there, blinking doe-eyed into the distance, that radiant smile still plastered over her face. She did not seem to notice the dust on her cheeks nor the twig that had knotted itself in her hair.

"Ianthe?" said Eirene. Desperation made her voice break.

"I am very happy," said Ianthe brightly. Her eyes slid past Eirene and her expression became sultry. "I'm in love."

"Didn't I just tell you not to speak to her?" The man—Ianthe's *husband*—puffed himself up. Perhaps he thought it made him impressive. He looked like a broody hen fluffing up her feathers so as to appear intimidating. Eirene noticed for the first time the squat plain jar clutched in one spidery hand. "Now, if you'll kindly remove yourself from my path . . ." He turned toward Ianthe.

"What is that?" blurted Eirene. She felt sick to the depths of her stomach. Desire brandished openly. He was not even ashamed enough to conceal it.

"I beg your pardon?" His eyes flashed and his skeletal fingers twitched toward the flashy little blade strapped at his waist. What were the odds he didn't know how to use it? Or, at least, that he wouldn't dare to use it on her? It was a bet Stavros might take.

Eirene supposed she had more in common with her cousin than she thought. "Tell me what's in that jar," she demanded. "Tell me what you've done to my friend."

Peiros let out an audible snort. "I'll be going now," he said, addressing Ianthe's husband and totally ignoring both Eirene and Ianthe. "I'll see you in the summer." He turned on his heel and strode away, disappearing into the narrow backstreets without a backward glance.

The man barely seemed to notice Peiros's departure; he waved him off without looking. His eyes, fixed on Eirene, had narrowed with astonishment at her impertinence. "Perhaps that sour face of yours is a blessing, girl," he snarled. "You will never know the taste of Desire. Oh, you are lucky that Leandros is already set on a wife. How I'd long to see you brought to your knees before him—"

"So there is Desire in that jar, is there? Of course there is." Eirene hurled the words at him as if they were stones. "How else could you convince Ianthe to marry such a dried-out old fish of a man? The Ianthe I knew would *never*—"

She had gone too far. But it was too late and an instant later she found herself flung against the rough walls of the brothel, her head colliding with the aged wood before she crumpled to the ground. He had *slapped* her across the face. A stinging backhand that left a smoldering patch of fire behind it. Stunned, she dropped Phoebe's medicine into the basket with the dyes. She put her hand to her flaming cheek. Tears—of pain, of a *fury* that encompassed her until she was shivering with it—welled in her eyes.

Her tongue had become a dead, leaden thing. She could not stand, let alone manage a single word as Ianthe's husband dragged his silent wife to her feet and marched her away. Eirene watched them go, tears stinging her eyes. There had been nothing left of her friend in that doe-eyed obedient girl. The Ianthe that Eirene had known was gone.

IV

BORN AND BROUGHT FORTH

Eirene

Eirene returned to a quiet house, the door propped open with a sandal—one of Phoebe's—to let the cool air in. The downstairs room was empty, the hearth burning low and the air sweet with the scent of drying herbs. It was a comfort, but Eirene could not escape the memory of Ianthe's blank face, nor of Peiros slinking away into the shadows.

Eirene kicked off her sandals. Clutching her basket to her chest, she began to creep up the stairs. Her feet were light and practiced; she could have been a spirit moving soundlessly across the earth. That was until the side of her foot collided with something round and solid that went skittering loudly down the stairs, shattering the silence. The stopper for one of Stavros's wine jars. Eirene swore under her breath, frozen in place as it clattered onto the floor downstairs.

If she was lucky, Stavros would be sleeping again, or at least would have no interest in emerging from his room to investigate his cousin's comings and goings.

She was not lucky.

Stavros's door banged open and her cousin stumbled onto the narrow landing. His eyes, bloodshot and unfocused, slid over Eirene and back again before settling on her face. His features twisted in a sudden, fierce anger. "And where have you been?"

Eirene lifted the basket up in a hopeless sort of shrug. "I was at the market, Stavros. I go there almost every day. I—"

"Don't patronize me!" He stumbled down the stairs toward her. Was he *still* drunk? The sour smell of wine reached her and her belly writhed with revulsion. There had been a time, the merest of memories now, when Stavros had been kind and mild-mannered. *That* Stavros would never have spoken to her like this. But that was before the symposia and the brothel and the drinking and the debt.

"Where is it, then?" snapped Stavros. He had reached the step above her; there was an arm's breadth of space left between them.

Eirene blinked upward. Stavros was not a tall man, but he towered over her like this. "Where . . ." She cleared her throat. "Where's what?"

Stavros's face twitched and Eirene fought back the urge to cower beneath his furious gaze. "The money," he snarled. "You've been at the market all morning, no? What do you have to show for it?"

"I—" Eirene couldn't help it. She glanced at the basket nestled in the crook of her left arm. The little jars of dye and the medicine for Phoebe were clearly visible. And her purse was almost empty because of it.

When she looked back at Stavros, his eyes were fixed on the dyes. "Eirene," he said quietly, "I consider myself a reasonable man. Don't you think so?"

"Yes," said Eirene. Her hands were trembling. Slowly, slowly, she moved one foot backward, feeling for the step beneath her. She could run. If the wide black expanse of his pupils was anything to go by, the previous night's drinking still held Stavros firmly in its clutches. He might not catch her—

Behind Stavros, the door of Eirene and Phoebe's room opened a crack. Eirene glimpsed a pale strip of her sister's chiton, a flash of dark eyes and hair. Slowly, Eirene returned her foot to the step. She would be brave now, for Phoebe. If she couldn't stand her ground against Stavros, she'd have no chance against Leandros if he came for her sister.

"Explain this to me, then. What's in the jars?"

She could have lied. But Stavros's mother had been a weaver too—the finest in the whole of the Ionian Islands, if Phoebe was to be believed. Stavros knew what dyes looked like.

"Dyes," she said hesitantly. "For Phoebe's weaving. The brightly colored pieces sell for much more, so I thought—"

"You *thought*?" interrupted Stavros. "Eirene, you can *think* when it's your money that you're spending."

But it is! What have you ever done to earn a single coin? Eirene swallowed down the furious words. Her priority now was Phoebe, half hidden behind the door, listening. "I'm sorry," she said. "I can try to take them back. Or sell them on. And"—desperately grateful that she had not stopped into the brothel to pay off Stavros's debt there, she dug in her purse and pulled out the few remaining coins—"there's still this!"

Stavros put his hand out wordlessly and she pushed the coins into his palm. He pulled open his own purse and dropped the handful of bronze inside. Eirene fought to keep her expression neutral as he yanked the ties closed again. Those were *her* earnings, Phoebe's earnings. He had no right to them. She clenched her fists and stayed quiet.

After a lengthy, agonizing silence, Stavros spoke. "I trust this will not happen again?"

Eirene shook her head. "It won't."

"Good." He moved without warning, shouldering past Eirene and stumbling down the final few stairs. Eirene leaned against the wall. Her shoulders were trembling—with fear or fury, she was not certain. She did not move until Stavros had disappeared from view, until she heard the slap of his footsteps on the hard ground outside and knew that he was heading for the village with a purse full of Eirene's coin. How little of it would be left when he returned? Eirene knew the answer to that question. She scowled.

"You shouldn't have done that." Phoebe pushed the door fully open and stood in the frame, her arms crossed, her spindle tucked beneath them.

Eirene sighed. "Done what?"

"The dyes." Phoebe nodded at the basket. "I don't *need* bright dyes. I just—"

"I meant what I said," Eirene interrupted. "The colorful pieces do sell for more. I'm *investing*." She stamped up the remaining stairs and skirted past Phoebe into their room. "Besides, Stavros can't spend dyes."

Phoebe made a noise in her throat, half irritated huff, half sigh of resignation. "*Must* you aggravate him? He is not all bad, and—"

Eirene was not really listening. There was something off in the room, something sweet and burnt and faintly rotten hanging in the air. She sniffed. "Do you smell that? What *is* it?"

Phoebe broke off from her defense of Stavros with a splutter, swiftly moving to stand in between Eirene and the window and the little brass brazier that stood beside it. The stick she used to walk when she was unwell leaned against the wall. "Nothing," she said, her cheeks darkening with the lie. A soft plume of smoke was rising from the brazier.

"You're a terrible liar." Eirene turned to deposit the basket of dyes by the loom. In between burning whatever was still smoldering by the window, Phoebe had clearly been busy; something was hung out on the loom, threads pulled tight with the weights Phoebe had inherited from their aunt, bright colors woven in between them.

Eirene reached out for the loom and ran her fingers absently over the wooden frame. Then she turned back to Phoebe, narrowing her eyes as her sister shifted awkwardly where she stood, her stance wide, the spindle now clutched in one hand like a weapon. "What did you do?"

"I—" Phoebe faltered. It was clear that she was debating whether or not to lie again. Then she wilted and stepped aside. "It was the plum," she said miserably. "I thought it'd be a nice gift, you know, since I like to offer something to Athena before I start weaving, and the plum looked so golden and tasted so wonderful that I—"

Eirene frowned. "A burning plum doesn't smell like that."

"Well, that's what I thought too, but—" Phoebe gestured help-lessly to the grate.

Eirene crossed the room and peered into the brazier. She was half expecting to see the singed wing of a moth or the blackened tail of a mouse. *Something* that would explain the scent of decay that only grew stronger the closer she got. But that wasn't what she found. In fact, it took her a moment or two to understand exactly what she was looking at.

"Oh," she said. The plum hadn't burned, exactly. It had *melted* into a thick brown sludge that was emitting sporadic puffs of smoke. The stone, intact amid the remnants of the flesh, was gray and wizened. It was surrounded by a few charred sprigs of rosemary—Phoebe had clearly tried to disguise the smell with another slightly less revolting one. "I'm not sure Athena wants that." She forced herself to smile even as her insides churned. She had known there was something wrong with the fruit Leandros had sent. Next time, she was throwing every bit of it in the river. But what if *next time* was already too late?

She looked closely at her sister, searching for some sign of poison or enchantment. But all she found was her own worry reflected back at her in her sister's eyes, her mirror image in this and everything.

"Stop *examining* me." Phoebe shoved Eirene away. "Do you want to do something useful? This wool needs spinning. Then I can try out these dyes and put the best ones aside for your tapestry." She offered Eirene the spindle.

Eirene obediently took it, letting it hang from her hand, clutching the distaff in the other, feeling for the tension. It was a process as familiar to her as breathing; automatically, she ran the whorl along her thigh and set it to spinning. The rough wool twisted into perfect thread as she leaned back against the wall, relaxing into the position she knew she could hold for hours, feeding the wool in with a practiced ease. Here, in this room, with Phoebe at her side and the thread spinning between her fingers, she could almost forget the threat that lurked in the world beyond.

"There," said Phoebe, sounding relieved. She took up her own position at the loom, seated on a high stool. The loom had been meant for a standing weaver, but Eirene had hacked it apart then put it back together at half height. Phoebe checked the tightness of the last woven row and the position of the staves before lifting the shuttle with its trailing tail of blue thread. "I love this color, don't you?" She pushed the shuttle through the gaps in the columns of taut thread. Eirene hummed her agreement. She wrapped the spindle with the new thread and set her whorl to spinning again.

Then she paused. She recognized that shade of blue; Phoebe had been delighted when she'd pulled the spun threads from their bath of dye. She'd kept it aside, as she did all the best colors. *For your tapestry, Eirene.*

She narrowed her eyes at the tapestry—rows of wavering greens and blues, a pale brown foot taking form. The detail was intricate; Phoebe would never normally take such care. "Phoebe, what are you making?"

Phoebe's shoulders stiffened but she did not turn around. "Your tapestry," she said lightly. "I'm always talking about it, but I've barely made any progress. I'm always so consumed with making things to sell, and I just—well, I thought that *this* should be my priority now."

Her priority . . . *now.* Eirene swallowed. Phoebe had always intended this tapestry to make up Eirene's dowry. There was certainly no urgency *there.* So Phoebe must be worried for herself, for her own ability to continue. Could she know about Alexandra? Poor dead Alexandra, who had left her widower in want of a new wife.

"Oh," Eirene said. She could not bear to argue now about money and priorities and how she wasn't sure she'd ever get married anyway. "What's it going to be?"

Phoebe relaxed a little. "You'll see," she said. "It'll be beautiful, I promise. Now get back to spinning. I want to see how that pink color you've brought takes to the wool."

"Yes, *mistress*," said Eirene, but she did as her sister asked, swallowing down the rest of her words. They worked in companionable silence, content just to be together, consumed with their own tasks and their own thoughts, the soft sound of twisting wool, the click of the shuttle against the frame of the loom and the clay weights bumping together. Eirene considered asking Phoebe what she knew of Alexandra. But that would mean breaking the quiet satisfaction of the moment, of making something together, perhaps to deliver news that did not need to be shared. Phoebe had nothing to be afraid of, not really.

Eirene would make sure of it.

V

FALSE AND DISOBEDIENT BEAUTY

Eirene

Eirene awoke with a terrified jolt to pounding on the door downstairs.

"What—" mumbled Phoebe, and the bed shifted under her weight as she lifted herself up onto her elbows. She was cocooned in her blanket, her dark hair falling from the neat braids she slept in. "What's that?"

"Someone's outside," said Eirene groggily. She hadn't bothered to braid her own hair, and pieces of it were stuck to her face. She spat out a curl. "But who—"

Leandros. The name tore through Eirene's hazy thoughts like an arrow through a rabbit. It could be no one else. Before, his gifts had been left silently. But today something was different. She didn't pause to think; she bolted upright and hurled herself from the bed. Her chiton had become unpinned in the night and she swore as it slipped from her shoulder. There was no sound from the other room—Stavros must still be sleeping, but he would not be for long. The pounding came again and Eirene jolted like she'd been struck by lightning. She grabbed at the folds of her chiton, pulling it up to cover her chest.

"My brooch," she shouted at a bewildered Phoebe. "Can you see it?"

"Er." Phoebe, sat up, lifting the mess of their blankets. "Yes, it's here. I—"

"Throw it!" Eirene's heart was racing like a prize stallion and she knew she must seem wild. Phoebe would not understand her panic; Phoebe did not know about Alexandra.

Phoebe's expression was exasperated. She pulled the brooch from where it had caught on Eirene's blanket. "*Eirene.*"

"Throw it," snarled Eirene. She cupped her hands and held them out. "Oh, never mind." She darted back to the bed and snatched the brooch from Phoebe. "Get *up*. Leandros is here. He's here; he must be." She fixed Phoebe with her most urgent look, wishing she'd had the courage to say this the previous night. "Listen to me. Alexandra is dead."

She didn't wait for Phoebe's response. She turned away from her sister—not fast enough to miss her face twisting with grief and understanding and terror—and hurried back across the room, shoving the brooch through the fabric at her shoulders. She snatched up her sash from where she'd discarded it the previous night, yanking it tight beneath her breasts. The pounding on the door had stopped. She had to get there before Stavros. She didn't know what she would do when she got there, but she would do something.

She sprinted out of the room and onto the stairs. There was still no sound from Stavros's room and she allowed herself to feel a momentary thrill of victory. She had beaten him. Now she just had to outsmart whoever was at the door, which couldn't be too difficult. Eirene had always been sure of her own cleverness.

The punishment for this hubris was swift and decisive. Eirene skidded to a halt halfway down the stairs as she heard the main door opening. *No.* How?

"Leandros," said Stavros, his voice slurred with sleep and surprise. *No, no, no.* Leandros had come himself. Even if Eirene had wanted to move, she wouldn't have been able to. "What—er, good morning to you." She could hear a rustling of clothing as Stavros talked—she could picture him hastily rearranging the chiton he'd slept in, doubtless wine-stained and crumpled. The drunken bastard must have fallen asleep on the floor of the main room. Today of all days. "Will you come inside? Have a drink?"

"Stavros, my friend," came a clear, cool voice. "If only I had the time to drink with you in your *charming* little house. But I have other business to attend to."

"Of course," said Stavros quickly. "I do not recall you at the tables of late, but if this is about some debt—"

"Debt? Stavros, you are a wit." Leandros let out a sultry laugh that made every hair on Eirene's arms stand up. She crept silently down the stairs, her heart in her mouth. She had to stop this, somehow. She had to—

"You surely know by now what I wish to ask of you," said Leandros. "But if you are somehow unaware, allow me to enlighten you. There is something of yours I crave greatly for myself; I hope you will be willing to share it with me."

There was a low animal sound behind Eirene. She turned sharply to see Phoebe behind her on the stairs. There was naked fear in her face. Wordlessly, Eirene reached her hand out and Phoebe took it gratefully. Her skin was clammy, her grip tight; Eirene could feel the violent hammer of her pulse.

Downstairs, Stavros was mumbling something incoherent:

"What's mine is yours, my friend," and "What I could possibly have that you do not already—"

"I speak, of course," interrupted Leandros, "of your fair cousin. Phoebe. Her beauty is renowned, as is her gentleness and her skill on the loom. Give her to me as a wife, and I will be honored if you too will call me cousin." He lowered his voice. "I will let you think on it. Three days, then you will bring her to me, I hope."

For a moment, there was silence, no other sound but the wind and the birds and the terrible screaming gaining strength in Eirene's mind. Then Stavros spoke, the words falling over one another in their haste to escape his mouth. "Yes," he kept saying. "Yes, of course. Yes. You will have her. Whatever you want, Leandros; it is yours. And we will not make you wait three days. Tomorrow, my friend, tomorrow. I would be honored. Phoebe, too, I'm sure will be—"

"I'm glad to hear it," said Leandros smoothly. "I have brought a final gift for my bride-to-be."

Stavros let out a surprised *oof.* Leandros must have handed him something heavy.

"She may not be certain at first," Leandros went on. "It is a hard thing to leave your family for your husband's house." Eirene had to strain to catch his parting words. "I hope you will let her know how sincerely I . . . *desire* this match."

Eirene's heart stopped. The threat was clear to her—Phoebe would become Leandros's wife of her own volition or she would be enchanted into wanting him anyway.

"Goodbye, Stavros," said Leandros. "I will see you tomorrow." The door slammed shut.

Eirene pulled her hand free from Phoebe's and threw herself down the last few stairs, startling Stavros so much that he dropped the gift Leandros had just bestowed upon him.

"Eirene," he snarled. "You'd better not have been eavesdropping."

Eirene said nothing. She dropped her gaze to the ground, where the last of Leandros's gifts lay.

Her stomach twisted. It was a pomegranate. The biggest pomegranate Eirene had ever seen, ruby red and glistening wetly like some enormous hatchling fresh from its shell. It should have been grotesque, but there was something bizarrely enticing about it. Eirene didn't realize she'd begun to move until she was stooping to scoop it into her arms. "Stavros," she said softly, cradling it like a lamb. How she wanted to tear it open, to gulp down the sweet seeds. She forced herself to look away from it. "Stavros, you can't—"

"That is for Phoebe," said Stavros sharply, cutting her off as if he hadn't heard her. "It is a gift from her betrothed." He smiled suddenly and the effect was ghastly. "Phoebe is to marry Leandros."

"It is decided, then?" Eirene spoke through gritted teeth. "Phoebe's fate is decided for her, and you can't even pretend that she had the slightest choice in the matter." Stavros's face darkened as she spoke. "She is not a sheep to be taken to market and—"

"Eirene." Phoebe emerged from the stairwell like an apparition, her footsteps silent, her feet bare, her face drained of its color. Her expression was no longer fearful, just perfectly, horribly blank.

"Phoebe," said Eirene, but Phoebe's eyes slid past her to fix upon Stavros.

"Stavros," she breathed. Her voice quavered on his name. "I cannot marry him. Alexandra is *dead*. Did you know that? Please, don't—"

"*Don't?*" echoed Stavros. "Don't?" His voice grew louder. "You do not command me, little cousin. You forget your place; I am head of this household and you will go to him if I demand it."

Phoebe shook her head and backed away. Her eyes were bright; she blinked rapidly, dislodging a single tear from her lashes. It trickled over her hollow cheek. "He does not want me," she said. "He doesn't know me."

"Know you?" Stavros laughed. "Why should that matter?"

Another tear slipped down Phoebe's face, then another. Eirene's chest seemed to be caving in on itself to see her sister like this, to have no way to stop it. Leandros's words rang through her mind over and over in his cool, cruel voice. *Let her know how sincerely I . . . desire this match.*

Stavros spoke now. "Cousin," he pleaded in a low, desperate tone. "He is a descendant of Eros, a demigod. He has a magic of his own. Think what such a marriage would mean for us."

"For *us*," repeated Phoebe. "Are you marrying him, too, Stavros?"

"So you will do it?" He could be gentle when he wanted to be. Kind, even. But there was always that glint in his eyes, and he could return to spitting rage between one breath and the next.

"She will *not*," exploded Eirene.

"I can speak for myself, Eirene!" snapped Phoebe.

"Phoebe."

Phoebe sighed and wiped her eyes on the sleeve of her chiton. She was deliberately not looking at Eirene. She straightened again, pulling her shoulders back with clear intent. "I don't have a choice. I think we all know that. I would rather go to Leandros with my own mind."

No, no, no, no, *no.* Eirene's grip on the pomegranate had grown fierce and white knuckled without her noticing. It gave way beneath her hands, the thick skin tearing open with the wet noise of a knife through the throat of a goat at slaughter. It felt like a huge mutilated heart in her hands—sun-warmed and wet against her skin, as if it had been yanked fresh from her body. Thick ruby-red juice dripped down her arms, coating her from wrist to elbow in the time it took for her to inhale sharply and drop the foul thing to the floor. It rolled against the hem of her chiton, leaving a bloody print behind.

Stavros smiled that awful smile of his again. "Good. Then it's settled."

"You can't," said Eirene. She and Phoebe stood at opposite ends of their room, glowering at each other. "You cannot go."

"You act as if I chose this," snapped Phoebe. "You know what Leandros is, Eirene, what he's capable of. If he wants me, I have no choice but to be his."

"We could run away," said Eirene desperately. "Tonight."

"Run?" Phoebe's laugh was cruel. They could be vicious with each other when they needed to. "Of course you'd think about running. You're the one who can still run, whose body can still do anything you demand of it. We have no horse, no donkey, no cart, and no money to buy them. It will be weeks before I could have anything new to sell. Besides, every man for miles will recognize us and return us to Stavros the moment we are spotted."

"Perhaps not," said Eirene, but Phoebe would not be interrupted. She was flushed with emotion.

"And what if we did get away? I would lose my loom, you would lose your garden, and we would have *nothing*. And you cannot imagine that Leandros will waste any time pining for me if I were to be gone. We don't have any friends left to condemn in my place, but *someone* must go, Eirene. Leandros will have a wife, some poor girl locked up in that house of his. Better that it be me."

Finishing her tirade, she sucked in a pained, gasping breath and sat down abruptly on the edge of the bed. She was shaking all over.

Eirene stared at her sister, at the person she cared most for in the world. She would die for Phoebe, had always whispered it in her prayers to the gods on the nights where Phoebe seemed to cling to life with only her fingertips. *Take me instead*, Eirene would tell the sky. *Let me die, so that she might live.* She had meant it then. She meant it still.

"I will go," said Eirene.

Phoebe lifted her head slowly. "*What?*"

"I will go," repeated Eirene. "If someone must go, let it be me. Disguised as you, of course," she added. "Stavros will never agree." And Leandros would not want her as a bride, she knew that. She was too short and too strong and she scowled too much. And she needed to stop cutting all her hair off. That's what Damon had told her, anyway, after she'd told him she was scared of being married off and he'd laughed in her face.

But Eirene was certain she could convince Leandros to keep her. He was an ambitious man. She could use that.

"You cannot go," said Phoebe.

"Did I not just say the very same thing? What makes this so different?"

"It is different because you do not *have* to, and I—"

"Listen." Eirene hurried to her sister's side, grabbing Phoebe's hands in her own. "I will not be Leandros's wife."

Phoebe shook her head, exasperated. "Eirene, a wife is what he *wants*."

"Not forever, I mean," said Eirene. "Just long enough for you to finish my tapestry. You said it yourself, we have no money and no way to make it, but if you finish it then we *will*."

Phoebe shook her head again. "Eirene, no. That tapestry is *yours*. It's for—"

"I was never going to need it anyway," said Eirene gently. "And if I do, then perhaps you will be so good as to make me another one. But for now I will go to Leandros in your place and, when the weaving is done, I will slip away and we will sell it and then we will take the money and *leave*."

"Leaving Leandros to prey on some other poor creature."

Phoebe's voice was doubtful, but Eirene could see that she could be convinced. She pushed ahead.

"I will be in his house," said Eirene. "There must be a secret to Desire. I do not believe that so distant a descendant of the gods could have such innate power. I know about herbs and medicine— this cannot be so different. So I will find what makes Desire. I will destroy it. Then we will be safe—and every other girl on Zakynthos, too."

"What if you can't? What happens then?"

"I *can*. But I need you to finish your weaving, Phoebe. Stavros will be so angry. We will not be able to stay here."

"And why can't you be the one who stays? Who earns the coins?"

"What can I do in a matter of weeks? Plant some seeds? Grow a really big rosemary? No, it has to be you that stays."

Finally, Phoebe nodded. Slowly, uncertainly, but a nod nonetheless. "You will need a veil," she said carefully.

"Yes," agreed Eirene immediately, even if she wasn't certain what the veil was for. She would have agreed to anything, so long as it kept Phoebe from throwing herself into Leandros's clutches.

Phoebe raised an eyebrow, her composure returning. "To hide your face. So that you are believably me."

"Ah," said Eirene. "Right. We can use an old cloak, perhaps?"

"Yes," said Phoebe. She stood up and dashed to the chest that held their clothes and blankets, ready to be piled back onto the bed when the cold weather returned. She threw it open. "Here!" she said triumphantly, digging out a faded blue shawl. "No time to redye it, so we will have to make do. It'll hide your hair, though I wonder . . ." Her eyes darted around the room, landing on the loom and the knife that lay beside it, the little blade she used to cut the loose threads when they were tied off.

"No," said Eirene, understanding immediately.

"I'll cut my hair. I can braid the pieces in with yours, somehow," said Phoebe. "I will have to pretend to be sulking in bed, of course, but if Stavros looks in, shorter hair will make it much more believable that I am you . . ."

"No," said Eirene again. Phoebe loved her hair. She rubbed oil into the ends every evening and pulled the curls into loose plaits to protect them. Eirene valued her own hair very little, but she could not take Phoebe's from her. "The veil will hide my hair well enough," she said firmly.

Phoebe bit her lip. "But what if—"

"No," said Eirene again. "Promise me you won't."

Phoebe signed. "Fine. We will just need to pin the veil very carefully."

"And I will need my herbs," said Eirene. "Perhaps I will need to sedate Leandros. Or"— she smirked—"incapacitate him. Some Alexandrian senna will do nicely, I think."

"You are a monster," said Phoebe, but she was grinning.

Eirene grinned back. "When I need to be."

That evening found Eirene's satchel lying by the door of their room, stuffed full of herbs. The veil was folded neatly beside it. Eirene herself sat up in bed and squinted at them through the half dark. Phoebe lay beside her, breathing quietly, utterly exhausted by their afternoon of frantic preparation. Stavros had disappeared into the village. Even his cousin's impending marriage could not keep him from the brothel.

Eirene crept from the bed silently, repinning her chiton and tying her sash tight. The realization had come to her slowly, but now she was certain of it: it had to be tonight. There was too much that could go wrong if she waited until the morning for Stavros to march her to Leandros's house himself. There were too many opportunities for him to discover the ruse and force Phoebe to go in her place.

So Eirene would go tonight, alone, and she would make sure that Stavros could not bring her back.

She wound the veil around her face and hair as Phoebe had shown her, then shoved half a dozen pins into it haphazardly, doubtlessly ruining the whole effect. She picked up the satchel and moved as quietly as she could toward the door.

A hand caught her by the wrist and yanked her back.

Eirene smothered a frightened yelp. She'd been so occupied with the veil that she had not heard her sister waking. "*Phoebe*," she hissed.

She could not make out Phoebe's features through the dark, but she heard the pain and anger in her voice. "You were going to leave without saying goodbye."

"I *have to*," said Eirene desperately. "I have to go now, before Stavros can stop me. You know I have to. What if he makes me take the veil off? What if he tries to make *Eirene* accompany us to the house and discovers that Eirene is a dirty rotten liar? There's too much at risk, Phoebe."

She had expected her sister to argue. But Phoebe, who had been woven from the same threads as Eirene, who was as she was and who thought as she thought, knew the truth of her words. "You're right," she said simply. "You have to go tonight." Without warning, she yanked Eirene into a tight embrace. "But you'll come back alive, or I swear on the Styx I'll bring you back from Hades just to kill you myself," she hissed into Eirene's ear.

"I will come back," said Eirene. She could not quite bring herself to swear it.

"I know."

"Then let me go."

Phoebe loosened the tight circle of her arms a fraction. She sighed. "I hope you know what you're doing."

Eirene gently detached herself from her sister's grip. "So do I."

VI

SERPENT DIRE AND FIERCE

Lamia

From the pitifully small window in her tower room, Lamia could see all the way into the village, so she was the first to catch sight of the girl struggling up the path.

The girl? Lamia blinked. She had been half asleep, leaning out into the cool rain and dreaming up patterns in the shifting shadows, but now she was wide awake. A *girl*. Surely not. The figure must have been a phantom, an apparition, some figment of what her father would affectionately call her *overactive mind* and *weak eyes*. After all, what girl would come here, alone, at night, and in such a torrent?

Lamia turned deliberately from the window and fidgeted with the linen bandages encasing her left hand as she cast her eyes over the room. It was dark, lit only by the single lamp her father allowed and the silvery moonlight, but there was her bed, her small chest of clothes, the rickety wooden table in the corner with its heap of ancient knucklebones, and the shelves piled with curling papyrus and sticks of charcoal worn down to stubs. All things she was certain of, that she could see and touch and know to be true. Unlike the girl.

But she had looked so *real*. Lamia turned back. The wind had the night itself trembling; one of her shutters had been stolen away by a storm much like this, but she braced a hand against the one that remained and peered out again into the dark.

Not a phantom. That much was clear, as the clouds shifted in the sky and a beam of moonlight shone on the trees and the path and the girl upon it. She was short and sturdy looking; her hands were clenched fists at her side, her face was turned from the wind. She had hidden her hair beneath a clumsy veil, but each fresh gust pulled free a tangle of dark curling strands.

Lamia's stomach gave a little leap of excitement, followed almost instantaneously by a rush of trepidation. What business could this girl have *here*, alone as she was? The last person to walk up that path—alone, at night—had been the physician, and he had come to take Alexandra's body away.

Still the girl came closer and closer, each step bringing some new detail into view. She wore a neat white chiton. The raiment was clean, and Lamia could see no holes in the fabric—though perhaps she was merely too far away to see—but it was too short; it hung only to the middle of the girl's calves. Her veil was dark blue, and she had a leather bag slung over her shoulders.

The girl walked with a quick, determined gait. It would not be long until she reached the door. There was no servant waiting there—as there never was this time of night, the pale-faced serving girls and rowdy kitchen boys were all sent back to their homes in the village—so she would have to knock and wait for Peiros to come. Lamia's pulse quickened. The door was usually barred at night, but Peiros had become forgetful in the aftermath of Alexandra's death. She had not heard him come tonight. And there was a hiding spot in her rose garden that would give her a perfect view of the girl's arrival, so long as she got there in time.

It was too marvelous an opportunity to pass up. She left the shutter open and crossed the room as quickly as she could. The sheepskins thrown across the floor muffled the thump of her boots, that distinctive sound that betrayed her uneven gait, and stopped her from slipping on the stone beneath them.

The tower stairs were another matter.

Lamia thrust open the door to her room—a sad wooden affair many years past its prime—and stepped cautiously onto the small circular landing. Sometimes she liked to wait here for a few moments, to prepare herself for the task ahead. But she didn't have time now. She walked to the top of the stairs, took a sharp, quick breath, and began.

She descended the steps slowly, both hands—one wrapped in yellowed linen bandages—clutching the rope that ran along the outer wall of the tower. It was a laborious task on a good day, and today was a bad one. Because of the storm. Her leg didn't like the rain.

She stood facing the rough stone, lowering her injured leg—her left, stiff and inflexible at the knee—onto each step, pushing down on her toes to make sure she had a sure footing before following it with the other. She moved cautiously, more slowly than she needed to. She had learned not to rush the hard way—slipping on a slick patch of stone and tumbling to the foot of the tower, breaking one wrist and spraining the other. The worst of the damage had been done to her leg.

Her father had been beside himself when he'd reached her—bounding down the stairs in a panic, hauling her up by the broken wrist and crushing her against his body. She remembered the way he'd held her, petting her hair as if she were a kitten, and how he'd trembled with rage and terror. "What if you'd *died*?" he'd whispered as she'd screamed into his shoulder, her left leg dangling uselessly beneath her. "Lamia, you are too precious to lose. What would I do without you?"

Lamia remembered staring blankly at her ankle, wrenched sideways and already purpling, and at her knee, which didn't seem to be where it had been before. Five years later, it had never healed; she could hold the cap between her fingers and move it about, push it back into its old place for a moment before it slipped off again. She bound it every morning to keep it stable, but it still hurt. It never stopped hurting.

There was another landing halfway down the tower, another small space in front of another battered wooden door that Lamia kept a careful distance from, and she paused there as she always did, an arm's length from the warped panels. Her leg—as it always did when she hadn't left her room all day—was seizing up, cramping painfully.

She braced her foot against the wall and grunted as pain shot up through her calf. If she didn't press the cramps out here, she knew her leg would crumple beneath her the instant she tried to take another step. But the *girl*. Lamia could not miss her. It was worth the risk. She pushed off the wall and put her weight back onto her injured leg.

This pain was a crack of lightning. Too hasty, as she always was. The leg gave way.

Lamia fell backward, throwing an arm back instinctively to break her fall. Her hand connected with the door. Lamia gasped, but it was too late to redirect her fall and she tumbled bodily into the wood.

She fell from the door to the floor in a crumpled heap, scrambling back as swiftly as she could. The door hadn't moved, as she'd known it wouldn't. In all the time she'd lived here—and that was as long as she could recall—it had been locked. But in her nightmares, in dreams that were hazy and slippery and suffused with terror, Lamia stood upon this landing. The door was always ajar, just a little, and her heart knew that something monstrous lay behind it.

Lamia yanked herself to her feet, fingers curling into the grooves in the stone wall. The cramps had subsided somewhat, but in her hurry to return to the stairs she was still close, too close, to falling again. It was impossible to see it from the ground, but the tower tapered as it rose, and the lower steps were slightly less steep. Her leg spasmed, shooting pains traveling up from her ankle to her hip, so she went the rest of the way on her rear. Her father hated it when she did that, but he was not here to see.

At the bottom of the tower was a third and final landing. Lamia stood, keeping as much of her weight on her right leg as possible. As far as Lamia knew, the door off this landing wasn't locked, but she had just as little desire to test it as she did the one above. Beyond the door lay a room and that room had belonged to Alexandra. Just the sight of it was enough to bring the memories rushing in—the day her father had brought her home, the tenderness with which he presented his young wife to Lamia. *What do you think, my sweet girl?* Alexandra's gentle smile, the dimples in her cheeks and the kindness in her round brown eyes. Her slender arms. Her curled bloodless fingers.

Lamia recoiled from the memory.

They'd never let her see the body, but her mind had still conjured up some horrific vision of it, and sometimes she dreamed of Alexandra sprawled out in the storeroom they'd found her in. Lamia could almost see the blood soaking her pale peplos, could almost taste it—hot, coppery—in the air.

A distant knock split the quiet of the night air. The girl! She was here. Lamia scrambled to the tower door and opened it as quietly as she could, inhaling deeply before slipping out into the night. She crept down the narrow path that cut through the gardens, the roses curling above her, until she reached the wall of the main house. She clung to the wall, taking her weight off her injured leg, and peeked around the corner.

She had meant to hold her breath, to stay as silent as possible, but hardly a heartbeat had passed before her stunned exhalation was a white fog in the cold air. But Lamia didn't care. She barely noticed; she was too busy gazing out at the girl.

With so little distance between them, she could see that the girl was not just a curiosity, she was a wonder. She was even shorter up close, and prettier than Lamia had dared hope. Lamia liked pretty things. From what she could see of the girl's face beneath the drape of the veil, she had light brown skin, a long straight nose, thick black brows, and dark curling lashes. The satchel slung across the girl's body was stuffed so full that she'd not been able to buckle it. A sprig of some kind of plant was hanging out of the side.

The wind had pulled almost all the girl's hair from her veil now, and Lamia watched as she raked her hands—elegant long-fingered hands—through the curls before shoving them back beneath the veil's drape. She huffed audibly and turned her face to the trees, away from Lamia. Lamia's stomach twisted in disappointment. Even with the veil concealing so much, Lamia had hoped to memorize every visible detail of the girl's features before she was gone again.

Her father would think her strange for it—had said as much, his eyes raking over her face, the curl of his lip unreadable, when he'd found the stack of messy drawings hidden hastily beneath her blankets. Portraits. Hundreds of them. Every girl Lamia had ever laid eyes on.

"I like drawing," Lamia had explained to him. And there were always men streaming in and out of the house, the same faces over and over, but the women were rarer, did not seem to stay so long. Drawing them was a way to see them again. And it passed the time.

Now, she kept the drawings in the chest with her chitons, where her father could not look at them with scorn in his eyes.

The door opened and Lamia shrank back, hiding from Peiros's searching gaze as he stepped out of the house. When, he spoke, he sounded uncharacteristically uncertain. "Oh. It's you." How did Peiros know this girl? Lamia risked poking her head around the corner again.

"My name is Phoebe," said the girl. Even muffled beneath the veil, her voice wavered—if it hadn't been such an innocuous little thing, just a name, Lamia might have thought she was lying. But what was in a name? "You've met my twin sister, I suppose. We are very alike."

"Phoebe," repeated Peiros. "You are *very* alike. I thought—"

"Your master is expecting me, I believe," said the girl. Said *Phoebe*—though the name did not seem to quite fit her. She lifted her chin in an unmistakable gesture of insolence. There was a little of Lamia's father in her arrogance. In him it could be frightening. But in Phoebe it was a wonder. Lamia liked *her* very much. "Tomorrow, I admit, but I could not wait another moment. I come at his request, for I am to be his wife."

VII

PILLARS OF GOLD

Eirene

Eirene felt as if she had stepped into another realm.

The entrance hall was enormous; what she had assumed from the number of windows and the height of the walls would be two stories was a single room. And what a room it was.

It was lit with hundreds of lamps, each glowing a soft, captivating yellow. The light spilled onto the floor, less a floor than a work of art—the grandest mosaic Eirene had ever seen. What must have been thousands of tiles had been painstakingly laid to give the impression of a garden. Roses swirled about Eirene's feet, attended to by a swarm of perfect tiny bees. Twisting green foliage burst up around the blossoms; beneath the overlapping curves of leaves there was the distant impression of thorns. Step carefully, they seemed to say. Eirene tore her gaze away reluctantly.

The rest of the room was no less grand. Every bit of wall not taken up with windows and heavy wooden doors was draped in vibrant cloths. A gigantic tapestry covered the entire left-hand wall. Eirene recognized Aphrodite lounging nude in the clearing of a forest, her body entwined with the supple limbs of a man, his face hidden in her thick hair. The colors were vivid and lovely; Eirene could not fathom how much such a piece could have cost. The tapestry shifted in the breeze blowing in from the open door behind her. No, not a tapestry, Eirene realized, drawing closer, a *curtain*.

As the curtain rippled, she glimpsed a narrow corridor behind it. A shadow flashed on the floor—a servant moving silently through the house, perhaps—before the curtain fell back once more. The most astounding piece of weaving she'd ever seen, and Leandros was using it as a curtain.

Across from Eirene, the room opened out onto a dimly lit courtyard. There was no curtain there, no wall at all, only a procession of columns, intricately carved and painted in the brightest of pigments. Eirene could not make out the precise details, but she imagined she could see the curve of a woman's thigh, the drape of a swan's wing, the majestic jut of a stag's horn.

Birds—doves, their plumage pearlescent in the lamplight—fluttered sleepily about the tops of the columns, where the carvings made recesses for nesting, and called to one another with soft melodic coos.

Something large shifted in Eirene's peripheral vision and she turned automatically to look. Her sense of awe and wonder vanished in an instant; her hands flew to her mouth just in time to stifle a sharp, involuntary scream.

At first, all she could see was an enormous mass of shifting sand-colored fur marked with what seemed in that moment to be a hundred black staring eyes. Something—a tail—lashed impatiently against the floor. A leg stretched out, claws scraping against the edges of the tiles. Eirene's heart skipped in her chest, then doubled its pace. Then the creature, the monster, whatever it was, turned in a neat circle. It lifted its massive head to stare at Eirene with a final set of eyes, this time huge and golden, and blinked slowly, deliberately. Its wide jaws seemed to unhinge and Eirene found herself looking into a dripping pink maw edged with vicious yellow teeth.

Eirene laughed, a startled sound that might have been a cry.

The cat—because somehow it was a cat, a massive, beautiful cat with an elegantly spotted coat, a hundred times bigger than any cat had the right to be—finished yawning and fixed its eyes again on Eirene. There was a surprising humanity in its expression. It looked, Eirene decided, a little offended.

"I wasn't laughing at you," she told it quickly. "I was just surprised. I thought you were a monster."

"She is a monster," Peiros said sulkily. He had closed the door and moved to loom over her shoulder, keeping a careful distance from the cat. "Just wait until she's hungry. She doesn't shut up."

The cat, who had up until then been silent, looked from Eirene to Peiros, narrowing her eyes. "Mrow," she commented. The sound was wholly unexpected, halfway between a rumbling growl and a toadish croak.

"Shut up, Daphne," said Peiros, but there was a waver in his voice. He edged away.

Eirene couldn't help it; she began to laugh in earnest. What *was* this place? It was nothing like she had expected.

"If you're quite finished," said Peiros irritably, "I will take you to my master."

Leandros. Eirene sobered immediately, and she kept quiet as she followed Peiros into the courtyard and across it. The cat—Daphne—crept silently along beside her, her tail swishing back and forth. Eirene took in the grandeur here less excitedly. The fountain was, like everything else, massive and intricate and beautiful, but it was owned by Leandros. It had been bought, there was no doubt, with the wealth that came from the sale of Desires. There was the faint smell of old wine in the air, and the sand that covered the courtyard was cold and coarse and kept working its way in between Eirene's sandaled toes.

At the far side of the courtyard, Peiros swept aside a curtain, smaller but no less grand than that in the entrance hall, and led her back into the house proper. The rooms on this side were smaller, lower, stacked one on top of the other. Peiros ushered her toward yet another curtain, plain this time. This part of the house was not, it seemed, for guests, and Leandros had abandoned some of his pretentions for practicalities. Still, the enormous cat padding at Eirene's side served as a reminder that this was not a normal house.

Peiros pushed her through the curtain and into a small untidy room. It was some kind of study, with a wide wooden desk and yet more curtains—thick and dark blue—by the window and shelves upon shelves of scrolls and quills and assorted oddities. Eirene tried not to look like she was staring too hard. This room was a trove of not just wealth but knowledge; she might have spent hours, days, *weeks* here were she left alone.

And yet all of it had come at a price—a price paid not by Leandros, but by the village girls as they disappeared one by one into the houses and beds of rich men. Perhaps this trinket or that one had been bought with the money from Ianthe's new husband. Perhaps this little brass statue at the edge of one shelf—a dancing girl, her leg kicked back—was the value of Clyte's life. Daphne padded across the room and batted at the bottom of the blue curtains, where they pooled against the stone floor. Then, apparently finding something of interest there, she made a low grumbling sound and vanished behind the draped fabric. Eirene felt her absence more keenly than she had expected—the monstrous creature had put her peculiarly at ease.

"Sit." Peiros directed Eirene toward a modest, uncomfortable-looking chair with a blanket hanging over its narrow back. When he made no move toward it, Eirene picked up the blanket herself, shook it out, and arranged it over the chair. A vicious thrill surged through her at the sight of a single red stitch among the cream. Phoebe's mark. This was her handiwork, then. Perhaps she should make some pretense of pleased recognition—she was supposed to be Phoebe, after all. But when she snuck a sideways look at Peiros, he had already moved back to the curtain, one hand reaching to pull it closed again.

"Stay here," he said shortly. "I will find the master."

Eirene debated hurling some kind of scathing retort his way. If Leandros had actually been expecting her, rather than her sister, she might have done it. Instead, she settled on silence and sat down primly, her hands folded in her lap to indicate her preparedness to wait. She had a plan—she'd gone over it a hundred times as she'd walked here—and she would stick to it. *She* would be Leandros's wife. She would find out everything there was to know about him and the Desires he sold. And then she would use that knowledge to destroy him. A wide smile spread across her face.

Peiros disappeared into the hall, the curtain swishing shut behind him. Once she was sure he was gone, Eirene yanked the veil from her face—the relentless brush of fabric across her skin had started to make her feel sick—and settled down to wait for her husband-to-be.

She was not left waiting long. She had just begun to fidget, debating investigating where Daphne had vanished to, before the curtain was thrust open and Leandros strode in. Daphne emerged immediately, bounding across the floor and running into the hall Leandros had just come from. Leandros ignored her. "I knew you'd come," he announced to the room at large. He did not look at Eirene, and she used the opportunity to inspect him closely.

He was beautiful, yes, as lean and leonine and lovely as everyone

said, but it was ruined by his preening; smugness seemed to ema-
nate from him like an unpleasant smell. "Was it the pomegranate
that swayed you at last? I am partial to them myself, you know.
Of course, I should have expected such fine taste from my future
wi—" The word "wife" never quite made it past his lips. He had
turned to face her and sheer astonishment seemed to render him
temporarily speechless. His brow furrowed over his clear blue eyes.
His full pink lips parted in a bewilderment so charming it must
have been deliberate. His hand had been outstretched toward her,
the fingers curled as if to beckon her forward. Now his arm fell to
his side again as he gazed at her.

He claims he is a descendant of Eros. Eirene could believe it.
Leandros's unnatural loveliness had no other explanation. It made
her skin prickle with unease.

Leandros seemed to recover his senses at last. He made a show
of blinking away his surprise, his long golden lashes fluttering.
"Phoebe," he said. There was an edge of irony in his voice. "You are
just as beautiful as your cousin boasts."

As your cousin boasts. Stavros was such a bastard. Eirene picked
at the blanket and said nothing, trying not to linger too long on
Leandros's disbelieving tone. She knew she wasn't as pretty as the
rumors would have said, because the rumors were talking about
Phoebe.

"I must confess, though, my dear Phoebe," Leandros added,
once it seemed to become clear to him that Eirene had no intention
of responding, "I had expected your hair to be longer."

It was going to be such a joy to ruin him. Eirene lifted her head
and offered him a bare-toothed grin. "I cut it," she said. "I like it
short. Phoebe's is longer, as you say, and she is beautiful. But I am
not Phoebe."

This time, Leandros's surprise might actually have been genuine. He gaped at her like a speared fish, if the fish was somehow blessed with the radiance of a god.

"My name is Eirene. Phoebe is my sister, my twin, but I have come in her stead."

Leandros recovered some small part of his composure. "As her delegate? You carry a message from my wife?"

Eirene squared her shoulders. "No. I come for myself." She paused, then added, as boldly as she dared, "And Phoebe is not your wife. Not yet, anyway."

Leandros's face twitched. She wasn't sure if it was in anger or something else. He wasn't even looking at her anymore; his attention had settled on something behind her—something at floor level, by the room's only window. She resisted the urge to twist about in her seat and follow his gaze. And then, to her great astonishment, Leandros laughed—a rich, ringing sound that filled the room.

"All right, then," he managed at last, between charming peals of laughter. His eyes returned to meet hers. "Why have you come then, Eirene, sister of Phoebe, who is not *yet* my wife?"

"I come with a proposition," said Eirene carefully. She needed to be slick and convincing, every bit as snakelike as she knew he was.

"Oh?" He raised an eyebrow.

"Don't marry Phoebe." There. Perfect.

"*Oh?*" The second eyebrow joined the first. Then his astonishment seemed to abate. He relaxed his brows and flashed her a vicious smile, a mouthful of white teeth. "But I am in want of a wife, my dear Eirene."

Eirene took a deep breath. "Then marry me." Before he could

say anything, she plowed onward, the words spilling out of her like seeds from an upturned sack. "We shared a womb; we are of the same flesh. We are the same age, of course, but I am much cleverer. Phoebe, she is . . . she's gentle and kind and sweet. But you seem like a shrewd sort of man and I doubt you will find her an adequate companion." It hurt to slander her sister so unfairly. But Leandros needed to want *Eirene*. "*I*, however"—she found that she was leaning forward in her chair, her palms upturned as if to offer the vulnerable flesh at her wrists to him—"I can read and write faster and better than Phoebe. I can do arithmetic—add together coins and that sort of thing—and manage an income. I know how to turn a profit. And I know about herbs. Everything that grows within a week's walk I can find and name and grow myself if you give me a few winters to get the conditions right." This, where the rest had not, seemed to catch his interest. His expression of disdainful feline amusement softened. His eyes narrowed and he drifted a little closer. Mirroring him, Eirene leaned forward even farther. Her words came fast and high and she forced herself to slow down. To sound considered and careful. "And I know they're good enough for your needs. Only yesterday, Peiros bought every herb I had. I'm a fast learner and I'm determined. I'll complete any task you put to me. I can run fast and I'm strong."

She sucked in a final triumphant breath. "Phoebe can weave, but she will still weave for you if I am your wife, so long as I ask her. Whereas *I* will do nothing for you if she is yours instead. I will never sell to your servant again. I will poison your wife against you; I'll poison *you* if I have to. Phoebe trusts me, and I am *very* persuasive. Think on what you would lose."

There was a pregnant pause. Leandros's brows had shot up again. "You seem better suited to be some sort of apprentice or assistant than a wife," he said at last. "Don't you think?"

"A good deal for you, then, don't *you* think?" Eirene hurled the words back at him. "Multifunctional." And then, when he made no reply: "So what if I would be a better apprentice? I'd be a perfectly fine wife too. What would Phoebe have on me?"

"She is prettier than you," said Leandros mildly. "With more hair, I gather."

"You are pretty enough on your own," said Eirene flatly. "No woman will look anything but plain as your wife. At your side I am as lovely as my sister is." She was near shouting now. She softened her words abruptly. "That is, not lovely at all."

Leandros gave her a long hard look. Then, without warning, he turned and strode to the other side of the desk, where he sat down, rested his elbows on the polished surface, and made a temple of his hands. "Well then, Eirene," he said, "you have convinced me."

She stared at him. Surely it could not be that easy. This was Leandros—he was a liar, a wicked charlatan who was clever enough to have a whole island hoodwinked. There was a trick here. "I have? I mean . . . that's . . . well, that's . . ."

"Wonderful?" offered Leandros. He picked up a pen from atop a neat stack of papyrus that would have cost Eirene a month's earnings and spun the slender length of reed between his fingers. "I will send word to your cousin, informing him of my choice. First, though, I have just a few terms."

"Terms," repeated Eirene. "What do you mean . . . terms?"

"I am sure you have heard the rumors."

Rumors. Well, Eirene certainly had heard rumors. That Leandros knew how to capture desire itself. That he could make the ugliest of courtesans beautiful again and change even the most faithful of hearts. And that he sold this magic to the highest bidder—rich men in want of pretty young wives to promenade about, or greedy brothel owners desperate to make their girls the loveliest. And to charge their patrons the highest fees. Eirene had not just heard the rumors, she'd seen the evidence with her own eyes—in the desolate market, in Ianthe's vapid gaze and her happy words.

Eirene was suddenly afraid. What if Leandros's terms involved the Desires he brewed? What if he expected *her* to drink them? To be as Ianthe had been: a hollow shell of her former self, pronouncing herself *in love*. Her throat tightened; she clutched the arms of her chair, digging her fingers into the blanket that Phoebe had woven. That brought her back to her own mind somewhat. She was doing this to make sure Phoebe didn't have to. If Leandros wanted a stupid, enchanted wife, he would take one—terms or not.

So, yes, she had heard the rumors. And she could not let him know exactly how much they frightened her. She rubbed her fingers over the knot in her throat until it loosened enough for her to say, quietly, "Which rumors, exactly?"

"That I am a son of Eros, of course." Leandros beamed. "A son of a son of a son of *the* son. The son of Aphrodite herself."

Oh. Was that it? Eirene's derision must have been clear on her face because Leandros's bright smile slipped.

"I've heard them," she said politely. "Are they true?"

Leandros tossed his head of perfect golden curls. "Of course they are true." The wild head-tossing disturbed the pen he held enough to flick a drop of ink onto the topmost sheet of papyrus.

Eirene fought back the urge to roll her eyes. "All right, then," she said. "The terms?"

"You don't seem interested in the story of my ancestry."

"It is late," pointed out Eirene. "And if I am to be your wife, there will be much time to discuss it later." His *wife*. It seemed only hours ago that she had been in the apothecary, crowing over her good fortune and the weight of the coins in her purse. How had it all gone so badly wrong? And so *quickly*? She stroked little circles over the blanket and counted her breaths in and out. She was doing this for Phoebe; once in Leandros's clutches, she would have been lost forever.

"Four tasks," said Leandros abruptly. "As Aphrodite gave to Psyche, so that she could prove her devotion to Eros. To show that she had earned him as her husband."

Eirene frowned, racking her memories for the story. Four tasks . . . it was familiar. But what had the tasks *been*? Her frown deepened. Hadn't one of them been going into *Hades*? Eirene was hardly capable of that. "What tasks?"

"Ah, you must allow me *some* secrets, my dear Eirene." He tapped the side of his nose with the top of the pen. Was the little spot of ink it left behind a calculated move? It was endearing, adorable. And it drew attention to the perfect symmetry and sharp slant of his nose.

If Eirene had ever had an interest in the beauty of men, his might have swayed her. But she hadn't and it didn't. In fact, all this pageantry only made her dislike Leandros all the more. She didn't trust a move he made or a word that came out of his mouth; it was all a carefully constructed illusion. Perhaps there was Desire in every breath she took. In the pomegranate he'd sent. In the plums Phoebe had eaten.

She swallowed down the bile that had risen in her throat and forced herself to smile. "Surely a little more information than *that* is permissible."

"Four tasks," repeated Leandros. "Set by myself, though I can promise you that I'll be reasonable. Upon their completion, you will be allowed to stay here. As my wife."

Eirene did not allow herself to relax yet. "Your wife," she echoed. She narrowed her eyes. "And you will leave Phoebe be. Swear it."

He laughed. "As you wish."

"Swear it."

Leandros sighed theatrically. "Your mistrust of me does you no credit, my dear." When Eirene did not cease her glaring, he threw his hands up in mock defeat. "I swear it." He nodded toward the statues that flanked the hearth—a woman, beautiful and naked and smiling knowingly, and a man, as nude as his mother, clutching a bow and gazing dreamily into nothing. "Let my ancestors be witness to my promise. If you complete all four tasks to my satisfaction, you will be my wife. If you fail, you will leave this house and I will have your sister, as I originally intended. Satisfied?"

If there was a trick, Eirene could not detect it. She nodded shortly. "Satisfied."

VIII

THE DIVINE APPOINTMENT

Lamia

"Satisfied," said Eirene curtly.

The bargain was struck. Thank the gods—Lamia couldn't stand to stay concealed for much longer.

From her hiding place behind the curtains, she shifted uncomfortably. Her foot was cramping again and she ground her toes into the floor, stretching out the jerking muscles. If she'd had a little more time, she'd have chosen a better place to eavesdrop from, somewhere she could *sit*. But, as it was, she'd hardly stepped behind the curtain before the door had banged open and the girl Eirene—Lamia had *known* that she was lying about her name—was being ushered inside. Lamia had worried that Daphne, who had smelled her immediately and rushed behind the curtain to greet her, would give her hiding place away. But Daphne had disappeared the moment Lamia's father had arrived.

"Good." She heard rather than saw him getting to his feet. His chair creaked. "I will allow you to sleep on your decision—"

"Wait," interrupted Eirene. There was a new note of panic in her voice. "One more thing."

A pause. Then the chair creaked again. "Yes, Eirene, dearest? What is it?"

"My cousin," said Eirene hesitantly.

"Your cousin?"

"Stavros. When you've sent word, he might—he might come. To try to see me."

"And you would have me turn him away?" Lamia's father tutted. "I suppose as your husband I must take some responsibilities for your family."

"Just—just don't tell him of our bargain. He won't allow it. Just don't let him take me away," said Eirene. There was a shuffling sound as she moved. "Tell him I was overwhelmed with love." An ironic note entered her voice. "Tell him I was overcome with *desire*. He will be happy to be rid of me, I'm sure, if you just tell him that. Please."

If only Lamia could *see*. It was infuriating not to know what was happening in each of these long pauses. But she could not risk being spotted. She was not explicitly prohibited, but—

"Very well, then," her father was saying. Lamia squirmed where she stood. "And what will you have me tell him when you fail and I come to claim Phoebe in your stead?"

"I will not fail." Eirene's voice wavered, the same way it had as she'd lied about her name.

Lamia's father laughed softly. "I will call for Peiros, then, and have him take you to your room. Unless you have any more demands to make of me?"

From the silence, Eirene did not. Lamia heard her father placing the pen down and then a distinctive metallic ring. The little brass bell that always graced his desk. At the sound, the curtain to the room opened instantly with a smooth swish.

"Ah, Peiros. Will you take our guest to her room? The lower tower room will do."

A pause, one that might have gone by unnoticed by anyone else. But Lamia, like Peiros, had frozen at the words. Her heart had skipped a beat and it stuttered to a start again as her mind whirred. The lower tower room was Alexandra's. Her father was putting Eirene in *Alexandra's* room.

Alexandra's gentle smile, the dimples in her cheeks and the kindness in her round black eyes. The memories always returned in the same order. Lamia bit down on her cheek, hard enough that her mouth was soon filled with the taste of copper and salt. Painful but it did what she needed it to. The memories slipped away. She did not see Alexandra's pale hands. The hopeless grasping fingers.

In the room beyond, there were footsteps. Peiros's—heavy, certain—and then Eirene's. Hers were lighter, hesitant at first, but she seemed to grow bolder as she was led away. "Good night, Leandros," she called, and there was a note of challenge in her tone. "I look forward to your first task." The door closed with a soft thud and Eirene was gone.

The study fell into quiet again. Then—

"Come out, Lamia."

Lamia went still. Stiller than she had been before; every muscle in her body was tense and immobile. He couldn't—surely not. How could he know? She'd been so *quiet.*

"*Out.*" This time it was a command. "You're lucky I let you stay and listen. You wouldn't have liked it if I'd dragged you out in front of our guest, would you?"

What else could she do? She was like a mouse in a trap. Slowly, Lamia pulled the curtain back and stepped out into the room. On instinct, she hunched her shoulders, bowed her head, and clasped her hands. She stared fixedly at the floor as her leg screamed its protest. It rarely bore weight for this long.

"There you are, my sweet girl," said her father. He did not *sound* too angry. Tentatively, Lamia lifted her gaze from the flagstones and looked directly at him. He was . . . smiling. "Sit," he said invitingly, gesturing to the chair Eirene had just vacated. The rush of relief was instant; Lamia sagged into it gratefully.

"I am sorry." The words fell from her lips in a garbled rush. "I only wanted to see her. I heard her saying that she was to be your wife, and I just—I wanted to see her. To see what she was like."

"And?" Her father's smile grew.

Lamia searched his face for a hint of the answer he wanted from her. Nothing. "And . . ."

"And how did you find her? Are you well pleased with the addition to our little household?"

"Oh!" Lamia allowed herself to relax. "I—yes. I can't see how I wouldn't be. It is as she said herself. She is clever and strong and *very* determined. And she knows all about herbs—picking and growing and brewing. She'll help you, won't she?" She was rambling, she realized, and she shut her mouth with an audible snap.

Her father had pulled a knife from his belt and was cleaning under his nails. He did not look at her. "You think she's pretty."

Lamia had no answer to that. None that she was willing to share. Did she think Eirene was pretty? Lamia thought all the women that she'd seen in her life were pretty in their own ways. But Lamia had only seen Eirene briefly, half her face veiled. It was Eirene's voice she liked most and the whetted resolve that each spoken word held.

"Well," she said eventually, "does it matter?"

Her father hummed as he dug dirt from his under his thumbnail. When he was finished, he dropped his hands, though he did not replace the blade in his belt. "I suppose not," he said.

"All right," said Lamia.

"But you like her?"

"I suppose I do."

"I'm glad." He leaned against the desk, stretching his limbs out lazily like a cat. "Lamia?"

"Yes, Father?"

"If I catch you spying on me again," he said pleasantly, fixing her with his warmest, gentlest smile, "I'll rip out all your fingernails. One by one. And stay away from Eirene. Is that understood?"

Lamia shivered, a sudden chill flooding her limbs, and flexed her bandaged fingers. She refused to glance down at the blood-spotted linen. It was not an idle threat. "Yes, Father."

IX

QUICK SONS OF THE GROUND

Eirene

Eirene woke with a start to banging on her door. She bolted upright, scrabbling to pull her chiton back into place; she'd been tossing and turning all night and it was rucked up around her waist. "Phoebe?" she muttered blearily before she remembered where she was. Not back at home, in the room she shared with her sister, but in the small dark room at the base of the tower. In Leandros's house. She shivered, though the air was warm.

The room was dusty and bleak, little in it besides the long narrow couch she lay upon. The unlit hearth was a shallow indent in the floor in one corner, ringed with raised stone, and a rickety table stood beneath the single window. There was a broad brass bowl set atop it alongside a small oil lamp.

"Eirene?" There was another bang on the door and it flew open to reveal Leandros. He held a bulging sack in each fist. "Good morning, Eirene," he said brightly. He strode to the center of the room and slammed the sacks down onto the stone floor. One sack toppled, the loose ties falling open, and its contents spilled across the floor. Eirene blinked at it in bewilderment. It was an erratic mix: lentils and wheat berries and—she narrowed her eyes—what looked like thousands of fine black seeds. All of them were coated in a layer of dust and sand.

"Your first task," announced Leandros, and Eirene snapped her attention back to his unnervingly lovely face. He looked very pleased with himself. He pulled a third empty sack from his belt and tossed it down beside the others. "You must sort the contents of these sacks. Poppy seeds in one. Lentils in the other, wheat in the third. The sand you can leave. I'll have you sweep it up later."

Eirene had the peculiar sense that she was missing something. The sacks were large, of course, and the contents thoroughly combined—it would certainly be a tedious task, several weeks on her hands and knees picking out seeds, but not a difficult one. Well, the poppy seeds might be a challenge, but—

"You have three days," said Leandros.

"*What?*" Eirene stared at him, aghast.

Three days? *Three days.* She looked again at the sacks, at the sprawl of seeds. She had estimated weeks, but there must be ways to speed up the process. Perhaps tossing them up in a bowl to bring the lighter pieces to the top. Or water. Did lentils float? She didn't think so. She tried to remember tipping them out to soften in a battered pot of boiling water. Perhaps—

"And three nights if you need them," said Leandros, as if this made much of a difference at all. "But by the morning of the fourth day, I expect them all to be separate."

"I—"

"And you'll be confined to this room, of course. These tasks are yours alone, to prove that you truly possess the strength and intellect you claim you do. If we see that you've left the room, you will have failed."

"But—" Eirene's plan to borrow every sieve in the village fizzled out like kindling dropped into a puddle.

"Or you can leave now." Leandros's gaze darted from Eirene to the seeds to Eirene again. He was smiling—a wide, vicious display of teeth.

Oh, the bastard. He was so *convinced* that she wouldn't agree. She wanted to slap that smug look off his face. Instead, she did the next best thing; she yanked the blanket aside, stood from the bed, and did her utmost to keep her surprise at just how cold the floor was from her face as she stalked across it to Leandros.

She stopped an arm's length away and glared up at him. "I'm staying here," she hissed.

Leandros looked back at her, a smile playing over his mouth. His eyes were so very blue. He didn't look human.

Eirene refused to look away. She couldn't let her fear show. Not now. She gestured to the heaps of seeds and sand. "How"—she cleared her throat—"how did they all become mixed like that?"

If she hadn't been watching him so closely, she might not have noticed the shadow that passed over his features or the brief angry twist of his perfect mouth. "Something got into the storeroom," he said shortly. "An animal. Some kind of wild thing."

X

GARLANDS OF ROSES

Lamia

The roses were whispering again.

It was only the wind, really, Lamia knew that, but there was something in the way their heads seemed to turn to her, to dip in toward her, petals rustling, that made her feel that they were trying to tell her something. She reached out through the window for the nearest rose—a glorious pink—and pulled it to her. "Look at you." She cooed to it as if it were a fledgling, tracing the petals. "So pretty. So—" She broke off, frowning, her fingers stilling. She peered closely at the rose, searching for the imperfection she'd felt beneath her fingertips. *There.* A small rip in one of the inner petals. Perhaps one of the birds that nested in the tangled thicket had done it, catching her claws as she flew to her young.

Lamia could fix it.

She adjusted her grip. Then she pressed the tips of her bandaged fingers against the thorns that sheathed the stem of the rose. Blood bloomed where she had broken the still healing skin open again, and the pain was so sudden and bright that it brought tears to her eyes. Lamia cried easily; she had to. She brought her free hand—undamaged, unbound—to her face and brushed a single tear from her lashes.

She paused, cocking her head. She could just make out the murmur of voices from the tower below; it snaked up the stairs, growing fainter and fainter until she could distinguish none of the words. But she knew from the familiar rumble of one voice that her father was speaking, and from the higher, sharp sound of the other that Eirene was replying.

Eirene. Still here.

How long would she stay? Perhaps she would stay as long as Alexandra—perhaps there would be four short lovely years when Lamia would not feel quite as alone. And maybe it would end, as it had before, with a cold white body and a terrible ripping emptiness.

The voices had stopped. There were footsteps on the landing again. Lamia strained to listen, her every muscle tense and still as she waited for the sound of boots upon the stairs, the sound that would tell her that her father was on his way with a small bronze bowl in his palm and a blade in his belt and that he would not leave again until he had what he needed from her. His secret ingredient—the one that united every Desire he brewed.

The tower door slammed, far below, and there was silence.

Not today, then.

Lamia lowered her hand, the tear clinging, pearl-like, to her index finger, and held it out into the sunlight. The roses that grew up from the garden curled around the window; the young birds in the vines chirped hungrily. "Me too," she told them. Hunger was beginning to gnaw at her belly. She could go to the kitchen, of course—her father always reminded her that the main house was her house too and that she could go where she pleased—but she couldn't forget his words from the previous night. What if he caught her sneaking bread from the hearth and thought she had come to spy on him again? Would he really pull out her fingernails? There were still eight left, after all.

No, she wasn't that hungry. Not yet.

The tear still sat, a perfect dewdrop, atop her finger. Lamia drew in a breath and kept it, concentrating, her eyes on the tear where it shone in the sun. In her other hand, she clutched the stem of the rose with its single imperfect petal.

A heartbeat. Then the tear began to glow.

First like the light of a lamp, flickering faintly as she fought to take hold of it. Then a torch, then brighter and brighter and brighter, flaring up endlessly until it seemed that there were two suns before her: Helios blazing in the sky, and the inferno burning at her fingertip. It was warm, growing more so with each moment until it was uncomfortable to hold. It began to hurt. The light blinded her; she squeezed her eyes shut against its assault.

An instant later, it winked out, the magic of the tear already spent. The heat receded. Lamia let go of the rose so that it sprang back, brighter than it had been, perfect once more, and allowed herself at last to exhale.

There was a single crust of bread left from the day before. It would be rock solid by now, but as the sun climbed and then began to fall, Lamia kept catching herself staring at it, wondering whether she could soften it in yesterday's equally stale water until it became something close to edible. No, she wasn't hungry. She *wasn't*. But the crust clung to the corner of her vision like moss to a tree.

She could bear it no longer. She retrieved the crust and sat back in the patch of light at the window, crumbling it between her palms. She tossed the crumbs out into the air and watched a throng of songbirds rise and dive and scrabble over the scraps. Though the birds themselves were plain, their flight disturbed the rosebushes, until the whole garden was swaying with reds and pinks and oranges. Eventually, the crumbs ran out and the birds quietened and the sun set in a glorious wash of color; far below, there was a muted clang as Peiros barred the door for the night. Lamia knew he would not be forgetful again. She had free rein of the gardens and the main house in the day, even if she did not use it, but the night held countless dangers for a girl like her. You could never know what was waiting in the dark, her father always said. Better the tower be shut up, better she be alone.

A final flutter of wings broke the quiet, the last sparrow settling into her nest, tucking her ugly little pink babies beneath her wings. Lamia swallowed down a sudden surge of longing for her father. He could be kind, sometimes, and her birds were not true company. Her father loved her as much as he hurt her; he protected her, he only used her magic to keep them safe, and—besides Peiros, who Lamia despised and distrusted in equal measure—her father was the only person left in the house at nighttime, now that Alexandra was gone.

Except that wasn't true. Not anymore.

Lamia sat bolt upright, the last crumbs falling from her skirts to the floor.

It was only when she was halfway down the stairs, pressing the cramp from her toes, that Lamia paused to consider her plan. Her father had only prohibited her from spying on him, nothing else, and yet creeping around the tower at night still felt like such a betrayal that her body trembled with it.

The tower is mine, she reminded herself. *It's mine and I can go where I please, whatever time of day it is.* In fact, it seemed even more hers at night than in the day. None of the dangers her father always warned her of would ever reach her here—not the men from the village, captivated and disgusted by her magic in equal measure, or the philosophers like her father, who sought her tears and would stop at nothing to get them. And these philosophers, her father would tell her, his face still and serious, were not kind and gentle like he was. They would not protect her; they would steal her away to use her power only for evil.

Her father used it to make things beautiful. He used it for love. And though he would never risk letting Lamia out to meet them, he assured her that she was the reason that a dozen young women were happily married to generous and wealthy husbands that adored them. He made it clear that these young women were very keen on the idea of husbands, even if it was one that had always baffled Lamia.

Still, her father had a sincere appreciation for beauty. He would not begrudge Lamia this excursion, not when she went to witness what must surely be the most startling example of loveliness that had ever set foot in his house.

The cramps subsided and she set off again, considerably buoyed by this argument. Even clutching her lamp—an addition that meant she could not hold on to the stair rope with both hands as she tended to prefer—she made it down the final flight of stairs without too much difficulty. The stiffness of her joints the previous day had eased a little with the weather.

She stopped on the lowest landing and stood, head cocked, listening. From Alexandra's room—Eirene's room now, she reminded herself—she heard nothing. In the main house, someone was snoring, a low, regular rumble.

She crept toward Eirene's room. It had been barred from the outside, so Lamia had no choice but to pull the bolt out of its bracket, wincing at the metallic scraping sound. The door, mercifully, was far quieter; it swung open on oiled hinges. It was as if it had been prepared for her to pass through, silent and unnoticed.

She moved toward the couch, skirting the cold hearth and the handful of humped shapes scattered about the room. What were they? She dipped the lamp and frowned as its light fell upon . . . Were those seeds? Seeds and sand mixed together in messy piles. There was a brass bowl half filled with yet more seeds, abandoned beside a heap of empty woven sacks and an extinguished lamp. Strange things to adorn the floors of a bedchamber, but Lamia was not dissuaded. She stepped over a final pile and drew level with the couch. At last, Lamia's lamplight reached the girl curled there. At the sight of Eirene, the blanket pulled above her shoulders and her face turned toward the tower wall, Lamia's heart skipped. She hadn't realized she'd been holding her breath; she let it out slowly, loath to allow the sound to rouse Eirene.

She wanted to see *more*. She had to.

She leaned closer, captivated by the arch of Eirene's brow, by the sweep of her cheekbones and the dissatisfied curl of her mouth as she slept. She had a squarish jaw and full, perfect lips. She seemed to glow with vitality—here was a girl who lived in the light.

The orange flicker of the lamp caught on Eirene's long lashes, fluttering as she dreamed, and the little scar above the bridge of her nose and the fine dusting of hair over her cheeks. Lamia would never have been able to see such detail from a distance. It took her breath away. She could have watched Eirene forever; nothing could have disturbed her admiration.

Except, of course, it could.

As Lamia leaned in closer—precariously close, too close—a single drop of oil spilled from the lamp and landed in the center of

Eirene's flushed cheek. Lamia drew in a sharp breath and swung the lamp away. The light flickered wildly and the next droplet of oil fell into the ragged skirt of her chiton. But it was too late; the damage was already done.

For a single heartbeat, Lamia thought that Eirene might not wake. That, somehow, she would not have felt the oil now cooling on her skin and would slumber on, lost in her anxious dreaming.

But then Eirene opened her eyes, and her dark gaze fixed itself upon Lamia.

XI

THE NIGHT AND DARKNESS

Eirene

Eirene awoke to a phantom bending over her, its pale face horribly close to hers.

Naturally she shrieked, a pitiful gasping sound issuing from her throat as she scrabbled back against the wall, kicking off her blanket, and attempting to put as much distance between her and this . . . this *thing* as she could. "Stay *back*," she panted. Her eyes adjusted slowly to the light and she cast about wildly for a weapon. "Don't think I can't hurt you." The empty lamp was on the floor, somewhere out of reach, and her knife was back in her satchel, tucked beneath the far end of the bed. She sucked in a determined breath. No matter. If it came to it, she'd use her teeth. Very few people expected to be bitten by a girl her size.

"I don't think that you *can't* hurt me," said a hesitant voice. "But I do wish you wouldn't."

If Eirene had expected a voice, this was not it. It was far too . . . human. Soft and young and unmusical. Eirene squinted in the direction of its owner.

She exhaled. It was not a phantom. It was a girl.

A mistake easily made, it had to be said; the girl was tall and very slender, with a long, gaunt face and thin reddish-brown hair hanging to her waist in limp strands. In the flickering light of the oil lamp, her skin was pallid—olive washed out so that it was almost gray. Eirene could see through to the blue-green tracery of veins beneath the surface.

With her back pressed against the wall, Eirene put a hand to her breast and sucked in harsh breaths until the frantic flutter of her heartbeat returned to its usual steady thud. Her fright gave way to annoyance. "What do you mean by sneaking in here like that?" she snarled. Her voice broke on the last word. "And in the middle of the night, too! What is *wrong* with you?"

"You're angry," said the girl. Her eyes were very large. Her nose was ever so slightly crooked, as if it had been broken and clumsily reset. She chewed on her lower lip.

"Of course I'm angry! You can't just materialize and—*oh*." Eirene clenched her fists. "How did you get in? The door's barred!" She remembered the screeching protest of metal as Leandros had pushed the bar into place.

The girl looked bewildered. "It's barred from the outside. And I came . . . from outside."

Eirene wished she had something clever and scathing to say, but a large number of her thoughts were still wandering, lost, through a fog of sleep. She settled for a furious glare.

If the girl noticed, she did not let it bother her. "I'm Lamia," she offered, and she took a hesitant step closer. "And you're Eirene."

"I know who I am," said Eirene hotly. "And I don't *care* who you are." Then she narrowed her eyes. Everyone knew that Leandros dismissed his servants at nighttime. And if this girl was not a servant . . . "Sorry," said Eirene, "but who are you?"

Lamia furrowed her brow. "I'm Lamia," she said again. Then, with a small, bright smile playing at the edges of her mouth: "I thought you didn't care."

"I changed my mind," said Eirene. She inched closer to Lamia, scooting over the stretched skins of the couch and plastering a broad smile onto her face. She had been sorting the seeds one by one before, blowing the sand from each individual lentil and making slow, painful progress. But there would be easier ways. Perhaps this strange waxen girl could get her the things she needed. "Are you a servant?"

Lamia deflated. "I suppose he didn't tell you about me?"

"Who didn't? Leandros?"

"I suppose he didn't tell you about me *yet*." This Lamia seemed to be saying to herself more than to Eirene. "But that makes sense. Because he can't trust you . . . yet."

"All right." Eirene was struck by a sudden mortifying thought. If Lamia wasn't a maid, was she something *else* to Leandros? Something closer? "You're not his . . . lover, are you?" she demanded. Lamia looked young—fifteen, sixteen *perhaps*—and certainly too young to bed a man like Leandros, who must have been nearing thirty. That said, Eirene herself was just sixteen and was meant to be *marrying* Leandros. Only the fact that she intended to destroy him and flee before that could happen would stop the match; after seeing Ianthe with *her* husband, she was not so sure little things like age mattered to men like that.

"Lover?" spluttered Lamia, who seemed to have taken several long moments to process Eirene's question. Her face was incredulous. "I'm his *daughter*!"

"Oh." Eirene relaxed her jaw. Then she frowned. "Wait, *daughter*?"

Lamia dropped her chin a little. "As I said," she mumbled. "He really didn't tell you?"

Eirene had not once heard tell of Leandros having a daughter. But here she was. Damn. It wasn't too likely that Lamia would be willing to help Eirene defy her father, then. But Eirene would try to convince her anyway. "Look," she said quietly, in the low, gentle voice she reserved for Phoebe when she was pulled under by her worst fevers. It was a voice that, beneath the words, said *please, trust me.* "He probably didn't tell me to . . . protect you. Somehow." It was a feeble excuse, but Lamia visibly perked up. Eirene hurried to continue. "I have a sister, a twin sister. Her name is Phoebe, and I'm doing this"—she indicated the floor scattered with grains—"to protect *her.* You understand family, Lamia, I can see that."

Lamia narrowed her eyes at the mess of lentils and grain and poppy seeds. Her lips parted, her features shifting into an expression of slow realization. "This is your first task?"

Eirene startled. "You know about the tasks?" Damn again. There was no chance she could just trick Lamia into working against her father, then. She knew what Eirene toiled for and it would have to be outright defiance.

Lamia ignored the question. "Why don't you want Phoebe to marry my father?"

"Because Phoebe is—" Eirene broke off. Lamia was *tall* and Eirene felt at a peculiar disadvantage hunched up in the bed as she was, her suspicions sprouting and blooming. She sat up properly, swinging her legs over the edge of the couch and peering up into Lamia's narrow face. "But how do you know I didn't want her to marry him? Did—did Leandros tell you?"

Lamia's waxy skin bloomed with sudden color. She ducked her head. "He didn't . . . tell me, exactly," she admitted.

"And what *exactly* does that mean?"

"I . . . overheard?"

Eirene shot to her feet. How much did Lamia know? How much did she know about *Eirene* when Eirene knew nothing of Lamia in return? "You *eavesdropped,*" she hissed. "Is that what you're saying?"

Lamia backed away, her hands up. "Why are you so angry? If I know what's happening, I can—I can help!"

Eirene stopped dead. Lamia was still backing away, her eyes darting to the ground and then back to Eirene with each step.

"You can help?"

"Leandros didn't say you couldn't have help," said Lamia. "Not that I heard. I don't know what you're doing with the grains, but maybe I can be of use. I'm an extra pair of hands at the very least." She offered Eirene her palms as proof. One hand was wrapped in pale bandages. The fingertips were dotted with dark color. Eirene looked away quickly, meeting Lamia's eyes again. They were wide and hopeful and an inexplicably captivating shade of light brown.

An extra pair of hands, Lamia had said. An extra pair of hands attached to a body that wasn't locked inside this room. Eirene narrowed her eyes at Lamia's outstretched palms and let out a soft huff of breath. She could do this. She *would* do this. "Can those hands get me a sieve?"

"A sieve?"

"A sieve!" Repeating the word only strengthened Eirene's conviction. "And water. I need to wash the sand off the seeds once I've separated them. And it'll need to be a fine sieve—for wine if you have one?" She'd seen Stavros use such a sieve each time he drank through to the bottom of a jug of wine, where the grape seeds and skins collected in a dark sludge. He'd pour the last dredges of wine through the sieve and into a bowl, then he'd sit by the hearth and tip the bowl back to his mouth, draining it in a single swallow. His eyes would be bright and empty. Eirene shook off the memory and continued. "It won't separate the lentils and the wheat berries, but"—the plan solidified in her mind with each word she spoke—"but I can use the water! The lentils will sink and the wheat berries will float!" She paused, frowning. "No, that's not right. They only float if they've been hollowed out by insects. But you'll be there to help me and the bigger seeds are easier to sort by hand. You can see I've already done a good number of the lentils, and—" She looked up at Lamia, her words swallowed up by the grin she couldn't stop spreading across her face. She was going to complete the task. She was going to save Phoebe.

But Lamia was shaking her head. "Can't you . . . ?" She looked down, twisting her hands in the skirts of her chiton. There was a messy stain in the material. "Can't you ask Peiros?"

Eirene blew out her cheeks in exasperation. "Of course not. I'm sure that he wants me to fail; he would never bring me such things. And if I leave myself, I forfeit the whole thing. It is clear that he does not wish me to succeed, and he will certainly not help me do so."

"I can't leave either."

Eirene stared. "What?"

Lamia's flush deepened until her whole face was pink. "Not right now, anyway. It's nighttime."

"*So?* Everyone will be sleeping, then! You won't even be seen!"

Lamia's lip trembled. "The tower door is locked at night. To protect me"—she brightened—"to protect *us*."

"So unlock it."

"Locked from the *outside*. With a bar."

Eirene laughed. It was a hard, vicious sound. "Locked from the *outside* to protect you? Do you know why my room is locked from the outside, Lamia?" She did not wait for Lamia to reply before plowing onward. "It's to keep me *in*."

"My father doesn't need to keep me in," protested Lamia. "The door is locked for my safety."

"Using a bar?"

Lamia's eyes darted from side to side, as if she sensed the trap. "Using a bar," she confirmed eventually.

"So why don't *you* have the bar on *your* side? Lock yourself in every night. That would be far safer, no?"

Lamia's face hardened. "What if my father needed to get in?"

"Why would he?" challenged Eirene. "What could be so urgent that he could not just call for you and have you unlock the tower yourself? It seems to me that you're making excuses, Lamia, and—"

"I can't leave," snapped Lamia. She was trembling, bright tears glistening in the corners of her eyes. "So I can't do what you want. There's no need to . . . to *taunt* me. To question me. I've been nice to you."

Eirene rolled her weight back onto the balls of her feet. She'd been leaning forward without meaning to, as if ready to spring onto the shaking girl standing before her. They regarded one another silently for some time. Then—

"Please," said Eirene. Her voice cracked—a nice touch. "Please, Lamia, just try. I *need* you to try."

She hurried over to the bowl she'd left on the ground, half the lentils picked out, the wheat berries and poppy seeds and sand still a hopeless mess. Her lamp had burned out before she'd had a chance to pluck out the remaining lentils, and she'd had no choice but to give up for the night. "Look," she said. "If I could just sieve out the sand and the seeds, then I could—"

"No," said Lamia.

Eirene froze, her hand hovering over the bowl. "No? You won't even try?"

"I can't. I can't disobey my father."

Eirene lifted her head very slowly and fixed Lamia with her most hateful look. "Can't? Or won't?"

Lamia said nothing. She lowered her head, refusing to meet Eirene's eyes.

How could she refuse when she knew what was at stake? When she knew how much Eirene had to lose? Her cowardice was infuriating; Eirene could not bear it. "Get *out*." She thrust her hand into the bowl and threw a handful of seeds in Lamia's direction. "Useless, disruptive, interfering *wretch*."

Lamia twisted away from the spray of seeds. "I *can't*," she protested miserably. "But, Eirene, we can still be friends. I just can't—"

"*Out!*"

When Eirene reached for the metal bowl at her feet, Lamia made a startled noise and scurried for the door. There was an awkward tilt to her gait—one leg that swung out a little with each stride.

"Coward!" Eirene yelled after her.

"I'm sorry!" wailed Lamia. She pulled the door open and tucked herself behind it, her pale frightened face peering around the edge. "I *want* to help. I just—"

"No, you don't." Eirene turned her face away. Her rage had petered out into exhaustion. She shouldn't have allowed herself to hope like that, so recklessly, that Lamia could help her. That Lamia wanted, *truly*, to help her. When she spoke again, she directed her words at the dusty stone floor. "Just go. Please."

She did not look away from the stone for a long while. When she finally lifted her head, Lamia was gone. She'd left her oil lamp behind, carefully tucked into the corner beside the door. A pitiful gift in the face of what she *could* have given Eirene. But it was something. And Eirene was rapidly running out of choices—and time.

Eirene sighed, watching the echo of the flame through the curved bowl of the lamp. Then she got slowly to her feet and went to retrieve it.

XII

FALSE AND FORGED TEARS

Lamia

For the first night since her death, Lamia did not dream of Alexandra. What she did dream, over and over, was the look of surprise and fright and then disgust on Eirene's face as she had looked upon Lamia. Each iteration of the memory sent a thrill of self-hatred through Lamia, so that it was almost a relief to be yanked out of sleep by heavy footsteps on the tower stairs and the familiar sound of her father calling her name.

"Yes!" Had there been a touch of irritation in his voice? Lamia fought free of her blankets, fear already pressing at her stomach. He must have found out about her visiting Eirene and he would punish her severely for it. Her fingertips prickled. Lamia drew in quick shallow breaths. She'd fallen asleep in her clothes; the brooch at one shoulder had left a stark mark on her skin, but at least she would not have to keep her father waiting as she dressed. She perched on the edge of the bed and carefully retied the wrapping around her knee, wincing as she bent the sleep-stiffened joint. Then she pulled on her boots. Her fingers only shook a little as she yanked the laces tight and knotted them deftly. "Come in," she croaked.

The curtain was flung wide and her father sauntered in. "It's dark in here," he said, glancing about. Lamia froze. He must have noticed the missing lamp. He moved closer, so that the light from the small window found his features. Lamia blinked. He didn't look angry. In fact, he was smiling. "I must get you another lamp, my sweet girl." He beamed at her, flashing his teeth, but Lamia's eyes had already slid down to his hand and the little bowl dangling from his fingertips. Ah. That was why he was here. The prickling in her own fingers sharpened and she was relieved to feel tears already welling in the corners of her eyes. At least he would not have to hurt her so very badly today.

"Hello, Father," said Lamia reluctantly, picking at the bedframe and bracing herself for the pain that must soon come.

But her father did not stride over and haul her to her feet as he usually did on days like these. Instead, he took a few more leisurely steps toward her and regarded her with what might have been fondness. "I do not say enough what a jewel you are, my dear Lamia."

Lamia's gaze flicked back to his face. He was *still* smiling, his features lit with genuine happiness. "I—thank you?" she managed. She let herself relax just a little. Her father's joy was infectious; he glowed with it.

"Yes." He took another step toward her. "I am not a reflective man—it is a flaw, I know—and I allow myself to frequently forget what we have accomplished together."

"Ah," said Lamia. It seemed better to be concise given she had no idea what he was speaking of.

"We are beloved here," said her father grandly. "We have brought contentment, beauty, *love*, and the villagers gladly give up their coin. They revere my name, as they would yours if they were wise."

If they knew it, thought Lamia, remembering Eirene's confusion.

"But we must know this adoration is not for us alone." His face was suddenly serious. His fingers twitched on the bowl. "And *they* must know this, too. My next symposium will be a celebration of our beloved foremother, Aphrodite, reminding my guests who the love they cherish is truly from. I will urge them to turn to her in worship, too, to burn the thigh bones of sheep and pour out their wine in libation."

This did not seem to have anything to do with Lamia. She nodded warily.

Her father let out a dramatic sigh. "It will not be a small undertaking. My sweet girl, I must beg of you your tears."

There it was. Lamia raised her shoulders in a wordless half shrug. There was no need for him to make such a show of asking. She had never denied such a request. She could not.

"Ah, you are my most precious thing," he said, fixing her with his most adoring stare. "Lamia, I would give you the world if I could. It is what I owe you." He lifted the bowl. "It will be quick. I have business in the village."

Lamia nodded slowly. Her father's words were clear. Lamia was valuable; this was a partnership. The thought filled her with sudden confidence. Eirene's words kept ringing in her ears: *It seems to me that you're making excuses, Lamia.* She could leave. If she wanted. But did she want to? Lamia felt her courage waver. "Can I come with you?" she blurted before it could flicker away completely.

He looked like she'd coughed in his face. "Come with me? To . . . to the village?"

"Yes, the village," said Lamia. She got to her feet so that he was not looming over her quite so much, so that she felt less like a small child, and took a hesitant step toward him. "Don't you think it's time?" She tried for a smile. "I'm all grown up now, and I have to see the world eventually."

Her father did not return her smile. He was frowning, a furrowing of his golden brow that deepened with each second. Slowly, he began to shake his head. "Lamia—" She had never heard him so hesitant. "Lamia, my daughter. Perhaps, in my enthusiasm, I spoke too highly of our fellow islanders. There are so many of them, and they are . . . they are not like you and me. They were born here, they will live their whole lives here, and they will die here. They have not seen the world as we have. They are fearful—easily driven to hatred and violence against that which they do not understand."

Lamia didn't remember anything of the world. But she understood what her father was saying.

He sighed. "Still, if you are *very* eager to go, I will not stop you. I suppose I cannot protect you forever."

All Lamia's courage had trickled away again. She remembered again the look on Eirene's face when she'd awoken to find Lamia standing over her, how it had made Lamia want to curl up into a ball and hide. And that was just one girl. How would Lamia feel with an entire village looking at her like that? Ogling her otherness: her leg, her awkward gait, the sallow features of her face. Lamia sagged. "No," she said. "No, you're right. I suppose I wasn't thinking."

"I suppose not," agreed her father. He stepped forward and enfolded her in his arms. She leaned stiffly against him. "Poor Lamia," he said to the top of her head. "Don't think I blame you. Of course you're curious. Of course you want to see the world. But the world is not kind to girls like you, you must understand."

When she said nothing, he pulled her harder against him, wrapping his arms more tightly around her until it was an effort to breathe. "You are so breakable, my sweet girl, but they would only see your peculiarities and think that *you* are the danger. They aren't kind to things that are different, things that are ugly. They would see you gone just to feel safe, or make a public spectacle, a mockery, of you and your strangeness."

Again, Eirene's face flashed in Lamia's mind. She shrank into herself. Her father was right; of course he was. Who but her own father could have any kindness for her? She pressed her face against his chiton so that he would not see the tears prickling in the corners of her eyes.

"But I won't let them. Of all the world, I am the only one who will *always* protect you."

He gently pushed her away from him, moving his hands to her wrists as he looked her full in the face. His eyes went to hers, then lower, to trace the path of a single tear over her cheek. His mouth twisted just a little. "But I can't protect you alone. You have to help me, Lamia. Can you help me?"

Lamia nodded wordlessly. She knew what was coming, and she was grateful that the rest of the tears came easily when he moved his fingers over the delicate insides of her wrist, where her pulse fluttered—a moth trapped in a jar—and pinched hard, his fingernails cutting into her flesh like butter.

Afterward, he held the small brass bowl to her face and coaxed her tears into it. Then he left and returned a short while later with a tray laden with olives and figs and bread. It was plain food, but when Lamia took her first bite of fig, her mouth filled with saliva and she was suddenly ravenous. She tore into the bread, sweeping pieces through the small dish of olive oil that accompanied the food.

She ate one-handed while her father wrapped a white linen bandage around her injured wrist. She tried not to look at it; the sight of the blood blooming in the five crescent-shaped wounds set her stomach twisting uncomfortably. It was not his fault. The tears needed to come, somehow.

When he was finished, he pressed a kiss to her forehead and left the room, leaving the curtain open. Lamia looked down at the tray. Her hunger had dissipated as quickly as it had come; the last bite of bread tasted stale and clung to the roof of her mouth.

She was desperate for air. She took the tray to the window and shook the crumbs out into the tangle of roses. The birds took up their usual fluttering and frantic chirping, but Lamia barely heard them. Her hands were sticky from the figs when she put them to her cheeks, rubbing her palms over the skin of her face until they too were tear-damp and shimmering. Then she cupped them together and watched as the shimmer became a glow that became brighter and brighter. Lamia turned back to the room. It always seemed to exist in half shadow, hiding the best and worst of it; Lamia's light fell upon dusty corners and charcoal stains on the blankets and crumbs on the poorly kept skins spread out over the floor.

The light cupped in her palms was growing uncomfortably warm. Lamia drew in a shuddering breath and the light pulsed brighter, the heat flaring with it. It *hurt*, badly, but she did not let it go—not until the pain was as sharp as a knife against her skin, until she could focus on nothing else. Even then, she acquiesced its power reluctantly. There was nothing quite like the feeling of magic, the shining of the light on her skin and the way it thrummed and danced and *burned* inside her.

As the light fractured and dissipated, Lamia looked down at her palms. One was still wrapped in bandages, with pinpricks of blood at the tip of each sore finger. The other, though, was bare, the skin uncovered, red raw and blistered.

XIII
MOST MISERABLE FORTUNE

Eirene

Eirene had had enough of lentils for a lifetime. After two days of sorting the wretched things, the air had assumed their earthy scent and Eirene kept finding them caught in the folds of her chiton, between the sole of her foot and her sandal, even in her hair. The sky was flushed with sunset when she tossed the last brown seed into the sack, and she was gripped with such euphoria that she managed to forget for a moment that there were still thousands of wheat berries and poppy seeds to sift through. And barely one day—and two nights—left to do so.

She stood, stretching out her shoulders and arching her back against the tightness that had come from so many hours folded over the piles of seeds. She paced twice around the cramped little room, rolling out her wrists and wincing at the stiffness in her knees. After another day of this, she'd barely be able to stand. She thought of Phoebe on the other side of the village. Was she stretching out her tired joints, too? Smearing salve on her fingers to soften the calluses? Eirene would make sure that whatever they both suffered was worth it. She *would* be victorious.

Eirene ducked down to the floor again and reached for the lamp Lamia had left. Eirene paused, her hands cradling the cool earthenware. Lamia. The thought of her made Eirene feel itchy. She wasn't entirely sure why. Perhaps, deep down, she knew she had been unfair; none of this was *Lamia's* fault, after all, and she hadn't deserved to be screamed at so viciously. If Phoebe was here, she would be eyeing Eirene with pointed displeasure, arms folded across her chest.

"She's a coward," Eirene would argue, hearing the whine in her own voice. She always knew which arguments she would lose the moment they began. "You would never leave me like that, just because it risked angering Leandros."

"Yes, but, Eirene, not everyone is the same. You don't know why she acts that way—perhaps she has her reasons."

"Stupid reasons," Eirene would grumble.

"You don't know that," Phoebe would say gently. "She was afraid, and you only frightened her more. Why should she help you? You thought only of yourself—"

"And you!"

"You let your anger get the better of you," Phoebe would say. "You have to apologize."

"Gods damn it," said Eirene out loud. Because Phoebe—or the part of Eirene that Phoebe always occupied—was right. Well, there was nothing she could do about it now. Eirene shrugged off the memory of Lamia's wide hurt eyes and lit the lamp. The oil was running low, but dark had fallen and Eirene could hardly see what she was doing without the lamp's steady shine. She rolled her shoulders once more, banished any last lingering thoughts of Lamia, then resumed her work.

She was making good progress. The wheat berries were easy to sort from the poppy seeds and sand—she had swiftly developed a method of tossing the mix up in loosely cupped hands, allowing the smallest pieces to fall through her fingers. She would be left with a handful of gritty wheat berries each time, which she deposited into a gradually filling sack. The hours crept by and the heap of wheat at the bottom of the sackcloth grew slowly but surely. Exhaustion became a steady drumbeat against her eyelids. There was no time to sleep. Eirene shook her head hard in an attempt to clear it, slapped her cheeks, and rubbed her gummy eyes, hissing as sand crept in between her eyelids.

She emptied another bowl of its wheat berries and thrust the empty dish into the dwindling heap of unsorted seeds. When she dug her fingers into the mixture, they felt something that was certainly not grain. A rough, stiff fragment that fitted easily into the palm of her hand. She frowned and pulled it out.

In the flickering lamplight, she could make out a neatly woven piece of fabric. Its edges were jagged, as if it had been ripped from a larger garment without care, and a stain marred its surface. The stain was long-dried, and when Eirene brought it to her nose and gave it a tentative sniff, it smelled of little but lentils. Eirene tossed it away with a scoff. It vanished into the dark shadows beneath the couch.

"Probably the only scrap left of the *last* poor soul set this task," she said out loud. This amused her, and she managed to sort the grain from almost another full bowl before the boredom and the fatigue crept into the edges of her consciousness again. She tossed the remaining poppy-seed-and-sand mix onto the floor and groaned.

When would this be *over*? Her mouth was dry with sand and grit, and running her tongue around her cheeks and across her lips did little to alleviate the discomfort. Her head, too, had begun to pound in time with her heart. Her eyelids were so heavy they might have been made from stone; each of her blinks seemed to last longer and longer until finally she closed her eyes and could not bring herself to open them again.

Relief washed over her, followed an instant later by a crashing wave of exhaustion. She was so *tired*. Her head dropped forward and she bolted upright again, snapping her head back. Her eyes shot open, but her vision was a dark blur. She had to rest. She *had* to. How could she work like this—all but blind and slumping over every few minutes?

Just a little while, she promised herself. If her eyelids had been heavy before, now they were even more so. She doubted Atlas himself could have held them open. She'd just rest them for a moment.

Through her eyelids, she could see the soft light of the lamp. It faded into a smudge of the night sky swirling with stars. "Just . . . ," she said aloud, the word dissolving into a yawn as the sky opened its maw to swallow her.

. . . a moment.

Eirene woke with a jolt.

It took her a while to orient herself, to understand why every part of her ached as it did. She was curled into a tight ball on the stone floor of the tower room, her head pressed against the cool surface. The lamp had burned out, but the room was bright.

Her ears seemed to echo with the memory of some recent sound. It had woken her. The pattering of something—feet, per- haps, on the stone floor. *Lamia?*

Her head snapped up and she looked about wildly, squinting into the sudden harsh light. But Lamia was nowhere to be seen. As the world swam into hazy focus, she saw that the door was closed. Not Leandros either, then. Or Peiros. So what had it been?

She shifted and something hard pressed into her knee.

No. Oh no.

Slowly, slowly, Eirene looked down.

There were lentils everywhere, scattered over the stone and clinging to the rough fabric of her chiton. The sack—the sack she had finally, *finally* filled—had toppled over, spilling its contents everywhere. They mixed with the unsorted heap, sinking in among the sand and seeds.

All that work. All that time. A waste.

Eirene let out a soft wail and scrambled onto her hands and knees, scooping up handfuls of lentils that had not become mixed again and thrusting them back into the sack. What time was it? How many precious hours had she lost—and, more importantly, how many remained?

She staggered to her feet and stumbled to the window, craning her head up to the sky. Her breath was rapid and uneven and the sun was a bright blaze of light above the tower. Even as she watched, it seemed to creep lower. Past noon. Well past noon. She had slept away most of the day and set herself back half a day more in her careless upset of the lentils. She would not finish in time now. Not unless . . .

Eirene largely considered herself an honest trader. She only overcharged those she knew could afford it—who only wanted her tinctures to soothe some invented complaint, anyway—and she hardly *ever* sold a cough cure that was nothing more elaborate than a teaspoon of honey dissolved in water. With a sprig of rosemary tucked into the jar for effect, of course. She tried to be ethical when she could afford it. But she certainly could not afford it now.

She threw herself back down on the floor and scooped up a handful from the unsorted heap. Sand and poppy seeds spilled beneath her fingers as she dashed to the window again. Once there, she went very still, chewing on her lip until she tasted blood. What would Leandros do if he found out? It could not be worse than what would happen if she failed. Phoebe would be here instead in this disgusting little room, and Eirene would be left with Stavros and his foul temper.

Eirene set her jaw. Her heart writhed like a songbird in a trap; her panic had settled in her throat, digging its claws into her flesh. She could hardly breathe. She could lose everything if Leandros knew of her deception. But everything for Eirene was very little now.

She cast the handful of seeds and grit from the window, flinging them as far from her as she could. There was a short, merciful moment in which the seeds showered to the ground and seemed to settle. Then there was an *explosion* of sound, of movement—the fluttering of what must have been thousands of wings as birds burst from the trees, the shrubs, the carefully maintained rosebushes. Thrushes, wagtails, sparrows, and finches all descended on the meager scattering of seeds. They seemed to be *screaming* at one another in an unbearable cacophony that was trapped inside her skull and furiously trying to escape, turning her mind to pulp, shattering her bones.

She backed away, pressing her hands to her ears. But it was too late. Everything, all of it, was too much. The noise, the task, the failure. Phoebe, Leandros, Lamia. Too much to do, too much to prove, too many depending on her. Too many destroying her. Even the touch of her hair on her cheeks and the brush of her chiton over her skin was a sudden and unbearable agony.

Too much, too much, too much.

Eirene cried out—an awful anguished sound that she could hardly believe was her own—and then she crumpled to the floor and sobbed.

XIV
THE NIGHT IN WEEPING

Lamia

The cry split the air as a sharpened blade might part flesh—a raw animal sound of agony.

Lamia shot to her feet, staggering as the pain in her knee flared beneath this sudden assault of weight-bearing. She leaned against the wall. She had been stretched out on her bed all day, massaging her temples against the vicious pounding of a headache.

The cry came again, quieter, more human, thick with despair and, this time, recognizable. Eirene. *Eirene.* What had happened? Was she hurt? Was she ill? Did she need help?

Another cry. Lamia clenched her hands into tight fists. No, that wasn't a sound of pain, not the physical kind anyway. Lamia was not quite sure how she knew, but she did; this was the sound of grief, of the deepest, most desperate kind.

Understanding came gradually to Lamia as she remembered Eirene's words: *Her name is Phoebe.* That helpless gesture toward her impossible task. *I'm doing this to protect her.* This sound was one of failure, then, of knowing that she had not managed to save her sister. She had not completed the task.

But there was time left, wasn't there? The situation could not be completely hopeless. Not yet, anyway. Water and a sieve. That was what Eirene had asked for.

Lamia looked out of the window, to the sun, where it tipped

heavily toward the horizon and then onto the path. She could certainly make it to the kitchens and back before the tower door was locked for the night. There was no sign of Peiros making his return. And even if her father caught her, he would understand, wouldn't he? Eirene did this for her sister, because she loved her, because she wanted to protect her. Lamia's father would do the same for her. She knew he would.

That decided it. She changed swiftly into a clean blue chiton, pinning the shoulders with the brooches her father had gifted her long ago, and made for the door.

The stairs were their usual painful labor; when Lamia reached the landing in the center of the tower, it was an immense relief to lean against the wall and stretch out the cramps in her foot. She could still hear the soft sounds of Eirene's pain from the bottom of the tower. *I'm coming*, Lamia told her silently. *Just wait.*

Lamia thought she'd been caught, two steps into the garden, when a shape melted out of the bushes and fell into step beside her. She gasped, hands flying to her mouth, heart leaping from her chest and into her throat. But it was only Daphne, with a small dead bird in her mouth and an air of smug self-satisfaction.

"Hello," said Lamia through her fingers. "I wish you wouldn't eat my sparrows."

"Mrow," said Daphne, through a mouthful of feathers.

With Daphne at her side, it was almost too easy for Lamia to walk through the garden to the little side door leading to the main house, push it open, and step inside. It led to a quieter part of the house, her father's rooms, where the servants—except Peiros—were never permitted. Today was not a symposium day, which meant that the rest of the house would be similarly deserted.

Besides her uneven footsteps and Daphne's soft padding, there was nothing to be heard as she crept toward the back of the house. Her father's chambers and the workshop she knew existed some-where beyond—below?—were divided from the rest of the house by a heavy wooden door, in front of which was hung an even heavier curtain. She had asked him about it once, when he was in a fine mood and she thought he might humor her questions with a response.

"I am not a heavy sleeper, Lamia," he had told her gravely. "And this is not a quiet house. Would you have me waking up at every sound?"

She had rarely known the house to be anything *but* quiet. Still, she kept her step as light and slow as she could as she passed her father's curtain and made for the kitchen.

She couldn't stamp down the fear that he would emerge from his rooms, or Peiros would return from his errand and catch her. And it would be perfectly fine if they did, Lamia reminded herself sternly; she was doing nothing wrong. She was allowed in the house before dark, even if she rarely went. It wasn't worth the painful descent of the tower stairs just to—what? Irritate her father by hov-ering over him as he tried to work? He labored all day, brewing his Desires and searching for new ways to protect *her*. He did not want to be harassed by his naive little daughter.

She walked into the kitchen and stopped dead, frowning, her eyes darting over the room. Lamia had a vague sort of awareness of her father's comings and goings; she watched him stride away from the house almost every evening, so she probably should have real-ized earlier how rarely he ate in his own home. The kitchen showed this neglect starkly. The great hearth had burned down to all but embers; the air—which smelled not of sweet herbs and honey and sizzling fat but of must and the slightest note of rot—was barely warm. A handful of skewers lay beside the smoldering ashes, each coated in a thin sheen of congealed grease, and the piles of beaten metal platters and pans stacked on shelves were covered in a thin layer of dust. As for the door to the storeroom where sacks of grains and beans were stored, it was . . . gone. Lamia blinked.

The door had not just vanished. It had been *removed*. This removal had clearly been done with some force; the stone was crumbling, gouged away, where it had once been joined to the wood of the door.

Lamia barely registered taking the few, stumbling steps toward the storeroom before she was brought up short by a sudden, violent surge of nausea. It came on so abruptly that she had no time to suppress it, to brace herself against it. She doubled over, gagging, feeling that there was something monstrous and rotten nestling in her stomach that had chosen this moment to fledge. Her mouth tasted of copper, as if she'd been running hard, as she hadn't done in years, until she was panting and exhausted. Her heart beat a frantic rhythm from somewhere near her ears. Lamia had never felt nausea so brutal.

She staggered back from the empty doorway and collided with Daphne. Daphne made a startled, furious sound and bolted. Lamia fell hard, head spinning, landing gracelessly on her back. Pain jolted through her and she let out a breathless howl of anguish. Lamia knew what it felt like when something was broken, and this was not that feeling. It was enough to snap her out of the awful haze of nausea; with a final twist that made her retch, the grip on her stomach let go. She lay on her back, splayed like a slaughtered lamb, until her heart had slowed enough that she would not faint when she sat up. Even so, she pulled herself upright cautiously, hissing through her teeth as her back screamed a constant note of protest.

She had to get out. She was halfway to the door leading back into the house when her mind caught up to her limbs and she slowed, coming to a stop a few paces from the doorway. She eyed the corridor beyond with sick longing. But she could not go back, not yet. Eirene needed her. A sieve and water.

Reluctantly, Lamia turned around. She kept her face turned pointedly from the storeroom and skirted the edge of the room, toward the precarious heap of empty wine jugs piled by the door that led outside and the trough where rainwater for washing was collected. They had clearly been left with some intention of rinsing that had never been executed; the smell of vinegar was sharp and unpleasant and blessedly sobering. Lamia walked closer, breathing in the acrid fumes. She could have cried when her gaze fell upon a little sieve discarded beside the jugs. It was clogged with the silt that clouded the bottom of wine jars. It smelled terrible, but it was perfect. Lamia snatched it up before, like the storeroom door from the wall, it could be torn away. She pulled the silt out with her fingers as best she could before thrusting the sieve through her belt. Now for the water.

She picked up the biggest jug she thought she'd be able to carry once it was full, which was not that big at all, and maneuvered it and herself out through the open courtyard door on the opposite side of the room. It was cool and dry outside, but the fountain bubbled away merrily. A trio of ducks eyed her suspiciously from the basin. Daphne, now lounging in a patch of sun, lifted her head and narrowed her eyes at Lamia. She was clearly still unhappy about having been tripped over.

"Sorry," Lamia told her. She set the jug down, then reached

over the ducks with her hands cupped, into the streams of water cascading from the fountain's centerpiece. She brought the dripping handful to her mouth and drank deeply, washing away the bitter bloody taste. She could not wash away everything, though. The memory lingered like a bad smell. What had happened? She was ill often, and did not always remember the details afterward, but she could not recall ever feeling like that. It was frightening, disorientating. Would it happen again?

She ducked down to retrieve the jug. When she was safely back in her room, she would have plenty of time to think it over. Time Eirene didn't have. Lamia's hands trembled as she dunked the jug into the trough and watched the water rush inside. Once it was full, she cradled it against her chest and hurried back into the kitchen. Her grip was lopsided and water sloshed over the rim. The sieve in her belt slapped against her flesh and her chiton grew more soaked with each step she took, but she could not bring herself to stop to adjust it. She just wanted to leave this kitchen and the awful fog of dread that hung invisibly within it.

She stepped out into the corridor, then shrank back into the shadows, pulse climbing higher, as something moved at the far end of the passage. Peiros. He would have seen her, she was sure, had his attention not been directed at the curtain that usually concealed her father's rooms, now thrust aside. She could see her father's golden fingers wrapped around the bright cloth.

"Returned . . . the brothel." Peiros was speaking in a low, urgent tone. Lamia could hardly discern every second word. ". . . the new price . . . expensive . . ."

"Too *expensive*?" She had no such problem discerning her father's words—she could have almost believed that his clear, scornful voice was audible all the way down in the village. Lamia shrank farther behind the curtain. "The price I offer them is more than generous. They don't really believe that it's the natural charm of their girls or the foul vinegars they call wine that bring the clients back, do they?"

"It seems that way."

"Ha!" The sound was entirely devoid of amusement. "It would be a pathetic excuse for piss, let alone wine. Half the girls are missing their teeth, and they'd be just as plain with them. It is *Desire* that brings those slobbering drunkards back. Desire and nothing else."

"That's what I tried to tell them," said Peiros. "But they would not listen."

Lamia frowned. She understood the individual words, but strung together like this she could make neither head nor tail of them. What could Desire have to do with drunks? And she had no idea what a brothel was, but that didn't sound relevant either. Desire was for helping people to be happy. It was for helping them fall in love.

"I will speak with them myself," announced her father. The heavy tread of his boots receded as he moved toward the courtyard. Lamia allowed herself to exhale. She had been so close to being caught. "Get your cloak."

A pause. Lamia peeked through the gap in the curtain. She could only see the side of Peiros's face, but his craggy features were twisted with bewilderment. "My cloak?"

"Yes, your cloak, Peiros! You're coming with me. I need someone to stand silently in the doorway and look thuggish."

Another pause, this one more offended than confused. "Of course."

There came the shuffling of cloaks and the creak of the main door as it was wrenched open. Her father was still muttering furiously; the words "ungrateful" and "exploiting my good will" seemed to feature quite a lot. Peiros was making calming noises of agreement. The sound stopped abruptly as the door slammed shut.

Lamia waited, concealed behind her curtain, for a full fifty heartbeats before she dared to step out into the open again. She hadn't been caught. She *hadn't been caught*. She let out a surprised, delighted laugh. It echoed in the empty hall, the space ringing with her jubilance.

Her heart racing with the thrill of her victory, water slopping over the edge of the jug with each painful step, Lamia made for the garden, for the tower. For Eirene.

Eirene was still working. Through the door, Lamia could hear the rustling of her skirts as she moved and the gentle patter of seeds falling into their sacks. Every so often, there came a miserable little snuffle. A thin strip of light shone in the gap between the door and the wall.

Propping the jug of water up on her hip and jamming the sieve in under her arms, Lamia yanked at the bolt on the door with her free hand. And all movement on the other side ceased.

"Eirene?" she called out softly. "Eirene, I have brought—"

A rapid slapping of footsteps and then the door was yanked open a sliver. Eirene—barefoot, her hair pulled untidily back from her face—stood in the opening and looked up at Lamia through the gap, her dark eyes narrowed and her arms crossed. Lamia had forgotten how short she was.

"What do you want?" demanded Eirene. She had been crying. Her face was puffy and her lip trembled; there was no venom in her voice—not like last time. She gripped the edge of the door so hard her knuckles were white.

Lamia stuck her knee in the gap and tried to push the door open. Eirene stubbornly resisted. "Let me in! I brought the things you asked for. I don't have a bowl, but I've got the sieve and the water, and once my hands are free I can go—"

She all but fell into the room as Eirene abruptly stepped back. She was saved from hurtling to the floor—and subsequently smashing the jar—by Eirene. She caught Lamia by the top of her shoulders and held her steady until she could find her footing again. She was alarmingly strong. When Eirene released her, Lamia had to resist the temptation to look down at the flesh of her arms, to see if Eirene had left a mark. She wouldn't have minded.

"You're too late," said Eirene simply.

Lamia gave her what must have been a blank look. "But—but I thought you had three days. Until tomorrow morning, I thought. How can it be—"

Eirene cut her off before she could finish. "It's not long enough," she said miserably. "I *tried*, Lamia. I tried. But it's just too much and it's *too late*." Her face twisted with sudden fury and she glared at the items bundled in Lamia's arms. "Leandros will return to me tomorrow morning and he will find my task incomplete. If you'd only brought me what I'd asked for earlier, maybe I could have done it. I could have saved her, but now—" Whatever she had meant to say was swallowed up in a soft sob. A single tear streaked over her grimy cheeks, leaving a trail in the dust and sand that clung to her skin.

"It's *not* too late," said Lamia stubbornly. "I'm here now. I can . . . I can help!"

"Help," repeated Eirene dully. She wiped the tear from her face with the back of her hand.

"Yes, *help*," said Lamia. "Think about it! There's an hour or so of daylight left, and then the whole night. There's not too much left to do, is there? With two of us and the sieve and the water—well, I don't quite understand what those are for, but you seem to know—with all those things together, it'll be *easy*." Eirene was gazing at her with utter despair. Even like this, she was beautiful. Luminous. Lamia had the urge to touch her, to press her mouth to the hollow where the line of Eirene's throat met her shoulder, where her pulse flickered. It was a good thing that her hands were still full, preventing her from doing anything so strange. "It'll be easy," she repeated, her voice filled with more conviction than she truly felt. "I promise."

"The lamps have all burned out," said Eirene. "I—I fell asleep and left one burning. Unless you have another one, maybe two, it doesn't matter how long the night is so long as it is *dark*."

"Light?" Lamia grinned with a heady rush of pleasure. Water and sieve aside, *here* was a way she could help. She knew about light. "You leave that to me."

XV

ABOVE IN STARRY SKIES

Eirene

Eirene would just have to take Lamia at her word. She didn't have a choice.

"Fine," she said stiffly. "And you'll help me?"

Lamia's smile was wide. When she wasn't lurking in the dark like a scared little mouse, she was actually quite pretty. There was a little more color in her cheeks, a brightness to her light eyes. "If you'll let me."

The joy on her face was too precious to destroy. Eirene grunted. "Come on, then. You can separate the poppy seeds."

While Eirene used the sieve to remove the last lentils and wheat berries, Lamia sat by the couch and dumped handfuls of sand and poppy seeds into the water bowl. When Lamia swirled her slender fingers through the slush, the poppy seeds would rise to the top, leaving the sand behind. Then Eirene paused in her sifting to scoop off the layer of little black seeds and spread them out atop her blue shawl to dry. The number of seeds increased steadily and Eirene dared to allow herself to hope again. Maybe, *maybe* they would make it in time.

Lamia was a steady quiet presence. Eirene stopped watching her like a snake that might strike at any moment and started watching her just for the sake of looking. She relaxed; her mind wandered. Perhaps that was why, when Lamia pushed her hair back from her face and left a streak of poppy seeds and sand across her cheek, Eirene didn't think twice before reaching out. It was only when her thumb touched Lamia's cheek, her other fingers resting beneath the hard jut of her jaw, that her mind caught up. She froze. Lamia, too, had gone perfectly still, a flush rising on her skin, her lips parting.

"You've got a bit—" said Eirene stiltedly. What the hell was she doing? She forced herself back into motion, swiping her thumb across Lamia's cheek and brushing away the seeds. She sat back, clearing her throat. "All gone," she said, as casually as she could.

Lamia gazed at her with eyes so wide they were almost perfectly round. Her lips were still parted; Eirene could see the white gleam of her teeth. "Thank you," she said.

Eirene cleared her throat and swept the poppy seeds from the surface of the bowl, turning swiftly to deposit them on her shawl, grateful for the excuse to hide the flare of heat in her own face.

"You're defying your father to do this," she said suddenly, staring resolutely at the seeds.

"Yes," said Lamia. "I know."

"That's brave," said Eirene. "Before, when I called you a coward—"

"I am a coward," said Lamia. "I shouldn't have left you. I've never been brave."

"You're not," said Eirene. "You came back."

There was a pause. Eirene shot a surreptitious look at Lamia, watching the rise and fall of her thin shoulders as she breathed. "Maybe a little," said Lamia at last. She smiled. "Not as brave as you."

Eirene laughed softly. "I'm terrified of heights and spiders. Hardly heroic."

"You came here instead of your sister. You're doing my father's tasks. That's not easy."

Eirene shrugged. "I don't see it that way. I don't have to be brave. I just have to keep going."

Lamia said nothing, a strange expression on her face.

Eirene cleared her throat again and returned to sorting her seeds.

They faltered in their rhythm again when Peiros came to lock the tower door for the night. When they heard the rattle of the bar, Lamia went very still, her hands braced on the floor beside her, as if she was preparing to thrust herself to her feet. Her face twisted with something Eirene recognized from Phoebe: pain, swiftly suppressed but unmistakable. Eirene waited for the tower door to open. But there was no further sound beyond the twitter of nesting birds. Clearly, Leandros was not worried about the girls he'd locked inside the tower. Though he should have been.

Eirene cleared her throat. "Are you all right?"

Lamia had already returned to her sifting. She looked up, brow furrowed. "Why wouldn't I be?"

"Um," said Eirene. "You winced just then."

"Oh. Yes, well." Lamia flushed. "My leg. My knee, really."

"It hurts?"

Lamia looked uncomfortable. "I suppose."

Eirene eyed her satchel, tucked beneath her bed behind the sprigs of herbs she'd tied to the frame to keep them dry and to override the dank, dusty smell that the room had had when she'd first arrived. In the bottom of the satchel was a cluster of neat little jars. "I might have something that'll help, if you'd like?"

Lamia looked bewildered. "Help?"

"Make it hurt less, I mean. It might not work; it's a bit old, since Phoebe has the fresh batch, but . . ."

Lamia was still looking at her as if she'd suddenly revealed herself to be a hydra and grown a handful of extra heads. "But I need to help you with the seeds," she said slowly. "You only have a little time left."

"It won't take long," said Eirene. "I have a paste—something I make for my sister for her wrists. She weaves. You just have to smear it on. It's made with saffron. Um, then hyoscyamus bark, poppy juice, hogweed, resin." She counted them off on her fingers. "Then wax and lamb fat. Soil."

"Wax, lamb fat, and *soil*?"

"It's a *paste*," said Eirene defensively. "That helps everything bind together."

"And it won't make me sleep?"

"No?" Eirene felt distinctly that she was missing something. "Why would it make you sleep?"

"I just thought—never mind. That's very kind of you to offer," said Lamia stiffly. "May I see it?"

"Yes," said Eirene, relieved. She stood, stretching out her sore muscles, and went to retrieve the satchel. "Here." She found the jar and passed it to Lamia.

Lamia lifted the lid and peered doubtfully at the dark clumpy paste inside. She stuck her finger into it and examined the admittedly quite unappealing blob of gunk with interest.

"I know it looks disgusting," said Eirene quickly. "But just smear it on your knee and it might help. I can do it if you like?"

Lamia's shoulders stiffened. "Oh. Thank you." She scraped the blob of paste on her finger back into the jar and wiped her hands clean on her skirt. "I don't think I'll use it now, actually. Would you mind if I took it with me when I go?"

"Oh," said Eirene, pushing down a flare of hurt. "Yes, that's fine." Lamia didn't want her medicine; that was fine. Phoebe would have told her not to take it so personally. The paste did look like river mud, and Eirene had definitely made Lamia uncomfortable by offering to apply it herself. What had compelled her to do *that*?

"It's getting dark," said Lamia abruptly. "I promised you light."

"Oh," said Eirene. "Yes. Please." She had to focus on what was important: finishing the task, saving Phoebe, finding the secret of Desire and destroying it. "If there are lamps in your room, I can go and get them, or—"

"Not lamps," interrupted Lamia. She tucked the jar into the sash at her waist. A sly smile twisted the edges of her mouth and her eyes shone like a cat's in the dark.

Eirene wasn't quite sure what to say to that. She nodded slowly. "All right. Not lamps. Torches, then?"

Lamia's smile only widened. "No, not torches." She spread her arms wide, an echo of Leandros's sickening showmanship. On her, though, it was somehow endearing. No false bravado—she was perfectly earnest, her face lit with childish delight. "Just wait." She leaned over and grabbed Eirene's knife by the handle, where it had been peeking out from the satchel flap.

Eirene stared. "What do you need that for?"

Lamia waved off the question, maneuvering herself back into her sitting position. She examined the blade closely before wiping it clean on her skirts. "Tell me about your sister," she said.

Eirene blinked. "What?"

"Your sister," repeated Lamia. "This is for her, isn't it, and so was that paste. So I want to know about her. What is she like?" She leaned forward, playing idly with the knife. "What makes you love her enough to sell yourself to my father?"

Eirene swallowed. "Phoebe is . . ." She pictured her sister's careful, measured stare. The dance of her hands on the loom. The words caught in her throat. She missed her. Had they ever been apart this long? Three days felt like forever. Was Phoebe all right without her? Eirene cleared her throat and tried again. "Phoebe is a weaver. People don't realize how hard weaving is. It's not just making pretty things. It's mathematical and technical and incredibly physical, and Phoebe is the best."

"The best?"

"Besides Athena," amended Eirene. It was not wise to claim weaving prowess over Athena. "I wish I could show you one of the things she's made."

"Are you close?"

"She's my best friend," admitted Eirene. She looked down at her hands. "We didn't grow up here and our parents are dead, so I suppose it feels like Phoebe is all I have to remind me of them. She's the only proof that I existed before Zakynthos and . . . and all of this."

"Where did you grow up?" Lamia's voice was strained.

"Ithaca," said Eirene. "My parents started planning to leave the moment that we were born. You don't—well, back then, you didn't keep two daughters on Ithaca if you could help it. My uncle—a merchant—lived on Zakynthos, so it seemed to make sense to come here. We left Ithaca when I was seven." She snorted. "Ironic, really."

"Ironic?" The word was clipped.

Eirene shot Lamia a quizzical sideways look. "Well, the curse—" She broke off, as her mind caught up with her eyes and was appropriately horrified.

Lamia was holding the knife between her hands like a bridge, the handle pressing against the soft skin of one palm, the tip of the blade pushed against the other. Blood dribbled from a small wound.

"Lamia," said Eirene. "Lamia, stop."

She did not get to finish. With a sudden, decisive movement, Lamia thrust her hands together and the knife entered her flesh with a short slick sound. Her face twisted.

A strangled, shrill noise tumbled from Eirene's lips. She jumped to her feet, lunging for Lamia as if she could undo the blow, close the wound, push the blood already dribbling over Lamia's wrists back in her fragile veins.

"Leave it!" Lamia's body curved protectively over the knife and the blood. Tears glistened on her cheeks among the fingerprint streaks of sand and stray poppy seeds. "It's shallow!"

"What the fuck are you *doing*?" Eirene snatched at the blade and Lamia blocked her. "I can't believe you just stabbed yourself, you—" She let out a string of filthy expletives.

"Why are you being mean again?" Lamia shuffled away from Eirene as well as she could with both hands still braced on the knife. "I'm helping you! Can you just—"

"By impaling yourself on my knife? Is that a joke? Give it to me!"

"Fine!" Before Eirene could react, Lamia gave the knife handle a vicious twist and pulled it free at last. Blood splattered the floor as she tossed the knife aside. Eirene dove for it. Lamia made no move to stop her—whatever she had hoped to achieve, she seemed satisfied that it was done. Still, Eirene held the knife childishly behind her back and glowered at Lamia.

"What. Was. That?" She ground the words out between gritted teeth.

Tears were streaming down Lamia's face in earnest now, blood dripping down her arm. She wiped her hands roughly on her chiton, leaving sandy, bloody smears on the light blue. Then she touched her fingertips to her wet cheeks and dropped her chin in a short, satisfied nod. "I'll show you," she said simply.

She clambered to her feet, leaving another bloody mark on the floor, and crossed to the window. Her body blocked the moonlight, and the room darkened further, until Eirene could see little but Lamia silhouetted against the night.

What was she *doing*? Knife still held behind her back lest Lamia try to recover it, Eirene took a small step toward her. Then another. And another and another until she stood at Lamia's shoulder. Together, they looked out at the darkened garden and at Lamia's hands, outstretched in the night air.

Was something supposed to be happening? Eirene had the impression that it was. She counted her heartbeats as she waited, reaching fifty before the silence and the anticipation grew too much.

She opened her mouth to speak, but Lamia got there first. "Promise me that you won't be afraid." Her voice was very small and earnest.

Eirene's heart jumped. Not with fear, as Lamia seemed to antic-ipate, but with an anger that shocked her. Who had told Lamia that anyone could ever be afraid of a girl like her, with her goodness and fearfulness, who would only wield a knife to turn it on herself? Her outstretched fingers were pale and so thin that Eirene could see every bone. She could have snapped them like twigs. Perhaps someone already had—Eirene remembered the bandages, gone now, that had encased Lamia's hands the first night they'd met. She clenched her fists.

"*Promise*," said Lamia again, cutting through Eirene's spiraling thoughts.

"I promise," said Eirene quickly. "I promise. I won't be afraid."

Lamia looked at her then, a lightning-quick flash of the whites of her eyes. "Good," she said.

This time, the wait was only a single heartbeat.

The tears clinging to Lamia's fingers began to glow.

At first, Eirene could do nothing but stare dumbfoundedly. The light grew slowly, pulsing faintly, spreading over Lamia's hands until she might have been Midas, her touch brilliant and golden. When it began to curl *outward*, ribbons of starlight dancing between her fingers, Eirene could not stay silent. She drew in a sharp breath.

Lamia lifted her head at the sound, tilting her face toward Eirene's. Her eyes were cautious as they searched Eirene's features. Eirene could not have guessed what Lamia was looking for there, and, besides, she stood no chance of schooling her expression into a more appropriate one anyway. She was sure every feature revealed her naked awe.

The corner of Lamia's mouth quirked up and then she was *beaming*, as radiant as the light cupped in her palms, as the starlight dancing up her arms and dripping between her fingers. Her eyes, when they met Eirene's, were like molten gold. "Are you afraid?"

Eirene shook her head mutely. She should have been. This was magic, real magic, magic that should have belonged only to the gods and their kin. But wisps of light floated away from Lamia like shining threads of fog and it was so enchanting that Eirene could have watched forever.

But she didn't have forever. She only had a night. She realized she had been leaning forward, her own fingers stretching out toward Lamia's. Their hands brushed.

Lamia startled and a shower of sparks fell into the dark. Eirene snatched her hands away. "The seeds!" she said breathlessly, ignoring the strange fluttering in her belly. "I have to—we have to go back to the seeds. There's not much time left."

Even illuminated in the sparkling, spiraling light, Lamia's face was unreadable.

XVI

SOFTLY IN THE VALLEY

Lamia

It was the birds that announced the day, breaking the silence of night with their high chatter and jolting Lamia from her reverie.

Her lights had unexpectedly lasted the night; she'd been afraid she'd need more tears and had spent the last few hours scheming a way to wrestle the knife back from Eirene, but somehow her magic had burned steadily on and on without a fresh bout of pain. She could feel its strain on her, though, building like a slow pressure in her head. She was going to have an appalling headache later. Her mouth was painfully dry and her stomach ached. It was worth it.

"It's morning," said Eirene, almost dreamily. She looked down at the heap of unsorted seeds before her and Lamia followed her gaze. A few handfuls at most. They had nearly made it.

"Morning," echoed Lamia.

The full impact of the word struck her a heartbeat later. *Morning*. She sat bolt upright, a clump of sand and seeds falling from her slack fingers into the water bowl. If it was morning already, her father would be returning soon to assess Eirene's completion of her task. He could not find her here. Lamia pulled in a trembling breath, forcing air through a throat that was tight. The stubs of her ruined fingernails seemed to pulse, an echo of pain.

Eirene, humming as she worked through the shrinking pile of lentils and wheat before her, hadn't noticed Lamia's distress.

She tossed a handful of wheat berries into their sack and turned to grin at Lamia. The smile slipped from her face at the sight of her; Lamia's distress must have been clearly wrought in her features.

Lamia sat very still. "I have to go," she breathed. "I should never have stayed this long."

Eirene blinked. "What?"

Lamia stood, using the couch as a crutch. Her leg was stiff and sore and trembled alarmingly when she tried to put her full weight on it. "What if my father finds me here? When did he say he'd come for you? I have to go!" She slashed her arm through the air in a sudden movement that was almost as unexpected to her as it was to Eirene, who reeled back, eyes wide. The tendrils of light that had been floating about the room, casting a comforting glow over them as they worked, vanished in an instant. Lamia's eyes went to the small pile of unsorted seeds. Her words came out strangled with their own urgency. "Can you finish without me? Will you make it?"

"You're leaving now?" The haze of confusion in Eirene's eyes cleared slowly to be replaced with grim understanding. "If you're going, you have to take the sieve," she said urgently, thrusting it up toward Lamia. "And the jug."

"But you still need them." Lamia indicated the remaining heap of unsorted seeds. And where would she hide them? She was already dreading the ascent to her tower room; it would be twice as hard carrying the jug.

"Gods *damn* it," snarled Eirene. She scooped the pile into the sieve clumsily and shook it over the bowl. Sand and poppy seeds showered into the water. Eirene gave it a final forceful shake before tipping the mess of lentils and grain that remained onto the floor. She jumped to her feet and crossed the distance between them in three long strides. She pushed the sieve into Lamia's hands. "It'll be fine!" she said, although whether the words were intended for Lamia or for herself, Lamia wasn't quite sure. "Leandros won't come right away. I'll make it in time." She ducked down to retrieve the jug.

Lamia wavered. "Are you sure?"

"I'm sure that you getting caught here or Leandros seeing these things wouldn't be good for either of us. *Go.*" Eirene balanced the jug on top of the sieve. Then she put her empty hands on Lamia's shoulders and gave her a little push. "Go *now*. Quickly."

The dismissal stung, even though it was Lamia herself who had decided it must happen. Her leg screamed its protest as she took her first step, but she was long used to pain by now. She lifted her chin, ignoring the first of the tears prickling at her eyes, and left Eirene alone.

XVII
CRUEL AND CONTRARY FORTUNE

Eirene

Hurt flashed across Lamia's face as Eirene pushed her toward the door. *I didn't want you to leave*, she wanted to snap, her hackles already raised. *Don't look at me like that. I wanted you to stay.* It was a ridiculous thought. If Leandros returned to find his daughter here, he would know that Eirene had not completed her task alone. He would cast her out into the cool morning and then he would go for Phoebe.

Eirene put her head down. "Bolt the door," she said to the floor, as Lamia slipped through the door, the sieve and jug clutched awkwardly in her slender arms. Lamia made no reply, but Eirene soon heard the telltale scrape of the bar being pushed back into place.

Eirene threw herself back to the floor, hands already outstretched to skim the poppy seeds from the surface of the water in the bowl. She didn't bother to dry these ones, just threw them straight in the sack with the rest. Let them rot. Distantly, she heard the uneven thump of Lamia's steps on the tower stairs. There was a curl of unease in her belly as she thought of her; what kind of creature was she, to have such power? She was Leandros's daughter, but Eirene had never heard rumors of him plucking light from the air as if it were mere daisies from the grass. And what else could Lamia do? What other secrets were there to discover here?

She could not dwell on that now. She had to finish her task. It was only these three days of practice that allowed Eirene to work as quickly as she did now, her fingers plucking out seed after seed. She blew a few stubborn grains of sand from a handful of wheat and tossed it into the sack. Almost there. She was so close. Lamia's steps had faded away.

That was when she heard it—the clatter of the bar blocking the tower door as it was lifted from its brackets. No. *No.* She would not fail like this—with half a handful of lentils and wheat berries left to separate. She cast about wildly for a place to hide them. Not under the narrow couch—far too obvious. She could bury them in the cold ashes of the hearth, perhaps, but a cursory examination of the pit would yield her deception. In her satchel? No, ridiculous. And casting them from the window would do her no good; the maddening twittering of the garden birds still came from the garden. They would descend on the seeds as they had before, shrieking, and Leandros would know of her treachery in a moment.

There was only one thing for it. Eirene scooped up the little heap of seeds and tipped it into her mouth just as the bolt to her door rattled. She dashed across the room and blocked the swing of the door with her foot, her mouth still full of the gritty mixture. She tried to swallow and almost choked.

The door banged against her foot, crushing her littlest toe. She was grateful for the mouthful of dry seeds and sand—it muffled her low cry.

"Eirene! The door, if you please!" Leandros sounded irritated. "You cannot prolong your task just by keeping me out." His voice became soothing and kind. "It's all right if you've failed. No one will think any worse of you. Honestly, I'm not sure anyone was expecting anything else. Just let me in and we can work this out together." Eirene's hatred for him flared, bright and furious. How dare he speak like that when she knew what he was? How dare he feign humanity while he threatened her sister and imprisoned his own daughter?

Eirene grimaced as the door smacked into her foot a second time. She managed to choke down a little of the seed mixture. Sand scraped against the back of her throat. She should have washed down the seeds with some of the filthy water left in the bowl.

"*Eirene*. That's enough now."

She *would* win this. She would beat him. Eirene forced herself to swallow again and again. The sensation of grit and the vile taste brought a memory bubbling to the surface—she and Phoebe, so many years ago, sitting by the riverbank and making cakes from the mud. Their parents had still been alive then, and they'd shrieked with laughter when Eirene had returned, sobbing, to the house with grime all over her face. Phoebe had duped her into sampling their creations, and the rough slab of mud had not tasted of honey cake as Eirene had so naively believed it would, but of mud.

"*Eirene.*"

Eirene choked down the last of the seeds and finally stepped back from the door. It flew open, narrowly missing her face, and Leandros all but fell inside. His usual smooth gold complexion was blotchy with his irritation.

Eirene pushed her hatred down inside herself and gave him her sweetest smile—mouth closed, lest he notice the sand she could feel stuck between her teeth. She cleared her throat and put her hand over her mouth in what she hoped was a coy gesture. "Sorry," she said. "My hair was a mess."

"What?" said Leandros, distracted. His eyes had passed over

Eirene and focused upon the three neat sacks of seeds and grain piled together in the center of the room. At first, he didn't seem to be able to process what he saw. Then, once he'd looked from grain to lentils to poppy seeds back to grain again half a dozen times, incredulity slowly spread across his face. Eirene's heart gave a smug little skip. While he wasn't looking, she surreptitiously wiped her teeth on her chiton sleeve.

Eventually, Leandros turned back to her. He'd schooled his expression into something closer to his usual tranquil superiority, but she could still see disbelief in his eyes. Disbelief and the first spark of suspicion. And then something else. He looked almost . . . impressed? Pleased, in that smug, feline way of his.

"I have done as you asked," Eirene announced cautiously. "They are sorted. What is my second task?"

"Your—" Leandros shook his head. "You're already thinking about your second task? You are eager, little Eirene."

Eirene scowled at him. How was she ever going to find the secret to Leandros's power and destroy it for good if she was stuck in this room? She *needed* to finish the tasks. And she could not deny that she'd felt a cold thrill of satisfaction at besting him, at completing what he'd clearly believed to be an impossible challenge. "I don't like to be idle," she said eventually.

"Nor do I," said Leandros. His eyes were wide and blue and framed by thick golden lashes; they darted about the room, lingering on the hearth, the couch, the windowsill. Eirene had been right not to try to hide her failure there, no matter how uncomfortably the grit and seeds were sitting in her belly. "But, alas, your second task must wait. I have important business tonight, and—"

"What business?"

Another young wife robbed of her mind and rewarded with a

husband twice her father's age? Another girl stolen from her sister, her father, her friends?

A shadow passed over Leandros's features. When he spoke again, his voice was as cold and as deadly as a viper, coiled to spring. "I do not know when I impressed on you this idea that you can interrupt me, but let me correct it now. The blood of gods flows in my veins, and if you seek to be my wife, you *will* show me the proper respect. Must I show you my hand?" With inhuman swiftness, he raised his arm to strike.

Eirene flinched, squeezing her eyes shut and turning her face from the blow so quickly that something twinged painfully in her neck. But the impact did not come. Instead, it was a featherlight touch. Leandros traced the line of her jaw with the soft pad of his thumb. She could hear the slow rhythm of his breathing as he cupped her face and gently turned her back to him. "There, that's right. You stay quiet." His grip on her skin tightened, pressing into her cheeks and forcing her mouth into a parody of a pout; she had the sudden terrible fear that he could crush her skull like an eggshell in his perfect hands.

Did he want her to speak now? She could not bring herself to, so she shook her head in as much as of a nod as she could manage with his fingers still digging into her cheeks.

"Good." At last, he released her.

It took all Eirene's willpower not to flee to the opposite end of the room. If she did, she felt certain he would pursue her, like a cat playing with its food. She had to be meek, uninteresting. She slowly opened her eyes and, too afraid to meet his gaze, stared fixedly at the end of his nose.

"Since you asked so nicely, I will tell you, my little wife-to-be." Leandros's tone was light, conversational. It was as if the past few minutes, with their threats of violence and retribution against Eirene's insolence, had never happened. "I am holding a gathering. I'm sure you have heard of my symposia, and this will be the grandest of them all, with free-flowing wine and a troupe of actors from the mainland and the best cuts of meat burned on braziers in honor of my goddess. It will be a glorious celebration." His expression was one of distracted self-satisfaction, his eyes half lidded and one corner of his mouth pulled up. "Aphrodite will smile kindly upon me when she sees how I have led these people to their knees in worship of her." He fondled the shining cuff on his wrist: a single rose cast in gold and bent into a perfect little circle.

If she hadn't feared his immediate retribution, Eirene might have asked why exactly Leandros seemed to seek Aphrodite's favor. Was he not of her blood? Though, Eirene supposed, she shared blood with Stavros and she despised him. Perhaps Aphrodite felt the same about Leandros. It was a pleasing thought.

Leandros clapped his hands together and Eirene's attention snapped back to him. "Well," he said cheerily, "I shall leave you to your day in peace, little Eirene. Go where you will; this will be your house soon, after all." He moved to leave but paused at the door. "If you survive the next tasks, that is." The door shut behind him with a soft thud.

Survive the next tasks. Not *finish the next tasks* or *complete the next tasks.* Eirene couldn't stop the convulsive shudder that ran through her aching body. It was followed by a wave of fatigue so fierce that she stumbled. How much had she slept these last few days? A few hours each night at best, tossing and turning fretfully. She took an unstable step toward the couch, then another.

She should use this time to find out more about Leandros and his secrets, to expose whatever nefarious source his magic had. She did not believe that Aphrodite would have gifted such a talent—love itself, or something that made a cruel mockery of it—to a man such as Leandros. He was too sly, too smug, too sudden in his rage. Though Aphrodite did keep Ares as a lover, so perhaps she did not fear the rage of men as mortal women must.

And then there was Lamia—his daughter, but so utterly different from him. And her powers—her fantastical control of light borne of pain. What kind of goddess must her mother have been? Eirene would have to ask her.

Exhaustion guided Eirene to lie down and draw the moth-eaten blanket over herself. She should wait until the symposium began to go snooping, anyway, until the house was bustling with activity and no one would notice her slipping into Leandros's private rooms. And she was so very, very tired. She hadn't meant to close her eyes, but she could no longer see the dingy little room before her.

Instead, she saw Lamia. Lamia, as she had been when the light had first blossomed between her fingers. Eirene was not sure she could have erased the image from her mind if she'd wished to: Lamia, beaming down at her hands, starlight shining in her cupped palms.

Eirene found herself smiling. It couldn't hurt her plans to grow closer to Lamia. Perhaps she knew something of Leandros's power that would otherwise take Eirene weeks of searching to uncover. Maybe all Eirene really needed to do was gain Lamia's trust—by showing her what her father deprived her of. By bringing her out into the world that existed beyond the gray walls of the tower. Eirene would like to see what she looked like in the sun.

XVIII
THE BIRDS AND WILD BEASTS

Lamia

By the time Lamia mounted the final stair, she was more exhausted than she remembered ever having been. Staying awake all night and the strain of using her magic for so long threatened to overwhelm her and she all but fell through the curtain to her room. It took every bit of her restraint not to throw herself down on the bed and fall fast asleep, but there were many things she had to do first. She hid the sieve in the chest that held her clothes, which she knew her father would never touch. The jug she set down on the far side of the bed, so that it would be concealed from someone standing at the door but would not look suspicious if discovered. Then she attended to herself.

There were dark crescents of sand and poppy seed beneath her fingernails. The thought of her father seeing them, of realizing how she had betrayed him, was enough to keep her wide awake. She picked at her nails until they were something like presentable. She changed her chiton swiftly, ran a comb through her thin hair, and twisted it into two neat braids. Then, when she was at last content that she looked as she always did, like a girl who rarely left her tower room and had certainly spent the night there, she pulled off her shoes and got into bed.

The jar of Eirene's ointment pressed into her belly and Lamia pulled it out from her sash, lifting the lid to examine the thick brown paste once again. Surely it couldn't work? The only one of her father's medicines that had ever touched the pain in Lamia's leg had also dragged her into sleep. What could this do?

But it was worth trying. Lamia pulled her skirts up above her knee. She carefully unwound the wrapping around the joint then dipped her finger into the jar and smeared it over the exposed skin. She swallowed, remembering Eirene's offer to apply the ointment herself. It had felt too vulnerable a thing, exposing herself like that, letting Eirene touch her here. Still, as Lamia massaged the paste in, she couldn't help but wonder what it would feel like if Eirene's hands instead of hers were carefully circling the slipped kneecap, Eirene's fingers brushing the pale skin of her thigh, Eirene replacing the lid of the jar and rewrapping the joint in strips of pale linen.

Lamia hid the jar among her bedclothes, then nestled beneath the blankets. When she closed her eyes, she saw Eirene's face.

If Lamia had hoped for an easy sleep, she had hoped in vain.

She dreamed of a room where the walls were made of gray rough-hewn stone, where a woman towered over her with a riot of flames burning around her face, casting her features into shadow. All except her eyes—huge, shining, golden. They were enchanting and lovely, and somewhere in the back of Lamia's mind they invoked a strange pang of recognition. Blood dripped from the corner of the woman's mouth. She smiled. She reached for Lamia and somewhere, far away, something thudded.

Lamia bolted upright, smothering the scream that bubbled against her lips.

She could not have been sleeping for long. The light outside was still the soft glow of morning and Lamia felt just as tired as she had before. What had woken her? Somehow, Lamia was sure it had not been the dream. She had nightmares all the time, and only rarely was she granted the escape of waking. Instinctively, she reached for the stack of papyrus that always graced her bedside and the slim stick of charcoal atop it. The dream was fading, as dreams were wont to do, and Lamia felt an urgent need to capture it.

Once the charcoal was cradled between her fingers and the papyrus spread out on her lap, Lamia's movements became automatic, instinctive. She sketched the arc of the woman's neck and the curve of her chin in long light strokes. The cut on her palm from the knife and the night before was still sticky; it seemed only logical to tear it open again and use her fingertips to daub the swirl of the woman's hair and the bright slash of her mouth. But it was wrong. She discarded the sheet and started on another. Then another. And another.

So absorbed was she that she didn't hear her father's ascent until his footsteps clattered on the top landing. Belatedly, she realized that it must have been his entrance to the tower that had awoken her, and that he must have just come from Eirene. *Eirene.* Had she finished her task in time? Had she made it? There was no time to worry about that now. Lamia scrambled to hide her drawings beneath the mess of her blankets, wiping the charcoal from her fingers as best she could.

She was just about presentable by the time her father pushed the curtain aside, stepping into the room and spreading his arms wide. The brass bowl for Lamia's tears dangled from his fingertips. His eyes met hers and he beamed.

"There you are, my sweet girl. I have a favor to ask."

It was only sheer exhaustion that lulled Lamia back into sleep, her wrists smarting where her father's nails had cut into them. This time, she dreamed of fire, of a roiling in her belly that bent her double. When footsteps on the stairs brought her back to waking, it was as if she'd been yanked from the sea, from drowning. Was it her father, come again? Lamia sat up, threw her legs over the side of the bed, and strained to listen over the sound of her own racing heart and deep, panting breaths.

The steps were too light to be those of her father, and for a moment she thought it might be Alexandra. But of course Alexandra was gone. Lamia's stomach twisted, bile rising in her throat. Not just gone. Alexandra was dead.

A slim hand with calloused light brown fingers rounded the edge of the curtain and paused there, digging into the woven fabric. A throat cleared. "Um," said Eirene. "Lamia?"

"Oh!" said Lamia. Eirene was here. Eirene was *still* here. Her heart leaped. Surely, then, she had been successful. "Yes. It is. Lamia, I mean. I'm Lamia." She bit down on her lip. What was *that*?

"Right," said Eirene from behind the curtain. "So can I come in?"

"I—one moment. Sorry." Lamia scrambled to pull on her boots, lacing them tightly over her knees. She had expected her injured knee to be especially bad after the night spent sprawled on the floor of Alexandra's—now Eirene's—room, but it was no sorer than usual. Stiff, but the sharp pain she had feared didn't come. Eirene's ointment, Lamia realized. It had actually helped a little. She sat on the edge of the bed. "Come in."

Eirene pushed the curtain open and took a tentative step inside. When her foot came down on the sheepskin floor, she jolted, pulling her leg back. She looked down, frowning. "Nice floor."

Lamia ignored that. She was too busy taking in Eirene—her stocky frame, her dark curls falling just past her chin, her wide stance. "You did it," she said.

"What?"

"Your task. You did it. You won?"

Eirene shot her an incredulous look. "Of course I did. *We* did." Her expression softened and she offered Lamia an uncharacteristically sweet smile. "We make a good team, don't we?"

Lamia's heart fluttered. She swallowed. "I think so. You know, I tried your paste. On my knee. It hurts a little less."

"Oh! Good." Eirene's smile widened. "I didn't think you wanted it."

Lamia shrugged. "Well, I did."

"Be careful with it," cautioned Eirene. "Even if the pain is numbed, its cause will still be there."

Lamia shot her a withering look. "I know that; it's my leg." She stood, letting it take her weight slowly. "It's better that I move it—it stops it from stiffening up so much."

"Right." Eirene nodded. "That makes sense. Maybe we could— maybe we could go for a walk then? I was hoping you could help me with something, actually."

"Another task?"

"No, no." Eirene shook her head emphatically. "No, this is something *fun*."

"Something fun," repeated Lamia doubtfully. There was a brightness to Eirene's eyes that made her think there was more to this than Eirene was saying.

"Yes, something fun," said Eirene. She bounded over to Lamia and took her hand, fixing her with a beseeching expression. "Now that I'm no longer confined to my room, I'd love to see the rest of the house. Maybe you could give me a tour."

"This is *not* fun," wailed Lamia. She dangled out of the window in Eirene's room, panting and sweating and staring with abject terror out into the darkening rose garden. When she'd agreed to show Eirene around the house, she hadn't realized that Eirene had meant *right now*. Her father had guests—she could hear their distant chatter from the main house—and he always barred the tower door when they were around. He didn't want them bothering her. But, as Eirene had cheerfully pointed out, that meant the only way to leave was *this*.

"Do you need help?" Eirene sounded unconcerned. "I can push this foot—"

Lamia felt the softest brush of fingers against her uninjured leg before she snatched it away. "No!" She wriggled herself through the narrow window as quickly as she could, toppling into the garden. "*Ow.*" She managed to avoid landing on her head, but one hand caught the thorny stem of a rose.

"Lamia!" Eirene stuck her head through the window, frowning when she saw Lamia sitting on the ground. "I could have helped you."

Lamia tried not to look sulky as she pulled the thorn from her palm. Why had she agreed to this? "I didn't need help. Are you coming?"

"Obviously." Eirene wiggled through the window with a fraction more grace than Lamia had. At least she managed to avoid the roses. She stood up, wiping mud from her skirts. "Come on!"

"Are you sure my father won't see us?" Now that she was here, outside and breathing in the cool scent of nighttime, Lamia was beginning to regret her ready agreement. Was she truly so easy to manipulate that Eirene only had to smile and ask and Lamia would do whatever she wanted? She felt her shoulders sag. She had proved her father right—she was easily led, weak-willed, and stupid. She would never survive a day on her own.

"There'll be a hundred people here at least, if my cousin's reports are to be believed," said Eirene confidently. "And there's no easier place to go unnoticed than a crowd."

"My father is an observant man," said Lamia quietly, following Eirene toward the side of the house.

Eirene waved a dismissive hand. "He'll be far too busy with his rich merchant friends to look too closely at the unwashed masses."

"I'm not unwashed," said Lamia, stung.

"It was a figure of speech," said Eirene. "Come on, let's see how many people there are." Without waiting for Lamia's response, she marched on, heading toward the front of the house. Lamia took the opportunity to sniff at her chiton. Perhaps she was a little unwashed.

Eirene came to a stop at the side of the house, the same place where Lamia had paused mere days ago to watch *her* arrival. Together, they peeked around the corner.

Eirene's cousin had been faithful in his reports of the numbers of attendees. People were pouring inside in a steady stream, all dressed in bright clothes; the moonlight glimmered off the gold that adorned their wrists and throats and brows. Daphne wove between them, a gold collar studded with gems wrapped around her muscular neck. It had made her irritable—she pressed herself too closely against legs, nipped at the trailing hems of gowns, swiped at sashes. When an elegant man in a deep-blue chiton reached out a hand toward her, fingers crooked and beckoning, she snapped at it viciously. The man yelled in surprise. Daphne made a chuffing noise, like a laugh.

Eirene let out a whistle. "Leandros knows how to draw a crowd." She turned to Lamia. "I've already seen the main entrance and the courtyard. Let's go in another way." Her eyes darted away, just for an instant, as she said with a casualness that seemed somehow feigned, "I'd love to see your father's workshop. You know that I'm a little of a potion-maker myself, medicines and things. To be able to see the place where Desire itself is made . . ." She trailed off suggestively.

"I can't show you the workshop," said Lamia, horrified. "That's beneath my father's private rooms." At least, she was fairly sure it was. She'd never actually been there herself.

Eirene frowned, opened her mouth, closed it again. Her lips twisted as if she'd made a decision. "What can you show me, then?"

Lamia considered it. "The kitchens," she said eventually. "The menagerie."

"The *menagerie*?"

"It's not so much of a menagerie anymore. Daphne ate the deer. And one of the swans." Eirene stared at her wordlessly. Lamia tried for a smile. "The other one's fine. And the dolphin is still there."

"Daphne didn't eat it?"

"Daphne doesn't like getting wet."

Eirene sighed. "The kitchens sound fine."

"All right." It was Lamia's turn to take the lead, walking back to the rose gardens at the rear of the house. There she paused, frowning. She could hear voices—female voices—ringing into the night. "More guests, do you think? But why are they using the back entrance?"

"Not guests," said Eirene wryly. "Servants and . . . performers, I'd wager. Women aren't permitted to join symposia. Not as guests, anyway."

"Why?" Lamia felt a burst of indignation. She had no interest in the symposium—that kind of crowd terrified her; if she thought about it for too long, she would fall into nightmares of them turning on her, pointing and laughing, driving her out with flaming sticks as her father had always told her they would. But the exclusion of *any* woman felt profoundly unfair.

Eirene patted her shoulder. "Excellent question. I wish I knew. I'm assuming the kitchens are this way?" She moved away from the walls but kept her head low, hiding her face. Reluctantly, Lamia followed.

Eirene had been right that there were no guests here; the lack of jewels and finery was a stark contrast. There was a group of girls in plain dresses weaving in and out of the broad back entrance that led to the kitchen, unloading flagons of wine from a cart. Another cluster stood by the wall, murmuring as they leaned into one another, heads down.

As Lamia and Eirene grew closer, Lamia began to pick out snatches of the conversation.

". . . a little on the eyes and the lips does the trick . . . ," one girl was saying urgently.

"A dab atop your collarbones," said another.

"So they'll stare at your breasts," giggled a third.

"A smudge between the legs," someone suggested in a sultry voice. "And you'll take home more coin than you ever have before. I'll get you a good price, girls. I buy from Leandros himself."

"What are they talking about?" asked Lamia uncertainly.

Eirene shot her a quick sideways look. "I don't know," she said without her usual confidence. "I thought you were showing me the kitchen—" She broke off, her eyes wide and fixed on the entrance to the kitchens.

Lamia followed her gaze. A girl had just walked out of the house. A girl with thick black curls that fell halfway to her waist, huge brown eyes and high cheekbones, and a thin, almost fragile frame. Lamia looked from the girl to Eirene. From Eirene to the girl. Her own mouth was already shaping the name when Eirene, looking as if she'd seen a ghost, finally said it.

"Phoebe," she breathed, and then she had taken off, sprinting toward her sister.

Phoebe looked up just as Eirene barreled into her, catching her in her arms and crushing her against her chest.

Lamia wavered where she stood, uncertain whether to follow or stay back. She settled on slinking closer, tucking herself into the shadows beneath the eaves, and leaning against a wall.

"What are you doing here?" Eirene demanded in a low, urgent voice. "Are you stupid? Have you lost your mind since I've been gone? What if Leandros sees you?"

Phoebe stiffened and pulled away. "It's not stupid to worry about you, Eirene," she hissed. "They always need more serving girls at these things; they don't care at all who I am. I'm just here to pour wine."

"Those jugs are enormous," said Eirene. "Phoebe, I'm worried about you. You look—"

"I'm fine," interrupted Phoebe. "I've just been weaving lots. And I'm not actually carrying the jugs. I just needed a way to be let in so I could look for *you*."

"Leandros could still recognize you," said Eirene stubbornly. "So would Stavros. Is he here?"

"He's here," said Phoebe shortly. "I expect he wants to try to catch a glimpse of you. You should have seen him when he realized you were gone. And then when Leandros showed up—"

"Leandros went to the house again?"

"To say he'd changed his mind. That he wanted you instead."

"He kept his word." Eirene sounded surprised.

"I wasn't sure you'd convince him," admitted Phoebe. "At first, I thought he was coming for me. And I was so scared, Eirene. And then I felt like a wretched creature for being relieved that he wasn't. I can't believe I let you talk me into this. It should be me here."

"We've been through this," said Eirene. "What the hell could I do at home?"

"Well—" began Phoebe, but Eirene was already speaking again.

"How is the weaving coming along?"

Phoebe seemed to light up. "Oh, it's beautiful," she said, beaming. "It's turning out just as I always hoped it would. I've never made something so lovely; just wait till you see it. The *colors*, Eirene."

"I knew it would be," said Eirene, laughing. "It'll fetch a price like nothing you've imagined."

Lamia felt a peculiar fluttering in her stomach. She longed to make Eirene laugh like that.

Phoebe's smile faltered. "I hate to think that soon it will be gone."

"We'll steal it back, one day," said Eirene. She squeezed her sister's shoulder. "I promise. All in good time."

"Yes, well." Phoebe chewed her lip. "Eirene, I have to remind you, these things take time. It will still be a few weeks until I am finished. A few weeks at least."

"It does not matter," said Eirene, waving off the words. "I am safe, as you see, and a matter of weeks cannot change that. Take the time you *need*. I really do worry about you."

"Don't be patronizing," said Phoebe. "Not while you're putting yourself in so much danger." She leaned closer. "Are you close to discovering—"

"Wait!" Eirene stiffened, then whipped about. Her eyes searched the dusty yard until they found Lamia. "Phoebe," she said, her voice full of false brightness, "let me introduce you to Lamia."

Eirene beckoned and Lamia approached slowly, cautiously, feeling as if she were a feral cat still distrustful of humans. Phoebe's eyes narrowed.

"Phoebe, this is Lamia," said Eirene, her smile forced. "She's Leandros's daughter. Lamia, this is Phoebe."

"Hello," said Lamia.

Phoebe opened her mouth, then shut it again. She and Eirene exchanged a look. "Hello," she said.

"Good, now we're all friends," said Eirene. "Phoebe, *please* go home. You've seen me. I'm fine."

"I won't—" began Phoebe, but Eirene cut her off.

"Go, please," she said. "I don't want you here."

Phoebe flushed. Even Lamia—though the words hadn't been for her—felt the sharp sting of rejection.

"I mean," said Eirene, gentler, "I don't want to be worrying about you." She touched her sister's wrist. "I want to know you're safe. Please, Phoebe, just—"

She broke off as a man, a stranger, loomed out of the doorway, glowering down at her. "Where's your wine jug, girl?"

"We—" began Lamia.

"You too!" He turned on her. "Get those jugs and get inside."

When none of them moved right away, he advanced on them.

Lamia let out a squeak and made for the cart stacked with the stoppered jars of wine. They really were enormous. She awkwardly lifted one into her arms. Then Eirene was at her side, doing the same. Between one moment and the next, Phoebe had vanished.

"Inside!" bellowed the man.

Lamia and Eirene did as they were told. He followed them into the kitchen and flapped them toward the courtyard. "There are cups that need filling. Quickly!"

Eirene drew up beside Lamia and leaned into her, so close that Lamia could feel the warmth of her breath. The jug was heavy and Lamia's knee twinged in protest at the new weight. "Follow me," whispered Eirene. "Walk to the farthest corner of the courtyard, then we can dump the jars. If you see Peiros, or your father, turn around. Don't let them see your face." She squared her shoulders and marched into the courtyard. Lamia followed close at her heels, weaving across the courtyard and around the fountain. There were two ducks bobbing about in the water. Drunken men kept tossing them grapes, which they fought vigorously over.

They reached the far side of the courtyard and Eirene stopped, glanced around, then shoved her jug of wine under a table. Lamia followed suit.

The man who had shouted at them was still standing by the entrance to the kitchens, scowling out into the courtyard. "Keep your head down," hissed Eirene, scurrying away from the abandoned jugs. Lamia ducked her head obediently, the circlet of braids atop her head bobbing with the movement, and followed close behind Eirene. Their hands were still tangled together.

"Careful," whispered Eirene as she tugged Lamia behind a lush display of foliage.

"Ow," said Lamia, though the sound was muffled as Eirene

pulled her face first into a large fern.

"Sorry," said Eirene. She let go of Lamia's hand. Lamia hadn't realized how warm Eirene's fingers were; their absence was like leaning into a cool wind. "We can wait here until he goes away."

Their view of the wooden stage was mostly hidden by a rowdy group of men who were clearly intending to drink as much of the free wine as they possibly could. They took great gulps from their cups between slurred words and staggered into one another each time they moved. Every so often, one would upend his cup onto his clothes to a great chorus of jeers. They took no notice of the two girls lurking in the shadows behind them.

Lamia adjusted her skirts compulsively.

"Are you all right?" whispered Eirene. She was distracted, her eyes darting around the courtyard, drinking in the crowds.

"I'm not sure," whispered Lamia back. She fussed with her skirts again, checking that they covered as much of her legs as possible. "You're certain we won't be seen?"

"I'm certain. Look, it's almost time for the theater." Eirene nodded toward the stage. "No one will be looking over here soon and we can slip away."

The drunken group in front of them had begun to holler some kind of drinking song, but Lamia hardly noticed them. All her attention was now fixed on the troupe of actors that were wandering across the stage, tapping their bare feet against the floor and frowning, talking quietly to their companions. There were three of them: all lithe young men with round cheeks and soft curls and lips that were full and feminine. There was something fascinating in the way they moved, almost dancing over the smooth wooden veneer of the stage. Lamia flexed the fingers of her free hand; she longed for the familiar feel of charcoal between them. How would she capture their grace, their serenity? A smudge to their limbs, perhaps, to hint at their etherealness.

Light flared suddenly from the stage and the chatter in the courtyard faltered. The actors stilled. The drinking song came to a clumsy, tuneless end. Someone dropped a cup and the resulting clatter might have been a strike of thunder. Lamia found herself holding her breath until the last clang faded into nothing.

"My dear friends." A loud, clear voice spoke into the quiet. The words filled the space like an unpleasant smell, crowding in among the clusters of drinkers who seemed to stand a little taller, to tighten their grips on their half-empty cups. Only one man on Zakynthos could have that effect. Lamia's grip on Eirene's fingers tightened for a split second before going slack, a compulsive sort of shudder. If she tried to leave, he would see her. That was the only thought that kept her from dropping Eirene's hand completely. It had been a mistake to come here. A terrible, foolish mistake. How could she have ever thought to stay hidden from him?

"Welcome," said Lamia's father, striding onto the stage and turning his keen blue gaze upon his audience. "I am so pleased you could all be here tonight."

XIX

THIS PLACE OF PLEASURES

Eirene

The actors hurried from the stage, disappearing behind the draped curtain. As the curtain fell back into place, Eirene caught sight of the room it concealed. Clothes and masks and props covered a low blocky table.

"Let us not waste time with pleasantries," declared Leandros. "You know why you are here—to drink, to eat, to laugh, to celebrate the glory of the gods who grant us such a life." The crowd cheered and Eirene found herself so caught up in the energy of the moment that she almost whooped along with them. She'd spotted Stavros face down on a table, his upturned cup spilling wine over the wood, and the relief of having one less person to fear was a comfort.

"We gather tonight in honor of Aphrodite and her divine son Eros," proclaimed Leandros. "My beloved relatives," he added with a coy wink. "Enjoy the performance and drink deeply, for the wine flows freely tonight!" More cheers. Leandros nodded to the crowd, his eyes sweeping the faces of those closest to him. There was no way he could pick the two of them out from the crowd, but Eirene still ducked instinctively behind a broad leaf. Really, they should leave. But they could watch for a few moments, surely. . . .

Eirene peeked out to see Leandros descend from the stage and throw himself into an empty chair at the frontmost table. He made a lazy beckoning gesture and a very pretty woman in a flowing blue peplos materialized beside him. He said something to her and she laughed and climbed into his lap. Eirene pulled a face.

"Who is that?" asked Lamia quietly.

Eirene quickly smoothed her features. "Um," she said. "A friend of your father's, I suppose." She was fairly sure it was one of the women they'd seen outside, discussing where to smear Desire so they would be irresistible.

Leandros pressed his face into the woman's neck. His hand crept beneath her loose skirts and her eyes fluttered shut.

"*Friend?*" repeated Lamia in a horrified whisper.

Eirene was saved from replying by the striking of a gong. The sound reverberated through the hall as the shortest of the actors retook the stage, now clad in a woman's robe belted above the waist. His face was hidden behind a mask carefully painted with full lips, long lashes, and cheeks that were dusted with pink. Someone in the crowd wolf-whistled and the actor threw them a coquettish glance over one shoulder. When he spoke, his voice was high. "I am Psyche!" he declared. "Most beautiful of mortals. And this is my tale, and that of my husband, the great god Eros."

Eirene knew that they should be leaving. But she could not help it; she wanted to watch. Lamia was completely still at her side. Daphne slunk past them, a limp white duck hanging from her mouth.

Another actor charged onstage. He was enormously good-looking. When he saw Psyche, he fell to his knees in awe, clasping his hands together. "Why, you are the loveliest creature I ever beheld. Has fair Aphrodite walked these lands of late, dropping her own sweet rose petals in her wake? Or are you perhaps a *new* Aphrodite, born not from the sea but from the land? If that is so, I must call upon my brethren to come and worship you, for roses are nothing to the rare flower you still possess." A snigger arose from the crowd. Leandros's head, which had been buried in his lover's dark hair, came up sharply. The actor didn't seem to notice. He winked and vanished offstage.

The third actor took his place. Like the first, he wore a woman's robe and face, though his mask was even finer. In his hand he held a perfect red rose. "I am Aphrodite!" he proclaimed. There was another high whistle from the assembled drinkers and Eirene saw Leandros's shoulders stiffen. The woman on his lap had noticed his displeasure. She tried playing with his golden curls and he shook her off irritably.

"Who dares to call herself lovelier than I?" Onstage, Aphrodite stalked over to Psyche. "This plain, mortal thing? Bah!" The actor gesticulated violently with the rose as he spoke. A single petal drifted down to the stage. "I'll remind the people of this land what power a true goddess holds. Where is my son? *Eros!*"

The second actor returned. Now he had a bow in his hands and a smoldering expression. "Mother, I am here." He winked again and the crowd whooped and jeered.

Eirene watched Leandros take a sip of wine. His jaw was tense. This performance was, apparently, not what he'd had in mind, but it was too late to do anything about it. With this many guests, he could not make a scene over something so utterly beneath him.

Aphrodite pointed an imperious finger at Psyche. "You see that girl?"

"Oh, I absolutely do." The actor that was Eros winked yet again, quirking his eyebrows, and Eirene frowned at him. He winked too much.

Aphrodite smacked him. "I'm not pointing her out as a conquest for you. This stuck-up little bitch"—at Eirene's side Lamia made a mortified noise—"thinks she's better than me. I beg you, my sweet son, to aid me in my revenge."

As she outlined her plan to make Psyche fall in love with some hideous beast of a man using the power of Eros's magic love-making arrows, Lamia turned to Eirene and whispered, "Eirene."

Eirene sighed. Despite the fact she was watching through a plant, she'd actually been enjoying the show. Particularly because Leandros didn't seem to be. "Yes?"

"That's Aphrodite?"

"Yes."

"She doesn't seem very nice."

"She's Aphrodite," Eirene whispered back. "She isn't nice. She's a god."

"Well, yes, but she's the goddess of beauty."

Eirene threw her a scathing sideways look, then softened her expression when she saw how bewildered Lamia looked. She patted Lamia on the arm. "Being beautiful isn't the same as being nice."

Lamia didn't seem to have anything to say to that, so Eirene returned to peering through the leaves. Onstage, Psyche had lain down to sleep for some reason. Aphrodite's actor had come back on dressed as a sort of mangy bear. Eros was creeping theatrically across the stage, bow and arrow at the ready.

"Eirene."

"What!" hissed Eirene at Lamia. It took her a half second of staring into Lamia's wounded face before she realized it hadn't been Lamia who had spoken. She whirled around and came face to face with Damon.

The sight of him was so wonderfully familiar that she could have wept. "Damon!" She pulled him into a tight embrace. He hugged her back, though it was a little lackluster.

"Damon, it is so good to see you." She released him, grinning.

Damon's face was guarded. "What are you doing here?"

Eirene shrugged, but her relief at seeing him was draining away as quickly as it had come. "I go where I like," she said shortly. She glanced back at the stage in time to see Eros trip, fall, and stab himself in the leg with his arrow. The crowd hooted. "Are you enjoying the show?"

Damon shook his head incredulously. "The show? Eirene, is that really all you have to say?"

"What would you have me say?" Eirene would have crossed her arms if Lamia hadn't chosen that moment to slip her fingers between hers and squeeze gently. Eirene squeezed back.

Damon's shoulders were hunched. "I suppose that it is true you are living with Leandros now? That you are . . . you are his wife?"

Eirene's stomach churned. "I—"

"That is what people are saying," Damon went on. "Stavros boasts of it nightly." Ah, of course her cousin couldn't shut up about his new relations. "Eirene"—Damon grasped for her free hand and clutched it in his own—"tell me he is lying."

Eirene carefully pulled her hand from his. "Damon, it is—it is not the whole truth. I can explain. Just be quiet. Leandros will be"—well, she wasn't entirely sure how he'd react, but she knew it wouldn't be good—"furious if I'm discovered here."

"Not the whole truth? But it is part of it. You really are married to him?" Damon's usually cheerful face was twisted with worry and distrust. The creases around his mouth deepened as he caught sight of Lamia, shrinking back into the shadows, her fingers still entwined with Eirene's. His suspicious eyes lingered on their joined hands. "And who's this?"

This was not exactly going to plan. "She's Leandros's daughter," said Eirene stiffly. "Damon—"

"Daughter?"

"Keep your voice down."

"Sorry, sorry." Damon raised his hands defensively. "You're just springing a lot on me here, Eirene. Suddenly, you're married, a stepmother—"

"I am *not* a stepmother," cut in Eirene hotly. Her face flushed with fierce heat. She was not actually married to Leandros, and had no intention of ever being so, but the suggestion of being Lamia's *stepmother* filled her with a unique kind of horror.

Eirene and Damon glared at each other in furious silence, punctuated by the proclamations of the actors on the stage and the laughing of the crowd in response. They'd reached the part of the story where Psyche had vowed to kill Eros in his sleep and instead realized how incredibly attractive he was. Eros was yelling at her for betraying his trust, flapping his arms about for emphasis while Psyche tried to kiss him, grabbing at his face and his crotch. Eirene wished she could pay better attention—she wanted to see every one of Leandros's reactions to this obnoxious display.

Damon sucked in air through his teeth. "Eirene, I don't like this. There's something you're not telling me."

"There's nothing," insisted Eirene. Lying to Damon was a distinctly unpleasant experience. "Really."

"Just the marriage and a conjured daughter of Leandros, then?"

Eirene sighed. "Damon—"

He put his hands up to stop her. "Don't, Eirene. I don't need to hear another lie. Just"—he ducked his head—"promise me you're safe? Next time my master is called to that house . . . I don't want it to be *your* bloodless body he's collecting."

Eirene frowned. *Bloodless.* A particular, peculiar word. "What do you mean by that?"

"I mean, I don't want you *dead*."

"No, not that." She waved away his concern as if she were swatting a fly. "*Bloodless body.* Why did you say that?"

"You mean you didn't know?" Damon's expression was stricken. "Eirene . . . I thought I told you."

"Damon," said Eirene. Dread was an icy claw around her heart. "Told me *what*?"

Damon's eye flicked past her to Lamia. "Well . . ."

"Tell me!" hissed Eirene.

He set his shoulders. "When my master collected the body . . . he said it had been drained of blood."

Eirene went very still. Lamia made a small horrified sound and dropped Eirene's hand. The voices of the actors seemed very distant now, the words slurred and softer, as if spoken underwater. Aphrodite was commanding Psyche to sort a heaping pile of grains and Psyche was wailing in despair. Alexandra had been drained of blood. *Blood.* But why? And by what?

Or, thought Eirene, and it chilled her to her core, *by who?* Poor sweet Alexandra. If Leandros was responsible, then she'd never stood a chance.

"Eirene?" said Damon.

"Give me one moment," said Eirene faintly. She forced herself to breathe deeply and focus her attention back on the actors and the stage, where Psyche had completed her grain-sorting task with the help of a swarm of helpful ants. Despite everything, Eirene found herself gritting her teeth in irritation. Ants, really? *She* hadn't used ants. She'd sorted the wretched things by hand for three days straight until she was so tired that she was near delirious. She wasn't entirely sure that she wasn't a little delirious now. "I have to go," she said at last, more to herself than either Lamia or Damon.

"Really?" said Damon.

"Wait, no." Eirene wavered. "I want to watch the performance." Grain sorting, what was next? Maybe it could help her prepare for her own upcoming tasks.

"The *performance*?" It was clear Damon thought she'd lost her mind completely.

"I have these tasks," said Eirene. "I think they're going to be the same as Psyche's. I had to sort grain already, and if I stay, maybe I can work out what he'll have me do next?"

"Didn't she have to go to Hades?" said Damon at the same time as Lamia perked up and said, "I know the tasks. We don't have to stay."

"You do?" said Eirene.

"Of course," said Lamia. "This is the story of my family. My father didn't tell it to me in quite the same way, but I know the tasks. The next is retrieving the wool of a flock of man-eating sheep—"

"Tell me tomorrow," said Eirene, her mind made up. "Right now, I need you to do something for me." She had been feeling progressively guiltier as she'd tried to come up with a way to trick or convince Lamia into showing her to Leandros's workshop. It was nice to be straightforward instead.

Lamia's face paled; it was clear she knew what Eirene was going to ask.

"Things have changed," said Eirene. "You heard Damon. Something is wrong here, Lamia, and I have to find out what it is. I need you to take me to your father's rooms. I need to know what happened to Alexandra." Her heart was hammering. She met Lamia's gaze and held it, desperate to convey how urgent her request was.

Lamia's expression was anguished. "Eirene—"

"Please, Lamia." She voiced the terrible thought gnawing at her insides. "I don't want to be next."

Leandros was confident to the point of arrogance. The door Lamia led Eirene to—though she refused to go inside herself—was unlocked and the workshop's location so obvious it was laughable. Behind a huge lushly blanketed bed was an archway leading to a set of neat steps descending down.

"You really won't come?" she called back to Lamia.

"No!" Lamia's terror was clear. "I have already defied my father in bringing you here. Don't make me go any further."

"Go back to the tower, then," Eirene instructed her. She didn't wait for a response before shutting the door. She allowed herself a moment to square her shoulders and draw in a deep, calming breath. Then she made for the stairs and hurried down them, emerging into a musky-smelling low-ceilinged room. Leandros's workshop.

The workshop was exactly what it should have been—the very image of an evil lair, down to the golden bust of Leandros glowering at her from what seemed to be a sort of shrine on the far wall. Someone—probably Leandros himself—had draped it with a crown of fresh flowers. Eirene let out a snort of laughter.

The room was long and dimly lit by two narrow windows high up in the walls. Its centerpiece was a huge wooden table, large enough to seat a dozen men on each side. But there were no benches tucked beneath it, and the only chair was a vast throne-like thing looming over a heap of stained and faintly scorched cloth. The air smelled sour. The near end of the table held an enormous stone bowl, but that wasn't what drew Eirene's attention. The surface of the table was glittering faintly. Eirene moved closer and the shine resolved itself into a fine layer of silvery powder. *Desire.* It could be nothing else.

Eirene ran her finger over the stained wood. It came back silver, Desire clinging to the grooves in her skin. If only there was *more* of it, perhaps she could somehow work out what made it. She touched her finger to the tip of her tongue. It tasted mild, sweet, and metallic—nothing distinctive. She wiped her tongue on her sleeve—so little Desire could hardly hurt her, but she didn't want to test that theory too thoroughly. Eirene pulled her knife from her belt and cut a small piece from the bottom of her chiton. Phoebe would be annoyed, but Eirene was used to annoying Phoebe. She swept the rest of the powder into the little scrap of cloth and twisted it closed, then tucked it and the knife back into her belt.

Peering into the enormous bowl revealed a little more. Charred sage, shaved pieces of bark, a handful of brightly colored leaves, poppy seeds, and a number of small white bones. It had to be Desire in the making, but Eirene could discern nothing truly extraordinary in the mix of ingredients. The final step, whatever Leandros would do next to transform this mess of detritus into shining, terrifying powder . . . *that* was what Eirene needed to know.

Eirene hurried over to the shrine next, bracing herself for what she might find there. *Alexandra had been drained of blood.* Perhaps that blood would be here—a vile offering to Leandros's patron gods. But beside the flowers, the candles, and a heap of fresh fruit, there was nothing there. The bust, Eirene realized, after looking closer, was not of Leandros. Its cheeks were rounder, its lips fuller, its curls tighter, and its eyes wider. Eros. It appeared Leandros was not exaggerating his resemblance to his godly forefather; they were uncomfortably similar if the sculptor of this bust were to be believed.

Eirene shivered and stepped back.

The wall opposite was lined with shelves. Those in Leandros's study were nothing to these ones; they were filled with an array of pots, jars, papers, and obscure artifacts. Eirene approached them cautiously. There was no way to prepare herself for what she might find here. After all, if he did not offer it to his gods, had Leandros used the blood to make Desire? Did one of these jars hold the last of Alexandra's life, ready to be weighed and mixed and distilled into one of those detested powders? She hoped that was not the secret of Desire. The world was full of blood trapped inside mortal bodies, ready to be harvested; she would never be able to stop Leandros from taking it. She swallowed down a swell of nausea. When she lifted her hands to her mouth they were shaking.

She started with the jars, lifting the lids of each and peering inside. She was greeted by an array of liquids and powders and pastes. One was full of rose petals so pungent Eirene sneezed. Another held a glittering, clear liquid that smelled of the sea. Another was full of salt, yet another with pepper. Cinnamon, ginger, yellow saffron. From hooks on the ceiling dangled bundles of drying herbs tied together with fraying brown twine. Eirene recognized the neat knots as her own. There was no blood. Apart from the little jar of a sparkling liquid that Eirene dared not to touch, nothing would have been out of place in a physician's store.

She rifled through the larger things crowding the lower shelves. She glanced dismissively into a woven sack of dark seeds, then paused, struck by the familiar scent. Surely not . . . she reached into the sack and withdrew a handful of lentils. They were unmistakably those she had spent all those days sorting; sand still clung to their rough surfaces. What use could Leandros possibly have for them? Eirene let the handful of lentils fall back into the sack and moved on, pushing down her unease. Leandros had so many strange possessions; she could not fixate on a few seeds. Wrapped in a square of worn gray cloth, she found a leg skillfully cast in brass with curling toes and a smooth muscular calf. The top edge of the leg was rough—it must have been sawed off some statue. Eirene replaced the fabric. Something about the leg made her stomach turn. Beside it was a wide bowl full of—was that *hair*?

Eirene gagged. Then, fighting down nausea, she leaned closer. Yes, it was hair—deep, coppery curls twisted loosely together. Again, it unsettled Eirene to her core, though she couldn't explain why. There was something shoved beneath the bowl, a curling corner of papyrus. Trying to avoid looking directly at it, Eirene lifted the edge of the bowl and tugged the papyrus free. She took a step back from the shelves and the leg and the hair, and then, once she was comfortably far away, she looked down at the papyrus.

It was a drawing.

The woman in the drawing was extraordinarily lovely. The artist had given her huge round eyes and a strong sharp nose. She smiled as if there were some private joke between them. Her chiton was short, like a man's, and it clung to her full breasts and soft waist. Her hips were round and broad, her arms were crossed, and she stood with her legs apart, her stance unassailable. Her thighs were glorious. Eirene scoffed—trust an artist to draw such an impossible, perfect woman.

One thigh continued to an equally extraordinary calf. But the other . . . the other ended in a vicious slash of color. Ocher—Eirene had bought the pigment for Phoebe enough times to recognize its hue. Strange. The rest of the drawing was in plain black ink, all but one final detail—her hair was coppery red. It swirled around her face as if she stood in the center of a storm. The drawing brought to mind the stories Eirene and Phoebe's mother had once whispered to her daughters, when the nights grew cold and they all huddled together in the dark. *Never go out alone after dark*, their mother would always begin, before telling them some story of sirens luring sailors to their deaths, the snake-bodied drakaines who had the faces of beautiful women but would swallow men whole all the same, or the brass-legged, flame-haired, shape-shifting, and illusion-casting empousa—daemonesses who would charm young men to their beds and then feast on their flesh.

But we are girls, Phoebe would always remind her cheerfully, *so there is no danger to us.*

Maybe some of the daemonesses have a taste for little girls! their mother would reply, reaching out to tickle Phoebe's round belly.

Eirene peered closer at the drawing in her hand. She had not noticed it before, but a thin line had been daubed onto the woman's face—a trail of red dripping from her lips. "Huh," she said out loud.

As if in response, far above her a door crashed shut.

Shit. She had lingered too long. Eirene shoved the drawing back beneath the bowl and ran for the stairs, ascending them as quickly as she could without making enough noise to alert whoever had slammed that door to her presence. She emerged into Leandros's room just in time to hear the furious rumble of his voice in the entrance hall and Peiros's nasal reply. There was no way she could sneak out of the room now. They'd see her right away.

Eirene cast about for a hiding place and then, seeing no

alternative, dove under the bed. She lay there in the cramped dusty space and strained to listen. Leandros and Peiros were coming closer. Eirene stayed still and tense. Would Leandros retire to bed immediately? Would he sense her the moment he entered the room, or would he go blithely about his evening ablutions? Then what? Would Eirene have to stay here all night?

"*Ungrateful, disrespectful.*" Leandros was seething as he came in. Eirene allowed herself a smile even as she shrank against the floor, desperate to conceal herself from his notice. She had known he would be angry about the actors and their performance, with its mocking portrayal of his family.

"You should punish them," said Peiros. "Punish them as your foremother would—drive them mad with lust for the same woman. Or for each other. Better yet, for the leopard."

"One word from me and Daphne would tear them to pieces." From the tone of Leandros's voice, he seemed to be considering it.

"Do it now, before they flee beyond our reach," urged Peiros.

There was a long pause. "No," said Leandros eventually. "No, my Desires are precious things. I will not waste them on such scum. Especially not now, when we are so close."

"You truly believe the girl will be able to find the grove?"

"She has proved that she will do anything for her sister," said Leandros. His voice grew soft, considered. "And if she is half as clever as she is determined, there is a chance that she can find it. The Fates brought her to me, Peiros; there must be a reason."

Beneath the bed, Eirene was still and silent as the grave. She had assumed that Leandros's tasks for her were ridiculous displays of his power over her and nothing more. And yet it seemed he had some greater plan in mind.

"Ensure there are no stragglers left in the house," instructed

Leandros, returning to his usual slick authority. "I have work to do." He moved across the room, coming closer to Eirene's hiding place until she could see his feet. His toenails were neatly filed. She wondered if he had Peiros do it. She held her breath. Discovery now would certainly be her destruction.

Leandros walked on, past the bed. She heard him clattering down the stairs to the workshop. A moment later, Peiros retreated to the main house, walking quickly and heavily.

Once his footsteps had faded into nothing, Eirene wiggled out from beneath the bed and rushed to the door, grateful for all her years of practice in moving about her own house in silence lest she wake Stavros. She slipped out into the corridor and ran back to the kitchen before emerging, breathless, into the night. Lamia had had to leave the tower door unbarred on her return. With a sigh, Eirene replaced the bar, then skirted the tower until she was standing in front of her own window.

Tomorrow, Leandros would set for her his second task— finding this mystical grove. Eirene was as prepared as she ever would be. All she could do now was worm her way back through the window, conceal the tiny twist of Desire at the bottom of her satchel, and sleep.

XX

DOWN IN THE NIGHTS

Eirene

At first, Eirene thought it was the wind that had woken her. She lay there in the dark and stared into the blankness, counting her own steady breath in and out. She was so *tired*; after three days of hardly sleeping, her exhaustion seemed to have permeated the marrow of her bones. And her neck hurt. She rolled it side to side and winced at its protesting twinges. Eventually, she pulled the thin blanket over her head in a vain attempt to block out the pattering of the rain.

Then the sound came again and she froze.

Not the wind.

It was a long, low moan, like the keening cry of someone in pain. Someone who was surely standing on the stairs of the tower, or perhaps in the little tower room that had been locked when Eirene had passed it.

The sound came a third time: thin, mournful, hungry. *Hungry?* Why was that the word that came so readily to her mind? But now it was there and she could not dislodge it. There was someone—or something—in the tower and it was *hungry*. It was that thought that finally broke her paralysis. She crept from her tiny pallet bed and crossed the room in a daze. The door could be barred from the outside, but what of the inside? She cursed herself for her failure to examine every tiny detail of the room in the light. Not a mistake she would be making again.

She began to run her hands over the wall. She traced her fingers again and again over the frame. Nothing. She would have to block it some other way. Stepping lightly, lest the hungry thing hear her, she returned to the bed to retrieve her satchel and the knife within.

Back at the door, she shoved the leather flaps and straps of the bag into every gap she could. Then, as a final measure, she shoved the flat of her blade in too, twisting it so that it would stick fast against any attempt to open the door. Eirene exhaled the breath she'd been holding for far too long. She was safe now, her door jammed against any stranger, and now that the danger was over, her fear abated somewhat. Of course there wasn't anyone in the tower. Of course there wasn't—

Clunk. A thudding on the stairs. A metallic sort of sound that shot a dart of fear straight through Eirene's chest. She stumbled back, tripping over the edges of the stone slabs that made up the floor.

She strained to listen, but whatever it was had ceased its movement. The silence did little to calm her. Those had been footsteps—clanging, heavy, and uneven, but footsteps nonetheless. She was sure of it. Eirene retreated to the far corner of the room and hunkered down there. If the thing outside came to the door and peered through the gaps in the slats, it would not see her here. Her bed empty, it would assume she had fled somewhere. It would not come inside. She hoped.

She waited for what felt like hours, pinching herself awake each time her head lolled forward. But three days with so little sleep had taken its toll. Every time she closed her eyes, it took a little more strength to force them open again. In the end, she was powerless to resist. Her exhaustion rose in a sudden surging wave, and, huddled up in her corner, face pressed to the wall, she fell into an uneasy slumber.

In Eirene's dreams, she was back at the door and the metallic thudding was growing closer and closer. This time, though, she did not reel back. She peered through the narrow gap, and, on the other side, a pale gold eye looked right back at her. And then the door was shaking beneath her fingers, rocking back and forth as the creature on the other side fought to get through to her, as the eye remained unmoving and stared and stared and stared. Eirene opened her mouth to scream, but no sound came out.

The eye blinked and vanished.

XXI

THE EARTH AND NOT THE SEA

Eirene

Somehow, the second task was even worse than the first. Eirene wasn't sure whether to laugh or cry. Or both. Leandros watched her closely, his expression politely bemused, as she took panicked, gulping breaths and tried to steady her racing heart.

He had arrived outside her room at the crack of dawn, announcing it was time for her to return to her labors. He'd been surprised to find his entry blocked—as had Eirene, jolting awake in the corner. She'd almost believed she'd dreamed it all.

"As I said . . . ," continued Leandros, "the crocuses only grow in crevices on the cliff face. Some attempts have been made to retrieve them, but after several . . . *unfortunate* accidents, those attempts were not fruitful."

"Unfortunate accidents?" echoed Eirene. Her heart wasn't just pounding now, it was throwing itself against her rib cage in a terrified attempt to break free before she destroyed it falling off a cliff.

"No deaths!" said Leandros, flashing her that smile of his. "But my understanding is that the injuries were"—he paused to examine his perfectly polished fingernails, long and filed until they looked sharp and dangerous—"life-changing."

Life-changing. Oh good. Eirene forced herself to keep dragging in breath after breath. She could do this. She *had* to. Phoebe was at stake, and she would do anything for Phoebe. Even scale down a sheer cliff face to retrieve a godsdamned magical crocus. Even knowing that Leandros would certainly have a plan for the flowers once she brought them back, some new way of brewing Desire. Or perhaps he was just setting her a task he knew would terrify her, playing games with her as if she were nothing but a child's toy.

Eirene took several deep, soothing breaths before forcing herself to bow her head in a short nod. Her voice was only a little high—and only cracked twice—when she managed to speak again. She hated him. Soon she would find a way to destroy him. But, for now, she could not defy him. "And how long do I have this time?"

Leandros's smile widened. "One day seems enough, don't you think?"

It was midmorning by the time that Eirene, two great lengths of rope slung over her shoulders, squared her feet on the golden sand of the beach and craned her neck upward. Peiros had brought the ropes to her. It seemed to make the task far too easy, but then, she supposed Leandros did not want her to fall to her death. He really did want these particular crocuses, though the jar of fine saffron threads in his workshop would have been enough to satisfy a king.

The cliffs towered over her—a seemingly endless expanse of pale gray that stretched up and up and up until the sky swallowed them. Eirene's throat tightened painfully and she shook her head emphatically, clutching her hands about her neck to force the fear back down. *Focus.* She blinked rapidly. Slowly, almost reluctantly, the cliff face yielded its details to her: lines that ran over great sections of the stone, patches of determined lichen, a hundred nooks and crannies that might each have housed what she sought. At last, she saw it.

It might have been just another of the ragged crevices in the cliff face—unassuming, cut into the rock, and shielding its contents in dusty shadows. But *there*. The blazing sunlight caught on something softer. Eirene narrowed her eyes, straining to see, and at last her gaze focused on a single white bloom, the only part of the plant not hidden deeper within the rocks. A crocus.

Good. She'd found one. Now she just had to work out how to *get* it.

She dug a short broad trench in the sand to mark the crocuses' location before commencing the long walk up to the cliff tops. Farther along the beach, the sand disappeared into coarse grit, then sharp pebbles, then huge boulders where seabirds perched and screeched relentlessly at each other. Eventually, all of it—sand, rocks, beach—was swallowed by the sea. There were caves at the base of the cliffs there, Eirene knew, hollowed back into the rock, but they were only reachable at low tide. Even then, they were damp and cold and utterly barren.

Her path took her in the opposite direction—along a broad stretch of beach until the cliffs softened into steep hillside, and the bottom of the sea path, flanked by tough rushes, came into view. This was safe; this was familiar. How many times had she come here in the aftermath of the sickness that had decimated the region, of her parents' deaths? She remembered bringing Phoebe, who had always loved the water.

"Show me something good," Phoebe would say, and she would sit on the beach, a blanket around her shoulders, while Eirene danced in the shallows, lifting her arms as high as she could. At that time, after that first, most terrible fever, Phoebe had seemed so small, so fragile, swaying like a flower in the wind with every faltering step. But each time they returned, her steps would be firmer and she would sway a little less. The first time Phoebe joined Eirene in the water, twirling through the shallows, Eirene had wept with something like relief, something like fear, her tears blending with the salt spray.

We will come again, thought Eirene fiercely, putting her foot on the first uneven step of the path and beginning to climb. It was a promise, a solemn vow, even if Phoebe was not there to receive it. *We will come again to the sea, another sea and another beach, when Leandros is defeated and we are far from here and there is enough coin to buy anything we need. We will dance in the shallows.* Phoebe would collect empty seashells and pieces of driftwood to festoon the garden paths and drape around their room. They would be happy and safe.

All Eirene needed to make it happen was a crocus.

By the time she reached the top of the cliffs it was nearly noon; the sun hung high in the sky and assaulted her relentlessly with its scorching touch. It was unusually hot even for the late springtime and she was not yet used to the heat. Her water skin had been full when she'd left Leandros's house. Now she tipped the last of its contents onto her dry tongue.

She was careful not to let her gaze stray too far as she busied herself with looping the first of the ropes once, twice, three times around the tree's trunk. Then again, around the tree behind it, just in case the first one suddenly sprang from the earth and threw itself over the edge after her. Eirene tied good knots. These were the best knots of her life.

She secured the shorter rope about her waist, just above the belt of her chiton with the knives thrust into it, and stepped cautiously toward the edge of the cliff. The second rope she kept loosely coiled around one forearm. She just had to throw it over the edge. Easy. She kept her gaze fixed on the sky beyond. She would not look down. She *could not* look down.

When she was close enough, when the grit kicked up by her feet began to tumble into nothingness, Eirene stopped. She laid both hands above her breast, her thumbs following the curve of her collarbones, and drew in a deep, calming breath. Her chest rose and fell beneath her fingertips; her heart steadied beneath her left palm. This was her flesh, her bone, her muscle. She was in control.

She opened her eyes. She looked over the edge.

A mistake. *Absolutely not.* Her heart surged again, bringing with it a wave of dizziness, and she stumbled backward. Her foot slipped on a loose patch of stone and a moment later she found herself sitting on the dry ground, her legs folded half beneath her and her tailbone smarting painfully.

Eirene swore loudly. She ground her hands into the dirt, dragging her fingers through the dust and leaving ragged trails behind them. The rope fell from her arm and coiled pathetically beside her. "Oh, *gods.* Gods*dammit.*"

Why couldn't she do it? It was an easy task, one she should have been grateful for. Scale halfway down the cliff. Rip a patch of flowers from their perch. Scale the rest of the way down.

It was a challenge of physicality alone; she did not have to be clever this time. Anyone could do it. Perhaps Leandros had thought it an easy task to set for her, though Eirene remembered the glint in his eyes as he'd told her what he wanted, and she wondered if somehow he had *known* that it would mean confronting the worst of her fears.

She longed suddenly for lentils and for scrabbling about on the floor in the mottled half-light. She longed for Lamia with her wide, bright eyes, if only so that there was a hand to reach for now. The thrumming of her heart seemed to reach a new feverish urgency and she felt her face twist in anger and shame. What a coward she was, that the mere sight of the cliff face and the sea below it could reduce her to *this*.

I don't need to be brave, she told herself firmly. *I just need to keep going.* She forced herself to her feet and checked the rope around her waist, searching for some flaw, some give, but it hardly shifted under the force of her furious tugs. It would hold. Eirene scowled at it—its surety seemed only to heighten her weakness.

She swore again—loudly, colorfully. And once more. Just for luck. Then she walked back to the edge and looked over it a second time.

This time, she was expecting the dizziness, and she rocked back on her heels with the force of it but did not fall. She looked down at the beach below, the glittering golden sand and the waves crashing over it at regular intervals. It was so far. So very far. If she were to fall, she'd break like a sparrow's egg tossed from a nest by its cuckoo usurper. She wondered if she'd live long enough to hear her skull cracking before the impact turned her brain to pulp. It'd leak through her ears like the yolk of that sad, broken egg. Was this how Icarus had felt fleeing the tower that was his prison? No wonder he had flown high to the sun when the sea was so fierce, so terrible, so enticing.

She let the long rope fall. Then she turned away from the sea and dropped to her hands and knees, the rope following the line of her spine. She forced herself to breathe steadily around the bite of the second rope that remained tight around her waist. Secure. She hoped. As an afterthought, she pulled off her sandals. She'd have a better grip barefoot. Though what to do with the shoes now? She couldn't well carry them, and they would be a nuisance—smacking into her every time she moved—if she tied them to her belt. But leaving them at the top would mean having to walk all the way up here again. Eirene considered the weight of the shoes in her hands then, realizing she was probably just wasting time deliberately now, settled for tossing them backward over the cliff's edge.

She did not look to see where they fell. She'd be reunited with them again at the bottom, anyway, with a clump of crocuses in her fist.

She crawled backward toward the gentle slope that led to the edge, biting hard on her lip as if the pain would somehow wash away the fear as she pushed the first of her feet out into open air. She dropped onto her belly and pushed the other foot out and over the edge. Then, her hands tight on the rope that would guide her from the top of the cliff and down, down, down to the bottom, she wormed her way backward, shuffling her hands down the rope one at a time. The strain on her arms increased until more and more of her was hanging over the cliff edge.

Eirene tangled her knees and ankles around the rope. No. That would do her little good. She had to find footholds, something firmer that she could push up on as she navigated her hands over the final lip of stone. She slowly unhooked one leg from the rope and dragged her foot over the cliff face. She should have thought this through more. She should have made sure to descend at a point where at least the first part of the climb was easy, the rock peppered with irregularities that nimble hands and feet could slip into.

When her foot finally settled in a stable hold, she released a breath she had been holding so long she was lightheaded.

She found a second foothold reasonably quickly. Just the hands now. One over the edge and onto the rope. Then the other. That was it—her whole body hung from the cliff face. She bit down on her lip and held the flesh between her teeth, relishing the pain.

Now what? A foot needed to move again. She shuffled her hands down the rope one at a time, her heart racing furiously every time there were fewer than ten fingers securely wrapped over the rough fibers. Then she was able to move her foot down to a nook some way below the first. She shuffled her bare toes as deep into the stone as she could and pressed down as hard as she dared. Her grip held. The second foot followed. Hand. Other hand. Foot again. She forced herself to look only where she needed to: straight ahead, occasionally permitting herself a glance at a particular tricky hold. How close was the sea? She didn't know. She didn't want to know.

Hand. Other hand. Foot. Other foot. On and on and on until the motion was all but mindless. Perhaps a little too mindless. Maybe that was why she grew careless with where she was placing her feet. Maybe that was why, when she shoved her left foot into yet another crack, she didn't test the strength of the hold with quite so much vigor as before. She pulled her other foot free, her weight transferring to that singular little gap in the stone. For one long moment, it held firm. The next, it did not.

She barely had enough time to scream as she *dropped*. It was only the instinctive tightening of her fingers on the rope that saved her. As it was, her arms were pulled straight, her elbows locking as she dangled. The only thing between her and certain death was the frantic hold of her hands on the rope. But her strength would not last long.

She swung her legs wildly for a foothold. Her hands burned, the rough surface of the rope scraping her palms as her weight pulled her downward. She couldn't hold on, not for much longer. She was going to fall.

Tears were slipping over her cheeks. The muscles of her arms were screaming their protest, her shoulders nearly popping from their joints. She slipped down another foot's length and felt her palms give against the rope, the skin tearing with a searing pain like she'd plunged her hands into hot ashes. She could feel blood on her wrist, a hot trickle of it. A high-pitched terrified sob forced itself from her throat. She gasped for air.

"Please," she choked out. She wasn't sure who she was asking. The gods? It had to be; there was no one else around.

But if the gods heard her desperate begging, they did not listen.

Eirene's grip failed, the rope slipped from between her raw, blood-slicked fingers, and finally, almost mercifully, she plummeted downward.

XXII

THE GOD OF ALL FIRE

Lamia

Lamia's skin was burning.

It was as if someone had taken a hot poker and run it over her face, her chest, her neck, and then thrust it down her throat for good measure. Vague shapes swam, dark and dreamlike, across her vision. Where was she? What was happening? She tried to force her eyes open and after a moment of struggle came to the realization that they had never been closed in the first place. But she still could not see. A film of fog had been laid over her; she was trapped inside it.

Help, she tried to say, but what came out was a dry croak that brought with it a sharp flare of the fire. Hot coals on her tongue, in her lungs, turning her to ash and dust and—

"Lamia?" The voice was shatteringly loud, as if her father had screamed it straight into the withered remnants of her ear. Burned away, all burned away. She tried to flinch from the sound but she managed only a feeble press of her head into the pillows that propped her up. *Pillows.* She was in a bed, then. In *her* bed? Slowly, the blurred shapes around her seemed to make sense. She could not see the fire that still raged through her body, but that rusty smear was her single shutter. The smudge of yellow light shining through the gap fell onto a shape that must have been her father. He was little but a blur of white and gold, shuffling with something laid out on the bed.

He must have sensed her watching him; suddenly the shape of him was looming over her and his voice was breaking through the dandelion fuzz of her mind.

"You're unwell, my sweet girl," he said. "But I'm going to make you better."

Unwell. But what of the flames? Could he see them? Could he put them out? She tried to ask him, to *beg* him, but she could make no sound but that same pitiful rasp as before.

"Here," he said. Something pressed against her lips. Cold and metallic. "Drink it," he urged her, tipping the bowl. "It will help."

Lamia *tried*, she truly did. But she did not seem to have gained control of her body yet, and though she tried her best to open her mouth, to drink whatever it was that he offered her, she couldn't. She *couldn't*. Something cool and cold slipped over her cheeks. In its path, the burning cooled and quietened.

"Ah, I see." Her father pulled the bowl back from her lips. *The bowl.* Yes, that was what it was. She could see it now, swimming into focus—the glint of the copper, the curve of the rim, its mud-colored contents—before it was pulled away.

"Wait." Her voice was cracked and quiet, but it was there.

Her father brushed his hand across her cheek. There was a white bandage on his arm, blood seeping through the wrappings. "I'm not leaving, Lamia. I know what you need." Lamia tried to turn her head to watch him. There came a sound like a gasp, a sharp inhale of breath, and then a *whoosh* of the exhale that brought with it a fine cloud of power. It settled over Lamia.

"*Breathe*," Her father coaxed her. "Breathe in, my sweet girl. It will help."

What could she do but trust him? What else had she ever done? Lamia did as she was told.

There was no telling how much time had elapsed when Lamia came to herself again. She was sitting up in bed, her blanket tucked around her waist, and the fire had gone out. Mostly. The embers still smoldered within her flesh but she was herself again, her mind clearer. Her fingers moved when she told them to, even if the gesture sent a flare of agony through her. The fog over her had thinned; she could see again.

Her father had not left her; he stood beside the bed, bent over a mess of terra-cotta jars and herbs spilling from twists of papyrus. He was speaking as he worked, muttering to himself. Or was it to her? She caught her name among the muddled sounds and strained to listen.

"What am I going to do with you, Lamia?" His voice was soft and unusually kind. Or perhaps that was only a conjuring of her fevered mind. Perhaps all of it was. Her father was still speaking in a gentle, soothing tone. "I should have seen that it was coming back," he said. "Oh, my poor girl."

He looked up at her then and froze when he saw that she was awake and watching him. The break in his composure only lasted a moment, then his face was splitting with a broad smile. "Lamia! You had me worried."

She returned his smile as best she could.

His brow creased with worry. "You are still unwell. Let me— here." He ducked down, sweeping something up from the floor. The little copper bowl from before, half drained. Lamia did not remember drinking from it, but she must have done so. "This will help, I promise."

He put an arm behind her and helped her to sit up straighter before bringing the bowl to her lips again and tipping it back. The tincture inside was an unpleasant greenish brown, and it had the consistency of mud. It tasted foul—bitter, earthy, metallic—but Lamia was too exhausted to do anything but part her lips and choke down the vile sludge.

"There," her father said. "There, that will help."

Lamia sagged back against the pillows, suddenly fizzy. The medicine's bitter sting unfurled from her belly, creeping through her veins until her whole body seemed to prickle and pulse with it. "What . . . is this?" Her own voice seemed to be coming from very far away.

"It will help," he repeated. He stroked her hair tenderly, pulling the loose strands back from her face. "It will help, my sweet girl. Sleep now. All will be well when you awaken."

"No," protested Lamia. Something shifted inside her. Her eyes fluttered shut and though she tried to open them again, she could not. Light flashed across the blackness, gone as quickly as it had come. Her head spun.

She had been here before—in this bed, with this bitter taste on her tongue. She tried to catch onto the memory. There was something there, just beyond her reach. The images came in flashing fragments. Slack fingers. Her own fingers? No, not hers. Someone else's. Someone else's fingers, white and unmoving and curved like a dead spider on its back. A spider in a pool of blood.

Blood? Lamia could have laughed. When would she ever have seen *that*? She was dreaming, of course, and frightening herself with her own imagination. She was safe and she had nothing to fear. The medicine soothed her frantic pulse until it was a steady drumbeat through her body. It cradled her in its warmth and she slipped into something like a dream, a dream in which a beautiful woman smiled at her, her face framed in flames. Her eyes were gold and Lamia was safe with her. What was it that she had been afraid of? She couldn't remember.

She couldn't remember anything.

Lamia slipped into dreams of fog and ash.

XXIII

THE FLOODS OF STYX

Eirene

For a split second, Eirene was in free fall, nothing holding her up, nothing keeping her from hurtling downward and smashing into the rocks. She was vaguely aware that her mouth was open and that the noise that escaped it was terrible and inhuman. Her eyes were squeezed shut; she did not want to see the water, her death, as it came to greet her.

Then the rope around Eirene's waist went taut and she came to a snapping halt in midair. Her eyes flew open just in time to watch the cliff face rapidly approaching her own. She turned her head as she slammed into the rock, hip and shoulder first, sending up a cloud of dust and dislodging a flurry of loose stones. She did not hear them hit the water below; the ear that had collided with the stone was ringing—screaming, really. Or was that her? Pain had torn through her body like an arrow.

She swung from side to side, bouncing against the stone. Each collision was gentler than the last, but that did not make them painless. She reached out blindly to stabilize herself and her hands met some kind of crevice. She scrabbled for handholds and pulled herself to an awkward, aching stop.

She clung to the cliff face, panting, sobbing like a child. Her hands burned as if she'd plunged them into fire; she ached all over, but she was alive. She was *alive*. Gradually, her breathing slowed, her tears dried. When her courage had returned, Eirene opened her eyes. And found herself face to face with a patch of silver crocuses.

"Oh," she said out loud. "Oh, you little bastards." Then she burst into tears again.

She hung there, the rope still painfully tight around her waist, her feet finally secure again in their footholds, buried her face in her red-raw hands, and sobbed.

At length, Eirene gained enough composure to examine her discovery. She groped around inside the crevice until she found two reasonably firm handholds, then dragged herself up into the hollow. There was just enough room for her to sit inside, her legs splayed out to avoid crushing the delicate little flowers growing from a broad fissure in the rock.

They were unlike any crocuses Eirene had seen before. Instead of the usual single blooms, or bundles of two or three, ten white flowers grew from a patch of long silvery leaves. Inside, there were no delicate masts of yellow and red but more of that same silver color. Eirene leaned in and gave them a cautious sniff. Nothing. The delicate scent and color these crocuses were usually prized for was lacking entirely.

All this for a patch of weeds. Eirene gritted her teeth. With the knife from her belt, she carefully dug the cluster of pale flowers and leaves from the soil, teasing the clumps of dirt from the roots with her dusty, bloody fingers. When she brushed a white petal, she left a rusty trail behind. She wouldn't try to wipe it off. Let Leandros see it. Let him know the lengths she was willing to go to. Let him know that she *would* win this.

Removing the rope from around her waist was both a relief and a new terror. Once she extracted herself from the crevice, there would be nothing preventing her from plummeting to the ground but the strength of her own hands. She was not confident they'd hold out against the second part of her descent. It was a small relief that she had perhaps a third of the cliff to go; a cursory glance over the crevice's edge had found the beach far closer than she'd expected. If she fell from here, she might get away with only a pair of broken legs. Maybe a black eye. She'd sprawl out melodramatically on her bed at home and force a long-suffering Phoebe to nurse her back to health.

Or Lamia.

Eirene reeled back, as if the thought was a physical thing—an insect that had flown in her face. Why on earth was she thinking of Lamia? Of Lamia *nursing* her? The girl had barely left her house. What could she possibly know of healing?

"Ridiculous," muttered Eirene to herself. It was the heat, the dehydration, driving her mad. She busied herself with cutting strips from the hem of her chiton to wrap her hands. She would need a new one soon. This one had been too short for a year or so now, and with great sections hacked out of the bottom it would be laughable. She brushed the dust from the rough weave as best she could and set to bandaging her bloody palms.

Once that was done, she leaned back against the wall of the hollow and breathed slowly and deeply, feeling her heart settle as the fear of falling became less immediate. As it seeped out of her, something else took its place: a coldness that seemed to reach into her very bones and a *pull*. Not out into the open air but farther into the dark crevice behind her. She felt an urgent compulsion to turn, to look, to crawl into the dark and leave the light behind. She shivered, her whole body shuddering, and it snapped her out of the feeling just long enough for her to decide that she should go *now*. Whatever had made the crocuses as they were was not for mortals.

Something terrible lurked in the cliff, and Eirene had no interest in meeting it.

The last part of the descent ended up being quite a bit easier, in part because Eirene was a little less terrified now that she realized that falling probably wouldn't kill her. The cliff face was rougher and Eirene passed at least a dozen more crags housing their own cluster of silver-white crocuses. Whenever she was close enough, she would hack at the flowers with her knife until her hands started smarting again, then toss the butchered blooms into the sea below. Whatever Leandros achieved with the crocuses she brought him, he'd have a hard time replicating it. She reveled in her petty rebellion.

She'd stuffed the crocuses for Leandros down the back of her chiton for safekeeping. The waist sash stopped them from slipping out completely, but they moved around far too much for her liking as she lowered herself, foot after foot, hand after hand, to the safety of the beach.

Her whole body was trembling by the time she made it. She dropped the final distance to the sand; her legs crumpled at the impact and she sprawled, face first, to the ground. She lay there for a moment, prone, her mouth and nose full of grit, before somehow finding the strength to roll onto her side. She was careful not to crush the crocuses—she refused to make it all the way down only to destroy them now. She tilted her face to the sun. A laugh bubbled past her lips.

She'd made it. She'd *made it*. Two tasks complete, and only two remaining. She couldn't wait to see Leandros's face when she sauntered back to the house, crocuses held aloft in a bloody fist like a torch of victory. She caught herself smiling, and all her joy and mirth vanished in an instant. Two tasks left? How had she fallen into the rhythm of Leandros's demands so easily? Her purpose here was not to complete the four tasks—to help Leandros in his endless pursuit of power. It was to save *Phoebe*; it was to keep Leandros away from her until her weaving was finished. It was to discover and destroy the secret of Desire, to take from Leandros the thing that gave him all his awful power, and to *run*. Leaving Lamia behind. The thought made her breath catch. She forced it swiftly from her mind.

Eirene raised herself to her knees and examined her hands. They were in bad shape to say the least. Bright red blood had soaked through the makeshift wrappings, and when she went to peel one of the strips away from her skin, the movement brought with it a searing flare of pain. She'd have to soak them off later, in cool, clean water.

Her feet were scraped and bruised and filthy, but it was all relatively superficial damage. The side of her face had been badly scraped when she slammed against the cliff. She trailed her fingers over the damaged skin and winced. She'd have to put together a poultice of yarrow and honey and pray that it didn't get infected. The shoulder on the same side was a mess of purple bruising. But all that could be addressed later. When she was back. When the crocuses had been presented to Leandros and he'd reluctantly admitted she'd succeeded yet again.

She staggered to her feet and cast about for the sandals she'd tossed down so long ago.

It would be a long walk back.

It was dark when she reached the house. She marched through the main door and into the courtyard—Daphne was stalking the remaining ducks, her tail swishing back and forth—making her way to Leandros's study. Peiros had heard her come in; he scurried after her like a rat, protesting loudly that she could not just barge in like that. Eirene turned sharply to face him. He flinched; she knew she looked terrible, her cheek torn and swollen. "I'd appreciate it if you would fetch Leandros," she said sweetly. She'd yet to replace the knife in her belt; she flipped it over and over in her hand, pretending that the tender flesh of her palm did not sting each time that she did. She thrust the curtain to the study aside, speaking over her shoulder: "And be quick about it. I've brought him a *beautiful* gift."

As sour as Peiros's departing face was, he *was* quick about it. Soon, Eirene heard Leandros's steady footsteps in the corridor outside. She felt the smallest prickle of fear. There had been no blood in his workshop that she could find, it was true, but *something* had happened to Alexandra, and *something* went into Leandros's Desires to make them so powerful. And here Eirene was, giving him something else he might be able to add to the enchantments.

She looked down at the crocuses in her lap with their tangle of muddy roots. Before she could convince herself out of it, she tore a single white bloom from the bunch and stuffed it into the sleeve of her chiton. She shoved the stem beneath the pin of the brooch at her shoulder and prayed it wouldn't fall out until she was well clear of the study.

She snatched her hand free of the sleeve just in time to receive Leandros. He pushed aside the curtain with his usual flourish and glided inside. "Eirene! I should have known you'd manage it." His delight seemed genuine. Then he saw her, and his warm smile changed to a melodramatic mask of horror. "Oh, Eirene, dearest. Look at your *face*."

Eirene waved a dismissive hand. The gesture pulled at her bandages and she had to suppress a grimace of pain. "It will heal."

Leandros's smile returned. "Well then," he said brightly, "you found my crocuses."

Eirene could have set them down on the desk or taken a single step so that she was close enough to merely drop them in his hands. She had a sudden urge to throw the bunch at him, to watch the mess of roots scattering soil over the floor as he threw his hands up just in time to snatch them from the air. But she was still afraid of him. She settled for reaching out and slamming the flowers into his hands with more force than necessary.

"*Careful,*" he admonished her. "These are precious."

"I know that," said Eirene pointedly, indicating her battered face.

Leandros seemed not to notice; his attention had already shifted to the flowers clutched against his chest like a child.

"There's a flower missing." He fingered the broken stem idly.

"I had to scale down a cliff with it," said Eirene, her tone as icy as she could make it. She was becoming a fine liar. "The rest are there and intact. It's enough for your purposes."

"And how would you know what's *enough for my purposes*?" He put on a high mocking imitation of her voice.

Eirene ignored the slight. "Am I wrong?" she challenged him. "Is the final flower so essential?"

Leandros tossed the plant onto his desk. Soil fell from the tangled mess of roots onto an unfurled scroll. "It will do."

"As I thought."

After Leandros had dismissed her, Eirene returned to the tower. She paused outside her room, then turned away from the wooden door and made instead for the stairs, kicking off her sodden shoes as she went. The steep spiral of the staircase did not intimidate her anymore, not since she'd scaled a cliff face. She did not stop on the landing with its locked door; she ran all the way up.

The curtain at the very top of the stairs was drawn half aside. Eirene paused there, breathing heavily. "Lamia?"

A small sound came from within the room. Taking that as permission to enter, Eirene slipped through the gap.

It took her a moment to see Lamia. She was huddled beneath her blankets, her face paler than usual, which was very pale indeed, and her hair was a wild tangle. When she saw Eirene, she pulled herself slowly into a sitting position. Her eyes were huge and bright, in the way that Phoebe's eyes would be when she had a fever.

"Lamia," said Eirene. "Gods, you look—are you ill?"

With a visible effort, Lamia shook her head. "Better now. I was sleeping. My father gave me medicine."

"Well." Eirene shuffled her feet. She should have visited Lamia before she left for the cliffs. Then she would have known she was unwell; she could have made her a tincture. "I brought you something," she said and thrust her hand forward before she could talk herself out of it. The flower—now battered and bruised from its time shoved into her chiton—looked rather small and pathetic in her palm. Eirene felt her cheeks grow hot with embarrassment as Lamia stared fixedly at her hand. She had thought to be sweet, but it was a pitiful gesture.

"Oh," said Lamia. Her voice was very soft; she spoke as if there was something caught in her throat. "Oh, *Eirene.*"

"I—" She had meant to say "I'm sorry," but Lamia's next words had the apology dissolving into nothing on her tongue.

"It's *lovely*," Lamia said, and burst into tears.

XXIV
IN SPIRIT AND SENSE

Eirene

Eirene waited until Lamia fell asleep, her breath growing slow and even before she left. She wanted to get into the workshop again, to search for clues she must have missed before. But no sooner had Eirene returned to her room than Peiros materialized outside her door.

"What do you want?" she asked suspiciously, peering through the gap.

Peiros spoke in his usual emotionless monotone. "The master requests that you join him for dinner."

Eirene gave him what must have been a completely blank look. "He requests *what*?"

Peiros ignored her question. "This way, if you will." He turned and marched toward the door that separated the tower from the main house.

"Wait!" said Eirene hurriedly. "Let me just—my shoes!" She grabbed the sandals from where she'd thrown them. They were still filthy, still wet with sea spray.

Peiros either did not hear her or he did not care. Eirene laced up her sandals in record time before racing after him, following the slapping of his footsteps ahead. He led her, eventually, to a room at the far side of the house, separated from the corridor by a large purplish curtain. Eirene had never been here before—it was an unpleasant reminder of how much of a stranger she was here and how ineffectual an investigator she was proving to be. She should have known the house from top to bottom by now. She should have discovered the secret to creating Desire. She should have destroyed it, not just stolen a tiny pinch of the enchanted powder and run away, her tail tucked between her legs.

"In there," said Peiros shortly, indicating the purple curtain, before vanishing through the nearest door. A gust of hot air came from the door, and it filled Eirene's nostrils with the most glorious scent she had ever smelled. Roasting meat, certainly, and garlic and onion and a medley of herbs. Her mouth watered and she was suddenly twice as hungry as she had been before. Was *that* what she was about to eat? The smell was irresistible, and she almost forgot that she was supposed to be going through to the adjacent room. She caught herself with her hand on the door to the kitchen and reluctantly turned back to the purple curtain and the room that lay beyond.

She plucked at the edge of the curtain. It was heavy, finely woven. It must have been astonishingly expensive.

"Eirene?" The voice, muffled but still distinctive, came from the room beyond. Leandros.

Eirene had not truly considered until now what Leandros might hope to gain from their dining together. Perhaps he was reconsidering their bargain; perhaps he wanted her as his wife after all, and now longed to win her favor through extravagant feasts and rousing conversation. Eirene fought back a giggle, her apprehension ending abruptly. *Not likely.*

Whatever it was, it could be nothing terrible. They had an agreement, after all, bound in blood and sworn under the watchful eyes of the gods. And Eirene was hungry. *Really* hungry. She squared her shoulders, yanked the curtain aside, and marched inside.

The room she entered was a vast entertaining hall that could have held more than a hundred men, and it was completely empty but for its single occupant. Leandros sat at one end of a long wooden table, his hand coiled lazily around his cup and an empty plate laid before him. He'd dressed up, Eirene was sure of it—his chiton was a rich blue, his hair was perfectly curled, and he had golden bangles spiraling up both his wrists. A wine jug stood before him and the creases of his lips were dark with drink. "Eirene." He greeted her enthusiastically. "Sit."

He indicated a chair that had been pulled up a little ways down from him. An empty plate had been laid there, too, and a matching cup. Eirene approached it cautiously and sat. She pulled her knife from her belt and put it beside the plate. Then, thinking better of eating with a knife still marred with soil and streaks of crocus stem, she wiped it clean on her skirt and set it down again. Leandros, who had been watching her with open curiosity, raised an eyebrow.

Eirene sat stiffly, her hands folded neatly in her lap, and said nothing.

The silence stretched out between them.

"You know," said Leandros eventually, with a sparkling laugh. He leaned forward, making a temple of his hands. "I must confess I did not expect you to still be here. I thought you were an arrogant little girl who needed . . . curtailing. But two tasks later, I think you might be proving me wrong."

Again, Eirene said nothing.

"Say 'thank you,'" said Leandros sweetly. He picked up the knife beside his plate and rested the tip on the tabletop, spinning it back and forth between his fingers. The threat was clear.

"Thank you," said Eirene. The words caught in her throat.

"Good," said Leandros, though he did not lay the knife down again.

Eirene startled as the curtain was thrust aside. Peiros skulked inside. He nodded to Leandros and took up position against the wall, a silent sentry.

"Peiros," called Leandros, his tone gently admonishing. There was a glint in his eye. "You forget your duties. Our guest has nothing to drink."

Peiros scowled, but he stepped forward obediently to fill her cup with wine before standing back against the wall.

"There, that wasn't so hard, was it?" Leandros picked up his own cup and lifted it in Eirene's direction as if he were toasting her. He brought the cup to his lips.

Eirene picked up her cup. The liquid inside was clear and dark and—though the color was not quite right—made her think immediately of blood. The blood that had trickled from Lamia's palms two nights prior, when she'd cut herself open to summon that astounding light of hers. The blood that had been drained from Alexandra. The blood she had found no trace of in Leandros's underground workshop.

"Eirene?" said Leandros. "Why do you frown so darkly? Is the wine not to your liking?"

"It is nothing," said Eirene quickly.

"Come now, we will be husband and wife. You do not think I would stoop to enchanting your wine?"

She hadn't, actually; she'd been too wrapped up in her thoughts of blood. Now, though—

"Let me put you at ease," said Leandros. He reached out and switched their cups, then drank deeply from Eirene's. He wiped the red from his mouth and smiled, his teeth stained as if with gore. Eirene flinched. "Your turn," Leandros growled.

He would not have poisoned his own cup, would he? Eirene lifted it and took a cautious sip. It did not taste as she'd expected. When Stavros came in, reeking of drink, it was always an awful sour smell. But *this*. This was sweet and floral and delicious. She took a longer drink. And another.

"Careful," said Leandros. He gave her a crooked smile. "Do you like it?"

Eirene ducked her head. "It's delicious," she admitted to the table.

"Just you wait. There's more."

He was not lying. For just then, the curtain was opened a second time and servants, hired from the village, she supposed, poured inside. Eirene barely looked at them; she was too distracted by what they held in their hands.

They were carrying the food.

The *food*. Heaps of puffy flatbread billowing steam from the tears in their sides. Some kind of large fowl had been plucked and roasted with garlic, thyme, and rosemary. It was still spitting oil. It was followed by a huge fish, its head and tail neatly removed and its skin peeled back from the succulent pink flesh. A platter of garnished chickpeas was placed beside it and Eirene breathed in the sharp scent of mint. Then there were fresh figs, apples, grapes, apricots, and a whole bowl of glittering pomegranate seeds. Asparagus stems and olives. A heaped bowl of walnuts. Eirene could do nothing but gape.

Leandros watched her with amusement. "What did you expect, my dear Eirene? That I would starve you, my bride-to-be? After you brought me such a fine bounty?"

Eirene made a face. The phrase "bride-to-be" made her nauseous, frankly, and, *yes*, she had thought he would let her starve. Or at least, that he would not feed her quite so well. She ran her tongue over her teeth and swore she could still feel the grit she'd choked down.

"You are halfway through your tasks, are you not? We do not celebrate things by halves, here." He didn't wait for a response before sweeping a golden hand over the food and grinning. "But I won't keep you from your feast with my idle conversation. Please, eat." He reached for the heaped pile of bread and took one.

Eirene followed suit. When Leandros cut a piece of fish, so did she, then pomegranate seeds and asparagus and everything else. Whatever Leandros took, she took. Whatever he was willing to eat seemed likeliest not to be poisoned.

When he took a fig, her heart flipped with excitement. She'd been eyeing them since they were set down. She selected the fattest, ripest fig she could find, its skin dark and stretched taut over its flesh. She followed this with a golden apricot, a bunch of dark grapes.

Leandros cut a glistening wedge of meat from the side of the bird and leaned over wordlessly to drop it on Eirene's plate. Eirene usually preferred the darker meat of the thigh and the leg, though she decided it'd be wise to keep this to herself on this occasion. She cleared her throat. "Thank you."

"Take more, if you like." Leandros cut himself a hunk of meat. "You must be hungry."

Eirene shrugged and did as he bid, tearing a leg from the bird and adding it to the pile on her plate. She supplemented this with another sprinkling of pomegranate seeds and another fig. She could smell its ripeness before she'd even pried it open.

She had a sudden memory of refusing to eat the figs and plums that Leandros had sent to the house for Phoebe. There was a reason, but she could not quite remember it now . . . Surely, there was nothing more insidious here than an appallingly rich man who had found a way to grow fruit out of season. Certainly, his roses always seemed to be in full bloom and they shouldn't have been out until it was almost summer. She relaxed a fraction and picked up her cup. Peiros had refilled it without her noticing and she drank eagerly. She had not realized how parched she was, and the wine really was delicious.

The moment she saw Leandros take his first delicate mouthfuls of bread, Eirene began to eat. She was as methodical in this as she had been sorting her seeds. First, she stripped the fish of the bones, picking out the delicate shards with her fingers. She heaped the bones on the edge of her plate. She tore bite-sized pieces from the bread and used them to shovel the flesh into her mouth. When that was finished, she turned to the rest. The chickpeas were warm and filling, the figs as sweet and ripe as she'd known they would be. The olives were salty, the asparagus stems tender and sweet. The pomegranates cut through it all with their sharp tang. She could taste the wine, heady and overpowering. She was so *hungry*. She ate ravenously, hardly pausing for breath. Leandros, thank the gods, seemed to have no interest in distracting her with idle chatter.

At last, she slowed. She took a half-hearted bite from the extra leg Leandros had bid her take, then replaced it on her plate. She'd vastly overestimated the number of olives she could eat; half a dozen lay beside a scattered heap of chickpeas and a pulverized fig.

"Keep eating," Leandros encouraged her.

Eirene laughed but obediently threw a handful of pomegranate seeds into her mouth. They were bursting with sour juice and slick with fat from the bird, though the richness was no longer quite as appetizing as it had been before. "I think that's all I can manage," she told him, tucking the seeds into her cheek as she talked. They were growing harder to chew, more fibrous now that she wasn't swallowing them down so quickly she hardly had time to taste them. She felt peculiarly giddy.

"Of course it isn't," said Leandros. "Keep eating."

"No, really." Eirene pushed her chair back from the table and rested her hands on her belly. It was round and firm beneath her fingers, such as it had not been for years. She laughed, a startled sound of satisfaction. "I've never eaten so much in my life."

"There are people starving in the village you came from, dear Eirene," said Leandros. His voice was as warm and friendly as it had been moments ago, but there was an edge to it now. "And I told you to keep eating."

Eirene stilled. Among the food and the wine, she had forgotten who she was sitting before. This was Leandros, a man who shilled vicious enchantments to snatch young women's wits from them and lead them into the beds of Zakynthos's foulest and richest. This was Leandros, who kept his only child locked away in a tower. Whose wife had been found drained of blood. Eirene risked a sideways look at him, and her heart leaped unpleasantly as his steady blue gaze met hers. There was no pretense there; his eyes were filled with smug cruelty.

Eirene looked away, back down at the food left in front of her. What had looked so appetizing half an hour before now might as well have been a heap of clay. The thought of taking another single bite was obscene. Eirene pushed the plate away and shook her head. "I can't," she protested weakly.

"You can," said Leandros. He leaned forward and reached out

to settle one of his perfect golden hands over hers, a spider crouching above its hopelessly entangled prey. Eirene's fingers were greasy and sticky from eating, but his were perfectly clean. It was only then that Eirene realized she hadn't seen him take a single bite of food but for those few restrained mouthfuls of bread at the beginning of the meal. Since then, he'd just sat there, sipping his wine, watching Eirene. His plate was full. His next words were cold and commanding. "You will."

What else was there to do?

She picked up the meat again and tore a chunk from the bone with her teeth. She made herself swallow. At least this was edible, she told herself firmly. Better than raw lentils and grain and sand. Even so, her body revolted as she took another bite and tried to force it down. It stuck in her throat and it took several wheezing gulps of wine to dislodge it. After that, she took smaller bites and alternated them with sips of wine. Even that had lost its appeal.

Eirene left as many slivers of meat clinging to the bone as she dared and set it down. Her stomach didn't just feel full now; it felt bloated, distended, like it had been forced to swell to twice its natural size. She could have sworn she could feel the food beginning to wrestle its way back up her throat. She tried in vain to swallow down a violent swell of nausea.

"I'm finished," she choked out.

Leandros tapped his fingers on the tabletop and offered her a dazzling smile. "Finished?"

She didn't dare repeat herself; she was sure that she'd retch. Was this how Phoebe felt when she was ill and all food made her queasy? Eirene did not know how she stood it over and over again. The wine was hitting her now, too. Her thoughts took longer to pin down and her vision blurred as she dropped her chin in a listless nod. Was this how Stavros felt, each night he struggled home from the symposium? If it was, Eirene could not understand why he always seemed so determined to return to his cups. She felt dangerously out of control.

"Oh no, Eirene, I don't think so," said Leandros. "There's perfectly good meat there. I know you were not raised to be wasteful. A few more mouthfuls and you'll be done." He leaned forward, his voice dropping. "In this house, we finish what we start. We *complete* things. We don't come back from the cliffs with a bunch of flowers missing a bloom."

Eirene made a sound that wouldn't have been strange in the mouth of a dying dog. Was that what this was? A punishment for a missing flower?

"Oh *dear*," said Leandros. "I think you'd better be getting to bed, my little bride-to-be. Just finish your food and then Peiros can take you back to the tower. Come on." He stood, a blurred shape suddenly looming over her.

Eirene felt for the greasy bone and brought it to her lips, pulling the last scraps of meat loose. She couldn't bring herself to swallow, this time; she chewed quickly and shoved the vile pulp of flesh into her cheek. It had a rotten taste to it now, like a bird that had been slaughtered in the morning and left to fester all day beneath the searing heat of the sun.

Eirene dropped the bone on her plate and slumped back in her chair. Leandros sat slowly, his edges still blurred, the details of his features lost in a fog. She blinked, trying to clear the haze that had descended over her vision, little stars dancing at the edges.

Her breath caught when she inhaled, a soft hitch of panic. Why couldn't she see? Was she going to faint? Leandros was talking, but she could not pick out the individual words.

"Please," she tried to say, but even to her own ears the word was just an indecipherable moan. "I can't—"

Leandros's voice grew louder and more urgent. A warm hand fell upon her shoulders just as her head slipped from her hands and she slumped forward onto her plate. The bones she'd picked clean pressed against her cheeks, but she was already too far gone to be disgusted. *Poison.* He must have poisoned her. Was she dying? Or Desired? Surely not—she hated him as much as she always had.

The stars in her vision surged and spread until she could see nothing but the night sky spread out before her. And then she was gone, lifted from the earth, spiraling among the stars.

XXV

THE SORROWFUL WOUND

Eirene

Eirene's neck ached.

"Ugh," she said aloud, rolling her head from side to side on the pillow and squeezing her eyes shut against the morning light. Clearly, her body was going to be slow to recover from the beating she'd subjected it to on the cliffs. And had she forgotten to close the shutters? But of course she had. "Ughhhhhhhh." She let out a long pitiful groan.

The previous night began to take shape in her mind in brief, mortifying flashes of clarity. Had she been . . . drinking? More than drinking. She'd been *drunk*. All those years of eyeing Stavros with superior disdain and she'd reduced herself to the same stumbling wretchedness. And it had not just been the wine. Eirene stiffened as the memory of the *food* hit her like a chariot. Her stomach twisted and for a moment she couldn't move; she lay on her back, completely still, her heartbeat pounding like a drum not just in her chest but in her ears and her hands and the depths of her belly, and she couldn't breathe because her throat was full of flesh and wine and pomegranate seeds and she could not swallow. She could not scream. She could not do anything. It was only another thrum of pain from her neck that wrenched her from her paralysis.

She sat bolt upright, gasping. Her mouth was as dry as a bone and tasted appalling, almost *rotten*. There was hair stuck to her face and her eyes were gummy. She peeled them open and blinked into the pale light that filtered into the room.

With her every movement, her body seemed to ache even more. She touched her fingers to the sorest spot—at the base of her neck, just above her collarbone. Her fingertips met something rough. When she drew them back, they were dusted with rust-colored flakes. Blood. What wound had reopened? Her face seemed the most likely candidate. Or the scrapes on both her hands, crusted with scabs and the grit she had not been able to pick out.

She stood slowly and stretched out her sore muscles.

When she turned her head, the ends of her hair brushed her shoulders. She clenched her teeth and forced herself to take a deep, calming breath. This really was the least of her problems. *It's only hair.* Doubtless, it had been this long for a little while, but pain and illness always made her like this—sensitive to even the slightest touch, the smallest sound. Automatically, she reached up and began to braid, pulling her curls back from her face. The action was a familiar one, repetitive and soothing, and it left her mind free to wander. Before she realized it, she was back at the table with Leandros, and his wide blue eyes were fixed on her as she tore meat from the bone and tried to choke it down.

Eirene dropped the braid she was holding. "All right," she said aloud, her voice a comfort in the empty room. "Let's try something else."

She found her knife—abandoned on the floor by the bed—and wiped the blade clean without looking at it, lest the shine of grease on it yank her again back to the memories of the night before and the long wooden table and the wine and the—

No. Eirene exhaled sharply. She would not think about it. Now, where was her bowl?

Once she'd retrieved it—again, from the floor, because apparently that was where she stored things now—she set the wide copper bowl on the table by the window, where the light was best, and peered at her warped reflection in the flat base. Phoebe usually cut her hair—with shears rather than a knife—but Phoebe and her shears were not here and if Eirene had to stand it like this for one moment longer she would weep. Even now, with the hum of pain in her body, tears of frustration and exhaustion clustered at the corners of her eyes.

Leaning over the bowl, she pulled half her hair into a bunch, one hand fisted around the tangle of black curls. There was something matting the ends together—more blood from her face? Blood was better than the other possibilities, Eirene decided, doing her best to shove down the memory of slumping onto her plate, of her face pressing into the bones she'd stripped clean. With her free hand she picked up the knife, trapping the hair between her thumb and the gleaming blade. Breathe in. Breathe out.

An easy movement, a twitch of fingers. A cascade of dark hair fell into the bowl, obscuring Eirene's foggy reflection. She dropped the knife and it clattered dully against the copper. "See?" she said out loud. "Easy."

Her hand trembled as she bunched the rest of her hair and picked up the knife again, bracing the blade against her thumb as she had before. Breathe in—

There came a sharp knock on the door and Eirene's whole body flinched. Was it Leandros, come with news of her third—her penultimate—task? But Leandros viewed a knock as a warning of his entrance, not a request. If it were him, he'd be inside by now. Was it Lamia? This made her brighten a little. She opened her mouth to call out a greeting.

The knock came again, harder and sharper. This time, it was accompanied with a voice. "Eirene. Are you in there?"

Eirene deflated. Peiros. She straightened again, flinging her shoulders back and thrusting her chest forward. She would not allow Peiros to see how badly the night before had shaken her.

"Yes, I'm here," she called back.

Peiros's only reply was to push the door open. Eirene swore under her breath, then steadied her grip on the knife as well as she could before hacking off the final chunk of hair. Doubtless, she'd cut both sides to different lengths and looked ridiculous, but at least she wouldn't have to stand the incessant brush of hair over her shoulders any longer.

"What are you doing?" Peiros's flat question lacked any genuine curiosity.

"Cutting my hair," said Eirene. She did not turn to look at him as she ran her hands through her curls, pulling away any loose strands and dropping them into the bowl. He must think her unaffected, unafraid. This house had no place for weakness. She laid the knife down.

Behind her, Peiros was silent. Then: "I have come to set you your third task."

Now Eirene did turn, spinning on the spot to frown at him. He stood just inside the door, in his usual grayish raiment. In one hand, he held a sort of package—a long, narrow *something* wrapped in coarse sackcloth. Eirene eyed it suspiciously. "Where is Leandros?"

Peiros set his shoulders. "I am not at liberty to disclose my master's business or his whereabouts. I am here only to deliver his instructions to you."

"When will he be back?"

"I am only here to deliver my master's instructions to you," Peiros repeated firmly. "And those instructions do *not* include making you privy to his private business."

Eirene folded her arms over her chest. "I don't believe you. My tasks come from *Leandros* and Leandros alone. I won't do whatever it is you tell me, not until I've spoken to him."

Peiros sighed. "As you wish. He will return tomorrow evening expecting his prize, but I suppose he will not be displeased to hear of your refusal. Your sister, I hear, is very beautiful."

Eirene made an incredulous noise. "My sister is none of your—" She steadied herself. Failure was not an option because losing Phoebe was not an option. "What prize?" she said at last.

Peiros fixed his eyes on some spot on the wall behind her and began to recite. "*A large silver ram terrorizes the near hills. He has silver horns and a silver coat. He stands at the height of a full-grown man, and his horns are the deadliest weapons. His coat resists the bite of any blade or arrow tip.*" This speech delivered, Peiros seemed to relax, returning his gaze to hers. "Your task is to collect wool from this ram—"

Despite herself, Eirene felt her mouth curl up at the side. A ram. It was almost exactly as she'd predicted, Psyche's tasks set as her own. And Lamia had told her exactly how to beat this one. She'd just need to follow the ram as Psyche had and collect the wool he had left behind, caught on twigs and shrubs. And she had more than a day for her task? It would be laughably easy.

"—and a horn," finished Peiros.

Eirene stilled. "A horn," she repeated. A *horn*. Such a thing could not be procured by sneaking and foraging alone. It would require proximity and force. And there was no chance that the ram would just *let* her saw off one of his horns. Would she have to kill him? Her mouth had gone dry. A stray curl came free from where she'd tucked it behind her ear and fell over her eye.

"You may need this," said Peiros. He offered her the mysterious package.

On closer inspection, it seemed about the right size and shape to be some kind of knife or shortsword. Eirene took it from him gingerly and teased the sackcloth open with her fingertips. Beneath was the glint of bronze.

Eirene's fingers found the handle and she allowed the wrappings to fall away from the blade. She frowned. Where she had expected to see smooth, sharp edges, the blade was instead rough and jagged, marred with irregular serrations. She looked up at Peiros, bewildered. "What is it?"

He returned her look with one of deepest derision. "It's a sword."

"Yes, I *see* that. But what—" She touched a finger to the edge of the blade and drew back with a hiss. Strange as it was, it was still sharp; blood beaded in its wake. "What is it *for*?"

Peiros shrugged. "Those are all the instructions the master gave me."

"How very useful."

He shrugged again. "If you've not got any more questions, I'll leave you to your task."

"Wait!" Eirene took a lurching step toward him. "No, I'm sorry. But that can't be all. A knife? Against a beast that size?" She'd seen it herself once, years ago, and had sworn never to return.

But Peiros was already leaving, his final smug words drifting through the door as it closed. "I look forward to informing the master of your failure."

XXVI

A BOLD HEART

Lamia

"Take me with you," said Lamia, once Eirene had explained it all. She stood from where she'd been sitting on the edge of the bed and grasped Eirene's hands. Her illness had passed now, she was sure of it. Her head didn't ache, her skin no longer burned, and her vision was clear. Her leg hurt, but then her leg always hurt. The bowl that had held the tincture lay empty at the bedside.

Eirene raised her eyebrows. "You seem better."

"I could say the same to you." The scrapes on Eirene's face weren't as angrily inflamed as they had been upon her return from the cliffs, and though her bare arm was patchy with bruises, they were already yellowing at their edges. There was a fresh scrape in the hollow of her throat and the sight of it made Lamia's stomach turn.

"Don't make me laugh. If I look even half as bad as I feel . . ." There was an edge to Eirene's voice. She put a hand to her neck, to the new wound there, and her eyes took on a strange distant sheen. When she swallowed it was with a visible effort.

"I think you look nice," said Lamia. She really did. She always did, even if there was a faint greenish tinge to Eirene's skin that Lamia hadn't noticed before and something dark matted in the wispy curl tucked behind her ear. Lamia blinked. "Did you cut your hair?"

"Oh." Eirene's eyes cleared abruptly and she dropped her hand. She lifted her chin a fraction, as if she were preparing for a fight. Clearly, Lamia had struck some kind of nerve. "Yes, I did," said Eirene, with an air of finality. Her gaze raked over Lamia, eventually fixing itself on the sheepskin-covered floor beneath her. "Were you wearing shoes in bed?"

"*On* the bed," corrected Lamia. It was her turn to raise her chin. "For efficiency. See, I am ready to leave at a moment's notice!" Eirene did not need to know the truth—that Lamia rarely took her shoes off, only to sleep. They kept her legs secure and concealed. Her father had told her, as kindly as one could say such a thing, how anyone else would react to seeing her without them. *You know that I think you are beautiful, Lamia*, he had said, *but the townspeople are cruel. They will look upon your . . . disfigurement with disgust. They will not be kind to you, not like I am.*

No, it was better that Eirene did not see. Not when Lamia could hardly bear to look herself.

"With my father gone, it should not be so hard to take me," she said quickly, before Eirene could press her further. Walking so far wouldn't be good for her leg at all. but she had some of Eirene's ointment left, which might stop it from hurting so very badly tomorrow. Either way, she doubted she'd be able to leave her room. But that was tomorrow. Now her knee was wrapped, her boot tied tightly over the bandages. And she wanted to go so badly; perhaps it was her glimpse of the symposium that spurred her, the way that neither Phoebe nor Damon had eyed her with anything other than suspicion. No fear, no hatred or disgust. Perhaps the world beyond her tower was not what she had always believed it to be. "Peiros rarely comes to see me; he will not notice I am gone. And I'm sure I can be a help to you, somehow. I can—" What *could* she do? It was daytime—her light would be no help. She cleared her throat. "Well, whatever you need me to do. Do you have a plan?"

Eirene bit her lip and Lamia's stomach somersaulted. She averted her gaze so quickly that the room blurred and she missed Eirene's first few words.

"—a tincture I made for my sister to help her sleep," Eirene was saying.

Lamia's stare was fixed on the empty bowl that sat beside her bed. Even looking at it filled her mouth with that foul metallic taste, as if she'd just been choking it down.

Eirene was still talking. "I don't know if it'll be strong enough for such a beast, but I don't really have any alternatives."

"Hmm," said Lamia. She ran her tongue over her teeth. If she hadn't known better, she would have sworn it was a memory. A memory that unfurled the more she thought about it—her father stroking her hair as he held the bowl to her lips. It was dark. Nighttime. The only light a feeble shaft of moonlight. The distant call of an owl. Her father's words in her ear: *Just a little more, my sweet girl. Drink and it will all go away. Drink and sleep. Drink and forget.* She had been crying—the sound ragged. She had seen something terrible. No, not just *seen*—

"Lamia?"

Lamia stood abruptly.

"Lamia!" Eirene reeled back before their foreheads could collide. "Were you even listening?"

"Um," said Lamia, racking her brain. Something about a tincture . . . a sedative. "It's a good plan."

Eirene crossed her arms over her chest. "I just explained all the reasons why it wasn't."

Gods, there was something seriously wrong with her today.

First her captivation with the hollow of Eirene's throat and the press of her teeth on her lip, now the merest glimpse of cleavage had her heartbeat lurching into a canter. She would have sworn she could feel the heat radiating from Eirene's skin. She sidestepped awkwardly so that they were no longer face to face and addressed the far wall. "The sedative doesn't need to put him all the way to sleep. It just needs to stop him from trying to kill us."

"Well then," said Eirene, "it cannot hurt to try. I have my herbs and a knife, and you have your relentless optimism."

"We?" Despite herself, Lamia turned back to Eirene, to look her full in the face. Her eyes were shining. "You'll take me with you?"

Eirene smiled, showing teeth. "You already had your shoes on; how could I say no? Now, come on. We only have a little time."

What felt like seconds later, they were on their way. Herbs and medicine stuffed into her satchel, Eirene led them both to the edge of the rose garden, then out into the open space at the front of the house. Lamia went straight for the cover of the trees that lined the path and pressed herself behind one, leaning against the trunk. She breathed in the warm morning air, reveling in the taste of freedom and the fragrant smell of the cypress trees.

Eirene joined her a moment later, announcing her presence with a soft press of fingers on Lamia's arm. "Here," she said. "There's a sort of path. Probably made by animals, but it's good enough for us, I think."

They moved off together, Lamia trailing a little behind as she picked her way carefully through the undergrowth. She didn't mind hanging back; it meant that Eirene would not see the flush burning in her cheeks.

By the time they broke out from the tree cover and onto the sprawling hills leading to the cliffs, she was not just a little behind. As well as she had felt that morning, she was not used to walking far or fast, and the familiar twinges of discomfort were beginning to shoot up from her knee. But Lamia was used to pain and she had known this would happen. She kept her eyes on the ground, placing her steps carefully where the grass looked smoothest. Even so, it was not long before she put her foot down on a deceptively soft spot and stumbled. A squeak of surprise burst from her lips.

Ahead, Eirene stopped dead, spinning on one foot, her eyes searching for the source of the noise. When they found Lamia, they widened. Her face dropped and Lamia's heart went with it, tumbling into her stomach.

Eirene stomped back down the hill. The huge knife in her belt smacked against her thigh with each step. "What are you doing?"

Lamia should have known that this would happen. They were barely at the crest of the first hill and the broad cypress that crowned it—if she looked over her shoulder she'd be able to see the house, the tower—and Eirene had already changed her mind. At least it wouldn't be too long a trek home when Eirene sent her away. "I—" she began, bracing herself for the rejection.

"Letting me march off like that!" Eirene's face had gone very pink. "Why didn't you say anything?"

Lamia blinked. "What?"

"I get lost in my own thoughts sometimes, all right? It's a bad habit, I know! Phoebe tells me all the time and I *try* not to, but I wasn't ignoring you on purpose, and I wasn't trying to lose you." Eirene pressed a hand to her sternum, her eyes fixed resolutely at a point just past Lamia's left ear. "Look, I'm really sorry for walking off. And, um"—her voice softened—"for shouting. But you should have said something!" She sagged. "Though I see why you didn't. Because of the history of shouting. I do feel terrible about that, you know. That first night I was so rude to you. I'm sorry. I just—hang on! I've got an idea. Wait there." Her expression frantic, she thrust her satchel into Lamia's hands and dashed off up the hill again.

Lamia watched her go, bewildered. "I can still come?" She addressed the patch of ground where Eirene had been standing moments before.

What was Eirene doing? She stopped before the cypress that stood atop the hill and examined the tree, her hands on her hips. She disappeared behind the tree and Lamia heard a tearing sound.

Lamia frowned and resumed walking. She might as well make some progress while Eirene was distracted.

Lamia reached the crest of the hill at the same time as Eirene danced out from behind the cypress, her face lit with a disarming combination of excitement and apprehension. In her hand, she held a long slender branch. Each end was ragged where she'd sawn it away, and she'd stripped it of twigs and leaves. She smacked it into the ground by Lamia with a satisfying thud.

"Here," she said. "A walking stick! For support. Phoebe uses one sometimes. I think it helps, and I thought . . . Well"—she shrugged—"maybe it was stupid. I thought maybe it might help."

"A walking stick," echoed Lamia. She'd made one for herself once, years ago, in the months following her fall. It had helped her with the stairs and with standing. Her father had taken it from her and broken it over his knee, scolding her for drawing attention to her injury. The world was not kind to those who flaunted their weakness, he'd said. Besides, he couldn't stand the noise it made on the floor. He'd told her that he'd break the next stick over her back.

Well, her father wasn't here now, and Eirene already knew

about Lamia's injury. Lamia slowly put her hand out for the stick and Eirene relinquished it. Her face was creased with anxiety.

"Will it do?" asked Eirene. She was chewing her lip again, her expression anxious. There was no need for her to look so pretty all the time.

Lamia hefted the stick in her hand. It was a little on the heavy side. She walked a few experimental paces, pushing the stick against the ground each time she had to put her weight on her weak knee. Gods, she had missed having a stick, even if she'd only had her first one for a matter of days. It did not take away all the pain and discomfort. But it helped. It really helped. A smile—half delight, half *relief* that Eirene did not intend to leave her behind, after all— broke across her face. "Yes," she said. "It will do very nicely."

"Good," said Eirene. Her smile was radiant.

She pulled the satchel from Lamia's shoulder and put it back over her own. Her fingers brushed Lamia's bare shoulder again. Lamia shivered and she knew from the dart of Eirene's eyes that she had noticed.

Eirene cleared her throat, suddenly looking anywhere but at Lamia. "Now, let's get going. We've a ram to mutilate."

They walked on in silence. At first, Lamia thought she was imagining the new tension between them—an awareness, like the edge of a blade—but when her fingers accidentally touched Eirene's and Eirene snatched her hand away as if she'd been stung, she knew she was not. She pulled the offending hand close to her chest and kept her gaze fixedly ahead. There was no sound but the distant twitter of birds and the rustle of small animals in the grass, the huffs of their labored breathing as the hill grew steeper, and the regular thud of Lamia's stick. Her leg was still sore, but it was in no danger of giving out. The stick made it easier to balance, too, and she could test the ground ahead with a hard poke whenever the grass looked suspicious.

Still, she could not ignore the flare of the sun as it climbed the sky. It was hot. Uncomfortably so. The path, too, was becoming an issue. Lamia had thought it might become easier as they neared the cliffs. It did not. Instead, as the trail curved toward the sea, it seemed to grow narrower and more muddied. By the time Lamia heard the first whispers of the surf crashing against the shore, it had vanished entirely.

"Just over this hill and we'll be able to see it," panted Eirene.

"The ram?"

"Wouldn't that make things easy? No, just the cliffs." Eirene paused to let Lamia catch up, breathing deeply, her face turned from the sun. She stood with her legs apart and her arms out, braced as if she thought the earth might try to shake her free. Her skin was flushed darkly, her lips parted, her hair pasted to her forehead and cheeks. The bright sunlight caught on a droplet of sweat clinging to the curve of her neck. Lamia stared at it a moment too long, a feeling like hunger curling in the pit of her belly.

"Thirsty?"

Lamia snapped her head down so quickly something in her own neck crunched. "I didn't see anything," she said quickly, staring resolutely at a patch of crushed grass. Eirene must have stepped there.

"What?"

"What?"

"I'm asking if you want water." Eirene's voice came closer. Lamia refused to look up. "I have it. You don't. We don't need to look for it. It's here."

"Oh," said Lamia. She rubbed her foot into the patch of crushed grass—Eirene's footprint and hers, indistinguishable.

"Well?" A water skin was thrust beneath Lamia's nose. At last, she looked up. Eirene stared back at her, her eyes as light as Lamia had ever seen them, the pupils shrunk down to pinpricks in the brightness of the open hills.

Lamia took the water. "Thank you," she muttered. She was sunburnt. Either that, or all the blood in her body had rushed to the surface until her skin flamed. She was certain that her face was bright red.

"We can stop walking," said Eirene. "Do you want to stop? Let's stop."

"Let's just get to the beach," said Lamia hastily. She knew that the moment she stopped, her leg would begin to stiffen. It was best to keep moving.

Eirene shrugged. "If you're certain."

"I'm certain," said Lamia. She tipped the water skin back and took a few inelegant gulps before passing it back to Eirene. "Come on."

They marched onward. They reached the top of the hill, then began to descend toward the cliff's edge. Lamia kept her eyes on the ground, thumping her stick rhythmically against the grass. They couldn't have much longer to—

"Oh, gods, it's there."

Lamia turned to the sound—a hoarse horrified whisper—just in time to see Eirene wildly fling out an arm. It collided with Lamia's stomach and the breath rushed out of her in a pitiful wheeze as her body crumpled. *"Keep quiet,"* demanded Eirene, her eyes fixed on some point in the near distance.

Lamia would have liked to respond with something reproach-ful—*I wasn't actually making any noise until you hit me*—but she was too busy panting for breath.

Eirene finally seemed to notice her lack of response. "Lamia?"

"One . . . moment," managed Lamia. "Let me just . . ." Whatever she had been about to say, she forgot it when she saw what Eirene had been staring at. Growing crookedly by the cliff's edge was a sprawling cypress tree. And, nosing around beneath it—

"Oh, gods," said Eirene. "I can't believe it. That's a *sheep*?"

Lamia took a long look at the lumbering animal. All right, he was a fair bit larger than she'd been expecting—at least twice the height of a normal sheep, his eyes would have been level with her father's if they stood face to face. But he was also . . . *beautiful*. He had a long, elegant body, muscular and lithe, more like a horse's than an ordinary ram's. His wool was spun silver. When he looked up, his gaze finding Lamia and Eirene instantly, his white face was long and graceful, set with wide intelligent eyes and framed by two spiraling silver horns. The horns took her breath away; if it had been somehow possible to straighten one out, it would have been longer than Lamia herself.

He watched them quietly, measuredly, and Lamia felt her first soft prickle of fear. If he felt threatened, he could run them down as easily as a cart horse. She pressed a hand beneath her breasts, to the hard bones at the bottom of her rib cage and the place where his lowered horns would hit her, should he choose to charge. "He's big, isn't he?" she said cautiously.

"Big? He's massive!" Eirene's voice was faint. Lamia turned to look at her and was appalled to see the green tinge to her skin, the naked apprehension in her dark eyes. "What if the draft isn't enough? I was going to just add it to the water he drinks from, but I don't know the dosage, and—"

"What's the use in worrying about that yet?" Lamia was

surprised by how certain she sounded. "We do as we planned and if we are unsuccessful, we think of something new."

Eirene nodded slowly. "I had planned on keeping him alive, but . . ." She narrowed her eyes at the ram. "I don't fancy our chances with a knife. But there are other herbs in my arsenal, and there are poisons among them. I don't want to see him dead, and the use of poison would prevent the use of his meat. . . . But we only need his horn and his coat."

"We try the sleeping draft first," said Lamia quickly. When she'd said "something new," she hadn't expected Eirene to pivot straight to murder. The ram had a gentle face, despite his vast stature. He had done nothing wrong and he didn't deserve to be killed. "I don't want him to die. Not if he doesn't need to."

"We follow him, then," said Eirene, her strength and certainty returning. She squared her shoulders and fixed the ram with a clear, unafraid gaze. "We find where he drinks and we *try*."

"And if not?"

Eirene's fingers twitched toward the jagged knife strapped at her waist. "I also brought aconite."

Aconite. A large enough dose could stop a man's heart in a matter of moments. "You'll need to use a lot," said Lamia. "Make it quick if you can."

"I'll do my best," said Eirene grimly. "But I cannot promise you he will go easily."

They tracked the ram for the rest of the morning, as the sun grew ever higher in the sky. Lamia kept to the shade where she could, but her forehead grew slick with sweat; fat droplets dripped down her neck and soaked into the folds of her chiton. As she yanked at the fabric for the hundredth time, unsticking it from her skin and letting cool air rush into the space, she forced herself not to wonder what her father might think, what he might *do* upon his return if he noticed the stained garment. She would have to think up some flimsy excuse. But she would not worry about that now.

She returned her attention to the ram. He seemed to be following the path of a small stream that cut through the valleys between hills, ambling leisurely between patches of grass, browsing the green shoots. As he chewed each carefully selected tuft, he kept his wide gray eyes fixed on Lamia and Eirene. Each time he lowered his head to the ground again, it was impossible not to notice the power in his great silver horns. This was a creature without fear. He did not watch their movements to know when to flee but when to charge.

"*There*," whispered Eirene at last. Her voice rasped from disuse.

Lamia's heart stuttered as she reluctantly dragged her gaze away from the ram. "There?" she echoed.

"Just beyond that patch of flowers, do you see?" Eirene extended an arm to point. "He's been walking east for some time. I think that's where he's going."

Lamia followed the line of Eirene's elegant fingers.

Just before the horizon, the stream they'd been following forked into two. One branch trickled on over the landscape. The other fed into a small sparkling pool. Rushes grew up around the edges and the surface of the water rippled enticingly. Lamia had not realized how thirsty she was until now.

"Come on," said Eirene urgently. "We can add my drug to the pool—it won't be washed away there. But we need to get there before him." She lengthened her stride and Lamia followed.

They cut a careful arc toward the pool, careful not to get too close to the ram. When they reached it, Eirene knelt gracelessly beside it and tipped half the contents of the jar into the clear water. It hung just below the surface, clinging to itself in a defiant clump. Eirene had to go in with her knife, sweeping it through the water in harsh lines before the medicine and the water finally began to mix.

"That looks disgusting," said Eirene.

She wasn't wrong. Their addition had turned the clear pool a pale, dirty brown. It didn't smell particularly wonderful, either. "Will he drink?" asked Lamia doubtfully.

Eirene shrugged helplessly. "For his sake, I hope so."

"Shouldn't you have used all of it?"

"It's strong, I promise, and I can always add more. But I'd rather be cautious. I don't want to kill him. I just—I can't explain it."

"It would be a crime to destroy such a creature," said Lamia. "He's so beautiful."

Eirene shot her an unreadable look. "Exactly."

They retreated to the nearest cypress tree to sit and watch the ram's progress. He took his time, wandering between patches of flowers. When he finally reached the water, Lamia's heart sank. He pawed at it with one shining hoof, then backed away, shaking his great head. He let out a dissatisfied snort and wandered over to a patch of dandelions on the far side of the pool, where he set about grinding the sweet yellow flowers into a pulp between his teeth.

"Shit," said Eirene glumly. "We should've just brought Daphne to eat him. Now we'll have to follow him to another water source. Then the aconite." She made to stand up.

"Wait." Lamia put a hand on Eirene's shoulder and pushed her down again. "No, wait." It was not the ram's fault that he didn't want to drink cloudy water that looked like it would give him at least three diseases. But Lamia could fix that for him.

She picked up her stick and pushed herself to her feet.

"What's that look on your face?" Eirene's tone was light, teasing, but her eyes were intense and fixed on Lamia.

Lamia squared her shoulders. "Let me try something."

XXVII

AND SORROW TO COMFORT

Eirene

They waited until the ram had wandered a little farther before approaching the pool again. Up close, it was easy to see why he had shunned it. It was even murkier than Eirene remembered, and the surface was littered with the bodies of insects. "This is going well," she said darkly.

"It is. You've got me." Lamia used her stick to lower herself to the ground. She plunged her hands into the water and muddled them through the murk, head cocked. "Talk to me about something."

Eirene blinked. "What?"

"Talk to me," repeated Lamia, "about something. Anything. And give me your knife."

"My knife?" Eirene stiffened, her hand flying to the handle. Of course Lamia wanted to use her strange light magic. The beautiful magic that was as awful as it was fascinating—that required pain and tears and a blade to draw forth. "Lamia—"

"Give it to me," said Lamia. She was sunburnt, her skin beginning to freckle. She'd never had so much color to her.

"No," said Eirene. "No. How can *light* help?"

Lamia withdrew her hands from the water and wiped them dry on her chiton. "I can do more than call light." She kept her gaze down but her voice was firm. "And you don't get to tell me what I can and can't do. If you're allowed to go falling off cliffs and scraping half your body up—"

"I didn't fall off the cliff." Eirene wasn't sure why she was arguing. The conversation would end the same way. They both knew that she would yield the knife and watch as Lamia drove it into her flesh because Eirene had to complete this task. She had to. She scowled. "I fell down. A bit. Clearly, falling *off* would be worse. And what do you mean, you can do more than call light? You didn't tell me that." Why did it send a prickle of hurt through her, to know that Lamia had kept secrets?

"Give me the knife and I'll show you," said Lamia. "You have no other choice. The ram must drink."

Her tone wasn't accusing, but her words still made Eirene's stomach lurch. She swallowed. "Fine." She knelt at Lamia's side and gave her the knife.

"Thank you," said Lamia. "Now look away."

Eirene did as she was told.

There was a long pause, then Lamia said peevishly, "You were going to talk to me?"

Eirene sighed. Then, because she'd wondered it before and because Eirene always wanted to know everything about the people she cared for and, well, if Lamia wanted to talk then they could *really* talk, she asked, "What happened to your mother?"

"My mother?" Lamia's voice was a startled squeak.

"Is she dead?"

"Thank you for asking that so sensitively," said Lamia. "I can tell you care a lot about my feelings."

"I *do* care about your feelings," protested Eirene. "How would you have preferred me to ask? Tell me about your mother—she's clearly absent because your father is going to marry me?"

"That wasn't kind either," said Lamia. "Try again."

"Fine," grumbled Eirene. Then, despite herself, she smiled. The frightened girl she'd first shouted at in the dark tower room would never have spoken to her like this. "Lamia, do you remember your mother?"

"That's better," said Lamia. She paused and Eirene heard her draw in a sharp breath. Her stomach twisted. Had the knife pierced Lamia's skin already? "I don't know."

Eirene frowned. "What do you mean?"

"Well, I'm not sure. I never thought I did. But lately I don't know . . . I sometimes have these dreams. Of being small and warm and of a woman standing over me, protecting me. I think—" She broke off and Eirene tensed, still staring fixedly into the distance. "I think she may not have been human," she said, as if she were making a confession.

"Why do you say that?"

"Well, she had these eyes—" This time, when Lamia stopped talking, it was to let out a hiss of pain.

Eirene shouldn't have looked. She knew what Lamia would be doing, but before she could stop them her hands were shooting out to snatch her knife back.

"Leave it!" protested Lamia. She had put the tip of the blade to her thigh and was pushing down on it, twisting slowly, her face contorted. She batted Eirene away with her free hand. "I need to cry! Leave it!" Her chiton concealed the wound itself, but the material was already stained with a jagged spread of red.

But Eirene had had enough. "If you need to cry, just—just sniff dust or something. Or get it in your eye." She made another attempt for the knife and Lamia moved her body to shield it. "Stop it!" She caught Lamia's bony shoulder and pulled it hard. Lamia was scrawnier than she was slender; her body was devoid of muscle, and she stood no chance against Eirene's stocky frame. The scuffle lasted seconds before Lamia surrendered the blade. Eirene stuffed it back into her belt and glowered. "I changed my mind. I'm not letting you mutilate yourself to help me. I'm not Leandros."

Lamia stiffened at the mention of her father. "It *works*," she snapped. "As dust in my eyes or my lungs never would, which I would have told you if you'd asked! It's not just about the tears; it's about *emotion*. Pain. Fear. Anger. And I was nearly there. If you'd just kept talking, I—"

"If I'd kept talking while you *stabbed yourself*?" Eirene's voice was pitched high with incredulity.

"I saw you after the cliffs," said Lamia icily. "Your face. The bruises on your arms. Sometimes the price is pain and it can't be avoided. My magic needs my tears and this is the easiest way to get them. It'll heal."

"I don't care if it heals. I won't let you." Eirene knew she was letting her fear and anger overwhelm her. But she couldn't stop.

"Can I decide anything myself? Or will everyone else always be making my decisions for me? First my father, now you." Lamia's eyes shone.

"Don't compare me to your father," snapped Eirene. Her fury spiked. "Your father is a vile monster and he has *ruined* my home. Don't you say I'm like him. Don't you dare—"

"This is all I can do and I want to help you!" exploded Lamia. "*Let me help.*"

"Not if it hurts you!" shouted Eirene. She would not be like Leandros, happy to cause pain so long as it benefited her. She would *not*.

"And what if hurting is all I'm good for?" Tears dribbled down

Lamia's face and her expression shuttered at the same moment Eirene felt something inside her break. It might have been her heart. "There," said Lamia. She touched her fingers to her cheeks and they came away wet. "See, you just had to shout at me for these ones. No knife involved. Is that good enough?"

Eirene stared at her wordlessly. If she spoke, it would be her own tears that fell next.

"Let me *help*." Lamia's voice softened. "Look, you *have* to get this horn. For Phoebe, remember? So let me help you."

Eirene's shoulders slumped forward. She wanted to send Lamia away, to refuse to use this awful, tainted magic. But what was the point in turning back now when the damage was done? She could not bring herself to make eye contact. "Fine. Help me, Lamia. Please."

"I learned to do this when I was ten, maybe eleven," explained Lamia from the ground. She wiped the tears from her cheeks and dripped them into the pool.

Eirene stood a short distance away, her fists clenched. "Oh," she said tightly, forcing the sound past the knot of guilt in her throat.

"I had a cat." Lamia trailed her hands through the water, and it seemed to grow clearer and more inviting with every sweep of her fingers. "She was called Nemea."

"All right," said Eirene.

"She was orange," said Lamia. "I found her abandoned in the rose garden, all tangled up in the thorns, and begged my father to keep her. She was half dead and she hated me, but I loved her anyway. After I'd had her for a few months—well." Her voice had a sudden edge to it. "I—I upset my father. Something silly; I'm not even sure what it was now. But he . . ." She seemed to be deliberately avoiding looking up.

"You don't have to tell me," said Eirene. She couldn't look at Lamia's face. "You had an orange cat. That's enough."

"He locked us in my room," said Lamia. "Nemea and me. And at first it was fine. She bit me and scratched me and she used to sit on my chest in the night and drool on my face. But after a few days . . . we were both hungry. And thirsty. And I tried shouting for my father. You can think what you will about him, but he *loves* me, I swear. All he does is to protect me. If he'd known it was that bad, he'd have come. But he mustn't have heard me."

Eirene's throat was shrinking in on itself. She swallowed hard, choked with fury. "He locked you in without food?" The words were a quiet hiss—the most restrained she could make them.

"He didn't know," said Lamia. The brittle edge to her voice hardened. "Don't think you can give your judgment when you weren't there."

Eirene just shook her head. Despite everything he'd done, it was *this* that made her hatred of Leandros reach its new peak. Even his daughter was not exempt from his cruelty and corruption.

"I had a bucket of water I'd washed in," continued Lamia. "It had been sitting there the whole time we were locked in, growing more and more enticing to me as the days wore on. I wetted my lips with it and then my tongue. I can still remember how foul it tasted. Stagnant and awful. I drank a little anyway and managed to keep it down. But Nemea—she wouldn't drink it. I was so *desperate*. I just wanted her to drink. I knew what I could do with light. How I could make things shine and become lovely. So I drove a pin through my thumb—"

"You did *what*?" Lamia had been doing this since she was *ten*?

Eirene put her hand to the knife at her belt, just to make sure it was still there, so Lamia could not take it up again. The water wasn't just clear now, it was sparkling and enticing, and Eirene had to fight the urge to jump in and gulp it down in desperate mouthfuls. She shook her head and looked away.

"That's hardly the worst thing. I needed to cry," said Lamia matter-of-factly. "And at the time a little pain like that was enough."

At the time. Eirene's heart gave a violent twist.

If Lamia noticed her silent horror, she did not comment on it. "I dropped a tear into the water and it was suddenly clean and clear. Nemea drank greedily, insatiably, and I was so relieved. But the water beneath the illusion was as foul as it had always been. I did not—I did not know how bad it was. By the next evening, she was feverish. Then she was dead."

"Gods," said Eirene quietly. What else was there to say? Something else turned over in the recesses of her mind, the memory of a plum, burned and shriveled, sluglike. Lamia's magic was not so different from Desire, then. And perhaps Eirene had been wrong. Perhaps there was no secret to Desire beyond what Leandros always claimed—the godly power that ran through his veins and his daughter's. Her skin prickled. If that was the case, how could she ever beat him? She'd have to kill him. There was no other way.

She would make it deliberately slow.

"And that's the story," said Lamia. Her voice was firm, but a fresh trickle of tears was cutting its way down her face. "I screamed myself hoarse. My father unlocked the door. I did not ask for another cat." She shook her hands of the shimmering water and picked up her stick. "There, that's done. Let's see if he drinks now."

XXVIII

BEAST OF ALL BEASTS

Lamia

The ram drank. Lamia had known he would. He drank just as Nemea had once—deeply, greedily, to his own ruination.

She and Eirene sat back beneath the shade of the cypress to wait for the medicine to topple him. Lamia gazed out over the hills, the distant woods, the smudge on the horizon that might have been her tower.

"I think," she said softly, "that this might be the farthest from the house I've ever been."

On the hills beneath them, the great ram lumbered about, the pool all but drained. Eirene had watched him closely for the first few minutes. She was clearly convinced that their plan had not worked, and she spent her time listing exactly *why* they'd failed— she had miscalculated, surely, and the drug was too diluted in the water to be effective. Or the ram was too big. Or he'd simply not been thirsty enough, even with Lamia's magic to tempt him.

Lamia was irate at this insinuation. The truth of her tears had cracked open between them and it seemed to make her feel everything so much more fiercely. She knew her own power. Her magic had *helped*; she was *useful*, and she would not allow Eirene to make her feel any less so. "Are you so eager to fail?" she demanded, putting both hands on her hips and twisting her face into the most vicious scowl she could muster. "You saw how he drank!"

Eirene put her hands up in mock defense. "All right, I'm sorry." She was smiling, but there was still a tension to her—a certain caution in the way she watched Lamia.

"He's slowing, I'm sure of it." Lamia held Eirene's doubtful gaze. The sun was blazing above them, but Eirene's eyes were still as dark as the night, the brown so close to black that it swallowed the iris. This was a dark Lamia could wander through forever if Eirene would let her.

"Yes, perhaps you're right," said Eirene softly. When had she last blinked? She was beautiful, with her sun-flushed skin, full lips, and stocky, determined frame. It seemed a fine joke that of the two of them it was Lamia who held the blood of Aphrodite in her veins.

She looked away, scanning the hills for the ram.

He was gone.

Lamia gasped, flinging out an arm. "Eirene!" Her hand brushed Eirene's arm and Lamia snatched it away quickly, as if Eirene's skin had burned her.

Eirene shot to her feet. "What is it?" she yelped. "What happened?"

"The ram," said Lamia. She stood too, casting about desperately for a glint of silver. "He's gone." She'd hardly taken her eyes off him and he had vanished.

She took a shaky step toward the place where she'd last seen him, and then another.

Oh. The relief was sudden and overwhelming, like plunging into a cold bath. There he was. From between the dry branches of a shrub, she could see the gleam of his fleece. His head was on the ground, braced by the cage of his great horns. One silver leg was stretched out to the side. As Lamia watched, the leg twitched and the fleece surged. He was trying to stand, but the effects of the drug were too great.

"Eirene," she whispered, not daring to raise her voice. She did not want to do anything that would risk disturbing the ram. "Eirene, he's down."

"I see him," said Eirene. "He's down. We brought him down." Her eyes were shining and she reached for Lamia's hand, entwining their fingers and squeezing. "We did it."

Lamia felt the corners of her mouth twitch up. "We did it," she echoed.

She took a step closer and the ram made a furious rumbling sound. He turned his great head toward them, scraping his horns through the dirt.

"Careful," warned Eirene. "He might still—"

The ram's great silver fleece surged again. He staggered to his feet.

"Oh, fuck," said Eirene. She took a step back, dragging Lamia with her. The ram took a wobbling step forward, shaking his enormous head.

"Lamia," said Eirene in a low voice. "Don't move."

"You just made me move," hissed Lamia.

"You know what I mean. Maybe he won't see us."

Lamia glanced back at the ram and stiffened. His enormous gray eyes were still clouded and fixed on Lamia and Eirene. He blinked once and then he lowered his head.

"Oh no," said Lamia.

The ram charged.

"*Go*," said Eirene. She set off at a run, dragging Lamia with her. "To the tree!"

"Let me go!" Lamia's stumbling footfalls were heavy and sent jolts of pain up her leg.

"I'm not leaving you!"

"I can't move properly with you dragging me, idiot. Let go!" Lamia shook Eirene off and ran as she hadn't done in years, her heart hammering, her leg screaming, her stick pounding the ground with every frantic step. She was going to suffer for this later, but for now she just had to get *away*. The ram was gaining on them; she could hear his heavy hoofbeats growing closer and closer.

They reached the base of the tree again. Eirene whirled. Her cheeks were dark, her eyes wide and terrified. "Can you climb?"

"I—"

"I'm taking that as a yes." Eirene made a cradle of her hands. "We won't be able to outrun him, so we have to climb. I'll lift you." Lamia glanced over her shoulder and a shock of terror went through her. Though each step he took was all but a stumble, the ram moved quickly. The drug had bought them some time, but it wouldn't be long before the ram reached them.

There wasn't time to protest. Lamia dropped her stick and put her right foot into Eirene's hands and Eirene thrust her upward. Lamia grabbed the closest branch and climbed onto it. The fronds of the cypress scratched at her cheeks. She hauled herself onto the next branch and then the next, her heart racing.

"Keep going!" yelled Eirene. "Higher!"

Lamia looked down and saw Eirene scrambling up the trunk, her hands digging into the bark. But she was too short, and without someone to help her up, she hadn't even reached the first branch. The ram would be on her at any moment and her legs were still dangling well within his reach. The first strike of his horns would crush her.

Lamia had to act. "You won't make it!" she screamed. "Throw me your knife!"

"*What?*"

"*Your knife.*" She didn't have time to explain. She just had to hope that Eirene would finally listen to her, finally trust her.

Eirene let go of the tree trunk and slid to the ground.

Lamia let out a shriek of terror. "Eirene!"

"I'm *doing it*!" Eirene yanked the knife from her belt and hurled it skyward. It arced toward Lamia and she reached out and caught it by the blade. She screamed as it cut through her palms. Blood poured over her wrists. The first tears cascaded down her cheeks.

Eirene was screaming, too, and scrambling up the trunk again. Her hands found a branch and she curled her legs up beneath her, her skin shining with sweat. The ram was pounding toward her, his head down, the silver of his horns glittering in a sudden brilliant light. He was going to crush her, he was going to kill her, he was going to—

"Eirene, *close your eyes*."

She didn't have time to see if Eirene had obeyed. Lamia thrust out her bleeding hands and the light surged free.

It lasted only a second, maybe two.

But it was enough. No impact came, the tree did not shake and topple as Lamia had feared it might. Eirene did not scream. When the light faded, she looked down, hardly daring to breathe. Eirene was still hanging from a branch, curled up as tightly as she could. She was whimpering.

"Eirene!" shouted Lamia, panic making her voice high and brittle. "Eirene, did he hurt you?"

"No," came the weak reply.

The relief had Lamia breathless. Eirene was unhurt. The ram hadn't hit her. She looked down at him. He had stumbled back, shaking his massive head. His pupils were tiny—the light must have blinded him momentarily—and he was panting, his hooves slipping on the grass. There were faint char marks on his silver coat.

"No match for our Lamia, are you?" Eirene said to him.

Our Lamia. Lamia's heart swelled.

The ram's eyes roamed wildly, trying to seek them out. Then at last, as Eirene's drug finally took its full effect, they rolled back into his head and he collapsed.

XXIX
SWEET AND FRAGRANT FLOWERS

Eirene

Eirene drew the blade toward her for what felt like the hundredth time, wincing at the metallic scraping that seemed to become more grating as she sawed deeper into the curling silver horn. She had the ram's huge head cradled in her lap and he watched her through half-lidded glazed eyes. His tongue lolled from the side of his mouth. Every so often he huffed out a hot, slightly damp gust of breath into her face. It smelled faintly of grass, except that grass tended to smell quite pleasant and this did not.

Gods, her arm was hurting. And she was barely halfway through.

At least there was no blood. She'd been worried there would be. She'd seen a ram's horn severed before; a young ram at the market had stumbled and fallen, breaking away a great curl of his horn. It had bled like an opened tap. But this ram was no ordinary beast; his horns were solid metal, as if he were a living, breathing statue.

She pushed the blade away again, then paused to sweep her forearm across her brow. It came away slick with sweat. A droplet she'd missed trickled down her cheek and clung to her chin like a tear.

Eirene couldn't help it, her gaze darted to where Lamia, her eyes squeezed shut against the sun, was curled against the ram's trembling body, her head lying on his back and her hair streaming out over his silver sides. Eirene watched as Lamia combed her fingers gently through the gnarls in his wool, murmuring platitudes against his body. She seemed to have forgotten he'd just tried to trample them.

In the bright afternoon light, Lamia's hair did not have its usual flat dark hue. Instead, pausing in the punishing work of sawing through the ram's horns, jagged movement after jagged movement, Eirene could have sworn she could pick out threads of color, of—

"Is your hair *red*?" she blurted out.

Lamia opened one eye. "What?"

"Your hair has red in it," said Eirene, already regretting that she'd spoken. She drew the blade back yet again. "I thought it was brown. But it's red."

"Oh." Lamia caught a few strands between her fingers. "It used to be. It goes red in the sun."

"It's pretty," said Eirene.

"Oh," said Lamia.

That wasn't quite the response she'd hoped for. Eirene cleared her throat. "How are your hands?" It was only when Lamia had dropped to the ground from the tree, her face very pale, that Eirene had seen the state of her palms. She'd insisted on wrapping them with the torn edge of her chiton, but blood was still seeping through the bindings.

Lamia shrugged. "Fine."

Eirene still couldn't fathom how something as lovely as Lamia's light could come from something so terrible. "They don't look fine."

"They'll heal," said Lamia succinctly. She shot Eirene a long look, unsure, then suddenly decisive. Her voice dropped. "They always do."

"Always? What do you mean, 'always'? How often are you . . . ?" Eirene trailed off, unable to say the words out loud.

"Whenever my father needs my tears, I suppose," said Lamia mildly, though there was an edge to her words.

"*Needs your tears?* What could he possibly—"

Eirene froze. Oh. Of course. *Of course.* The realization was a blow to the belly. How had she never seen it? Or maybe some part of her had, but had been unable to face it; after all, she had vowed to defeat Leandros by destroying the source of his power. "Desire," she said softly. "That is what makes it."

Lamia said nothing. Her chin was up, her gaze clear. She had wanted Eirene to understand.

Eirene stared at her and for the first time she didn't just look. She *saw.* She remembered. Lamia's hollow, wan face. Her slender body. Her bandaged hands that first night, blood spots on the fingertips where the nails were stubby and shorter by far than the rest. The scars inside her wrist that Eirene had written off as rose-thorn scratches but were so obviously something else. The way she had called the light, how she had turned the murky water of the pool clear and inviting. "It's your magic. And he takes it from you by making you cry. By *hurting* you."

There was a long awful silence. Then: "It always heals," whispered Lamia.

"Is that how Leandros justifies torturing his own daughter? It's fine because it heals?"

"It's nothing to do with you!"

"Isn't it?"

"No, it's not!" snarled Lamia. "For once, Eirene, will you listen to me?"

"Lamia—"

"Don't."

Lamia's chest heaved. Eirene stared at her in horrified silence. Her mind raced. If Lamia's tears made Desire, then what had Alexandra's death been for? Her body, drained of blood. Why? *Why?* She was missing something.

If it had been anyone else, Eirene would not have listened. She would not have stopped. But this was Lamia. Almost mechanically, Eirene resumed sawing. The motion seemed to have become ingrained in her muscles themselves, so when there was suddenly not as much as horn to cut through, and Eirene still moved with the same, considerable amount of force, it was only a very rapid pull back that stopped her from driving the knife's tip into the ram's nose. She was almost there.

She forced herself to look away from Lamia as she sawed through the last piece of horn. The huge grooved curl of silver fell to the ground and the ram let out a soft grunt. "Thank the gods," muttered Eirene, quickly working to extract her legs from beneath the ram's massive head. Her newly released legs prickled as the blood surged back into them. Eirene clambered to her feet.

"Let's go," she said shortly. "Where's my satchel? I hope this will fit."

"We're leaving?" Lamia looked past her shoulder at the ram's face. "What about the other horn?"

Eirene let out a short, harsh laugh. "The other one? Absolutely not. Leandros only said one horn, and if he wanted two, he should have—"

"I wasn't asking what my father said," interrupted Lamia. She reached out and petted the gigantic ram's head as she spoke. "You should take off the other horn."

"Lamia, I—" Eirene was so stunned that she struggled to find the words to articulate her disbelief. "That just took me *forever*."

"Phoebe said her weaving would take her weeks. This horn would sell for a lot, Eirene. Then you'll have the money you need. To run."

"Lamia—"

"You should do it, you know," said Lamia. "Run, I mean. My father is—" She shook her head. "I don't know what he is anymore. But he won't protect you, I know that. You could have fallen from those cliffs, and he sent you out knowing that. You'll be safer away from him."

"What about you? What about Desire? I can't leave now."

"Desire is not what I always thought it was," said Lamia quietly. "Those women at the symposium, using it to make themselves"— she flushed—"beautiful."

"Desire is a tool," said Eirene quietly. "In the wrong hands, it's a weapon. I have seen it destroy lives. I can't allow your father to keep making it."

"Perhaps I can convince him," said Lamia, her voice very small. "He is not an evil man, Eirene. And he loves me."

Eirene did not have the heart to contradict her. "Still, I will not leave you alone."

"Selling the horn will protect Phoebe, then, whether you stay or go. If the final task . . ."

If I fail it. "You're right," said Eirene. "You're right. It's a good idea. I'll cut the horn."

Lamia nodded. She looked down at the drugged ram, then

buried her face in his back, flinging her arms around his body. "I'm sorry," she whispered.

"Are you talking to the *sheep*?"

Lamia lifted her head, her expression hard. "I'm talking to him because he's probably scared because *someone* just tricked him into drinking poison and now he can't move and you've gone and cut a piece of his head off. And I just told you to cut off another bit!" Her face crumpled, her eyes shining.

"Oh no," said Eirene. "Don't cry, please."

"I can't help it. I'm an easy crier." Lamia wiped her eyes with her hands and examined her shimmering palms. Then, with a glance at Eirene that was so brief it could have been imagined, she began to comb her fingers through her hair. Beneath her touch, the strands shifted. The pale brown darkened, deepened, *reddened*, until Lamia's face was framed with auburn. It suited her. With her cheeks pink with sun and her hair like tongues of fire and her eyes still wet and cautious but undeniably brighter, she could not have been more lovely. It was exactly what Desire would have done.

Eirene looked away. "Why did you do that?"

"It's red," said Lamia. "You said—you said that was pretty."

There was a desperate plea in her voice. "I meant it," said Eirene gently. "But you didn't have to change it. I liked you—" She cleared her throat. "I like it just as it is."

"This *is* how it is," said Lamia quietly. A dark flush had risen in her cheeks. "How it should be. I mean, this is how I remember it being when I was younger. Before I—before I fell and hurt my leg and my father became afraid of what could happen if I were permitted to roam the hills like a wild thing." She laughed. Her eyes were soft, fixed on somewhere in the middle distance. Eirene suspected that she was not seeing the hills around them at all but somewhere else, lost in time and the naivety of childhood. "I forgot how beautiful it was out here."

Eirene stared at her wordlessly, appalled. *It goes red in the sun.* Lamia's earlier words made sudden sickening sense. When Eirene could finally shape the words, fury made them as sharp as arrow tips. "You mean your hair wasn't red anymore because Leandros doesn't *let you outside*?"

Lamia eyes refocused instantly. Her shoulders went up. "Don't," she said quietly.

"You aren't *defending* him?"

"No, I'm not. But I don't want to discuss this again. Not now, Eirene. I don't know what to say. I don't know what I think. There are so many things that don't seem the same as they did, so many questions I think I know the answer to. But—" She chewed her lip, blinking rapidly. "Well, he's my *father*."

Eirene nodded. "All right."

"Thank you." Lamia pushed her hair behind her ears and smiled shakily. "Don't you have a horn to be cutting?" Before Eirene could reply, Lamia turned away. She began to shove at the ram's great side, rolling him onto his back.

There was so much more Eirene wanted to say: that Leandros was a tyrant and a monster and that Eirene would kill him if Lamia would only ask; that she might kill him anyway; that she would take Lamia away from her wretched tower and build her a new house with her bare hands if she had to. A new house without a single staircase. A house with large windows and a rose garden and a hearth that they could tend together. But a single look at Lamia's face told her that Lamia would not be interested in hearing Eirene's grand plan at this precise point in time. She sighed and helped Lamia roll the ram over.

The second horn was easier. Eirene had the knack now, and she drew the blade back and forth with long well-practiced strokes. Lamia was as she'd been before, curled against the ram's side with her narrow arms flung over his shining fleece. She had her head nestled in the crook of one pale elbow. Eirene watched her closely, her eyes tracing the lines of Lamia's features and the soft waves of her hair. Alongside her inexplicable urge to follow the movement of her eyes over Lamia with her fingers, was a growing sense of discomfort. The longer she looked at the reddish strands, the more uneasy she felt until she could no longer stand it.

"Lamia . . . ," she said hesitantly.

Lamia opened one eye. "Yes?"

"How does it work, exactly? The tears. The light and the . . . what you just did to the water. And your hair. Desire wears off. Does this? Will it change back?"

Lamia turned so that she could look Eirene full in the face. She frowned and bit her lip. "It's hard to explain," she said eventually. "It's not a change, exactly. I don't think. I can sort of *feel* it, how it was meant to be. Underneath. I don't think I change the *essence* of an object, just how it appears. It's an illusion, I suppose, though it's not just how it looks. For the pool I had to make it smell better, too. And my roses." She flushed. "I like it when they smell nice. I don't know much about the Desires, though. My father is the alchemist."

"And you can make anything look different?" Eirene pushed her. "Smell different or . . . taste different?"

Lamia shook her head and Eirene's chest seemed to loosen. But the rush of relief was pushed down by Lamia's next words. "Not different. Only better." She laughed nervously. "More beautiful, I suppose. It is Aphrodite's blood in my veins, after all."

"Would it—" Eirene swallowed. She remembered the pomegranate bursting in her hands. Pomegranates were always so hard to get into, their skin tough and thick. But what if the pomegranate was stored from the previous summer, left to soften, rot, and decay, so that beneath its shining surface it was . . .

"The magic you used, the illusion. Desire. Would it work on food?"

Lamia shrugged. "I don't see why not."

"It could make something rotten look fresh? And smell delicious?"

Lamia nodded slowly. "I suppose so. Why?"

The grand banquet, when Leandros had touched nothing. Speaking it aloud would make it too real. Eirene looked away, back to her sawing. She was almost through and she picked up her pace. "No reason," she said, cutting through the last section of silver. The horn thudded to the ground. "There," said Eirene wearily. "Two horns."

Lamia reached for the shining horn, lifting it from the ground with a visible effort and setting it beside its twin. "It will keep Phoebe safe," she said. Her lashes were copper where they had caught the sun.

"It will," said Eirene, more abruptly than she had meant to. She had unsettled herself badly. She should never have asked about the food. All she could think of was what horrors Leandros had hidden beneath the illusion of roasted fowl and spiced chickpeas and in the cup of sweet wine. She pushed the ram's head from her lap and stood. "Now can we go back?"

As much as she could have stayed there forever—an eternity of hills and soft sun and Lamia—she could not forget what still needed to be done, much as she could not forget the glorious smell of the food at the feast Leandros had laid out for her, or how it had seemed to become rotten in her mouth as he forced her to eat and eat and eat.

No, she could not remain here.

She had to return to the house. From the moment she had understood what made Desire, she had known what she would have to do. She could not destroy the source of Leandros's power, and she knew that he would hunt it—would hunt *Lamia*—across the earth if she was ever stolen from him. And Eirene could never forgive him for what he'd done. To her, to his daughter, to poor little Nemea.

Leandros had to die.

XXX

NO FRUIT OF HONOR

Eirene

It was not especially easy to carry both horns. They were heavy and huge and most inconveniently shaped. Eventually, Eirene's solution was to jam one into her satchel as best she could, its sharp spiraling tip poking out from beneath the flap, sling the satchel over her back, and cradle the other horn in her arms.

They walked purposefully, stopping to rest only once they reached the trees lining the path that led to the house. While Lamia sat against the broad trunk of a pine and stretched out her legs, Eirene found a tree that had lost the center of its trunk to rot, leaving a hollow recess inside the rings of bark. She carefully tucked one horn inside. Leandros would be delivered precisely what he had asked for and this second horn would be her key to escaping him.

She paused by the tree, staring into its decayed core. Then, before she could doubt herself, she reached into the bottom of her satchel and pulled out the tiny package of Desire from Leandros's workshop. She unknotted the twist. Then she reached into the tree and rubbed it over a patch of rot, smearing the tiny amount of Desire into the decay. For a heartbeat nothing happened. Eirene relaxed a fraction. And then the surface of the rot shimmered and changed, melting smoothly into untarnished wood.

Eirene snatched her hand back, bile rising in her throat. She'd been right. All that dazzling, beautiful food . . .

"Eirene?"

Eirene stepped away from the tree and turned to face Lamia, forcing a smile. "We'll find a way to get this to Phoebe."

"Maybe she can visit the ram for us," said Lamia hopefully. "To check on him." She had spent the first leg of their return glancing back every few paces to see if the ram had shaken off the drug. Eirene couldn't help but think she'd been the more pleased of the two of them when he'd finally clambered to his feet in the distance, if only because Lamia's distress made her feel so wretched.

"Maybe," said Eirene. She had no intention of sending her sister anywhere near that damned sheep. "Come on. Keep to the trees." She offered Lamia her hand and Lamia took it, allowing Eirene to pull her to her feet.

"What will it sell for, do you think?"

"I'm not sure," Eirene said truthfully. She held a low branch out of her path, letting it snap back once Lamia was out of its reach. "It feels solid. If it's pure silver, it could be worth a lot. Maybe enough for a house. For me and Phoebe and—" She forced herself to laugh. The word "you" sat heavily on her tongue. But would Lamia even want to come? "I don't know where, though. Wherever we wouldn't need husbands or cousins or . . . fathers. Not any man," she finished, looking away.

"That sounds nice." Lamia's tone was almost wistful.

"I think so," said Eirene.

Soon, they were back at the house, back at the tower. Eirene threw the horn down on her bed, then trailed Lamia upstairs. With Leandros gone, there was nothing to do but wait, and there was no reason to do that alone. Searching the workshop didn't matter anymore when the secret to Leandros's power was sitting right in front of her. Lamia sprawled out on her bed, atop the mess of blankets, and leaned her new stick against the wall.

Eirene perched next to her, but something crinkled beneath her skirts as she sat. She frowned, reaching beneath the blanket to pull out a stack of crumpled papyrus sheets. They were swirled with charcoal—drawings, features forming in the dark smudges—and Eirene automatically averted her eyes. This felt private.

"What's this?" She offered the pile to Lamia.

"Ah," said Lamia. "Those." She reached for the topmost drawing. "Well, I suppose they're . . . they're dreams." She smoothed the curled edge compulsively as she spoke.

"Dreams," repeated Eirene. "What do you mean, dreams? Are you an oracle or something?" There was a knot of urgency inside her, tightening with each minute. And yet, Eirene could not help but smile playfully at Lamia, nudging her thin shoulder with her own. "What greets me in my future, oh wise one?"

Lamia did not look amused. "Not prophecies. *Dreams.* Although sometimes I—" She bit her lip and looked away.

Eirene stopped smiling and leaned toward her. This suddenly seemed much more serious than it had a moment before. "Lamia," she said softly. She pressed her hands to Lamia's, pulling Lamia's clenched fingers free of the papyrus. It fluttered onto the blanket between them. "You don't have to tell me if you don't want to. Your secrets are your own."

"It's not that." Lamia would not meet Eirene's eyes. Her hands were cold. "We spoke about my mother before. How I thought I remembered her. But it's only in dreams, and recently I wonder whether they're dreams at all. Whether they might be something else."

Eirene frowned. She looked down at the papyrus. It had landed face up, and she found herself staring into the smudged face of a woman skillfully rendered in charcoal. She was smiling.

It was not a welcoming smile, but nor was it threatening exactly. Eirene put it aside and looked at the second drawing. It was the same woman as before. This time, she was not smiling. Her teeth were bared and her hands were raised. A shadow approached her from a dark space at the edge of the drawing. The figure was barely a smudge, faceless and featureless. Among the black drag of charcoal, there was a strip left bare, one that seemed to glint as Eirene looked at it. The illusion of a bared blade.

Eirene put the drawing down. There was a malice to it, something in the scene that made her heart race and her throat tighten with fear. She flexed her fingers and turned her attention to the next drawing. A beautiful, furious face framed by a cascade of curls. Eirene pushed it aside. Beneath it was another—the woman crouched low, her eyes fixed again on a smudged assailant in the distance. She remembered the drawing of the woman in Leandros's workshop, the woman with the swirling red hair and the leg inked in ocher. She wasn't sure why, but she shivered.

"Are these . . . *all* of her?"

"I can never get her right," said Lamia. She was frowning. "I must have drawn her a hundred times but I can't—nothing can capture her. I had one that I thought was close, but—" She shuffled through the papers. "Still not right. She must be a creature of the gods or a god herself—more beautiful than you can imagine, but it's a beauty like a sharpened blade. As if just looking at her could draw blood."

"What does she want?"

Lamia's frown deepened. "Want?"

"In your dreams," said Eirene. There was something about the woman that she couldn't quite place. "What does she want?"

"I'm not sure. I'm never afraid of her, though. I don't think she wants anything. Not from me, anyway."

"Strange." Eirene ran a finger over the woman's crown of flames. Flecks of color came off on her fingers: muted, coppery. "What's this paint?"

"Oh," said Lamia, snatching the drawing back and hunching protectively over it. "Um. Shouldn't you go? Before my father gets back, I mean. You don't want him to catch you here."

The dismissal was clear. Eirene frowned. "You're suddenly eager to get rid of me." What was it with her today, managing to sound pathetic every time she spoke? She cleared her throat and got to her feet. "I'm joking. You're right. I should go."

"Be careful," said Lamia. She flipped the drawing in her hands face down.

"I'll try," said Eirene, trying for lightness, but Lamia's only response was a sort of grimace. "I'll tell you what I find." She slipped from the room and hurried down the stairs. She had known the drawings were private the moment she'd picked them up. So why had she pushed Lamia like that? Lamia had every right to withdraw, though Eirene could not deny that she felt the rejection keenly, like a bee sting inside her chest. Perhaps that was what had her so distracted that she hardly thought to look up as she marched onto the landing. By the time she had collided with a broad chest draped in purple, it was too late.

Leandros caught her by the shoulders and steadied her before she could fall. "Eirene!" he said. He smelled of outdoors and there was a bag slung over his shoulders. His sandals and the exposed skin of his feet were coated in a thin layer of gray dust. "Just who I was hoping to see."

"You—" Eirene swallowed down the words just in time. *You were supposed to be gone.*

What was he doing here? How long had he been back? He hadn't seen them return, had he?

"Look at you." Leandros's voice softened. He released his grip on one of her shoulders, though his other hand stayed where it was, clamped down on her flesh like a dog bite. "You're a mess." Without warning, he reached for her face. Eirene jerked back instinctively.

Swift as a striking snake, Leandros caught her by the chin.

Eirene's breath shuddered and then stopped as her whole body froze, every fiber of her being focused on Leandros's fingers as they pressed into the bottom of her cheeks. Her thoughts were suddenly tangled, terrified—the screaming of the wind in a storm. "Now, now, Eirene," Leandros purred. She could feel his heartbeat through his fingertips, that golden vitality pulsing within him. It was impossible to forget that he had the blood of the gods in him. "This is the touch of your future husband," he said. He had brought his face so close to hers that she felt his breath on her mouth as he spoke. He smelled of roses. "You should welcome it." He dragged his thumb across her lower lip, baring her teeth. For a horrifying moment, she thought he was going to kiss her. Then, mercifully, he released her, stepping back with a tinkling laugh that would make flowers bloom.

With considerable effort, Eirene forced herself to breathe. "I'm sorry," she managed, swallowing down her revulsion, her words little more than a squeak.

Leandros waved her apology away. "You will learn," he said

pleasantly. He looked her up and down, his eyes moving languor-
ously over her body. Her chiton was high-necked and only slightly
too short, but even with nothing but her bare arms and a sliver of
ankle uncovered, Leandros's stare made Eirene feel as exposed as
if she were naked. He tutted. "Dear me, your chiton is *filthy*, little
Eirene."

"You're right," said Eirene. "I will change it if you will give me
a moment."

"No need," said Leandros, in a tone that made it clear that she
was not dismissed. He smiled. "I don't object to filthy if it is you."
Eirene stared at him. "But of course," he continued, still smiling
that same, sardonic smile, "I prefer to be more presentable myself.
Do as you wish while I change my clothes, then bring that ram's
horn you're hiding somewhere to my study." He turned to go.

Eirene stared at his retreating back. "What— How—" Her
heartbeat surged as her veins were flooded with a cold, terrible
panic. If Leandros knew that the horn was in her room, what else
did he know? Did he know that Lamia had helped her? The tasks
had been intended for her alone. How long would it take him to
cast her out? How long would she have before he came for Phoebe?

"You stink of sheep," said Leandros over his shoulder. "I was
guessing you'd succeeded, and it seems from your reaction that I
was correct." She could hear the cruel smile in his voice. "I'll see
you in my study."

What else was there to do? Eirene knew that she had given herself away entirely. She returned, shoulders slumped, to her room to
retrieve the satchel. Then, feet dragging against the stone floor with
each despondent step, she made her way to the study.

She'd beaten Leandros there, but she didn't bother waiting outside for him. She slipped through the curtain, pulling it closed behind her, and threw her satchel down on the chair in the middle of the room. Eirene had once imagined spending hours losing herself in the seemingly endless baskets and bundles of scrolls. But she certainly didn't have hours now. She might not even have minutes—Leandros would be on his way at any moment. Still . . .

The intention was barely forming in her mind before Eirene was moving, maneuvering herself around the desk to the shelves behind it. There was a basket of well-worn scrolls on the lowest shelf. That seemed a good place to start. Eirene lunged for the first scroll and yanked it open. It was a simple drawing of a plant she didn't recognize, neatly annotated with its medicinal uses. She ached to examine it more closely, but this was not the time. She replaced it and retrieved the second scroll. She recognized the plant this time. Licorice root.

She rifled swiftly through the rest of the basket. More herbs with their uses carefully cataloged. Eirene threw them back with disgust. Next to the basket was a delicate brass statue—the tiny form of a dancing woman. Her hands were drawn up over her head, her face turned upward and her eyes closed. One slender brass leg was kicked out in an elegant arc. Eirene picked her up, the solid metal a cold weight in her palm.

There was something tugging at the back of her mind, something that worked itself free as she stared at the figurine, running her fingertips over the cool hard curves of her body. *A brass leg* . . .

A brass leg. Eirene went still, her fingers tightening over the statue. The room had gone hazy around her; all she could see was Lamia's monstrous woman, a phantom in smudged charcoal with flaming hair and dried blood on her lips. How could she not have seen it?

Hair of fire. Leg of brass. A strange unearthly beauty.

Empousa. Blood-drinker.

Eirene had a sudden awful vision of it, her mind bringing Lamia's drawing to life as a living, breathing woman. A golden-skinned woman with cascades of fiery hair and eyes like stars and blood dripping from her perfect lips. The empousa of Eirene's imagination had long sharp fingernails—almost claws—and her teeth were pearlescent when she smiled. Somehow, Eirene knew that they were as sharp as any blade.

She saw the scene as if it were before her. The empousa leaned over a sleeping Eirene, her breath stirring the stray curls that fell across Eirene's face. Her touch was gentle, loving, as she unpinned the brass brooch from Eirene's shoulder and tugged the fabric of her chiton away, exposing that vulnerable hollow at the base of Eirene's throat and the first swell of her breast. The empousa lowered her head and the gesture was almost reverent. Her hair pooled on the blanket. Red lips brushed brown skin. There was a flash of teeth—

A door slammed somewhere in the house and Eirene dropped the figurine as if it had burned her. It toppled with a clang she barely heard; it was as if some god had cast himself down from Olympus and surged into her bones. She recoiled from the figurine with stumbling steps backward that did not seem to be her own.

She collapsed against the chair with the satchel on its seat, where she had sat on that first night, bold and brave and completely *blind* to what went on here.

Her head was spinning and she was breathing fast, her breast heaving with each panicked inhalation. Without meaning to, she'd bitten down on her lip and her mouth tasted of blood. The pain of it had not yet registered. Her whole body thrummed with terror. There was a tightness in her belly; her thighs were tense.

The blood on her pillow, the clanking footsteps in the night, the staring yellow eye.

Lamia, pale and feverish the next morning. Alexandra, drained of blood.

There was an empousa in the house.

It was near impossible to maintain her composure when Leandros walked into the room. Once she'd regained a little of her sense, she set the statue upright, touching it as little as she could. It was just a statue, but the feel of the metal made her head swim. She'd forced herself to sit down in the chair, pulling the horn out of its bag into her lap, and now she sat hunched possessively over it. She concealed the shaking in her hands by stroking them along the horn's shining length.

When Leandros laid eyes upon the ram's horn, his face lit up with almost childish delight. "So you did get it!" Then he frowned. "But there's only one. And did you forget the wool?"

Eirene forced herself to smile back. She reached into the satchel and pulled out the tangles of silvery wool she and Lamia had collected. "The wool is here. And as for the horn, you only asked for one." She ran her hand over it again, pressing her fingertips into the tiny grooves that covered its dazzling surface. By now, she hoped, the drug would have worn off and the ram would be back to his contented rambling. Perhaps a little bewildered and off-balance— certainly, the horns were hefty enough that their loss would be disorientating—but *alive*. Alive and safe from Leandros, from the savage, wild creature he had under his control. Eirene shivered.

"You're cold." Leandros missed nothing.

It had unsettled her before and now it terrified her. What would he do when he realized what she knew? Chain her? Beat her? Set his monster on her?

"It's the exertion," she lied. "I'm fine."

Leandros shrugged and turned his attention back to her prize. "I will confess that I *had* hoped that once you killed the beast, you might bring *both* his horns. Once you've gotten one of the things, the other seems little more effort." She did not correct him but sat in rigid silence and watched as he strode over to her and made to lift the great horn from her lap. He was surprised by the heft of it, she could tell; his bare arms strained against its unmoving weight, then he was swinging it away from her, depositing it with a heavy thud on his desk.

"I could hardly carry two."

"Still." He was not looking at her. As she had moments before, he stroked his elegant fingers over the curves of the horn. She twisted hers together in her lap. "It's extraordinary. Without equal. I'd have liked the second."

Eirene sat upright in the chair, rubbing the blanket between her fingers. "If you wish it . . . ," she said, as boldly as she dared. She had to be as she always was. He couldn't know what she had discovered. "That could be the fourth task. I would not object to the repetition, I assure you."

Leandros let out a childish laugh and clapped his hands together. "You are so very amusing, dear Eirene, but I cannot do as you ask. Your final task was decided long ago." His smile chilled her to her core. "You will discover what it is soon enough." He turned his attention back to the horn and dismissed her with a casual flick of his fingers. "You may go."

Eirene did not need any encouragement. She picked up her skirts and fled. There were just two thoughts left in her mind.

One, that every day that she stayed here she was in danger of meeting the same wretched end that Alexandra had, drained of blood by a beautiful, deadly creature.

Two, that she had to tell Lamia.

XXXI
THE DIVINE BEAUTY

Lamia

Lamia sat perched on the edge of her bed, massaging her aching knee as she waited for Eirene to return. She had been gone a very long time now and Lamia tried to remind herself that this was not necessarily a bad thing. Eirene was clever. Cleverer even than Lamia's father was, perhaps. Clever enough to outwit him, run away and retrieve the silver horn and leave him far behind. And Lamia, of course, would be left behind with him. She slumped.

She straightened immediately at the scraping of the bar on the tower door. She heard the door being flung open, the thud of wood hitting stone followed by a clattering from the landing at the bottom of the tower, and the distinctive slapping of sandals on stone. Someone was going up the stairs—and they were *running*.

Eirene? Lamia's heart attempted a sort of backflip.

It couldn't be anyone else. Both Leandros and Peiros moved with far heavier footfalls. Besides, she had never known either of them to run. Certainly not to *her*.

Eirene was running for her. Lamia was flushed with pleasure at the thought. She stood from the bed and went to the curtain. As Lamia drew it aside the sound of Eirene's running became clearer and closer. She had reached the middle landing.

Lamia had a sudden brilliant idea.

Lamia slipped past the curtain and put her back to the wall beside the entrance to the spiraling stairway. When Eirene came thundering up, Lamia would be completely hidden from her. Lamia could picture the way Eirene's mouth would round in surprise, her hands flying up as Lamia materialized. She pressed herself harder against the wall, a hand to her mouth to stifle the giggles that threatened to burst from her lips.

The footsteps came closer and closer until Lamia could hear the rapid huffs of Eirene's breath. She held her own.

As Eirene came skidding out onto the landing, Lamia lunged for her, pushing off her stick. She caught Eirene by the shoulder and spun her into the circle of her arms.

For a moment, it was just as she had imagined. Eirene's head was tucked beneath Lamia's chin, her body cocooned in Lamia's arms. Lamia could smell her hair and the rose oil she daubed behind her ears in the mornings.

"AHHHHH." Letting out a muffled, frightened yell, Eirene swung wildly, her hand connecting with Lamia's face.

"*Ahhhhhhhh*," cried Lamia, cradling her cheek.

"*Ahhhhhhhh*," shrieked Eirene, still reeling backward, her eyes lighting up with horrified recognition. "It's you! I'm so sorry!"

"What was that for?" moaned Lamia, still cupping the side of her face. There were tears in her eyes—more of surprise than real pain. Her father hit her much harder. "You hit me!"

"I'm sorry!" Eirene's voice had gone very high-pitched. She shook her hand out, wincing. "Did that hurt you?"

"Not really," said Lamia.

Eirene regarded Lamia with a wild expression. "Listen, there's something I have to tell you."

"What is it?" asked Lamia. She understood that she should be afraid. It was a mild evening, but her bare arms prickled with cold.

Eirene's eyes darted toward the stairs. "Not here." She moved toward Lamia's chamber with quiet footsteps.

Lamia followed, making her own steps soft, putting down her stick as gently as she could.

Once they were inside, Eirene pulled the curtain shut. When she turned back to Lamia, her face was serious, her lips pressed tightly together and her dark brows low over her eyes.

"I know what's in the tower room," she said without preamble. "The empty one beneath us, in the middle of the stairs. Well, it's not empty, actually. Leandros is keeping a monster there."

Lamia gave her what must have been a completely blank look.

"The woman in your drawings. She's not a woman at all. It's called an empousa," said Eirene urgently. She drew nearer with every word until she was close enough to cup Lamia's face in her hands. She didn't, obviously. Her hands stayed firmly in place at her sides, balled into tight fists. "That's what he's keeping in that room, I'm sure of it! A beautiful woman who drinks the blood of young men—that explains why Leandros keeps no servants but Peiros. But this one doesn't just prey on men, it feeds on women, too. You—your dreams that aren't dreams must be memories of when she drank from you. And from Alexandra . . ." Her hand drifted to her throat. "And from me, I think."

"You think it's been feeding on us?" Lamia brought a hand to her neck, mirroring Eirene. Without thinking, she threw a glance over her shoulder, like this empousa creature could be lurking in the shadows behind her, ready to pounce.

"Yes," said Eirene grimly. "But there's only one way to be sure."

"This is a very bad idea," said Lamia for the fourth time. "She eats people. *We* are people."

Eirene straightened. She'd been trying to peer through the narrow keyhole into the room beyond as Lamia stood behind her, hands knotted together, nervous words spilling from her lips.

"You only have a knife," she reminded Eirene. "And she has—"

"Flaming hair and flesh-rending teeth. I know," said Eirene. "But she can't be like that all the time, otherwise we'd have realized before now. Leandros must have a way to keep her restrained and quiet. I've only heard her once, and the next night he *drugged* me so that she could *eat me*." This realization had come to her as they'd walked down the stairs, and her shriek of fury had been so loud that Lamia was surprised it hadn't brought Peiros running. "I'd bet anything he drugs her, too. With one of those horrible Desires of his. Well, I've got a desire for *him*. My fist in his—"

"How are you planning on getting in, then?"

Eirene had been miming something vicious and crude. She stopped ramming her fist into an imaginary Leandros and frowned at Lamia. "What?"

"It's locked," pointed out Lamia.

"I'll—" This seemed to be the first time Eirene had thought about it. "I'll smash it down."

"I think she might hear you, drugged or not," said Lamia. "If we have to go in—"

"We do."

"*If* we do, we should do it quietly. We need the key."

"The *key*?" Eirene looked stricken. "Lamia, where would we get the key? I've never seen Leandros with any keys."

"Tomorrow, then—"

"We don't have time! I could be given my final task at any

moment. Psyche's last task was retrieving beauty from the Underworld, so that could be anything. What if—what if it's something to do with the empousa? Lamia, I have to know. I have to know *now*."

Lamia pressed her hands together. Her skin still felt raw from the sun. Her stomach was tight. "Fine. I'll open it."

Eirene blinked. "You—what? You have the key?"

"I don't need the key," said Lamia. "The lock is wooden, is it not? So it'll burn."

"You want to set fire to it?"

"Something like that." Lamia knew that she was being deliberately obtuse, but she could not deny the prickle of satisfaction she felt with each of Eirene's questions. She did not often feel clever and she longed to savor the moment.

Eirene narrowed her eyes. "Well, come on, then. Tell me."

"Why don't I just show you?" Lamia reached for the knife at Eirene's waist.

Finally, Eirene seemed to understand. Her eyes widened and her lips parted, shaping a single word. "*No*." She swung the knife out of reach before Lamia could close her fingers over the handle. "Absolutely not. No."

"It's the fastest way," said Lamia. "I'll call the light, burn through the lock—"

"Over my dead body."

"If this is as urgent as you say, it *will* be over your dead body. Or mine."

Eirene's brows shot up. "There are alternatives. We don't need the key; we just need something like it. It'll take a little maneuvering, but anything narrow and hard, some kind of stick—"

"A needle?" suggested Lamia.

"*Brilliant*." Eirene beamed. "I have one that'll work perfectly."

She ran toward the stairs leading down to her room, then skidded to an abrupt stop at the top. She turned back to Lamia. "Don't you dare try anything while I'm gone," she said threateningly. "I won't have you hurting yourself just because you think it's the only way you can help. Not for this, not for anything."

As Eirene dashed down the stairs, Lamia looked down at her hands. The gash from the night in the tower room sorting seeds, when she had thrust the knife point into her hand, had scabbed over, but it still throbbed when she flexed her fingers. For a moment, she debated tearing it open again, using the pain to summon a beam of light to burn through the door before Eirene could return to stop her. She touched the edges of the wound with a tentative finger and the pain flared. Downstairs, the door to Eirene's room banged and Lamia let her hands fall back to her sides. There was no telling what lay in this room, beyond this door. Lamia could save her tears for now.

Soon, the tower rang again with footsteps and Eirene came barreling back up the stairs. She emerged onto the landing with a battered brass needle held aloft. Her lips were stretched wide in a victorious smile, but her eyes darted suspiciously to the lock and to Lamia's hands before they finally settled on her face.

"Here," she said, sounding very pleased with herself. "Let's get that door open."

"Keep your knife close," said Lamia.

"You can have it now," said Eirene. She drew the blade free and offered it, handle first, to Lamia.

"Generous," said Lamia with a snort, but she still took it, holding it tightly in her unscathed right hand.

She stepped to the side to allow Eirene to crouch beside the door, one eye squeezed shut, the other pressed against the keyhole.

"It's hardly worn at all," she announced, drawing back. "This shouldn't be too hard." She pushed the needle into the lock and worked it like a lever. She curled her free hand into the narrow gap beneath the door and tugged at it. "Come on," she muttered.

Lamia watched her silently, turning the knife over and over in her hand. If this failed, would Eirene let her use her magic? Perhaps she'd only care when it was convenient.

Lamia would never find out. With the sound of wood grinding against wood, the lock gave. Lamia braced herself, but all that happened was that the door swung back a sliver, allowing a narrow shaft of light through. No sound came from within—no snuffling of a drugged monster in sleep, no shriek as the empousa launched itself toward them, no clicking of talons as it stalked toward freedom. Lamia didn't actually know if it had talons, but she felt that blood-drinking, flesh-eating monsters *should* have talons, and the long skirts it had worn in her dreams could have concealed anything.

Eirene made a small satisfied noise and stood. "There," she said. Her voice only shook a little. "Let's see what kind of thing Leandros is keeping, shall we?" She offered Lamia her hand.

Lamia nodded wordlessly and took it. Eirene's fingers were warm where they curled around hers.

Eirene gave her a final grim smile and pulled the door open.

XXXII

THE END OF ALL FORTUNE

Eirene

The room was empty.

Eirene stepped inside and looked around. The hope that had filled her heart until it felt fit to burst was draining away as swiftly as it had come. She could feel it dripping from her ribs, pooling in her stomach. It was cold.

Set halfway up the stairway as it was, the tower room was only small; the shutters on the single narrow window had rotted away, and the dim evening light fell upon curved stone walls, a bare, uneven floor, and a hearth full of nothing but dust.

Eirene might have been a sleepwalker. The world around her had become blurred, dreamlike. A strange certainty had come over her—that she would pinch herself awake and find herself in bed. The tower room would still be locked, would still hold every secret she sought and *knew* must be found here. Where was the empousa? How could she have been so wrong? She took a stumbling step forward, then another, pulling Lamia—the only thing that anchored her to the world of waking—with her. Lamia's fingers were cold, her grip firm.

"Nothing," said Lamia glumly.

Eirene swallowed hard. She didn't trust herself to move, let alone speak. She wanted to collapse against Lamia, to cry out against her throat, *"How could you make me believe it?"* All of it—that they would find the answers, that they would somehow be free, and that they would do it *together*. She wanted to cry. She wanted to push her face into Lamia's shoulders and weep for hours, until Lamia cupped her hands around Eirene's face and smiled and leaned forward and—

Lamia let go before Eirene could do anything, gently pushing her away and detangling their fingers.

"I'm sorry, Eirene," she said, wiping the back of her hand across her cheek. She moved toward the window, perhaps drawn by the light there; shining flecks of it clung to her fingertips like so many jewels. "I truly thought—" Her final words were swallowed up in a shriek of surprise and fear as her foot caught in a dip in the floor. She thrust her stick out too late to stop herself and fell hard.

She collided with the stone with a yelp and a muffled clanging noise.

Eirene went very still. The world before her seemed to swim in and out of focus.

Lamia hadn't noticed. She was maneuvering herself into a wide-legged sitting position, grumbling and cursing under her breath as she examined her palms. The fall had scraped them raw.

Eirene looked down at her with silent horror. The sound had been unmistakably familiar. Hadn't it?

"Eirene?" said Lamia, looking up at last.

Eirene schooled her expression into something like neutrality as quickly as she could, but it was already too late.

Lamia's eyes darted across Eirene's face. "What is it?" Her own features—sunburnt and freckling—were suddenly drawn and afraid.

"That sound," managed Eirene. "When you fell, I—I heard a sound. Like metal on stone. What was it?"

Lamia's face went perfectly blank. "I didn't hear anything."

It was such an obvious lie that Eirene could have laughed. "That *sound*," she repeated.

"I don't know what you mean."

"You're an awful liar. I heard it. Just tell me what it was."

"It wasn't anything!"

"I know you're lying!" Eirene closed the distance between them in three long strides. When her shoe landed on the last footfall, a handspan from where Lamia sat, Lamia flinched. It was a pathetic gesture and it wrenched at Eirene's heart like a bird trying to pluck a particularly determined worm from the earth. "I'm not—" She swallowed. "Don't be afraid of me. I just want to understand." She lowered herself slowly to the floor beside Lamia.

Lamia looked pointedly away from her. She traced an aimless pattern in the dust.

"Can you show me?" Eirene asked at last. Then she could be sure. Then she would know how Lamia had betrayed her, how she had lied to her. What she would do after that, she didn't know. She didn't want to know.

Lamia looked down, her eyes wet and glittering. "All right." With trembling hands, she drew the skirts of her chiton aside to reveal the shoes she wore beneath.

They were the most peculiar shoes Eirene had ever seen. She'd assumed they were men's riding boots—supple leather that covered the whole foot, ankle, and a modest portion of the shin. But Eirene saw that Lamia's encased her entire lower leg, ending a little past the knee. They were fastened by way of leather laces that ran from ankle to thigh, where they had been knotted into a neat bow. A leather tongue lay beneath the overlapping ties, so there was not a single sliver of skin left visible.

Lamia's left leg was closest. Without thinking, Eirene reached for the knot.

Lamia flinched and Eirene snatched her hand away.

"No, I didn't—" said Lamia quickly. She swallowed visibly, seemed to steel herself. She stared at Eirene's hand with great intent. "You can. If you want. But it's—it's the other leg."

Eirene blinked. "Your right?"

"Yes." The word was an exhale.

"But you favor your left. When you walk."

Lamia bit her bottom lip. Her eyes were still fixed on Eirene's hand. "My right is stronger. When I . . . when I fall, it's harder to—" She had chewed through the delicate skin of her lip. Blood dripped onto her chiton. "It doesn't break so easily," she finished at last.

"I understand," said Eirene softly.

She was slower to reach this time. She worked the knot open with great care—her body seemed to thrum with something like fear every time her fingers brushed the cold flesh of Lamia's thigh—and plucked at the end of the ties. It was almost a shame to see the perfect bow fall apart.

She moved her hand down, fingers resting atop the crossed laces, and looked up at Lamia, a wordless request for permission. Lamia made a small gasping noise and ducked her chin in a nervous birdlike nod.

Eirene pushed her fingers beneath the ties just below the curve of Lamia's knee. It was impossible not to notice how unyielding the flesh beneath her touch was; she held on to some final, fleeting hope that it was even flesh at all. She looked again at Lamia, who had set her jaw and was watching her intently. Eirene did not break eye contact as she curled her fingers up, pulling the ties loose.

She could have stopped there. The empousa in the illustration had been ocher to her knee. Eirene could have pushed aside the top of Lamia's boot; she knew she would have found the answer there. But she couldn't bring herself to do it. She would not allow everything to come to an end like that—between one brief moment and the next, in one crude little gesture.

She moved her hands a little lower, then lower again, tugging at the ties until the full length of the boot was loose and all but falling open, the laces slack. Then, with another look, another nod, she rested one hand against Lamia's calf, found a firm grip with the other on her heel, and *tugged*.

The boot slipped off without resistance.

Beneath it, Lamia's leg lay bare. Eirene's eyes drank in the lean calf, the delicate ankle, and the narrow foot.

And then—impossible to ignore, for it was everywhere—the dull glimmer of brass.

XXXIII
SIRENS TO THE MOUNTAIN

Lamia

Lamia squeezed her eyes shut and braced herself for what she had always known must come. Eirene's lip would curl in disgust, she would jump to her feet and back away, horrified, her knife clutched in her hand and pointed straight at Lamia's heart. She would scream at Lamia, call her a vile, deformed creature. That was the picture that Leandros had painted for her again and again over the years until Lamia was sure that she could tear herself open to find the word "abomination" burned into her heart.

But Eirene did not move. She did not scream.

Lamia opened one eye. Eirene's mouth was hanging open, her pupils were blown wide, her gaze fixed on Lamia's brass leg. She was breathing slowly and deeply, her chest rising and falling with each rasping inhale, each exhalation.

"Eirene?" Was that flutter against Lamia's ribs . . . hope?

Eirene looked up slowly to meet Lamia's gaze. It seemed to cause her physical pain—she winced and looked away again, fixing her eyes somewhere behind Lamia. "It's you," she said softly.

This was not the reaction Lamia had expected. This wasn't hatred or disgust. Lamia wasn't precisely sure what it was, though. "What's me?"

"What?"

"*What?*" Lamia could hear a defensive edge to her own voice now. "Just tell me."

Eirene's face fell. "You don't know." It wasn't a question, more a slow, terrible realization. "How could you not know?"

"Know *what*?" Lamia's confusion was turning to irritation. "Stop talking in riddles, Eirene."

Eirene squared her shoulders and took a deep breath. "The empousa—"

Fear surged through Lamia's spine. She jerked away from Eirene, twisting about to search wildly behind her for the beast that must surely be lurking there. But the room was as empty as it had been before; they were alone but for the shadows. She turned back to Eirene, whose face had crumpled. She looked as though she might be on the verge of tears.

"No," said Eirene, answering the question that must have been clear in Lamia's eyes. "It's not here. I mean, it is here, but it— *she* . . ." She didn't seem to be able to go on.

Lamia gave her what she knew must have been a blank, stupid sort of look. Eirene was calling the creature *she*. Something was piecing itself together in the back of her mind—she could feel the truth fitting into place like a bolt slid across a door. "Eirene?" she asked quietly. "What is it?"

There was a long silence before Eirene spoke again. "When I told you of the empousa, I—I didn't tell you everything," Her gaze was fixed on her own lap. "I didn't think it mattered. I was so pleased with my own cleverness that I didn't think . . ." She laughed bitterly and covered her face with her hands. She was shaking.

"I don't understand," said Lamia. "There isn't an empousa?"

Eirene made a choking sound from behind her hands. "There is."

"Eirene," said Lamia urgently. She could not be kept in the dark any longer. "*Please*. Don't hide whatever this is from me. I can *help* you. What—"

"The empousa has a leg made of brass," blurted Eirene.

Lamia's heart seemed to still—a rabbit caught in the middle of a path. Eirene had dropped her hands into her lap, her face a mask of anguish.

At first, Lamia could do nothing but stare. Then: "No." She shook her head and put her hands up between them, as if to fend off the words that had spilled from Eirene's lips. But it was too late— they had already broken through. Eirene had begun to cry, silent tears slipping down her face. Lamia wanted to shake her. She was wrong. She had been wrong before—she was wrong now. She had to be.

"No," she said again. "You said—you said the empousa is a killer. You said she enchants men and she drinks their blood. I haven't—I would *never*." Even as she spoke, she saw Alexandra. Her limp white hands, the memory seared into Lamia's mind. Alexandra was dead. But Lamia couldn't have killed her, could she? She would never have hurt Alexandra. Gentle sweet-faced Alexandra, who had been kind to her. "She killed Alexandra. It can't be me. You said she's a monster."

Lamia's voice broke as she made her final desperate plea, with all the feeling of pressing her hands to a flickering flame, of being caught in the brief moment before the pain came. Her words were quiet and ragged. "You said she was beautiful."

Eirene looked right at her, her eyes flicking across Lamia's, dropping to her lips and back again. "She is," said Eirene helplessly, and the rush of agony was almost thrilling.

Lamia did not know just how long they stayed like that. Lamia, sitting on the floor with her chiton up about her knees and her brass leg splayed out in front of her like a shining testament to her monstrosity. And Eirene, kneeling at her side. Since those two awful, lovely words—"She is"—she had been perfectly, terribly silent.

Tears dripped down Lamia's cheeks. She had killed Alexandra. And she had not just killed her. She had hunted her, cornered her, drunk her blood. And then she had just . . . forgotten? In her dreams, she'd conjured up a woman of fire and blood to take the blame, to claim the crime so that Lamia could pretend that she was not the only vile monster in the world.

Eventually, Eirene moved. Just the smallest gesture, the slightest stretch of her hands, the fluttering of fingertips. "Can I—" She turned her face away, her cheeks darkening. "Can I touch your leg?"

"*Touch* it?" Lamia twisted her hands into tight fists, her broken, bitten nails digging into her palms. "Why would you—Eirene, you just told me that I'm—" She shook her head, unable to force the words out. "You should be running."

"Running? Are you any different from how you were yesterday?"

"Yesterday, you didn't know that I'd *killed* someone. Nor did I," she added, softer.

"You don't know that," retorted Eirene immediately, but she jerked her hand away from Lamia's leg. To Lamia's surprise, she rested it instead on Lamia's shoulder and squeezed. "We don't know everything. I think—I think there might have been another one. Another . . . empousa. Like you."

"Another one?" Lamia shook her head. "No, you know that doesn't make sense. We were stupid to think there was some creature hiding in here. How would Leandros keep her concealed from us? There's only me." She laughed, the sound entirely devoid of humor. "It's me."

"No, I don't think so," said Eirene. Her voice was firm. "When I went into Leandros's workroom, I saw something. I thought it was from a statue or something like that, but now I'm not so sure. No, I am sure. It wasn't from a statue."

"What are you talking about?"

"A leg," said Eirene. "A brass leg, like yours. There were other things, too. A jar of this gritty white stuff, like sand but . . . not. And hair!" Her hand tightened on Lamia's shoulder and Lamia made a soft noise of pain. "Sorry," said Eirene and released her. "Lamia, there was *hair*. Red hair, like yours but a lot more." She waved her hands about as if that would help Lamia understand. It didn't. "Orange," said Eirene at last. "Much more orange, and curly."

"Perhaps it was my hair," said Lamia. She couldn't remember a time when her father had cut her hair off, but clearly her memory had some significant gaps. A haircut was the least of her worries.

"No," said Eirene with an air of great certainty. "It wasn't. Unless it was your leg, too, there's another empousa. Or"—she winced—"there was."

Lamia drew in a shaky breath. So the only other creature like her was dead, dismembered. Still, if she was alone now, it was only as alone as she had been before. But for Eirene. "You can touch it," she blurted out. "If you want to."

Eirene met her gaze. "Really?"

Lamia nodded. She tried to laugh but only succeeded in sounding like she was choking. "It's just a leg."

"Tell me to stop whenever you like," said Eirene earnestly. She reached out again and rested her hand at the bottom of Lamia's thigh, where the pale olive morphed into metal.

Lamia's breath caught. Eirene's hands were cold.

"It's warm," said Eirene, her voice full of wonder. She moved her hands lower, tracing the shape of Lamia's knee with her fingertips.

Lamia made a soft sound. "Well, it's not just a lump of metal. It's part of me." She flexed her foot.

"Of course." Eirene moved lower, running her hands over Lamia's calf. She looked up at Lamia and Lamia was struck by her closeness, the smell of her skin, the warmth of her body. It was not the hunger of a monster, for flesh and blood and bone, that had Lamia leaning closer, but another kind of hunger, all too human. Her belly fluttered like a new flame, a heat that spread lower as the fire caught.

She should have heard them, the footsteps on the stairs, but she was so captivated by Eirene—Eirene's wide eyes, her trembling lower lip, the gentle caress of her fingers over Lamia's leg—that the rest of the world seemed to have faded away entirely.

It returned rudely, viciously, with a sharp smack as the door was flung open and crashed against the wall. Lamia's father paused in the doorway, his shining blue eyes taking in the scene. A broad smile spread across his beautiful face. He stepped inside.

Of the two of them, Eirene moved first. She snatched her hand away from Lamia, leaving only the residual burn of her fingertips and jumped to her feet.

"How long were you planning on keeping this a secret?" she demanded. She advanced on him, blazing and furious, but drew to a halt some distance from him.

Something eased in Lamia's chest. Her father was only a man, and yet Eirene shied from him. Moments ago the hands now fisted at her side had been soft and open and resting against Lamia's skin. She could not be so very bad a monster, could she, if Eirene was content to keep her so close? She picked up her stick and stood, moving to Eirene's side.

Her father brushed an imaginary speck of dust from the bright white of his chiton. "Not too long," he said. "You have one more task, remember, before you become my wife. There are some secrets too . . . intimate to be shared before such a position is granted."

Eirene's shoulders hardened. "You had no intention of sharing them."

The edge of his mouth lifted.

"Do you deny it? That you tricked me, drugged me? That you waited until I was sleeping and—" She shot a desperate look at Lamia.

Lamia's father followed the movement. The amusement on his face only grew. "And set her upon you?" he supplied. "Ah, Eirene, you know I cannot deny it. I would fall to my knees in earnest supplication if it would please you."

Eirene shifted but said nothing.

Lamia's grip tightened on her stick. She could use it to strike her father, if she had to, so that Eirene at least might get away.

"Would it?" he prompted Eirene. He rubbed his sandal against the stone and pulled a face. "The floor is dusty, but it is worth ruining my tunic if it will return me to your favor, sweetest Eirene."

"Stop that," snapped Lamia. There was a brief stunned silence. "Stop speaking to her like that."

Her father's eyes went to her, narrowing momentarily with fury. Then he laughed, soft, victorious. "And *you*. You think I haven't seen you creeping around the countryside, my precious girl? You think I don't know that you helped her with the grain, that you both defied me? I could have punished you for it."

Lamia couldn't help it. She flinched. No matter what she was, what she had done, she still felt like a helpless child in the presence of her father.

Her father's eyes slid back to Eirene. "I found the sieve in her chest with seed husks stuck inside."

Eirene stared at him. "You knew? You knew I'd failed the *first* task and you let me go on? For what? *Why?*"

He ignored her questions. "You really shouldn't have trusted Lamia to help you. She's a sweet girl but not very clever."

Lamia's chest ached. There was something stuck in her throat that she could not dislodge no matter how many times she tried to swallow it down. She had thought herself so brilliant for hiding the sieve where her father would never go looking for it. And yet she had never even noticed he'd discovered it. She wilted.

"Lamia's not stupid," snapped Eirene. "Just because she isn't vicious and cruel like you, just because she doesn't expect the worst in everything and everyone. Even in *you*. Now answer my question! Why did you keep me here if I'd failed your task?"

"You know why."

It was not Leandros who spoke, but his blue eyes brightened and he turned them to Lamia. She met his gaze before looking away, her mouth acrid with the taste of bile. "You know why," she repeated, more quietly. "Didn't we both realize it the moment you told me what I was? You were brought here as *fodder*." She spat the word and Eirene winced.

"Not *just* fodder," Lamia's father said.

Eirene's fingers curled around the handle of her blade. "What, then?"

He smiled. "Do you remember Psyche's fourth task?" he asked her softly.

Eirene's face twisted in bewilderment. "She . . . she went to Hades. To Persephone, I think. But I don't—"

She broke off as he leaned toward her with the air of someone about to reveal a particularly delicious secret. Lamia watched as Eirene swayed toward him, a willow in the wind; she seemed drawn to him as if commanded by the same power that calls the rolling surf to the sand.

"Beauty," he whispered. "Psyche was sent to retrieve beauty itself from the land of the dead. And that is the final task I set for you, Eirene."

Eirene gazed at him. Then her mouth quirked up and she barked out a short, derisive laugh. "Really, Leandros? Your delusion astounds me."

"You won't do it?"

"How could I? Mortals cannot simply walk into Hades."

"Or out," said Lamia quietly.

Neither seemed to hear her. They were so close, her father all but whispering into Eirene's ear.

"That's what I thought once," he said. "I have been searching long for the secret to true Desire, to beauty and to love. A search that led me here."

"To *Zakynthos.*"

"To Zakynthos," he repeated. He had taken on the tone of a storyteller, of someone repeating a tale he was told long ago. "There lies the entrance to the myrtle grove where walk the victims of love, where divine light will shine on you and all that is mortal will be burned away."

"What?" Eirene laughed again.

Was Lamia hearing things, or did she sound less certain this time?

Her father cocked his head. "Why do you laugh, little Eirene?"

"Where did you hear *that*? There is no entrance to the Underworld here."

"Oh, but there is. You know there is, Eirene. Just *think*. You collected those crocuses, did you not? Can you truly tell me that you did not sense it?"

What was he talking about? Lamia frowned as Eirene shook her head slowly, but she seemed hesitant. She drifted even closer to Lamia's father, caught by the intrigue in his words, her forehead furrowing. "No. It couldn't have been." She squared her shoulders and spoke again, louder. "Whoever told you to come to Zakynthos was clearly trying to make a quick coin off an idiot."

What feeling? Lamia wanted to scream. What had she missed?

"Shall I tell you how to find the entrance, Eirene? Shall I tell you how it is guarded, how to make your way into the Underworld? How to come *back*?"

"Go ahead." Eirene's voice was full of disdain.

"I will," said Lamia's father. "If we can make another bargain. Enter the Underworld. Bring me the myrtle that grows in the groves there. Return to me and I will forget how you have betrayed me in your previous failures. Return to me with the myrtle, and you will be free of me forever. As will your sister."

There was a long pause. Then: "And Lamia?" asked Eirene. "What about her? What will happen to her?"

"Don't worry about me," Lamia said quickly.

Eirene had been given another chance to save her sister. That was all she had wanted from the moment she'd come here. Lamia could not deny it to her, no matter how it would hurt her when Eirene was gone.

"Listen to Lamia," said her father. "She is not your concern."

"What will happen to her?" Eirene repeated stubbornly. She was so much smaller than him, and yet she advanced on him without fear. Her ferocity gave her words wings.

"She is my daughter. She will stay with me here, of course."

Eirene turned to look at Lamia. Lamia gave her what she hoped was an understanding smile, one that gave permission, one that said *leave me behind*. Eirene turned back to face Lamia's father. They were all but nose to nose now, Eirene spitting each word from her mouth to his. "I know your secret. I know where your power comes from. I could *destroy you*."

Lamia's father stopped smiling. "So you refuse? You will not fetch the myrtle for me?"

"Go to hell," said Eirene, "and get it yourself."

"A shame." There was a small leather pouch at his hip and he reached into it. When he pulled his hand away, there was something clutched between his golden fingers. He sighed. "This could have been so much easier for you, Eirene."

It was only when he opened his palm, revealing the fine silverish powder that had been concealed within his fist, that Lamia understood. As if from very far away, she heard herself shout a garbled warning. She lunged for Eirene, to pull her back, to shield her somehow, but she had realized too late. Her father smiled as he blew the powder into Eirene's face, and Lamia could do nothing but watch in helpless horror as Eirene recoiled, as she blinked against the sudden, swirling haze—as she opened her mouth in shock and breathed in the handful of Desire.

XXXIV

OF LIKE WRETCHEDNESS

Lamia

The effect was instantaneous. Even as Lamia yanked her back, Eirene went stock-still, the tension melting from her limbs, her raised hands falling limp at her sides. She blinked again, several times, and her mouth slackened into a slow, stupid grin. Her wide eyes were fixed on Lamia's father. "Oh," she said, and a laugh burst from her lips. Lamia had never heard anything quite like it: near hysterical, ringing like a bell.

"Oh," said Eirene again. "I feel so peculiar." Very abruptly, she sat down, pulling Lamia to the floor with her. From the floor, cross-legged like a child in the dust, she continued to gaze up at Lamia's father with open adoration.

"Eirene," said Lamia. She followed Eirene's gaze to her father. "What did you *do*?"

Her father ignored her. He looked down at Eirene with smug satisfaction. "Are you going to cause me any more trouble now, Eirene?"

Eirene shook her head.

"Good girl." Now he turned his attention to Lamia. "I call that one Loyalty," he said, with an air of great satisfaction, brushing silver dust from his hands. "It uses the essence of the saffron flowers Eirene so *helpfully* brought to me. An adjustment of my recipe for Devotion, which was more of a romantic bond." He beamed. "And

I didn't want that! Not for poor Eirene."

Lamia found her voice at last. "What kind . . . what kind of bond is this one, then?" This was what he had used her magic for? It was twisted and cruel; it disgusted her. She had known her father was not a kind man, but she had never thought him capable of this.

Her father lifted his shoulders in an elaborate shrug. "A simpler one. A dog and its master, perhaps." He put his fingers to his lips suddenly and whistled sharply. "She knows I will protect her. In return, she will do anything for me. Eirene! Come!"

Lamia felt sick with horror. She pushed herself to her feet to stand in front of Eirene, as if that could protect her, but Eirene jumped up eagerly and pushed Lamia aside as if she were mere furniture. She lurched across the space that separated her from Leandros. The moment she reached him, she crumpled to the ground again. She reached out a hand to pat the hem of his chiton, hooking her fingers into the fine cloth. "I am here," she said. Looking into her eyes was like staring out into the sky at night. Beautiful and empty, the space between stars.

"Good," said Lamia's father quietly. He dropped to his knees beside Eirene and lifted her chin with the tip of his finger. His face twisted with a peculiar expression—halfway between a smile and a strange, sad sort of grimace. "A shame," he declared. Then he looked up at Lamia. "She was a smart girl. If you'd left her alone, she'd have done well here."

Lamia gaped at him. "If I'd . . . left her alone?"

"Well, of course." He tucked one of Eirene's curls behind her ear.

"Stop touching her," snapped Lamia. She took a step closer, clutching her stick tightly. Her fear was a living thing inside her, coiling and uncoiling. She knew that he would not hesitate to hurt her; her arms and hands were scarred with the pale imprints of his fingernails. But she had to protect Eirene.

"This is all because of you, Lamia." Her father watched her with a lazy smile. "You know that, don't you? It's your fault."

"My fault," echoed Lamia. Her breath caught in her throat, her grip on the stick slackened. Because he was right. It was, wasn't it? All of it. It was her magic that made the Desires that Eirene had wanted so desperately to protect her sister from. And this was where Desire had landed her now. Tears pricked at her eyes. Her father knew exactly where to strike her, exactly how to reduce her to the helpless, terrified girl she'd always been.

Her father gave her a long look. "Oh, Lamia. Perhaps I shouldn't be so hard on you. Perhaps it's in your nature."

Perhaps it was in her nature. But what was *it*? Merely ruining lives—or ending them, too? She suddenly could not keep the question in. "Am I—" Her voice trembled and broke and she felt a hot tear slip onto her cheek. Her father's eyes went straight to it, his gaze sharp and predatory. Lamia cleared her throat and forced herself to inhale. She had to know. She owed it to herself, and to her old friend, to discover the truth. No matter how awful. "Am I really an empousa? Did I kill Alexandra?"

"Ah, Alexandra." He looked almost sad. "What a waste. I suppose her death was my fault in a way."

Lamia's breath caught. His fault? So perhaps . . . perhaps Eirene had been wrong: *Lamia* had not been the one to kill Alexandra. Perhaps the other empousa—the dead creature whose remains Eirene had seen in the workshop—had been responsible. But her father's next words sent her heart crashing back down.

"I should have known your appetites were changing." He spoke the words like a confession. "As you grew from girl to woman, you

were not so easily sated by a little blood. You don't remember it"—
he shrugged lightly—"of course you don't. I made sure of that.
I had only left you alone for a while, but when I returned, you
were . . . you were savage. Uncontrollable. Alexandra was already
dead, the poor thing, and there was nothing I could do but leave
you to drink her dry."

Lamia's insides churned with disgust and revulsion; her mouth
seemed to fill with the coppery taste of blood. Warm. Thrumming
with vitality. She saw it again, the image that had haunted her
dreams for so long—Alexandra's hand on the stone. The skin pale,
the fingers clawlike and unmoving. Not a dream, then. A memory.

"I didn't know." She choked on every word. "Why didn't I
remember?"

At first, he said nothing. He merely raised his arms and offered
his palms to her, still glistening with the silvery remnants of the
Desire he called Loyalty. It took her a moment to understand. "You
used a Desire on me?"

She could not have said anything more if she'd wanted to.
How . . . how *dare he*? The Desires were made using *her* magic,
her power, that she had bled and wept for over and over again. Her
father had said he used the Desire to protect her. But instead he had
stolen from her: first her magic, then her memories.

"I call it Lethe," he said. "It's not one I trade in much. Its
uses . . . They are too complex to grant to just *anyone*, though certainly many come seeking it."

"The daffodil girl," remembered Lamia.

He frowned. "Who?"

Lamia flushed. "A girl came here. Just before Alexandra—
before Alexandra lived here." When her father continued to look at

her blankly, she felt her lip tremble. "She was here! I *remember*." Or had it been a dream? How many of her memories were false? How many of her dreams were true? But he could not take this one away from her. Lamia remembered it as if it were yesterday. "There were daffodils outside, so it must have been spring. You met her inside and she said she'd heard you had magic. She was crying. She said she wanted to forget. And *you* told her she had heard wrong and that—and that you weren't fooled and you knew she was working with the other one—and you sent her away. Even though she said she didn't *know* the other one. That she didn't even know what you meant." Lamia did not mention that she'd waited for the girl to emerge from the house again. How, when the girl had fallen to her knees beside a clump of yellow daffodils to sob into their petals, Lamia had leaned out from the tower window and called for her as softly as she could. She'd told the girl where the other had gone— the tall, dark-featured girl with a proud chin and scars around her wrists who had said that she'd come seeking magic and been turned away just the same.

Lamia's father made a noise of recognition. "Oh yes," he said dismissively. "Her. One of many."

"You didn't help her."

"She was unpredictable," he said. As he spoke, he absentmind-edly reached for Eirene, her head still resting against his calf. He stroked his fingers over the top of her head. "Grieving. And marked with the touch of a deathless one. I daren't interfere in what the other gods have decreed."

"But you are not a god," snapped Lamia, her eyes on Eirene. She regretted the words as soon as they had passed her lips. But it was too late to take them back; they hung in the air like dust.

Her father's fingers stilled atop Eirene's head. When he spoke again, his voice was like ice. "You will recall, Lamia, that I set Eirene a task."

"I do," said Lamia quietly.

"It'll take a few weeks for the effects of the Desire to fade. By then, I'm hoping she'll be more amenable to aiding me." He grinned viciously. "But after what I've seen, I think I might have an idea of how to encourage her. Since threatening her *sister* was clearly not sufficient."

Lamia felt sick. What was he implying? That Eirene would do it for *her*?

"Still," her father mused, "while she's like this, perhaps there is something else she can help me with."

Before Lamia had time to reply, he was moving. Crouching beside Eirene, he caught a fistful of her hair in his hand. He twisted it into a knot and used it to pull Eirene's head back so that she was looking him full in the face.

Eirene whimpered.

"The tears of empousa," Lamia's father said. "Invaluable, powerful. But easy to obtain if you know how." He released his grip on Eirene's hair. Then he pulled his hand back and cracked it across her face with a sound like a jar shattering.

Lamia screamed.

Eirene's head snapped to the side with the force of the blow, his ring cutting into her cheek. She made a small noise—a bewildered mewling.

"No, no, *no*." Lamia scrambled forward, her anguish dizzying, making her stumble with each step.

Her father rose to meet her, blocking her view of Eirene.

She lunged for him, but he caught her easily by the shoulders and held her at arm's length. She lashed at him with her stick, but he barely seemed to notice. "Now, now, Lamia," he said, gently chiding, "behave yourself. You might be angry at me now, but I know you will come to understand. You risked everything, my sweet girl, everything that we've been working toward for so very long."

"*We?*" snarled Lamia.

"But of *course*. Everything I do is for us. Did you even consider for a second what would happen to you once dear Eirene knew your secret? She'd flee! She'd tell the world! Within the hour, there would be a village at our door, determined to stamp out the life of the *monster* they knew was beyond it. Eirene would run from you, precious thing." His smile was sad. "*Think* of what you are, what you have done. Would you blame her?"

"She wouldn't," said Lamia. "She *didn't*."

"She didn't *yet*," said her father pointedly. "You are young, sweet girl. And idealistic. But I know what the world is, and I know how fear can render a heart cruel. Eirene is *safer* now. She's happy. Look at her." He released Lamia and stepped aside to reveal the girl hunched on the ground behind him.

"Eirene," said Lamia. "*Eirene.*"

Eirene lifted her head. She was still smiling—achingly lovely and yet empty of everything Lamia had come to love her for. Gone was the determined set of her jaw, the intelligence of her eyes. She was a beautiful blank canvas, unmarred but for where the ring had torn her cheek open. Blood dripped from the jagged gash, shining and dark and—

Saliva welled in Lamia's mouth and she tore her gaze away. Her chest was tight with disgust at herself, at the monster she had not realized she was. Her throat was dry with a sudden thirst.

"*Look at her*," snarled her father, and she had no choice but to turn back. "She is *happy*."

She was hollow.

"And we are *safe*."

And Lamia was the one who had hollowed her.

XXXV

PROFANED AND MADE VILE

Lamia

It took Lamia all her strength to coax—then, when Eirene seemed not to understand, to drag—Eirene back up the stairs into her room. She sat her down on the sheepskin-covered floor, propping her against the wall. Her father had just . . . left. But not before he'd had Eirene take the small brass bowl from him and hold it against Lamia's cheeks until there was a shimmering pool of tears in the bottom. Lamia swallowed and tried to force the thought away.

She still had so many questions. Was she truly her father's daughter or had he just found her somewhere where horrors roamed and brought her here? Perhaps she had hatched from some monstrous egg, like Helen, if Helen had been an ugly sallow-skinned monster that drank the blood of its friends until it inevitably killed them. And who had the other empousa been and why did Lamia see her in her dreams? What had happened to her? And, above all, what was the *point*? Of Desire, of bringing girls to the house for Lamia to feed on? Was her father just another weak man who coveted gold and wealth and power? Despite knowing all that he had done, all that he had concealed from her, Lamia didn't want to believe it.

She had other concerns now, anyway. First, there was Eirene. Lamia had been trying not to look at her, at her empty gaze, but she would have to. She had to. She took a deep breath and turned to look at the girl she had destroyed.

Eirene's eyes were fixed blankly on the opposite wall. Her mouth was twisted into a tranquil smile; she didn't seem to be aware of the gash across her cheek, sticky and filthy, nor the blood dripping off her chin and onto her chiton. She didn't react as Lamia lowered herself awkwardly to the floor beside her, holding the warm bowl of water and a ragged strip of linen torn from her bedsheets.

"All right," said Lamia, swallowing down the lump in her throat. "This might sting a bit." She dipped the linen into the bowl, then carefully pressed it against Eirene's cheek. Eirene kept smiling. Her expression did not slip once as Lamia cleaned the blood and the dust from her face. By the time Lamia was finished, the linen was stained pink.

"That's all done then," she said. "How do you feel?"

Eirene turned to Lamia, her head tilted quizzically. "I feel wonderful," she said after a long pause. She let out a high ringing laugh. "Why wouldn't I? I love it here. Everything is so beautiful. You're beautiful."

Lamia wanted to laugh too. And cry. "Come on," she said softly. "Let's get you into bed." She took Eirene's hands and helped her up, pulling her across the room to the bed and helping her clamber up. Once she was settled, Lamia turned away. She couldn't bear to look at Eirene now—the living proof of all her failures.

Perhaps Lamia could have taken her and run. She could have dragged Eirene back down the stairs again and forced her to clamber through the narrow window in her room. But what then? Her father still had her tears; he still had his Desires. Eirene and her family would never be safe.

Lamia threw a despondent glance over her shoulder at Eirene. She sat at an awkward angle on top of the blankets, slumped against the wall and gazing blankly at her own hands. Without Lamia's father there to fawn over, it was as if she'd just . . . stopped. Like a bear hibernating for winter, unwaking until the springtime.

Lamia wished that she could join her. That she could breathe in a handful of Desire and feel nothing, *be* nothing, until someone came to save her.

"No one is coming," said Eirene.

Lamia stared at her. She hadn't realized she'd spoken aloud, or that the dazed, enchanted Eirene could understand her.

"What?" she said, but Eirene's attention had already drifted away again. Eirene stared out the window and at the roses swaying there. An absent smile played over her lips. Lamia made a soft, hopeless noise. Even in the clutches of Desire, Eirene had said aloud what Lamia could not begin to admit to herself.

No one was coming.

If she wanted to be saved, if she wanted Eirene to be saved, she would have to do it herself.

XXXVI

THE SWEET SLEEP

Eirene

The world had been draped in a blanket of glittering fog. Wherever Eirene looked was a dizzying array of color. None of it quite came together into something she could understand, but it was beautiful.

Eirene smiled and stretched her fingers out, making them dance through the air. The colors swirled in their wake. Blues and golds and greens.

A figure loomed suddenly from the fog. Its appearance was so unexpected that Eirene's heart leaped frantically in her chest, pushing her breath from her lungs. It passed her lips as a frightened squeak. She tried to skitter backward. Her back collided with something hard and she pressed herself up against it, her hands scrabbling against the floor.

"Eirene," came an urgent voice. The figure brought its face closer to hers and Eirene stilled. She had found herself staring into a girl's face, a girl with a pair of eyes that were wide and fearful. They looked like the forest in the sun. A soft brown and dappled gold; she could lose herself in them for days. "Eirene, he's coming. It's time to wake up, Eirene. Please. *Wake up.*"

This made no sense to Eirene. "You have lovely eyes," she told the girl dreamily. She reached out to touch them.

The girl recoiled. "My father is *coming*," she said. "Leandros, I mean. Please, Eirene, you have to—"

But Eirene had stopped listening. "Leandros is coming?" At the sound of his name, her body had the most peculiar reaction. First, she had tensed up all over, her mouth going dry, her hands springing into fists, her mind burning with a sudden flare of . . . what was that? It was gone before she could recognize it, to be replaced with a cool, soothing feeling. *You love Leandros. You would do anything for him,* said a quiet voice that came from nowhere and everywhere at once.

"Leandros is coming," she told the girl, who responded with a wretched sort of wail.

Eirene frowned. Poor girl. But Leandros would come and make it all better.

Yes, Eirene knew who Leandros was. He was all gold and roses and loveliness. She loved him.

You love Leandros, agreed the voice in her head. *You would do anything for him.*

A door opened somewhere, the sound a visible tremble in the glittering air, and the girl stumbled away from Eirene. She extended a slender pale hand, then disappeared again into the swirling, shining mist.

"Oh," said Eirene. "Where did you go?"

Someone laughed. A man with a deep, pleasant voice.

Eirene's body tensed in that strange, frightened way once more, but her muscles relaxed again, even faster than before. *You love Leandros. You would do anything for him.*

Was this laughing man Leandros? She squinted into the fog.

"Don't hurt her." It was the girl, and she was sad.

Eirene turned her head, trying to pick her out in the dazzling strands of color, but she was nowhere to be found.

"Don't hurt her, Father. I'll cry. I'll cry, I promise. Just leave Eirene alone."

Leandros laughed again.

Eirene smiled at the sound. *You love Leandros.*

"I'm afraid it's time you learned, Lamia," he said. "You aren't a child anymore. You can't behave like one, and if you defy me, I will punish you."

Eirene smiled wider at his words. *You would do anything for him.*

"You'll punish *Eirene*, you mean." The girl—Lamia—was angry. Eirene fluttered her hands in the direction of her furious voice, as if she could waft it away. She wanted Lamia to be happy. She wanted them all to be happy.

Except Leandros. She wanted him to suffer. She wanted him to burn.

Eirene blinked. Where had that come from? Already the thought was fading, soothed by that cool feeling. *You love Leandros. You would do anything for him.* She would never want him hurt.

As if summoned by her thoughts, he was suddenly before her, shining and golden and lovely. He was there to protect her. She knew that.

Perhaps that was why the blow took her so much by surprise. A sharp slap to the face snapped her neck to the side and sent a bolt of pain through her dulled mind. From very far away, she heard a girl crying out.

Eirene cupped her hand to her cheek, to the searing pain, and tried to rise to her feet. What was happening? Leandros couldn't have hurt her.

But of course he could. Leandros was a monster. She wanted him dead.

You love Leandros.

Eirene gave up trying to stand and put her hands over her ears, as if it would shut out the voice in her head. She didn't know what was true and what was not. The fog was not just around her; it was in her mind too.

Another blow came to the other cheek. The force of it sent her head back against the wall. She couldn't hold herself upright any longer and she crumpled to the floor, eye level with a sandal-clad foot. Leandros's foot.

She'd kill him.

You love Leandros.

She'd tear every hair from his golden head and force-feed the bloody mess to him.

You would do anything for him. The voice was insistent.

She'd take his daughter—*You love Leandros*—and with it the magic he depended on, and then she'd drive a knife into his heart. She'd smile as he bled out.

You would do anything for him. You love Leandros. You would do anything for him. YOU LOVE LEANDROS. The voice grew louder and louder, the fog around her growing thicker and brighter.

I'll kill him, Eirene told it. The fog was so beautiful, she wanted to plunge into it and let it take her. *I'll kill him.*

You would do anything for him, said the voice. It sounded almost sad.

Then the fog closed in and swallowed her whole.

XXXVII
MOTHER OF ALL THINGS

Lamia

Acid seared the back of Lamia's throat—the bitter taste of hatred. Her father did not seem to feel her furious glare; he only laughed as Eirene gazed up at him, her eyes wide and hurt.

"Oh, don't look like that, pet," he crooned, offering her his hand. "It's just a little game. Come on up, that's right."

Eirene seemed to soften as he helped her to her feet again, his hands tight on her upper arms. The downward twist of her lips relaxed; she tilted her head up to him and patted the weave of his cloak as if to comfort herself.

"There," he said gently. He reached into the pouch at his waist. "You're all right, aren't you? You know I'd never want to hurt you, Eirene." When he withdrew his hand, it was sparkling and silvery. Desire. But Lamia could hardly focus on it; his voice was still ringing through her head. There was something horribly familiar in his tone, in his choice of words. It took Lamia a moment to understand it. That was how her father had always spoken to *her*.

And he was lying. He *did* want to hurt Eirene—he had all but confessed as much to Lamia. There was not a grain of truth in any of his words, and his every tenderness toward Eirene was a facade. Lamia's mind took the reluctant final leap: he was lying to Eirene as he had lied to her, and somehow she had been falling for it for her whole life.

Had her father ever loved her—his daughter, his sweet girl, who had nothing in the world but his protection? Lamia understood little of love, and yet, watching Eirene lean into her father with pliant trust, she knew she could never do as he did. The pain on Eirene's face seemed to be multiplied tenfold in her own heart. She could never strike her, never make her bleed, never make her *cry*.

Lamia put her hands to her mouth to muffle the anguished noise that her lips could not help but shape. It spilled out between her fingers, a quiet sob of pain.

Not quiet enough. Her father let go of Eirene, her lips sparkling with the Desire he'd just tipped into her mouth, and turned sharply to Lamia. In the absence of his hands on her shoulders, Eirene crumpled gracelessly to the floor.

"Lamia." It was the first time he'd looked at her, let alone spoken to her, since his entrance. She had spent every moment of his neglect stoking the fire of her own righteous anger. Under the sudden scrutiny of his icy gaze, that fire sputtered and dwindled. She shrank back in on herself.

"Did you say something, Lamia?" he asked pleasantly. "You know that you can say anything to me."

Her fire wavered again. This time, it was not fear that altered it but a desperate *hoping* that made her chest ache. Perhaps her father was telling the truth this time. Now that his secret, her secret, *their* secret, was laid out before them, maybe he would listen to her.

She cleared her throat. "You're hurting her." She nodded her head toward Eirene. Then, in case her meaning was not clear enough, she said, "*Don't.*"

"Oh, Lamia." Her father tutted. He took a step toward her. "I'm not hurting her. Eirene doesn't mind. Look at her."

Lamia did as he bid, sliding her gaze past her father's bulk to

Eirene. He was right, she *didn't* seem to mind. Her mouth had broadened again into that vapid, silly smile. She had something in her hands—a compact earthenware jar—and was playing with it, tapping the lid against the lip so that the silence of the room was punctuated with a rhythmic *tap, tap, tap.* Dully, Lamia recognized it—the tincture that Eirene had used to send the ram to sleep.

It all felt like years ago. The ram, the cliffs, the bright sun. The thrill of triumph and then of something else as Eirene took Lamia by the hand and led her through the trees. Had it only been yesterday?

"Lamia?" The hand that fell heavily onto her shoulder was not Eirene's, which only made the grip of golden fingers even more unwelcome.

"Don't *touch me*," snarled Lamia, snapping at her father's hand with her teeth. They could rend flesh, she knew that now, and it was gratifying to see him flinch, his eyes flaring wide. He was afraid of her. Good. He should be.

"Lamia," he chided gently, recovering from his shock. "Is that any way to speak to your father? Another man might strike you for that." He offered her a smile. It was manufactured to elicit a reaction from her. *Look at how calm I am*, it said. *See how I am not overreacting.* "But I understand that you're afraid," he went on. "And though a whole day has passed, and you should really have come to terms with this by now, I understand that it can't be easy, Lamia. To have so much change. To discover that you're a monster."

"I am what you made me," she said. "You hid the truth from me. The truth of what I am. If I'd known—"

Her father cut her off with a short laugh. "I did what was best for you, because I am your family, and that is what family does. If you'd known what you were, you'd have turned out exactly as your mother did. A savage beast. A wild thing. I did the world a kindness in putting her down."

Putting her down. The world seemed to turn to ice around them. For a moment, Lamia could not speak. Then, her voice so small it might not have been there, she whispered, "You did what?"

Her father fixed her with his cool stare. "If you want *that* story, you'll have to earn it. I will return when you are calmer," he said coldly. "Until then, Eirene will have no food or water. When she cries out in thirst, *you* may explain to her why she is so deprived."

Not so long ago, his anger alone would have had Lamia weeping. She had always been so desperate for his approval—and fearful for the punishments that his ire invariably brought.

I don't want to do this, he would tell her sadly, as he wrenched her fingernails from their beds. *But you gave me no choice.*

How afraid she had always been, swallowing down her whimpers of pain as best she could. She was afraid of him still. But she would not give him the satisfaction of tears. She bit into the side of her cheek and felt blood pool in her mouth, the pain and salt mingling on her tongue. She smiled and knew from the minnow dart of her father's eyes to her lips that there was blood in her teeth.

Good. She smiled wider. Let him see it. Let him see her for what she truly was.

By the time her father's footsteps faded out of earshot, Lamia had decided what she was going to do. He had been using her to create his Desires for years and years; it was only right that she be the one to destroy them. But she needed help, and her father's words, *I did what was best for you, because I am your family, and that is what*

family does, had given her an idea of how she could start.

She dragged the brazier that had been smoking in the corner to the center of the room. The coals in its broad base had all but burned to ash and glowing embers. But coal was not the only thing that could burn. Lamia marched over to her basket of fresh papyrus. She reached for the scroll and paused, her fingers brushing the edges. For all her father's faults, he had always granted her this—fresh scrolls of papyrus, sticks of charcoal, the closest things she'd ever had to the gifts a normal child would receive from her normal, loving father. They had to go. Lamia ripped a piece free from the scroll, tucked the basket into the crook of her arm, and returned to the brazier. She put the torn piece to the smoldering remnants of the fire and blew softly. The papyrus resisted its destruction for barely a second, then the edge caught in a sudden bright plume. Lamia dropped it into the brazier. She followed it with the rest of the scroll, tearing neat sheets from it with a practiced ease.

"What are you doing?"

Lamia jolted. She'd been so caught up in herself, in the heat and the light and the smell of charred papyrus, that she had not noticed Eirene rising from the bed. Now she stood at Lamia's elbow and gazed up at her with wide blank eyes.

Lamia looked away. Bile rose in her throat. "I'm calling on Aphrodite," she said.

It sounded ridiculous now that she had spoken out loud. She had convinced herself that the flow of Aphrodite's blood in her veins would be enough to capture the goddess's notice. But she could not ignore the fact that that blood was presumably more a trickle than a torrent, having been diluted by generations of mortal women. And an empousa. Lamia clenched her fists. How had she deluded herself into thinking that this could work? She could never earn the goddess's attention. She would never escape her father.

"Oh," said Eirene. "Why?"

Lamia ripped the last curl of the scroll into two. "For my father," she said shortly. *And for you.* She retrieved a fresh scroll from the basket and shredded it, letting each piece shrivel into ash. The papyrus burned quickly; the flames would not last for long. She could not falter. She darted back to her bed and pulled another sheet of papyrus from beneath the blankets. Then she sat on the floor beside the brazier, her injured leg stretched out and the other, the brass leg, tucked beneath her. The secret had been revealed and yet it still discomforted her to see the glint of the metal where the rays of afternoon sun caught it. In her hands she clutched a pile of drawings. Years upon years of drawings. She swallowed. She looked down at the first one, one of the oldest—a black-eyed girl she'd glimpsed once at the door, before her father had turned her away. She dropped it into the fire. Then she followed it with another.

Drawing after drawing disintegrated into ash. Eirene, gone. The blank-faced girl with matted curls and her pathetic handful of daffodils, gone. Sweet-cheeked Alexandra, gone. They were followed by a clumsy drawing of a crocus. The broad body of a ram. An empousa, her teeth bared. "*Aphrodite,*" she whispered. The empousa, again, her eyes soft. "Heed this offering. I am of your blood. Come to me. Help me." Lamia's hands shook as she fed every last memory of her mother to the brazier.

It wasn't enough. Aphrodite did not come.

What else was there? What else was there that was loved and lovely? What else was a worthy sacrifice to the goddess of beauty herself? Lamia ran to the window, snatching the knife from her bed as she went. She had spent years nurturing the roses until they climbed this far, until their heads dipped drunkenly into her room and filled the space with their sweet scent. It took a few seconds to destroy them. Lamia dashed back to the brazier with a fistful of flowers. Blood dripped down her fingers where the thorns had cut her. "Aphrodite," she said again. She squeezed her eyes shut and dropped the roses. There was a wet sort of hissing noise as the flames took them. "For you."

Still nothing. *What else?*

She remembered Eirene smiling, leaning forward to catch a strand of hair between her fingers. *Your hair has red in it.* Eirene had thought it was beautiful. Maybe Aphrodite would agree.

Lamia knew that she was a coward, so the knife was back in her hand before she could think any more on it. She twisted her hair into a thick reddish rope and set to sawing at it. The coppery strands fell in clumps to her bare feet. When she was done, Lamia swept it all into her hands and began to feed it into the fire.

"Please," she muttered. As the flame caught on each new bundle of hair, the air thickened with foul-smelling smoke. Lamia tried to breathe through her mouth, but that was no better; she choked and spluttered, her tongue heavy with ash. "*Please,*" she tried again, more a wheeze than a word. She coughed into the loose fabric of her chiton and wiped her face with the filthy neckline. The last of the hair was burning. Beneath the crackle of the lessening flames, she could hear Eirene humming tunelessly.

"Aphrodite," whispered Lamia, "I have given you every beautiful thing I have. There is nothing left. Help me. I'm begging you, *help me.*"

Still nothing. *Nothing.*

Lamia let out a shriek of frustration and advanced on the flame. She could *feel* the goddess's eyes on her; she was sure of it. So why would she not show herself?

Perhaps this was how Lamia's father felt, hunched over his shrines, begging for recognition from the gods whose blood he shared, whose name he so gracelessly touted. *Aphrodite's name.* Perhaps that was it. Lamia leaned forward.

"He disgraces your name," Lamia hissed into the brazier. "He invokes your lineage at every opportunity so that *he* might be famous, so that *he* might be revered, when you should be." She remembered the actors at the symposium, the prancing Aphrodite who was bitter and petty. "He hires men who ridicule you to a drunken audience. He makes a mockery of love. Of *you.* He is not worthy of your blood, but *I am.* I could be. I just need you to help me." A furious tear dripped from her chin and into the flame.

At last, at *last*, a change. A thickening of the air, a slowing of time. The smell of the burning roses soared and sweetened.

Perhaps it was a trick of the light, but the flames in the brazier seemed to have solidified. Five tongues of fire licked at the air, like a slender hand reaching upward. Lamia found herself transfixed as a single glowing finger beckoned to her. She leaned closer until her proximity to the flames grew unbearable. The skin of her throat burned, but Lamia didn't care; her mind was somewhere else entirely.

The words had not been spoken aloud, Lamia was sure of that, they were just *there*. Hanging in the air where the smoke had been, searing themselves into her mind.

Aphrodite had heard her prayers. She had answered.

Daughter of sons, why do you call on me?

"I—" Lamia licked her dry lips. She was too close to the fire, too close by far, but she found that the heat did not bother her so much anymore. "I need your help. My father, he—"

Yes, you have told me of your father. The voice grew fainter, uninterested already.

"How do I break the hold of the Desires?" blurted Lamia.

A pause. *Why should I care to tell you?*

"They are false Desires; they tarnish what is sacred to you. They destroy those who use them and those who they are used upon. And they—"

And they have your Eirene.

Lamia swallowed. "Yes. They have Eirene."

Only the truth can erase a lie. Only love that is true can overcome the false Desires.

"True love?" Lamia's heart leaped. "That's all?"

Of course not. Aphrodite's laugh was like the chiming of a thousand bells. Beautiful and agonizing.

"Then what?"

Your father learned the secret years ago. The myrtle of the grove in the fields of mourning, where walk the victims of love. If he obtained it, he could master not just desire but love itself. Aphrodite sounded amused. *And it will break the hold of his counterfeit Desires, too. How ironic.*

"So I must go to the Underworld if I want to save Eirene," said Lamia. Another shining tear slipped from her chin. The greedy fingers of flames caught it from the air and devoured it. "Into Hades. I will never make it."

It is easy to enter Hades, daughter mine.

"Then I will never make it back!" cried Lamia. "What good is that to Eirene?"

There is a way. Your father knows it, though it has never admitted him. There is a path, but you cannot walk it alone. He who guards the way, guides the way.

Lamia shook her head slowly. "I don't—"

It is fortunate you left him alive. Even if you robbed him of his horns.

Lamia's lips parted in surprise. "The *ram?*"

You must go to him blind and trusting; the path is not for mortals to know. Offer him the blooms of rebirth and he will know that you wish to return. Take care that you follow him only to the grove and no farther. If you step beyond the trees, you are in the realm of Hades and we cannot help you any longer.

"Stay within the trees," said Lamia. "I understand."

The root of the myrtle is what you seek. With the root of the myrtle and a token of true love, you will break the hold of the false Desire.

"A token of true love," repeated Lamia. Her mind raced. "I will find one."

That will not be your greatest obstacle.

"My father will not allow me to seek the grove."

He will not.

Lamia smiled grimly. "Then I mustn't let him stop me."

She felt Aphrodite's agreement, her pleasure at Lamia's conviction. *You do not need my help for that, daughter mine. Remember, you must not lay eyes on the path. The moment you do, you are lost. Now go! You already have everything you need.*

Use it.

XXXVIII

MOST DREADFUL AND FURIOUS

Lamia

Lamia did not wait for her father to return. She went to him.

She took the stairs carefully, tapping her stick against the stone. She could not risk straining her tightly bound knee, with the last of Eirene's soothing ointment smeared over the skin; she needed all her strength for what she was going to do next. She went barefoot, her brass foot exposed. It made her steps surer somehow.

The little jar of Eirene's sleeping drug was tucked into her armpit, hidden beneath the drape of her chiton. Somehow, she had to convince her father to drink it.

She stopped in front of the tower door and banged on it with her stick as hard as she could. "*Father*," she screamed. "*Father*." Even when she heard the steps on the path beyond, she did not stop her screaming or the frantic drumbeat of fists against wood.

Her father opened the tower door almost into her—she stepped back just in time to avoid it smashing into her face. He reeled back when he saw her.

Lamia smiled and let her stick fall back to her side. "Father," she said.

"Lamia," he said. "Your *hair*." His hand twitched toward the blade at his belt.

Lamia made sure to give no indication of noticing the weapon. She might be able to taste her own fear on her tongue, but she could not allow her father, serpent that he was, to scent it. "I cut it," she said curtly. "To signify a change. A new start, I hope, if you will permit it. I have a . . . request."

Her father's eyebrows lifted. His eyes darted to her bare feet and back to her face. He looked interested. "A request, sweet girl?" What had once been an endearment sounded mocking now.

Lamia looked down at her feet and tugged on the sleeve of her chiton. The gesture would make her look shy, uncertain—better yet, it would prevent him from seeing the truth in her eyes. She had to be clever. Her father could not suspect what she intended for an instant.

"Now that I am more"—she paused, chewing on the possible words—"*illuminated* about everything, I hope we can be transparent with one another. We can work together, I think."

Her father seemed to consider this for a long moment. He lifted his hand to his chin and rubbed the golden stubble there thoughtfully. Lamia had never seen him with stubble. It was a gratifying break in his usual perfection; it was proof that the chaos of the last few days had thrown him off-balance. "What would you propose?" he asked her at last.

"Dinner," said Lamia promptly.

"Dinner?"

"And talking. Ideally at the same time." She attempted an ironic smile. It would be the simplest way to trick her father into drinking the sleeping drug. "I'm hungry."

Her father quirked a brow and she felt her smile slip.

"For food," she clarified quickly. "Just food."

Her father assumed a patronizing, kindly air. "You're allowed to be hungry for other things, Lamia. You know that, don't you? I'll confess, this is why I thought to shield your true nature from you. You've always been sensitive and caring—and, of course, it does you credit—but I knew there was a chance you'd be . . . squeamish."

"Squeamish," repeated Lamia flatly.

"It is time for you to embrace what you are, sweet girl. To *control* it." He gestured toward the stairs with an open palm and an earnest expression. "It is nothing to be ashamed of. I can make sure you won't hurt her. A little more Desire and she won't feel a thing—"

"No," snapped Lamia. Her fear for Eirene was a living creature. Without meaning to, she'd clenched her free hand into a tight fist. Her ragged nails were sharp; they cut into her palms and she felt blood trickle over her fingertips. She looked down in time to see a fat red droplet spatter onto the floor. "No," she said again, calmer, the word an even exhalation. "What I am hungry for now is *understanding*. I am sure you can imagine that I have questions. I hoped you would be willing to answer some of them." She ventured to look at him again, to meet his eye. She was a flame, come to burn him to the ground, and it was he who should be afraid. "Perhaps we can come to some arrangement for my future. For the future of Desire."

"Understanding," repeated her father slowly. He dipped his chin in a thoughtful nod. "Yes. There are some truths that I have kept from you. I have kept you in the dark. But perhaps you are right." He surged forward and took hold of her hands, squeezing them hard between his. The cuts on her palms stung, but she did not allow herself to flinch, even as her father smiled, crocodilian, and nodded again. "Yes, sweet girl. Perhaps it is time that you are illuminated."

※

After her father had ushered Lamia through the garden and into the main house, he bolted the tower door behind her. An unnecessary caution; it wasn't like the hopelessly Desired Eirene would be making a break for freedom. "I'll meet you in the hall, shall I?" he said, less a question than a command that he accompanied with a condescending pat on her head.

I know what I am now. You should be more careful. The words were bolder than Lamia dared and she swallowed them down. "You aren't coming?"

Her father tutted. "I remember when you didn't question my every move, sweet girl." Lamia said nothing and he rolled his eyes skyward before conceding. "Notice is generally required before dinner is served for one more. I have to inform Peiros and it may have to be a simple meal."

Lamia declined to point out that he had rarely given her anything but simple meals. She ducked her chin and brushed past him, heading for the dining room.

Inside, the long wooden table was bare but for a jug of wine. Lamia swore softly. She had been clinging on to some desperate hope that she'd have a moment of unsupervised access to her father's cup. The wine would have to do, and she'd just have to drink as little of it as she could. Would her own magic work on her? Or would it protect her from the effects of the sleeping drug? She wasn't sure and there wasn't time to experiment. She retrieved the jar from her chiton and dumped half of it into the wine jug. Then she sat at the table, hiding the jar in the folds of the blanket draped over her chair, and waited for her father to return. If this didn't work, she still had some of the drug. She could find another way.

She was not waiting long; within minutes he had blown past the curtain into the dining room with Peiros at his heels. Peiros was carrying a tower of flatbreads and bowls of olives and oil, two polished wine cups tucked under his arms. He set down the whole lot and stood back against the wall.

"Peiros," said Lamia's father. "The wine." He indicated the jug.

Lamia's heart did an unpleasant sort of somersault. The wine? Was it going to be taken away and replaced? She hadn't considered that. But Peiros stepped forward again and poured wine into the cups, setting one before Lamia and one before her father. Lamia let out the breath she had inadvertently been holding and felt her shoulders relax. She could do this.

Her father took up his cup and examined her over its rim. "You wanted to talk." He took a sip. "So let's talk."

Fingers trembling, Lamia picked up her cup. Her father was watching her closely. What did he suspect? She brought it to her lips. "Dismiss Peiros," she said, her voice sending ripples over the surface of the wine. "This is a private matter." She took the smallest sip she could, making sure to coat her lips with it so it might appear that she had drunk more.

Her father arched a brow at her request. Perhaps he was startled by her boldness, but it did not seem to displease him as much as she might have expected. He did as she asked, banishing Peiros with a wave of his fingers. He reached for the bread, tearing off a piece and tossing it into his mouth. He waved a hand in her direction now, as if to say *go on*.

Lamia waited until the sound of Peiros's footsteps had faded completely before leaning over the table toward her father. She lowered her voice. "I have questions. First—am I truly your daughter?"

Her father seemed to consider this question for a long while. He swirled the wine in his cup and took a thoughtful sip. She watched his face closely. "Yes," he said.

Lamia faked a sip of her own drink. She could smell the sweetness of her magic beneath the tang of wine. "And who was my mother?"

He leaned back in his chair. "You truly wish to know?"

Did she? Truly? Lamia nodded, not quite able to shape the word "yes."

"Very well." He took another drink from his cup. Soon, he'd have emptied it. Was one cup enough? Should she offer to refill it? Or would that arouse his suspicion?

"Your mother was an empousa," he said, "a monstrous seductress. You are not quite as she was—though, certainly, there is some of that creature in you." His lip curled. "Your leg. The blood drinking."

Lamia tried to keep the hurt from her face. Her father did not love her; he did not care for her. She knew this. And yet his visible disgust, his disgust at *her*, was still a knife wound to her heart. "You said it was nothing to be ashamed of." She sounded too defensive. She lowered her gaze quickly and reached for one of the pillowy flatbreads. It was calming to tear pieces from it and drop them onto the table.

Her father laughed softly. "I would not have you ashamed, though I will not deny that your appetites can be . . . distasteful. But I would never deprive you of your nature, dear little Lamia."

"What happened to her?" She was sure she knew the answer to this—Eirene had already told her of the leg in the workshop. Her mother was a brass-legged empousa. There was a sawn-off brass leg in her father's house. It wasn't too difficult to put the two together. Lamia put her cup to her lips and remembered only at the last moment not to drink. She swallowed the air in her mouth with an exaggerated motion.

"I killed her," said her father succinctly.

It should have hurt, but it didn't. Lamia barely remembered her mother; she didn't know what there was to grieve. She ducked her head to stare fixedly at the table. "Why?"

"Because she tried to kill me. I didn't take it well."

Lamia looked up at him in surprise. "She tried to kill you? But you had a child together. Why would she—" She broke off with some effort. Each word she spoke seemed only to shine a light on her naivety. Wives had been known to kill their husbands throughout history. Why should her father's be any different?

"Oh, sweet girl." His tone was indulgent. "She tried to kill me because she was an empousa. That's all she knew to do."

"How old was I?" asked Lamia quietly.

"Three years old or thereabouts."

"You didn't know how old I was?"

"I met you for the first time that day," he said. "You'll forgive me for it, I hope."

Lamia shook her head slowly. How could he have not met his own daughter until she was three years old? He had, it seemed, always cared as little for her as he did now. "I don't understand," she admitted.

Her father sighed. "My first meeting with your mother was limited to a single night. I lived on the mainland then, traveling from city to city in the company of a group of alchemists. The intellectuals of the cities liked to host us at their symposia, and we were grateful for the food and the wine and the women. Your mother was one such woman at one such symposium. She would sing there, masquerading as a beautiful mortal. Nobody had noticed yet that the men who accompanied her home were rarely seen again."

Lamia listened in silence.

"She took me to her home," continued her father. "A fine house in the hills bedecked with bright hangings and statues and the largest bed you've ever seen. I should have known then—no woman could live alone in such a place. But when I asked her if it was her husband's house, she only laughed at me. She led me to the bed and we—"

Lamia coughed into her wine. A little splashed onto her tongue and she was grateful not to have to hide her wince.

Her father laughed. He raised his cup to her in a mock toast. "And that is how you came about, sweet girl." He drank deeply, wiping his mouth on his sleeve before continuing. "But no sooner was I spent than the house dissolved around me, the fine furnishings fading into gray stone. An illusion. Without it, the house was a cave, and there were bones in the shadows of every corner." He paused dramatically, searching Lamia's face for a reaction.

She bit her lip and tried to keep her features blank. "And then?"

He shrugged. "It was only my speed—a relic of my godly blood, no doubt—that saved me. The beautiful woman I had lain with was suddenly a fearsome creature with hair of flames and teeth dripping in gore torn from my arm. I hit her with a stone, but she barely faltered. She lunged for me. I ran." He smiled, baring his wine-stained teeth. "When I returned to the cave the next day with a band of men and their swords, she was gone."

"But you found her again," said Lamia.

"I found her again," her father confirmed.

Were his words slightly slurred? Lamia's heart leaped.

"And killed her," supplied Lamia.

"She was an abomination," said her father. "Her fate was always to die on a hero's blade. It took me four years to track her down, following the whispers and the rumors and the disappearances, and then the bodies. She put up a hard fight. *You* were her final defense.

She asked if I would truly kill the mother of my child. She found out soon enough what the answer was."

Lamia swirled the wine in her cup and said nothing.

"I thought she was lying, you know." Her father spoke the words like a drunk's confession. He was slurring in earnest now. He drained his cup, dribbling wine. "But then I saw you—and the shining tears on your cheeks as you gazed at her butchered body— and I *knew*. I knew you were mine. I knew I could never let you go."

He reached for the wine jug and missed, upsetting a dish of oil over the table.

Lamia set her cup down with a thud. Finally. "Are you quite well, Father?"

Her father, his brows furrowed, was blinking hard at the wine jug. He looked around at her words, and she felt relief rush through her at the sight of his unfocused eyes—the pupils dilated until they all but swallowed the blue.

"Yes," he managed. "A sudden—" He put his head in his hands, bracing the weight on his elbows. Lamia caught the flare of surprise in his features when his arms gave way beneath him and he slumped onto his plate.

She did not have much time now. "Father!" she said, rushing to stand. Her head spun and it was her turn to brace herself against the table. She probably should have forced herself to eat more, but every bite had been an effort.

She scooped up the jar concealed in the folds of the blanket and hurried over to her father. She kept the jar hidden in her palm just in case he was preparing to shoot upright again; the drug and her tears were no match for his size and strength.

As she drew closer, it became rapidly clear that this was not the case. His curls had fallen into his face, and his mouth was slack. It seemed to take a conscious effort for him to fix his eyes upon her. Lamia could have pinpointed the precise moment he understood. Hatred flooded his features and he groaned a sound that might have been her name. His fingers twitched.

Before she could talk herself out of it, before the fear building in her chest could billow out and take hold of her entirely, Lamia stepped forward and pressed the jar to his parted lips. He tried to turn from her, and it was almost too easy to take hold of his curls with her free hand, to dig her fingers in between the silken strands and pull tight.

"It's easier if you swallow it yourself," she advised him. "But I can help." She forced his jaw shut and used her grip on his hair to tilt his head back, tipping the last dregs of the tincture into his mouth. When he still did not swallow, she clamped her hand over his mouth and nose. As he writhed feebly against her, she saw the bob of his throat. That would keep him sedated for a long time.

She released him and stepped away, bracing herself against the back of his chair as her knee twinged painfully.

"Peiros!" she bellowed. "Peiros! Come quickly! Something is wrong with my father!"

Her father tried desperately to rise from his slumped position, but the drug seemed to be taking greater hold with each passing moment. He managed to lift a trembling hand, but no sooner had it risen than it was crashing back to the table. "Lamia," he hissed, the words slurring, "what are you doing?"

"Be quiet," Lamia advised him. She picked up the wine jug from the table and crossed to the doorway, pushing herself against the wall. She raised the jug in preparation. She could hear Peiros's rapid footsteps growing closer and closer.

"Peiros," her father slurred, the words feeble. "Don't—"

"Hurry!" Lamia yelled, drowning him out easily. She hefted the jug over her head. "There's no time to lose, Peiros! Come quickly!"

The curtain was thrust aside. Peiros's eyes went wide as he skidded into the room and caught sight of the limp form of his master. He looked around wildly for Lamia. She didn't give him a chance to spot her.

She smashed the jug over Peiros's head with all the strength she had. He gave her a surprised, offended look and crumpled to the ground. Her father made a furious noise.

"I'm coming," she told him, trying to mimic the mask of endless patience he always assumed. She brushed the shards from her hands. "No need to shout."

"Lamia," he bit out. His skin had gone an ugly blotchy mauve. Lamia closed the distance between them in a few short steps. Her body hummed with power. Had she always been capable of this? "Lamia, what have you done?"

His eyes moved wildly from side to side. A silver string of drool fell from the corner of his lips, like the spool of some awful spider hidden within the dark wetness of his mouth. Beneath the tang of wine, his breath was fragrant with the sedative as she leaned in close to him. Her voice cracked only a little as she repeated the words that he'd spoon-fed her for years, watching her choke on their poison. "I'm doing this for your sake."

She did not know how long she had until her father stirred again; there was no time to waste. She wanted to be long gone, Eirene at her side, when the moment came for him to open his eyes again.

Lamia went straight to his rooms, pushing the door open and making for the stairs tucked away at the back. She followed them down to her father's workshop.

There was no time to marvel at the space, with its long table and the smell of copper and salt and rotting flowers. Lamia went to the rows and rows of jars and pots and began to lift the lids as fast as she could, peering inside. There was one thing left to find and one to destroy before she left this place forever. First, she had to find the crocuses Eirene had brought him—the flowers of rebirth, Aphrodite had called them. And then . . .

Her father was powerless without his Desires, and Lamia was going to take them all from him.

She found the crocuses quickly—a small bunch with only four of its blooms remaining. Lamia could see where others had been torn away, to make the Desire her father called Loyalty. Lamia tucked them into her sash and kept searching. She did not allow herself to falter, not even when she lifted a piece of gray fabric and caught the familiar shine of brass. The amputated length of leg was stiff and cold, and just the sight of it threatened to send Lamia to her knees. This was all that was left of her mother. But she could not stop. She had to take this grief, this anger, and use it to fuel her revenge. She covered the leg up and moved on, swallowing down bile.

She pulled open a sack and the smell of lentils transported her back to Eirene's room in the tower and those long hours sorting through the night. What a waste it had all turned out to be. No, not a waste—Lamia reached inside and snatched up a handful of the dark seeds. She quickly tipped out a pouch of fragrant petals on the shelf above and dropped the lentils inside. To break the hold of the Desire on Eirene she needed more than the myrtle. She needed a symbol of love, and what could be more perfect than the remnants of that first task? Three days of relentless, monotonous, exhausting work, because Eirene loved her sister.

It did not take Lamia long to discover the other thing she wanted to find.

The amphora was round and squat and small enough to fit in her palms when she cupped them together. The pattern was simple: a winged horse pranced atop a field of swirling flowers. The lid was loose and rattled against the lip of the amphora as she plucked it from its shelf and tilted it from side to side. Something sloshed around inside.

It was almost a formality to cradle it against her chest in one hand and to pluck the lid from the top. She knew what the amphora held; her magic sang to her as if it were a siren. Still, the sight of it—a glittering, sparkling pool of tears that almost filled the jar—took her breath away.

So many tears had been shed for this, and her father had not used them. He'd hoarded them, hidden them away. He had promised Lamia that her pain would be used for good, to spread love and joy. Looking down at the jar, Lamia realized at last how naive she had been.

She let it fall from her fingers. It bounced once on the hard stone floor, a crack marring the pretty painted surface. The second impact obliterated it; shards flew in all directions and the tears spilled over the stone in a shimmering pool. Lamia stared down at her distorted reflection, chest heaving. How much pain did this glittering puddle represent? How many tears had her father forced from her? She turned away. It didn't matter now. He would take nothing more from her.

She moved faster now that she had found the tears. Nothing else here was quite so significant. She peeked inside every pot, every jar, before sending them crashing to the ground. Soon, each step she took was accompanied by the crunch of terra-cotta beneath her thin-soled sandals. A piece embedded itself in the side of her foot, but she did not stop. She left splatters of crimson where she walked.

She left one thing standing—a golden bust of Eros adorned with a wilting headpiece of white flowers. Lamia pressed a kiss to his cold metallic mouth, then stepped back, casting her hand over the shattered remnants of her father's workshop. "An offering for you, grandfather," she said.

The candle in her hand flickered once before she cast it down.

The mess of rose petals and papyrus and herbs was soaked with wine and it caught as easily as a breath. Lamia smiled grimly. She was done here. She had the seeds, the flowers. It was time for her to return to Eirene and to take her away from this place forever.

She bowed once more to Eros. The gold eyes set in a face so eerily like her father's followed her as she slipped from the room, closing the door behind her and shutting out the hissing of flames as the workshop, her father's legacy, and her mother's body caught fire and burned.

XXXIX
VOYAGE TOWARD THE SEA

Lamia

When Lamia returned to the tower, she found Eirene waiting for her—sitting on the edge of the bed, kicking her feet. She was pale and Desired and still bleeding from her cheek, but she was *alive*, and Lamia was going to save her.

Eirene allowed Lamia to lace her into her sandals but made no move to rise. Lamia took Eirene's hands in hers and tried to coax her into standing. She couldn't leave Eirene here, for Lamia's father to find when he awoke. He would never have a hold on either of them again. "Come on."

But Eirene pulled away, shaking her head like a child. "I can't go," she protested. "I have to wait for . . ." The petulance drained from her in an instant, a dreamy smile spreading across her face. "*Him*. Leandros. I love him. I would do anything for him." To see her lovely features like that, drained of their sharpness and intelligence, was a knife to the belly. Lamia was slowly bleeding out.

But when she spoke to Eirene, she forced her voice to be bright. "We're going to do something for Leandros! He'll be so happy when he finds out."

Eirene perked up. "Really?"

Gods, it was agony to look at her. Lamia fixed her eyes on some point to the left of Eirene's ear. "He'll be waiting for us. You don't want to be late, do you?"

Eirene shook her head emphatically. This time, when Lamia tugged at her wrists, she stood quickly. Her expression was eager even if her eyes were still blank and dull. Lamia looked away, unable to see her like this for longer than she had to.

Eirene followed her obediently to the door and trailed her down the stairs. Lamia's entire body felt coiled and tense, fear like a tight cage around her chest. Each moment that passed was another moment when her father could wake and come after them with the full force of his fury. Lamia tried not to recall the vicious glint of his eye as he'd stared at her, slumped over his plate.

She shuddered as she led Eirene outside, into the rose garden, and then around the house to the path. Eirene followed complacently until Lamia pulled her off the path and into the woods. Then she resisted the tug of Lamia's hand. "This isn't right."

"Leandros is this way," Lamia lied. "We have to go find him. He's waiting for us."

"Really?"

Lamia had thought the Desire was meant to make Eirene mindless. Now was not the time to be subverting that. "Yes," she said firmly. "Come on. It's just a little ways through the woods." She would not risk being visible on the main path.

"Where's Leandros?" whined Eirene as Lamia hurried her through the trees. They skirted the path, staying just out of sight. It was a risk to remain so close, but despite living here for all her life that she could remember, Lamia did not know the woods. The path was the only guide she could depend on as she struggled to remember the way they had walked mere days ago.

"Not far!" she promised Eirene brightly, steering her around a fallen log. The words were as much to reassure herself as Eirene. *Not far*. Step after step took them farther from the slumbering

Leandros. Or perhaps—the thought curled snakelike into Lamia's thoughts—he was not slumbering now. Perhaps he was awake and shouting for Peiros to fetch him a mount, perhaps he was slamming open the door with a knife in his hand and fury in his heart, perhaps he was already thundering through the woods toward them—

No. No. Lamia bit down on her cheek, the pain emptying her thoughts momentarily of her father. The taste of blood in her mouth was an appalling sort of comfort; her stomach twisted expectantly and Lamia did nothing to suppress the shudder of anticipation that ran through her body in answer. This was what monsters were, she supposed. Always craving blood. Craving death. She could not look at Eirene stumbling along beside her, still flushed with vitality despite all that the Desire had stripped from her.

Her father would pay for that, Lamia promised the skies and the trees and the soil beneath her feet. Oh, Lamia would make him pay dearly.

It was this hateful resolve that drove her onward. Still, when the distant, scattered lights of the moonlight off the sea finally came into view, Lamia sagged with relief. She allowed herself to turn to Eirene for the first time in what felt like hours.

Eirene looked terrible. Her whining had subsided into the occasional whimper. Her eyes were half closed, her lips parted and cracked around each shallow breath. Her hair was full of foliage and the gash marring her cheek had been joined by a myriad of scratches and scrapes: the kiss of the pine needles Lamia had been dragging her through. She could feel the sting of the cuts on her own face and exposed upper arms.

"Eirene?" she said gently, shaking Eirene's shoulder.

Eirene lifted her head to look up at her. "Leandros?" she whispered. The hope in her eyes was agonizing.

"He's near," Lamia promised her. It might not have been a lie. Was that an animal moving through the trees some ways behind them? Or was it her father, creeping through the undergrowth as he hunted them? Lamia pointed to the sea. "You see that light up ahead?"

Eirene continued to gaze up at her. Lamia picked a twig from her hair and cupped her cheek, turning her head toward the water.

Eirene made a small sighing noise. "Leandros is where the light is." Not a question—a statement. An unfailing belief that Lamia would not lie to her. "That's where we're going."

"Yes," said Lamia, forcing the word through the sudden tightness in her throat. "We're going where the light is."

The closer they grew to their destination, the stronger Lamia felt. They were going to make it. Her father would not be able to stop them.

Her injured knee ached, but her brass leg was strong and unyielding, her stick hit the ground with a comforting rhythm, and her steps were surer than they'd ever been. Aphrodite's words guided her like a lamp in the night; she felt only the faintest twinge of surprise when they reached the beach at last, feet sinking into the loose sand, to find the ram waiting for them at the base of the cliff, his silver face luminous in the moonlight. It was as if he'd known to expect them. As if Aphrodite had sent word that a girl of her blood would soon need guidance to the grove he guarded.

Lamia stopped a healthy distance from him, pulling Eirene to a stumbling halt next to her, and eyed him warily. Aphrodite's blood in her veins or not, she couldn't forget the way the ram's eyes had once darkened as he charged them down, how Eirene had been so close to falling beneath the strike of his horns. And yet, looking at him now, she was not as afraid as she felt she should have been. He seemed diminished, somehow. It was not just the absence of his horns—though Lamia could have sworn they had started to grow back, the ugly silver stumps protruding far more than she remembered—but it was something else, too. Not a change in him. A change in *Lamia*.

The ram took a step forward. He cocked his head and huffed. He had been expecting them. He welcomed them. And now they were wasting his time.

Lamia lifted her chin and greeted him hesitantly. "Ram"—she should have asked Aphrodite whether he had a name—"I wish to visit the myrtle grove. I will go blindly, and trusting, so long as I am sure I will be returned to the light." She offered him the crocuses, stretching out the fistful of flowers into the distance between them.

"What are you doing?" Eirene sounded dazed.

"This ram will guide me to the myrtle grove," said Lamia. "The myrtle is what my—what Leandros seeks."

"Leandros," echoed Eirene. She brightened. "He'll protect me."

Lamia pushed down the urge to scream or turn on her heel and march back to the house to beat her father bloody for what he had done to Eirene. *I can undo the Desire*, she reminded herself fiercely. *I just need the myrtle*. And there was only one way to get it.

She shook the crocuses at the ram again. "I seek the grove," she said firmly. "I ask for your guidance."

The ram approached slowly, head low, coming closer and closer until his wet nose brushed Lamia's hand. He nudged at the flowers, then backed up again, cocking his head.

Lamia bit her lip. Was that it? What had Aphrodite said? *Offer him the blooms of rebirth and he will know that you wish to return.*

Well, she'd offered them. Now what? "I'll bring these with me, shall I?" she asked. "In case you need a reminder at the other end."

She looked to the ram for confirmation. He huffed. Then, very deliberately, he closed his eyes.

"Oh, right." The crocuses were not all. *You must go to him blind and trusting.* "I have to close my eyes?" Lamia guessed. "The whole way?"

The ram opened one eye, gave her a withering look, then closed it again. "Closed eyes aren't good enough, got it. Blindfolded, then?"

No response from the ram. Well, it was better than a haughty one-eyed look at least.

Lamia dropped the crocuses into the satchel—Eirene's satchel—slung across her body. She took up the hem of her chiton in her hands and tore a clumsy strip from it. She tied it around her head, covering her eyes. Light filtered through the gaps in the fabric, just enough to calm her racing heart.

"What are you doing?"

Lamia pulled the blindfold back up and looked at Eirene. Eirene gazed back at her, her eyes huge and black, her full lips parted. She was Eirene and she was not. Where was everything that had made her shine so brightly—her fierceness, her fury, her utter belief that everything would turn out as she wanted? Lamia wanted to shake her, hard, until that Eirene returned to her.

She looked away, reopening the satchel and drawing out the crocuses again. She held the silvery flowers in her palm. Perhaps she should wear them—a clear symbol to anything that lurked below the earth that she would not stay there. That she would return.

"I—" She'd been about to say *I have to go.* But she couldn't. She couldn't say it. And she wasn't sure she could go, either.

Her mother had been fierce and fast and powerful, and her

father had tracked her across kingdoms. He could certainly follow his own daughter's footprints a few miles to the sea. And he knew about the grove; he had sought it himself. It would not take him long to deduce her destination; he would come here when he woke, and he would come swiftly.

Almost without thinking, Lamia pulled the clump of crocuses in her hands into two pieces. She could not let her father find Eirene, Desired and alone and unprotected.

After a quick adjustment of the drape of her chiton at the shoulder, she pinned one clump of the crocuses to her own clothes. Then, with a murmured explanation, she attached the other half to Eirene's.

Eirene looked sick and confused. Her eyes darted back and forth across Lamia's face.

"I can't leave you," said Lamia quietly.

She took the ripped hem of her chiton in her hands and tore another strip from it.

"You must keep this on," she told Eirene urgently, as she laid the blindfold over her eyes and knotted it tightly against the back of her head. She tucked the loose ends of fabric into Eirene's braids, as if that would prevent her from tugging it free if she wished.

Eirene lifted her hands to touch it. "Why?"

"No!" said Lamia, making Eirene flinch. "Eirene, you mustn't. Here, hold this." She pressed her stick into one of Eirene's hands. Even though she knew it would make the journey that much harder, she'd need to hold on to both Eirene and the ram, so she could not use it. "And then you'll hold my hand when I tell you," she said firmly. "You mustn't let go."

She untied and retied the bandages that wrapped her knee, knotting the ends together twice over. She could not afford for them to come loose. Then she pulled her blindfold back over her eyes and grasped for Eirene's free hand. When she found it, she held it tight.

"Ram," she called, "we come to you as the goddess commands. Blind, trusting, with the flowers of rebirth. Will you take us to the grove?"

First she heard him walking across the sand toward them. Then she felt him—his wet nose against her hand. Then the butt of his horn. She grabbed onto the jagged stump, twisting her fingers into the wool that curled around its base.

The ram waited, patiently, until her grip was sure. Then he took a step forward. Lamia stepped too, pushing against his head, pulling Eirene along behind her. The ram took another step. So did Lamia. So did Eirene. Again and again and again until they were walking together in perfect synchrony.

The first change was the sand. Lamia heard the ram's hooves strike stone an instant before her own bare feet found it. Then the air began to cool, though there was no slope to the path they walked. They must be marching straight into the cliffside. Lamia could feel its punishing weight above her. Every so often, a droplet of cool water would strike her face or the tops of her shoulders. The path was narrow: leaves and the soft curves of petals brushed Lamia's cheeks, her arms, her feet as she went. More crocuses? As the foliage grew denser, Lamia longed to take her blindfold off. Surely they must be walking through some extraordinary garden, a tunnel that shone silver with strange, lovely little flowers.

This is not so bad at all, she thought.

Foolish.

The dripping of water suddenly ceased, as did the brush of plants. Lamia could no longer smell the ocean. The path beneath her feet changed abruptly, the roughness of the cliffs replaced by earth littered with detritus that worked its way between her toes. Her heart leaped with terror, her footing became less sure, and she almost stumbled. She tightened her grip on Eirene's hand and on the ram's head. She took a deep breath. And then they were descending, down, down, down, into the belly of the earth.

The incline was shallow and unchanging. They did not turn corners or weave through paths cut out by water; they marched on a path that was as straight as that of an arrow. Eirene's hand felt hot and small and rough inside Lamia's. She had begun to hum— softly, tunelessly. It might have been irritating, had it not served to alleviate the unnatural silence that had descended around them, a quiet so absolute that the rush of blood in Lamia's ears might have been the crashing of waves.

The light that had at first filtered through the coarse weave of her blindfold now faded away; they were walking through darkness, an endless darkness, one that would certainly remain even if she pulled the fabric from her eyes, defying Aphrodite and condemning herself to never make the journey back to the surface. She had slowed as this thought hit her, and the ram jerked his head impatiently to hurry her along. Her fingers slipped and she fumbled to retain her grip. She found it again in an instant, but the fear had already hit her and her breath came now in panicked pants. If she lost him, she too would be lost. And with her Eirene. Any mistake of Lamia's would condemn Eirene to an eternity of wandering in the dark. And Lamia could not allow it. Lamia forced herself to take deep, calming breaths. She knew she wasn't brave, but that didn't matter now. She didn't need to be brave. She just needed to keep going.

The air grew warmer and thicker, then colder, thinner, and colder and thinner still. Lamia felt Eirene shiver, her hand tightening on Lamia's. Lamia squeezed it, willing the warmth of her body to rush into Eirene's.

"I'm cold," said Eirene, her voice small and tired. They were both in thin clothes suited for the late spring; Lamia did not know how much farther they would be able to go if the air continued to cool.

"We're almost there," she said to Eirene desperately. "Not long now."

They must have been walking for hours. At some point, after she'd tripped over what felt like a tree root but could have been a snake or the skeletal arm of a corpse reaching out to her in the dark, Lamia's leg had started to hurt. Once she'd righted herself, her fingers clamped over the ram's horn in a terrified vise, she found herself contending with a sharp twinge of pain in her knee every time she lifted her foot to take another step. It hurt badly at first, as it always did, but at some indeterminably long time after that, the pain had seemed to merge with the rest of the horror—the crushing blackness, the endless tilt of the path, the occasional sound of wingbeats or the brush of something warm and damp and searching across her cheeks—and she found she did not feel it so strongly. After a while, her sense of it became so detached that—though she knew, distantly, that she was hurting—the pain did not seem to belong to her anymore. She clutched tight to Eirene and squeezed her eyes shut. That helped a little, with the fear; it kept the darkness at bay.

Her mind drifted pleasantly, floating away from her like a duck on a pond in a low wind. Somehow, it came to rest on a memory of her mother. One that had been buried deep in the recesses of her mind, pushed there by her father's unnatural alchemy. It must have been a memory from when she was very young. Her mother looked impossibly tall and beautiful, her long auburn hair cascading over her shoulders, and Lamia was curled in her lap. Her mother's hands were outstretched, and she was making shadows and sparkling colored lights dance together on a craggy stone wall. The lights resolved themselves into a glittering scene, a clear pool of water that rippled with movement as fish darted beneath its surface. Lamia watched now as she had watched then, utterly captivated. She almost forgot where she really was—walking into the Underworld, one hand clasped with Eirene's, the other resting lightly upon the jagged stump of the ram's horn. They kept pace so easily now that she hardly needed to hold on.

Then he came to an abrupt halt, pulling Lamia from the memory and back into the dark. His horn slipped out from beneath her hand. Lamia grabbed for him, lunging forward, slipping on the wet ground, dragging Eirene along behind her, but her outstretched hands did not find his head again. Her fingers didn't even brush a single curl of wool. He was gone. He had left her.

XL

BY A NEW CONCOURSE

Lamia

Lamia made a soft sound of terror. Her eyes were still squeezed shut beneath her blindfold, and now she pressed her free hand over them too. She was terrified to open them, to find that there was still nothing but darkness filtering through the cloth. She could not stand to hope that it might be something else, something more. That they had emerged once more into light. She strained to listen over her own ragged breath and her pounding heart. Eirene was quiet behind her, but was that the distant sound of water or the rush of blood in her ears? Was that the shuffle of footsteps on leaves? The whisper of a girl's voice?

No. Whatever it was, she had to calm down. Think of a plan. Eirene would approach this carefully, systematically, as she had all her tasks, and she would emerge victorious. That was what Lamia had to do.

"Ram?" she called, her voice cracking. "Ram, where are you?"

Nothing. Lamia swallowed. Either the ram had abandoned her at her final destination or he hadn't. Her next step was the same either way. She needed to *look*.

If she was lost somewhere on the path to Hades, she was already lost. But with the blindfold removed, she might be able to find the ram again. Then she could make him return Eirene to the surface at least; it was a comfort that one of them, the better of them, would live.

She held tight to Eirene and groped with her free hand behind her head, finding the knot. It was impossible to undo one-handed, and it had become hopelessly tangled in her hair. Eventually, she gave up on trying to pick it free and just yanked it down as hard as she could, tearing away what felt like a sizable clump of hair with it. It hung like a dead snake around her neck.

Lamia breathed deeply. Once. Twice. Three times. It was time.

She opened her eyes and light—*light*, soft and gray and a little greenish and so utterly welcome Lamia could have wept—flooded her vision.

They were standing in the center of a small marshy clearing. The sky was a wash of gray without sun or moon or stars, nothing but a steady pale light that filtered through a swirling fog. The air was cool but not cold, and sweet with a subtle floral scent. Moss covered the ground in a damp blanket and Lamia, relieved and exhausted in equal measure, fought back the sudden urge to lie down, to sink into it. On all sides of the clearing were shrubby trees with dark green leaves and hundreds of perfect white flowers. Behind those trees were more, their branches shifting in a wind that seemed to come from every direction and none at all at the same time.

Lamia could not help the smile that spread across her face. They were myrtle trees. She had made it to the grove.

The ram stood at the edge of the clearing, where one of a dozen swirling myrtle-bordered paths began. "You bastard," Lamia told him, startled by the swell of affection that had risen up within her at the sight of him. "You could have warned me that we were here. I thought you'd abandoned us."

He sniffed—a human sound—and stamped his hoof.

"Thank you," admitted Lamia. "You brought us to the grove

unharmed. We would never have made it without you." When the ram continued to look unimpressed, she offered him a stiff little bow. He sniffed again and retreated a little farther along the path. He stamped his hoof again, then put his head into the nearest cluster of myrtle flowers and began to eat them.

Lamia let go of Eirene's hand. Eirene made a high panicky noise. Her other arm, which had been hanging limply at her side, flew up and she beat at the air around her with the stick she still held. She took a few shuffling steps forward, her feet sinking into the marshy ground. "Lamia?" she whimpered.

"Here, I'm here." Lamia caught her by both wrists and pulled her closer. "Here, it's all right. You're safe. I'm here. Let me take that blindfold off for you." She reached behind Eirene's head and carefully teased the loose ends free from her braids, before pulling the blindfold clean off.

Eirene let out a relieved little sigh. Her pupils were huge and she had to squint in the low light. She clutched Lamia's stick, her knuckles white.

"Let me take that," said Lamia. She pushed it against the soft ground, comforted by the familiar feel of the wood. Then she unpinned the clump of crocuses from Eirene's shoulder and dropped it into the satchel. They might need the flowers to return, after all, and she wasn't sure she could trust Eirene with them.

"Stay here," Lamia told her. "I won't be long." *Root of the myrtle and a token of true love.* That was all she needed to return Eirene to herself, to return Eirene to *Lamia.* She had the token of love—the pouch of seeds tied securely around her neck. Now she just needed the root, and it was better that she was swift to obtain it. The clearing, with its fog and its flowers and the gentle rustling of the wind through the trees, felt too much like a dream. At any moment it could become a nightmare. They were in Hades, after all.

In the short time standing still Lamia's knee had stiffened, so she gave it a few slow experimental swings and hissed as the feeling returned—along with the pain. Typical. She squared her shoulders, pushed her stick into the wet ground, and marched toward the—

"Agh!" She let out a terrified yell and pitched forward as her foot sank suddenly, disappearing along with half of her shin. It was only rapidly whirling both her arms and reeling backward with the rest of her body that saved her from falling face first into what had looked like solid ground but had just revealed itself as a rancid bog full of tar-dark mud. She sat back heavily on the wet grass and tried to pull her foot free. The earth seemed to pull back just as hard; at last it relinquished her foot with a sickening squelch.

The leaves and little plants that covered the surface of the bog swirled and resettled.

Lamia breathed deeply. She could have sworn she'd just put her stick down there and that the ground had felt firm. But she must be mistaken. And yet, she could not shake the feeling that the earth had *moved* just as she'd stepped onto it, opening like the maw of a starving beast.

"Stop it," said Lamia out loud. She couldn't think that way. She pushed herself to her feet and continued on more carefully, probing the ground with her stick before she took a new step, retreating whenever she felt that it had begun to give. She did not fall again and she began to believe that she had been mistaken. The ground was not *moving*. More likely, Lamia was exhausted and terrified and she'd misstepped. Still, it was only when she reached the edge of the clearing and laid her hand tentatively against the leaves of a myrtle tree that she let out the long breath she'd been holding since her fall.

It was the myrtle root she needed—that was what Aphrodite had said. She knelt, bringing her face close to the base of the tree. "Don't let me down," she whispered to it.

She pushed her fingers into the soft wet earth and began to carefully scrape the mud away, teasing the roots free without breaking them. Her hair fell into her face and she pushed it back irritably, not caring that her hands were filthy or that they left a clammy trail where they had brushed her skin. Nor did it matter that the damp was seeping through her skirts or that dark crescents of dirt had already worked their way beneath her fingernails or that her aching knee was sinking deeper and deeper into the mud. How her father would have scorned to see her like this, and yet she had achieved what he had not. She had walked the path into Hades, she had entered the myrtle grove, and she would hold in her hands the missing piece in his desperate hunt for true desire and she was going to use it against him. She was going to save Eirene. She drew her knife and dug it into the arch of a root her digging had revealed. With a quick sawing motion that brought to mind those hours in the sun separating the ram's horns from his proud head, she cut the root free. Then another. And another. She collected them together into a bundle. Perhaps just one more—

"Lamia?" An appallingly familiar voice shattered Lamia's reverie and she jolted as if she'd been shot through with an arrow. With the bundle still clutched in her hand, she stood, her stick sinking into the ground. She drew in a sharp single breath and turned to greet the newcomer.

"Alexandra," she said. Each word felt like a bee sting as it passed her lips. "You're here."

"Lamia," said Alexandra again. Her voice was full of surprise, recognition and, beyond that, grief. Grief that ran so deep and wide it wounded Lamia just to hear it. "I thought it was you." She looked exactly as Lamia had remembered her—before the bloodless hands had curled like dead spiders, before the limp body was laid out on the sand. She looked dark-eyed and round-hipped and painfully pretty. She looked imagined. She looked dead.

Lamia made a wordless sound of misery. She had done this. Alexandra was dead because of her. The proof of her monstrosity stood before her in the shape of a girl.

Alexandra took a step closer. There was a peculiar quality to her when regarded this closely, like a woman woven into a tapestry. A lack of definition to her shape: a blur around her edges, a paleness to her features, a faint shimmer to her hair and skin, as if they were trying to dissolve into the air around them. She frowned. "You shouldn't be here," she said, the words like the wind. "What happened?"

I killed you. It was so simple, and yet Lamia could not say it, no matter how much Alexandra wanted her to. "I'm sorry," she choked out instead. "Alexandra, I'm so sorry. I didn't mean to. I never wanted to hurt you. My father, he—" A sob swallowed the rest of her sentence. How dare she cry when she was still alive, when she had the land and the sky and the sunrise and Eirene to return to, while Alexandra would be here forever?

"Lamia," said Alexandra. She put a hand on Lamia's arm. She was still warm.

"I didn't *know.*" Lamia covered her mouth with her hand to hide her grimace of anguish, to hide her teeth. "I didn't know. I'm so sorry, Alexandra. I know you will never forgive me, but please, please believe me. I didn't know."

"It doesn't matter," said Alexandra gently.

Lamia's legs trembled beneath her. It was almost a relief not to be forgiven. She did not deserve it. "Yes," she said. "You're right. It doesn't. It doesn't matter why I did this to you, only that—"

"It doesn't matter," said Alexandra again, more forcefully. She drew Lamia closer to her, pulling her into a tight embrace. The shock of it was too much; Lamia wept into her shoulder, unable to stifle her anguished gasping sobs as the grief and the guilt pulled her under again and again. Alexandra murmured into her hair, her warm breath brushing her cheeks, "I don't blame you, sweet Lamia. Without you, I would never have been free."

"You aren't free," said Lamia without thinking. "You're *dead*."

"What of it? There was no freedom to be had in a life like mine." Alexandra pushed Lamia away with a gentleness Lamia did not deserve so that their eyes could meet. "Do not cry, Lamia," she said firmly. "I do not blame you for anything and I cannot bear to see you grieving."

"You should hate me," said Lamia. "I killed you."

"Leandros killed me, with his Desires and his ambition. You *saved me*."

"And condemned you to spend eternity here."

"It is not so bad. A little wet. And lonely, sometimes, but there are others who walk the same paths, who offer comfort and company." Her eyes raked over Lamia. "But you are not one of them. You are—"

"I'm not dead," said Lamia. "If that's what you mean." Not yet, anyway. "I am only here a little while. I'm going to go back."

Alexandra smiled. "That is good," she said. "It grieved me at first to see you here. To think that you were gone. But now, I am glad to see you."

"Perhaps I can come back," said Lamia eagerly. "To see you if you are lonely. The ram brought me here once—"

But Alexandra was shaking her head. "I do not think so," she said carefully. "Now that I have seen you, that I have spoken with you, I have a great temptation to return to the paths of the grove, to become unknown once more. The dead, I think, cannot be too greedy in their pursuit of resolution."

"So this is our last conversation? Ever?"

"I think it must be." There was a weight to Alexandra's words; their truth made them substantial, undeniable.

Lamia bit her lip. "I wish it didn't have to be. I wish it was different."

"We all wish for something different." Alexandra squeezed Lamia's hand tightly. "When you go back, make sure things change, Lamia. For me, if not for yourself."

"I will," promised Lamia. "Alexandra, I—"

Her words were swallowed by a high terrified shriek that rang through the clearing, then cut out as swiftly as it had begun.

Lamia jerked around so fast she only just avoided smacking her forehead into Alexandra's. "Eirene!"

The patch of damp grass where Eirene had been standing was empty. But something was thrashing a little ways away, where the earth grew watery and treacherous. As Lamia watched, a mud-streaked hand burst from the boggy ground and grasped uselessly at the air.

"Eirene!" shrieked Lamia again. Eirene must have grown bored of waiting and followed her. She whirled to face Alexandra. "Alexandra, I'm sorry. I have to—"

"Go." Alexandra pushed her away. "I am glad I could see you one last time, Lamia. You were the kindest creature in that house. To the very end. Now go!"

Lamia did not need any more encouragement. She took one

last fleeting look at Alexandra, then she turned back to the path she'd carved with her footprints, back toward Eirene.

She reached her just in time to see that Eirene—Desired and bedraggled as she was—had the situation somewhat in hand. She'd clawed her way to the edge of the bog and, having maneuvered herself into a roughly horizontal position, was attempting to worm her way free.

"I told you to stay still!" wailed Lamia. She threw herself to the ground. Her knee screamed in protest but she forced herself to ignore the pain, tossing her stick aside and grabbing for Eirene just as Eirene lost her grip and went sliding back into the filth. "*Stay still*," bellowed Lamia.

Eirene gurgled something and did not stay still. Lamia found herself trying not just to pull Eirene free but also to sort of wrestle her. It was not easy; loathe to put it down, Lamia still clutched the clumsy bundle of myrtle root in one hand.

"Stay still," shouted Lamia for the third time. "I'm trying to stop you from drowning. Would you just let me?" At one point, she accidentally put her hand in Eirene's mouth—narrowly avoiding choking her with the myrtle root. Eirene spluttered, spitting out twigs and mud and Lamia's fingers. This gave Lamia a momentary advantage. She grabbed Eirene beneath her muddy armpits and yanked her from the bog. Eirene flailed and fought, but Lamia did not let go. She dragged her along the safe path she'd marked, smearing her own careful footprints, until they reached the relative safety of the myrtle bushes. She laid the coughing, spluttering Eirene out beneath their shallow cover.

Then, utterly exhausted, she collapsed to the ground next to her.

XLI

THE WATER OF THE RIVER

Eirene

When the glittering fog finally lifted and Eirene returned to herself, she found that herself was lying flat on her back covered in mud, feeling like she'd just been run over by a chariot. She was cold, her legs ached, her face hurt, and her mouth tasted like she'd not just been rolling in the mud but eating it too. Even in the fog's absence, her thoughts felt wispy and confused: cloudlike.

Someone was lying beside her; she could hear them breathing heavily, like they'd been running. Eirene had absolutely no idea who it was. She didn't know where she was or how she'd gotten there, let alone who had accompanied her, but there was a weight in her chest and a catch in her own breath, so she knew that she had been afraid. If the fog had been what she thought it was, then she had also, until a few moments ago, been under the influence of one of Leandros's Desires. Perhaps she should be still.

So she just lay there, perfectly immobile, and listened. It was not Phoebe at her side, that much was certain; she knew her sister's breathing as well as her own. Nor did she think it was Leandros. There was a softness to the sound that she could not reconcile with Leandros's sharpness. Surely there was only one person it could be, and yet Eirene did not dare to hope, not with the fog still clouding the edges of her vision and the sickly taste of fear still coating her tongue like honey. Better to find out for certain. She turned her head without lifting it and was rewarded with the distinctly unpleasant feel of mud squelching against her scalp. That hardly mattered, as she found that she was looking at Lamia.

The recognition and relief and sheer joy that surged through her at that discovery left her near breathless. Lamia was as filthy as Eirene felt—caked head to toe in a thick greenish sludge that had soaked through her clothes and seemed in real danger of becoming a permanent addition to her being. The reddish shine of her hair was barely visible through the filth that plastered it to her face, her neck, and the pale jut of her collarbones above her tattered chiton. It seemed they'd both been involved in a kind of altercation. Apparently, with the ground itself, which was cold and wet and generally unpleasant.

Lamia was not looking at Eirene. Her eyes were open, but they were fixed decisively on some point in the low branches stretched out above them. Her chest rose and fell as she breathed deeply; both her hands were pressed to her breast, to her heart.

Eirene waited for Lamia to notice her. When this seemed unlikely to happen in a punctual manner, she decided to alert Lamia to her regained consciousness. She pulled a twig out of her mouth—then a second; had they been fighting the bushes as well as the ground?—and considered how to begin.

She settled on "Oh, good, you're here too." Then, as Lamia snapped her head around to stare at her with a crunch like a snail shell underfoot, her hair stuck to her face, her eyes wide, her mouth falling open, Eirene offered her an apologetic smile and asked, "Where exactly are we?"

※

Once she'd recovered from the initial shock, Lamia hurled herself into Eirene's arms, getting even more mud in Eirene's mouth—and a little hair this time, as a treat. She clung to her like she was drowning and was determined to drag Eirene down with her.

"Well?" said Eirene to the top of Lamia's head. "Where are we? I didn't even know Zakynthos had a—what is this, a swamp?" She could not bring herself to ask about the Desire that had infected her mind. She did not want to know who she had been in that time or what she had done.

"A grove," said Lamia, her voice muffled in Eirene's chiton. Her grip was like iron. "A myrtle grove."

"A swampy grove, you must admit." Eirene considered the masses of little trees sprouting around them, continuing in haphazard lines as far as the eye could see, with renewed interest. "Myrtle," she mused, frowning. "That feels significant. I feel as if I were just discussing it with someone, though I cannot imagine why."

At last, Lamia released her, sitting back and grimacing. The mud smeared across her face was beginning to dry, cracking as it did so, so that she seemed to be covered in soft brown scales. "You don't remember?"

So Eirene had forgotten things. A lot of things by the sound of it. She decided not to let that alarm her. Her heart elected to ignore this decision; it gave an anxious little skip and redoubled its beating. "I don't," she admitted. "The last thing I remember is . . ." She trailed off. Lamia stayed quiet as she strained to recall. What was the last thing she remembered? She remembered sitting on the floor of the tower room with Lamia, her hand curved beneath Lamia's thigh. She remembered running her fingers over the shimmering brass where flesh should have been. She remembered the swell of tears in Lamia's pale eyes. She remembered thinking about kissing her. At some point, she had become enchanted by Desire, though she could not have said when. "The tower room," Eirene said hastily, rushing to fill the silence. She felt herself flush, her cheeks growing hot beneath the caked-on grime.

"You remember . . . me?" asked Lamia, her voice very small. "You remember what I am?"

"I've always known what you are," said Eirene. She remembered the discovery that Lamia was the empousa they had searched for. And, beyond that, she remembered how Lamia's face had crumpled, how she had seemed to shrink in on herself. "You're Lamia. You're kind and you're brave. You helped me."

"Yes, but—"

"I remember what you are," said Eirene firmly.

"And you remember my father finding us?"

Eirene nodded slowly. Yes, that was right. Leandros had burst into the tower room to find Lamia sprawled out on the ground, her brass leg bare and cradled in Eirene's hands. He had smiled. He had seemed amused. And then he had told them—

"No," gasped Eirene. The Desire. What had it done to her? She shot to her feet so quickly that her vision blurred and she crumpled to the floor again. "Lamia, no." The shrub beside them was splendid with flowers. Eirene grabbed for a handful of the white blossoms and brought them to her nose, crushing the delicate petals between her fingers. The scent was heady and sweet, unnaturally so. *No, no, no, no, no.*

"Lamia," she moaned. "This is the grove. The grove of myrtle Leandros talked about. Where walk the victims of love. Lamia, are we dead? Did we die? Did he kill us with the Desire? Both of us? Lamia, I don't remember."

They were dead. They were *dead*. All the tasks, the schemes, the hope, and it had come to this: Lamia and Eirene, in Hades together, covered in stinking mud. Dead.

The touch of Eirene's filthy hair against her skin had seemed so inconsequential moments ago. Now she was so aware of it that it made her sick, that she wanted to rip it from her skull in handfuls. Her clothes were sticking to her body; her feet were bare and cold. She doubled over, gasping for air, her throat too full of terror to make space for breath. She clutched at her neck.

"He didn't kill us!" Lamia was there, suddenly, pulling Eirene's hands from her throat with surprising strength. She tugged Eirene back from the myrtle shrub and folded her into her own arms, holding her tight against her chest. Then, with one arm still clutching Eirene, she pushed the hair back from Eirene's face, twisting it one-handed into a knot at the base of her skull. It was an instant relief—Eirene no longer felt as if columns of ants were marching across her cheeks and down the line of her neck. "He didn't kill us," insisted Lamia. "We aren't dead."

Still, Eirene shook her head. "This is the grove," she breathed. "Can't you feel it?" The cool wet air. The whisper of the wind, as if the voices of the dead stirred the leaves from the trees. The ground that seemed to be pulling them in. "This is the land of the dead."

"The living can walk there too," said Lamia. "And we are living."

"This is Hades," said Eirene.

"Yes." Lamia pulled back. "But we are *alive*, Eirene, wherever we are." She grabbed Eirene's hand and guided it to her chest, just above the slight swell of her breasts. "Here, can't you feel the beat of my heart?"

And mine, Eirene might have said. It was a wild thrumming

inside her. Her breath caught; Lamia was so warm beneath her touch. Her cheeks were flushed, her eyes were bright. She was beautiful, lovelier than the myrtle, than the sun Eirene would never see again, and her vitality was a torch that burned away some of Eirene's terror.

A little but not all; they were still here, in the grove, in Hades, and they both should be dead. "How?" Eirene asked at last. "How did we get here? Are we—are we stuck here forever?"

"The ram brought us," said Lamia. "And he will take us back, too."

"But *why*?"

"You were Desired," admitted Lamia unhappily. "I had to break it. I had to."

"Desired." Eirene shivered involuntarily. "Yes, I thought so. There was a fog in my mind, covering everything I saw and heard and *thought*. It kept telling me that . . . that I loved Leandros. That he would *protect me*." Her mouth twisted around the final words; she all but spat them.

"I learned how to break its hold," said Lamia. "That's why we came here. I was going to . . . But you said the fog is gone now?"

"Gone," confirmed Eirene. "You know how to break the hold of Desire?"

"It has always faded with time. I know that," said Lamia. "But when there is not time, there is another way. The very thing my father searched for."

"The myrtle?"

"The root and a token of love."

Eirene picked a small piece of twig from the corner of her mouth. "Myrtle root," she said slowly. Then, with a soft laugh, she looked at Lamia. She could not stop herself from smiling. "What was the token of love, then?" She posed the question as if she had not already guessed the answer. What else could it be but the root itself? The root that Lamia had traveled into Hades for, had risked her life for? Because Eirene had been under the thrall of Desire and Lamia had *had to* break it.

"I was going to use the seeds you sorted," said Lamia. "A token of your love for Phoebe. It was all I could think of." She reached into the pouch strung around her neck and pulled out a handful of grain.

Eirene's mind went blank. "Phoebe," she whispered. She looked from Lamia to the grain and then back to Lamia without truly seeing, her heart gripped in a fist of terror. "*Phoebe*, Lamia. Where is Phoebe?"

"I don't—"

"You ran from Leandros. You took me with you. What if he goes after Phoebe? What if he takes her, Desires her? He said if I ever left that he would! I have to go to her." She tried again to stand but Lamia pulled her down easily. She was *smiling*. How could she be smiling?

"He won't," said Lamia confidently.

Eirene glared at her. "And how could you know that?"

"Because he hasn't got any Desire left," said Lamia. "Because I went into his workshop and destroyed it. I burned it. All of it."

Eirene stopped trying to get up. "You—you what?"

"I burned it," repeated Lamia. "I found my tears and I poured them out and then I threw everything into a pile and burned it. All the Desire and everything he could use to make it. It's all gone." She squeezed Eirene's arm. "It's gone. We're safe. We're—we're free of him. The ram will take us back to the surface and you will find Phoebe safe and well. I promise you."

Eirene nodded slowly, her panic fading. "We'll get Phoebe," she said, "and we'll go."

"Go?"

"Somewhere—I don't know where, but somewhere away from here. All of us. Phoebe can weave and I can sell her weaving, and you, Lamia"—she grabbed Lamia's hands and held them tightly—"you can do whatever you like. You'll never need to shed a single tear again."

But Lamia didn't smile at this proclamation the way Eirene had expected. Her face fell and she turned away.

"What is it?" Eirene asked.

"I can't come with you," said Lamia.

"What? Why not?"

"I don't . . . I still don't fully understand what being an empousa is. What it means. I could hurt you. I've hurt people before—"

"You would never have hurt anyone if you knew what you were doing," interrupted Eirene. Her temper flared. She would not lose Lamia to *this*. She would not allow Leandros to hurt Lamia anymore. "You can't blame yourself. It's not fair."

"Life isn't fair," said Lamia dryly.

"Exactly," said Eirene. She stabbed her finger into Lamia's chest. Maybe she was getting carried away. But she was so *angry*. How dare Leandros do this? "And it's infuriating. It's always been like this—you've heard the stories."

"This isn't a story, Eirene," said Lamia. "It's my life."

"It was their lives, too. Scylla, Medusa, Charybdis, Arachne, a hundred more like them." Eirene's voice rose as she listed them off. "It is an unspoken truth, is it not? That the most appalling thing you can do to a woman is rob her of her beauty and her helplessness, turn her into some beast, some monster. Fashion her into something to be terrified of. Who cares that she was *made* that way, that someone did that to her? There is nothing worse than a woman made wild."

Lamia eyed her skeptically. "Arachne wasn't turned into a monster. She's just a spider."

"I hate spiders," said Eirene. "They're terrifying. But, Lamia, you aren't. I am not afraid of you."

Lamia only shook her head. "You should be. I know what I am."

"Do you?" said Eirene. "Really? Because a few days ago you didn't have a single idea of what you were, and I don't think it could change that fast. I don't think you've scratched the surface of your magic, and I don't think you know how your—your hunger works. How *could* you?"

"I know that I hunger for blood," said Lamia. "That that hunger is strong enough to make me a killer."

"Maybe it doesn't need to," said Eirene. "Think about it. The night I had dinner with Leandros, I woke up with blood on my pillow. I think you fed from me. And I'm still alive. Maybe with Alexandra, something went wrong. Your father miscalculated. But now that you know what you are, I'd bet anything you don't *need* to kill."

"That's an excellent theory," snapped Lamia. "Shall we just wait for the next time I go on a murderous rampage to check it?"

"We can check it now," said Eirene. "Bite me." She offered Lamia her forearm.

Lamia looked at her with abject horror. "Excuse me?"

"Bite. Me. Just on the arm, I'd prefer you stayed away from my throat. Drink a little and then stop. Keep your control."

"What if I can't?"

Eirene cast around for inspiration. Her eyes fell on the knife in

Lamia's belt. She reached out and snatched it away. "I'll stab you with this," she said. "Come on." She offered Lamia her arm again.

"Eirene . . . ," said Lamia. Her shoulders were high and tense.

"Lamia," said Eirene. "Do it."

"What if I don't want to?"

"I won't make you. I'm not your father. But I want you to come with me, Lamia. With me and with Phoebe and away from here. Will you try? For me?"

The moment that Lamia relented was obvious—she squeezed her eyes shut, then her shoulders fell slack. She let out a long audible breath. "Fine."

"Fine?" repeated Eirene.

"Fine!" said Lamia. She opened her eyes and grabbed Eirene's proffered arm, bringing it to her mouth. "Fine, I'll do it. But if I hurt you—"

Eirene waved the knife with her free arm. "Don't worry, I'm ready."

"Really?"

"Really." Eirene braced herself.

Lamia parted her lips, whether to speak or to bite down, Eirene didn't find out. At that moment, the ground shook violently and then opened beneath her.

Eirene shrieked, then spluttered, her mouth filling with mud as she tumbled into the bog that had appeared around her. Coughing and choking, she flailed for purchase, and found it—both hands closing over the warm hard flesh of Lamia's brass leg just as her head went under. Distantly, she could hear Lamia screaming. She pulled hard and managed to resurface, lifting her head above the water.

Lamia's screams resolved into words.

"I *knew it*," she shrieked.

As Eirene had caught hold of her, Lamia had thrown herself back into the embrace of the nearest myrtle bush and was hanging on to it, white knuckled. "Let her go! Let go!"

Eirene managed only an awful hacking cough. Mud splattered her chin. In response, the mud around Eirene's legs seemed to grow thicker. It *pulled*. She slipped, her hold moving from Lamia's calf to her ankle.

"*Lamia*," she choked out.

"Don't let go!" shrieked Lamia. "Ram, *ram*. We want to leave! Ram, take us back, *please*."

The swamp was still pulling and now the mud had begun to *climb*, tendrils of filth snaking around Eirene's forearms, creeping over her chin. She made a wordless sound of terror. All she could do was hold on.

"Ram!" bellowed Lamia. The myrtle was bending, leaning toward the swamp, unable to stand against the force of Lamia's desperate pull.

The mud reached Eirene's wrists, her fingers. It began to push its way beneath her grip, prying her fingers up one by one. "*Lamia*," she sobbed. A tendril of mud slid into her mouth. She spluttered and spat, but now the mud was surging into her nose, her eyes. One of her hands slipped from Lamia's foot. She desperately held on with her remaining hand, but that was sliding too, the mud working its way between her and Lamia. With a final victorious tug from the mud beneath her, Eirene let go and slipped into the dark.

For a moment, she was suspended in the pitch-black, being sucked down into the foul swamp of the Underworld. Then light—blinding, burning, as bright as the stars—exploded around her. The mud recoiled—Eirene could have sworn she heard a furious hiss. And then Lamia was there, hoisting her once again from the mud, light shining from her as if she were the sun itself. The dark mud shrank back from her.

Eirene coughed convulsively; mud splattered Lamia's face.

Lamia barely reacted. "Get up!" she shouted, yanking Eirene's arms. "We need to go!"

Eirene staggered to her feet, blind with filth, still choking up great wads of black mud. She tumbled and almost fell, but instead she collided with something warm and soft and silvery. The enormous silver ram let out a huff of what could have been a greeting but was probably exasperation. He ducked his head and bent his forelegs.

"Do you want—" Eirene managed to say before she was racked with another fit of coughing.

"Get up," said Lamia, already clambering up the ram's side. She found her seat easily, then stretched her stick down to Eirene. There was no time to question it—what was the *ram* doing here? Had they ridden him into Hades? Was Hades trying to *eat* them? Eirene grabbed the end of the stick and, partly climbing, partly being dragged, made it onto the ram's back behind Lamia. He stood fluidly and Eirene almost fell off. She flung her arms around Lamia's waist and clung tight to her. Lamia was still glowing, but the light was fading. Eirene looked down to see the mud beginning to snake toward them again, winding around the ram's back legs.

"Put this on," said Lamia. She pushed something filthy and muddy into Eirene's hands. "The path is not for mortal eyes." She patted the ram's head and he began to walk toward the edge of the clearing, easily kicking off the mud that tried to pull him back.

There was something besides fear and exhaustion in Lamia's voice. Eirene pulled the knotted blindfold over her head without complaint, but she left it tied around her forehead.

"I didn't cry," said Lamia abruptly. She looked at Eirene over her shoulder, her features tight with fear. Her eyes were shadowed and dry, but they softened when they met Eirene's. "I was so scared. I didn't—I just *reacted*. The light was just *there*."

"Well, we are in Hades," said Eirene tiredly.

"I suppose," said Lamia. "But I think it's time to go. Put your blindfold on." She pulled her own—filthy and mud-soaked—up from around her neck and over her eyes.

"Or maybe, now that you know what you are, your control over your magic is different," said Eirene. "Maybe it'll be the same with the hunger. You can bite me and—"

"The *blindfold*," said Lamia as the ram strode into the trees.

"You're blindfolded! You don't know that I haven't got mine on."

"Eirene."

Eirene looked around the grove one last time, drinking in the light and the trees and the perfect little flowers and the scum that still heaved and reached out tentative fingers toward them. She shivered, leaning closer into Lamia as she pulled the blindfold down.

She did not intend to return here for a long, long time.

"We're here."

Lamia's voice broke through the haze of exhaustion that had flooded Eirene's mind. Had they been moving for hours or days or years? She couldn't have said. Time did not seem real on the path—all that Eirene had been certain of was the terrified thrum of her heart, the steady movement of the ram's body as they climbed upward, and the unwavering warmth of Lamia's body against hers,

Lamia's fingers clutched between her own.

"What?" Eirene mumbled. Her mouth was horribly dry, like she'd bitten into a raw quince.

"We're here." Lamia tried to pull her hand free of Eirene's and Eirene responded, automatically, by clamping her fingers down so hard that Lamia let out a yelp of pain. "*Eirene!* We're here. You can let go."

"Are you sure?" rasped Eirene. She had had plenty of time to think about what might happen if they became separated on the path back to the surface—whether those lost there could die and free themselves, or whether they were destined to wander in the dark forever. She shivered.

"I'm sure." Lamia's voice was gentle. "We're here." Her voice softened further. "Come and sit with me. Take the blindfold off when you're ready." She helped Eirene clamber down from the ram's back. Eirene slowly registered that there was sand beneath her feet that was slipping under her battered sandals.

There was a huff behind her and she heard the ram getting to his feet and beginning to walk away.

"Where's he going?" she asked blearily.

"Back into the cliffs," said Lamia. "I won't watch. I don't want to know how to find that place ever again. Here, sit." She led Eirene a short distance, then guided her down to the ground without letting go of her hand. Eirene settled herself and breathed slowly in and out. She waited until her heart felt steady inside her, until she could hear the distant twittering of birds and smell the sea in every inhalation. If this wasn't home, it was something like it. She was ready to face it either way.

She reached up with her free hand and pulled the blindfold off. Lamia had not lied. They really were back. They sat side by side on the beach with the cliffs behind them. The sea stretched out before them. A tear slipped down Eirene's cheek and she wiped it away with the back of her hand.

They were home. They were alive. They were free.

She looked over at Lamia. Lamia's head was tipped up to the sky, her light eyes fixed somewhere far above them. Her hair was streaked with dried mud, but it shone coppery in the light. Eirene didn't think she'd ever appreciated how truly pretty she was—the slant of her cheekbones, the curl of her lashes, the flush of her throat. The scar beneath her ear, the light marks in her lips where she'd bitten them, the irregular line of her nose where it had been broken. It was a face Eirene knew almost as well as her own now.

"Lamia," she murmured, "I know what it was. The token of love."

Lamia did not look away from the sky. "Shh, Eirene," she said distractedly. "I'm wandering in the rose garden of dawn."

Eirene followed Lamia's dreamy gaze to the sky. The sun was rising over the sea, emerging like Aphrodite from the waves. Its reflection on the water was a glowing path. If the cliffside held the entrance to the Underworld, surely this marked the ascent to Olympus.

She tried again. "Lamia."

"I know," said Lamia. "We have to go soon. Just a little longer, Eirene."

"All right." Eirene leaned into Lamia's side and felt Lamia relax back against her. Tentatively, she rested her head on Lamia's shoulder. She felt Lamia's breath stutter and settle. "I'm still going to make you bite me," she said into her hair.

Lamia jerked her head away and turned to shoot Eirene an irritated look. "Really? This again?"

"Don't I smell delicious?" asked Eirene. She shoved her upturned wrist into Lamia's face.

"You smell of *swamp*," said Lamia, wrinkling her nose.

Eirene did not withdraw her arm. "Come on," she encouraged. She felt giddy with victory. They had been to hell and back. They were *alive*. A little biting could hardly kill her now.

Lamia caught Eirene by the elbow and tried to push her away.

"Bite me!" said Eirene. "I've still got your knife handy, don't worry."

Lamia glowered. "You really want to do this?" She brushed her lips over the delicate skin of Eirene's wrist and Eirene shivered, the muscles in her belly and thighs tightening convulsively.

"Yes," she whispered. "I want to."

"Then I'm sorry," Lamia said, and bit down.

"Why are you saying—*agh*." Eirene's final word was swallowed up by her own poorly concealed grunt of pain. "Gods*dammit*, that hurt."

Lamia withdrew immediately. "I said I was sorry," she wailed. Blood dripped from her chin in a thin stream. Her pupils were huge.

Eirene shook her head, biting back another sound of pain. "Try again."

"Again?"

"You've still got control, haven't you? Again."

Lamia wiped the blood from her chin. "I don't want to hurt you."

"It isn't that bad. It's more the shock than anything. Come on." Eirene lifted her arm and pressed the bloody bite mark to Lamia's lips. "Drink."

"Eirene, I don't know . . ."

"*Please*, Lamia. I want you to come with Phoebe and me, when we leave."

"But what if—"

"*Bite me.*"

"*Fine.*"

Lamia grabbed Eirene's arm and bit down hard, her teeth cutting easily into Eirene's flesh. Eirene tensed, biting down hard on her lip to smother the gasp of pain. It really did hurt, but Lamia had walked blindly into hell for Eirene. So Eirene could bear this, couldn't she? It wasn't so bad, actually. She breathed slowly in and out, forcing herself to think of anything but the pull of Lamia's mouth against the torn flesh of her arm. The pain was already fading into a dull throbbing as Lamia's throat worked, as she drank. She had Eirene's arm in both hands now, her knuckles white as she held it in a vise grip. There was a myrtle flower caught in her hair, a single bloom that had survived the journey from the Underworld. Eirene reached out absently with her free hand to pluck it free.

Lamia jerked her head back, teeth sliding from Eirene's flesh with a wet sound.

Eirene froze. They looked at each other, both breathing heavily.

"There," said Eirene at last. "That wasn't so bad."

Lamia's pupils were enormous. She blinked rapidly. "I didn't . . . I didn't drink too much? You're all right? You don't feel faint?"

"I feel perfect," Eirene assured her. "I mean, I could probably do with a bandage." She twisted her bloody forearm. The flow of blood was already slowing, the blood darkening and clotting. On closer inspection, the little puncture marks from Lamia's teeth were not too deep. "You were holding back?"

"Yes," said Lamia, the word a hiss through her teeth. She looked away from Eirene and busied herself with tearing a strip from the bottom of her chiton.

"But you kept your control," said Eirene. "Look, I'm fine." She thrust her forearm toward Lamia.

"I'd rather you didn't do that, thank you," said Lamia. She offered Eirene a muddy strip of fabric. "Sorry, this is filthy."

Eirene grimaced. "On second thought, maybe it just needs some fresh air."

"Good idea," agreed Lamia. The torn hem of her chiton fluttered in the soft sea breeze, exposing the filthy wrappings around her leg.

"Your leg," said Eirene. "Your knee—that can't have been good for it."

"No," said Lamia succinctly. She shrugged. "But better than it would have been if we'd had to walk back too."

"We should rewrap it," said Eirene. "Rinse the bandages in the sea. The cold and the salt water might even help with any swelling."

Lamia sighed. "I suppose so."

"I can do it," offered Eirene cautiously. She remembered the last time she'd offered something similar, how Lamia had turned her down without a second's thought.

But Lamia only sighed again, closing her eyes and tilting her head back. "I'd like that."

Eirene shuffled even closer. She kept her touch gentle as she pulled the knots that held the bandages apart, tugging the sopping pieces of fabric away from each other, listening to Lamia's breath's catch each time Eirene's fingertips brushed her flesh. Eirene kept her own breathing as steady as she could as she peeled the bandages away. Lamia's knee underneath was pale and muddy. There was some swelling, but less than Eirene might have expected. She could see where the kneecap had shifted, how it sat a finger's breadth from where it should.

"I'm going to wash the bandages," Eirene said softly. "And try to rinse some of the mud out of my hair and clothes. Come with me?"

Lamia opened her eyes slowly. "You go ahead. I'll be a moment."

"All right." Eirene walked to the water's edge, then waded into the shallows. The water was cool but not cold. A cloud of silt formed around Eirene as the mud was washed from her skirts. She waded out farther, then sank into the water entirely. The sun ambled upward and the water was bright and clear. Eirene raked her hands through her hair, feeling the grime lift and disperse, then surfaced, paddling back to the shallows. She sat in the knee-deep surf and swirled Lamia's bandages through the water. Her soaking chiton stuck to her skin.

A splash told her that Lamia had joined her. Eirene looked up with a quiet smile as Lamia walked past her. She did as Eirene had—plunging herself into the water and emerging to shake sparkling droplets from her hair. Eirene stood, the bandages now clean, and Lamia trailed her back to the shore, where she'd left her stick. Eirene picked it up and gave it to her, deliberately avoiding looking at the places where Lamia's chiton clung to her. The air felt charged. "Thank you," said Lamia softly.

"Of course," said Eirene. "Can I—would you like me to rewrap your knee?"

Lamia nodded slowly, wordlessly.

Eirene knelt before Lamia and carefully began to wrap the bandages around her knee. Her hands were trembling. Lamia gasped as the cold fabric touched her skin. "Hold still," said Eirene, cupping the back of Lamia's calf. She wrapped the bandages around a final time, then knotted the ends deftly together. "There," she said, and stood up.

"Thank you," said Lamia.

Eirene said nothing; words had escaped her.

Lamia was so close, her cheeks pink, her hair wet and hanging jagged to her chin. Her lips were swollen with cold. Eirene could not look away. Something held her still. It was not like the terrible pull of the swamp, or the control of the Desire; it was something soft. Something true. Lamia exhaled, her lips parting, shaping a smile. Eirene could not help it; she leaned forward, feeling the brush of Lamia's breath on her mouth.

"Isn't this lovely?" It was a distant call in the wind, one that could almost have been imagined. Eirene stiffened and stilled. Lamia turned, still smiling. The smile fell from her face in an instant, her eyes focusing on something far above them on the cliff tops. Eirene's heart dropped. Of course this couldn't last. The ram had brought them back to the world—and now they had to face it.

"Eirene," Lamia whispered.

"Yes." Eirene tried to drink in every aspect of the moment—the closeness of their bodies, the heat of Lamia's skin, the water clinging to her brow and cheeks—wishing it did not have to end.

"Look," said Lamia simply.

Eirene looked.

A man was leaning over the cliff's edge, gazing down at them. From this far she could not see his features clearly; it could have been anyone if not for the way the new sun caught on his curls and made them shine like spun gold. If not for the coldness she could have sworn she felt emanating from him even at such a distance. If not for the way she'd known, deep in the hollows of her heart, that he would be waiting for them.

"Hello, Eirene," called Leandros. The smile she couldn't see was evident enough in his voice. "Won't you come up here and talk to me? You have something of mine. And I think I have something of yours, too." He turned to speak over his shoulder.

"Don't I, Phoebe?"

XLII

WITH SWEET HARMONY

Lamia

Lamia's father was waiting for them at the top of the cliffs, wind whipping his curls back from his face. When he saw them walking hand in hand, Lamia's father raised his arm in greeting. He looked haggard. There was no one with him but Eirene and Lamia and a small slender figure all but concealed behind his bulk. There was no sign of Peiros.

Beside Lamia, Eirene stiffened. "Phoebe," she breathed. It seemed until then that she had not truly believed that Lamia's father had her sister.

Phoebe's eyes were wide and terrified and the skirt of her chiton was torn. Lamia's father towered over her; her brown wrist was firmly clasped in his fist. He tugged sharply on her arm and she stepped out from behind him.

"Phoebe!" This time Eirene shouted. Her panic and fear were clear. Her grip on Lamia's hand was tight and clammy.

"Eirene!" Phoebe's voice was high and terrified. "Eirene, you shouldn't have come."

Lamia felt sick. She had left her father alive because some part of her still loved him, still believed that there was good in him. But perhaps there was nothing left that was not rotted and corrupted.

"Hello, Eirene," said Lamia's father in his clear, cool voice. "I have your sister. I see you have my daughter. How would you like to trade?"

"Why can't you just let her go?" Eirene's words were quiet, but the wind carried them faithfully. When they reached him, Lamia's father smiled.

"I cannot let Phoebe go, because then I'd have to let *her* go," he said, nodding toward Lamia.

Lamia froze. His first true acknowledgment of her presence, and he hadn't bothered to use her name. "And you know I can't do that."

Lamia clutched the top of her stick. "What gives you the right to keep me?" Her voice wavered but she forced herself to keep speaking. She would not allow herself to cower before him any longer. "You've lied to me all my life, but I know the truth now. You told me you wanted to keep me safe, but I don't think you can do that anymore. It's time to let me *go*."

Leandros barked out a harsh laugh and Phoebe flinched.

"My father was an immortal," he said. "And his father was an immortal, and his father before him. And *his* father was truly deathless. A god."

"You've mentioned that before," said Eirene. "Several times."

Lamia's father wasn't put off. "Eros," he concluded. "I have lied about many things over the years, my dear girl. But I have never lied about that."

"No need to," said Lamia. "Why pretend, when the truth of one's parentage is so *tantalizing*?"

"Tantalizing and *disappointing*," said her father. His face contorted. He looked vicious and wild. "My grandmothers were demigods and dryads, nymphs and naiads."

That rhymes, thought Lamia at the same time that Eirene said scornfully, "Dryads and naiads *are* nymphs."

"*They were not human*," roared Lamia's father. "But my own wretched father begot me upon some common mortal bitch."

Lamia winced at the venom in his voice.

"Oh, he said she was a warrior, he said she was worthy, but her pollution has never been welcome in *my* blood. My blood should have been ichor, I should have been a *god*."

"So you're mortal?" hissed Lamia. "So what? You're powerful, you're rich, you're still young—"

"Still young?" His laugh was near hysterical. He must have tightened his grip on Phoebe's arm because she gave a gasp, her face crumpling. "When I found you, I was dying," he hissed. "Barely forty years old and already softening, already creasing, already weakening. My heart faltering, my beauty fading—"

His beauty. Lamia wanted to laugh. *That* was what had been so important to him, important enough to keep her locked up for her whole life.

"I am dying still, I suppose. You might see my Desires, those silly party tricks, and think *that* is power. But look at me"—he spread his arms wide and bared his teeth in a wolflike grimace—"*this* is true power. With each day I grow older, but I remain as lovely as ever."

"Beauty cannot keep you alive," said Eirene. "If what is inside is rotting."

Lamia's father did not seem to hear her. "Empousa command beauty; they are creatures of seduction and illusion, and none did it so well as your poor sweet mother." He fixed his eyes on Lamia and shook his head, a smile curling at the corners of his lips. "And, of course, *you*, my dear. The descendant of monsters and gods both. You are without equal. If only I could find another empousa. If only I could *replicate* such a miracle."

"Maybe this one would finish the job my mother started and *kill you*," snarled Lamia. Still, she could not stop her mind racing ahead. What if he could find another empousa and sire another child like Lamia? Another Lamia who could grow up to kill another Alexandra? She had to stop him.

"Here I am, then," she said out loud. She had proved that she could defeat him. He may not be so trusting again, but Lamia would not be so gentle. "If I am so essential to you, then give Phoebe up. Let her leave safely with her sister." She swallowed. "Then you can have me."

"Lamia," said Eirene. "No. You *can't*."

"Trust me," Lamia said softly without looking at her. "Please, Eirene. Trust me." Her eyes were fixed on her father. *Say yes.* He had to say yes.

"Oh, dearest Lamia, *no*." Her father giggled and shook his head. His eyes were bloodshot. "No, no, no, my sweet girl. Do you think I could trust you so easily? No, you will come to *me* first. Then I will let little Phoebe go."

"Do you swear?" asked Lamia. Eirene was breathing heavily beside her.

Her father smiled at her. "I swear."

"Lamia," whispered Eirene.

"Trust me," said Lamia again. She let go of Eirene's hand. Then she squared her shoulders and walked back into the jaws of the beast, into the arms of her father.

XLIII
CLAD IN MOURNING

Eirene

"Now it's your turn," said Lamia, once she was standing at her father's side. "Let Phoebe go."

Leandros nodded slowly. His lips curled into a benevolent smile that made her blood run cold. She forced herself to remain still. When Phoebe was safe, when Phoebe was clutched in her arms, then she could run. Then she could work out how she would ever get Lamia back. But for now she had to wait. Just a little longer to wait. "Let her go," she said again. "Please."

This part of the cliffside plunged straight to the sea; Eirene could hear the waves as they crashed against the unyielding stone.

"Yes, Eirene. I will let her go."

Eirene relaxed too soon. She had just begun to smile, the smallest smile of relief, when Leandros spoke again.

"You made things very inconvenient for me, Lamia, my sweet girl, when you burned my workshop. But I'm afraid you made an oversight. You should have checked my belt, I think." He brought his hand, clenched into a fist, out from behind his back and uncurled his fingers. "Phoebe, darling," he said, "the sea is calling you." In his open palm was a neat heap of purple powder. He blew it into her face.

"*No!*" The word ripped itself from Eirene's lips. She lunged forward, stumbling as she sprinted toward Phoebe. "*Phoebe.*" Her hands just brushed the edges of Phoebe's chiton as her sister smiled widely, turned to the cliff's edge, and stepped off.

Eirene screamed. She scrambled forward, her vision lurching alarmingly. She could climb down. She could climb. She had climbed before and she would do it a thousand times over for Phoebe, for the person she loved best in the world.

But there was no rope now, nothing but the pale face of the cliff and the rocks and the treacherous, churning waters below. And Phoebe—Phoebe, Phoebe, Phoebe, Phoebe, Phoebe. It was as if she had been struck by a Gorgon's gaze—Eirene could not move, could not breathe, could not think. Phoebe was drowning. But she could do nothing but stand there, frozen and afraid and trembling and—

There came a shout of alarm, a thick flailing arm in the periphery of her vision as Leandros flung himself after Lamia.

After Lamia, who had just thrown herself from the cliff top.

XLIV
THOSE PESTILENT AND WICKED

Lamia

The fall was longer than Lamia expected. It gave her plenty of time to come to terms with the consequences of her actions and to consider the very real danger of shattering herself against the waves.

As she fell, she crossed her legs as tightly as she could and kept her eyes fixed on the horizon. Something kept her from squeezing them shut—she did not wish to go to her death blindly, perhaps—but nor did she want to see the water rushing up to meet her. It would come all the same.

And come it did.

She hit the water feet first, the impact rocketing up through her bones. It was a sharp shock. Her breath rushed out of her all at once and her ears filled with an awful crackling, crunching sound. For a moment, she could not move—she was dimly aware of being fully submerged, of floating, weightless in the water. Was she dead? She tried to open her eyes and it was such a relief when her vision filled with murky blue that she inhaled sharply. That was a mistake; she spluttered and choked her way back to the surface. Her stick was made of a light, flexible wood and it floated, guiding her way up.

Lamia coughed, expelling the freezing salty water from her lungs and blinking it from her eyes. As her vision cleared, she saw the limp body of a girl floating face up near her, her dark hair spread out around her. Even as Lamia watched, she began to sink.

Phoebe.

Lamia struggled toward her. She wasn't a good swimmer; she hardly remembered how, but some instinct guided her arms and legs. Each kick was painful. Her soaking chiton pulled her down even as her stick kept her up, but sheer determination drove her onward. The current was strong, running parallel to the looming face of the cliffs, and by the time Lamia could reach out and touch Phoebe's cheek and lift her face from the water, it had swept them both toward the beach enough that her feet could touch the sand.

She wrenched Phoebe from the water. It was bright here on the beach, lit with the dancing reflection of the sun on the sea. In the shifting light Phoebe looked so much like Eirene that it hurt. Her eyes were shut. Her skin had gained an awful grayish pallor. Her lips were ever so slightly parted.

Please be alive. Lamia cupped her hands around Phoebe's face and turned her head from side to side. Was she alive? Was she breathing? She lowered her ear to Phoebe's mouth and strained to listen over the rhythmic rush of the water as it lapped at the rocks. Seawater dripped from Lamia's hair and face onto Phoebe's.

"Please," she muttered, more to herself than to the silent, still girl beside her. She pushed gently on her chest. "Wake up. *Please.*"

Phoebe coughed weakly.

Lamia jolted in surprise, just in time to avoid Phoebe's forehead slamming into hers as Phoebe shot upward, pulled into a sitting position by the force of the convulsions that racked her body. Water poured from her mouth in a torrent as she choked and coughed and vomited. Lamia could do nothing but pull her sopping curls back from her face and wait for it to end.

After what felt like hours but which could hardly have been more than a few minutes, the convulsions subsided and Phoebe slumped against Lamia, exhausted. Some of the color had returned to her face; her cheeks were flushed.

"The—" Phoebe tried to speak but the word was little more than a croak. She tried again. "The sea. Did I make it? I have to. I have to get to the sea." She batted weakly at Lamia.

Lamia's heart stilled. Phoebe's eyes were huge, her pupils dilated. The Desire had not released its grip on her yet.

"You made it," she said quickly. "We're there. Stay still."

Phoebe shook her head. "No. I have to go." She tried to stand but she was still stunned, her eyes unfocused; Lamia could hold her easily. For now. But she would be forced to let go when her father arrived. He would have run for the water the moment Lamia pitched herself over the edge. He would not be able to let her go. Selfishly, Lamia hoped that Eirene had followed.

She pulled a tangle of seaweed from Phoebe's hair. "You don't have to."

"I *have to.*" Phoebe bared her teeth and shook her head. "The sea is calling me. I have to go!"

Eirene, thought Lamia desperately. *Help me.* But Eirene was not here. Lamia had to break the hold of the Desire somehow, but with what? She still had the myrtle root stowed safely in the pouch around her neck with the seeds she hadn't been able to bring herself to throw away. No token of love for Phoebe. Unless—

Lamia let Phoebe go abruptly. Phoebe seemed so stunned that she just sat there, blinking before lunging toward the water. But Lamia had already retrieved a handful of root and seeds from the pouch. She caught Phoebe by the edge of her chiton—then, with a yelped "*Sorry!*", by a sizable chunk of hair—and hauled her back.

"Eat this," she screamed in the terrified girl's face.

Phoebe shook her head, pressing her lips together, her eyes

wide. But if Leandros had taught Lamia anything, it was this. She pushed Phoebe to the ground and climbed on top of her, pinning Phoebe's arms to the ground with her knees. Phoebe whimpered in pain and thrashed feebly, her mouth still tightly closed. With her free hand, Lamia grabbed her nose and squeezed it shut. Phoebe's eyes widened even farther. She had the same eyes as Eirene, huge and dark and deep enough to drown in, and for a moment Lamia did not see Phoebe but Eirene, staring up at Leandros with betrayal in her gaze and blood dripping down her cheek.

Phoebe gasped for breath, her lips parting.

I am my father's daughter, thought Lamia grimly. *I do what I feel I must.* She shoved the fistful of grain and grit and tangled roots into Phoebe's mouth.

"Swallow it," she commanded. She pressed her hand over Phoebe's mouth, the other pinching her nose shut, until she saw the desperate movement of Phoebe's throat.

She let go. Phoebe went limp. She stopped fighting. Her mouth was now open and slack. She stared blankly into the sky.

"A token of love," Lamia pleaded. "Eirene spent three days sorting seeds for you. She barely slept to get it done, all so she could marry a man she hates. But she did it for you. Because you're her sister. Because she loves you."

Phoebe blinked. Her eyes flickered from side to side, then settled and focused on Lamia. They were clear. "Eirene," she rasped.

Lamia could have cried. "Yes, she's near," she said. "She's near. Do you want her? You don't want to go to the sea?"

"Eirene," protested Phoebe, but the word was even weaker than before. Her eyelids fluttered and her body sagged. She wasn't Desired anymore. But she had just fallen from a cliff, and Lamia had no idea how badly she was hurt.

"I'll bring her," promised Lamia.

Phoebe made an exhausted noise. "I'm *cold*."

Lamia had been kneeling too long; a stabbing pain shot through her knee as she shifted her position on the stones. Phoebe was cold. That was something Lamia could fix.

Her tears were not hard to come by; it was just a matter of swiping them from the back of her hands. She closed her eyes and concentrated, conjuring up the memory of burning everything she loved in her tower room. She didn't want fire, just heat. She had to be softer now. She was not trying to destroy something; she had to preserve it. Her hands grew warm and she pressed them to Phoebe's shoulders.

At first, Phoebe shivered under her touch. But as the warmth continued to build in Lamia's palms, little puffs of steam began to rise from Phoebe's clothes where she touched them, and Phoebe visibly relaxed. When Lamia ran her hands through Phoebe's curls, separating the tangled strands, Phoebe pressed her cheek into the warmth of Lamia's palm. Her eyes fluttered open and closed again. The rise and fall of her chest was steady and pronounced. Lamia couldn't help it—she smiled, pride filling her own chest. Empousa, blood-drinker, it did not seem to matter so much. She had drunk from Eirene without killing her. And now she had saved her sister.

"Phoebe?" murmured Lamia.

"Yes?"

"Stay quiet, all right? Until Eirene comes for you. You have to stay quiet. Stay down." If her father thought Phoebe was dead, maybe he would leave her.

She could hear the distant slap of running footsteps against the sand and then a shout that might have been her name. Her father, come to retrieve her at last. Lamia closed her eyes tightly, as if shutting out the world beyond might make it disappear entirely. She did not want to face her fate, face *him*. She wanted to lie down on the sand and remain there, unmoving, unreachable.

But if she stayed here, she knew her father would find her, and she needed to keep him away from Phoebe. Lamia yanked the pin from her soaking shawl and pulled it from her shoulders. She dried it as quickly and thoroughly as she could, leaving brown handprints on the pale cloth. The smell of burning wool lingered in the air even as she tucked it around Phoebe, cushioning her head and wrapping it around her face so that she looked like a swaddled infant.

"Stay quiet," she said again.

Phoebe nodded. She was still trembling, but the color had returned to her face and her eyes were alert. She wiggled into an awkward sitting position, still wrapped in Lamia's shawl.

"Lamia!" This time there was no mistaking the bellowed word.

"Whatever happens, *don't* follow me." Lamia pressed her glowing hand to Phoebe's flushed cheek once more, then hoisted herself unsteadily to her feet with her stick. Her knee screamed in protest. The rush of adrenaline she'd felt as she'd jumped, as she'd dragged Phoebe from the water, was beginning to wear off and the pain was returning. She'd done something to it, something bad, when she hit the water.

"I'm coming," she called. She coughed, tasting salt, and called out again, stronger: "I'm coming!"

"Lamia?" Her father, closer now. Lamia felt an odd thrill of pleasure at the sound of his voice. His usual composure had slipped; he was breathless from running and he was *afraid*. Breathless from running to *Lamia*. Afraid that he had lost her. It seemed it was her turn to cause him pain. How she would *relish* it. Lamia staggered toward him, her lips pulling into what might have been a smile.

"Phoebe!"

Eirene. Lamia's stumbling steps quickened. She slipped on the sand, her stick little help on its shifting surface.

"Lamia!" Eirene shouted again, her words pitched high with terror. "Where's *Phoebe*?"

Lamia kept moving, pain shooting through her with each step. *Eirene*, her heart called, filled with equal parts longing and fear. *Eirene*.

And then Eirene was there, sprinting across the sand, her hair unbound and a cloud of golden dust flying out behind her, and Lamia's father hard on her heels. There was a knife in Eirene's hand and she held it out toward him even as they both slowed to a stop.

Lamia's father's face was furious, his eyes fixed on her. Lamia couldn't understand why he had allowed Eirene to follow him. And then it hit her. He must have run out of Desire. He'd used the last of it to enchant Phoebe and now, without Lamia's stolen magic, he was all but powerless. Lamia wanted to laugh with relief. Then her eyes met Eirene's and all mirth was gone from her in an instant. Eirene looked wrecked. Desperate. Wild.

"Please," said Eirene. Her voice cracked. "Lamia, where is Phoebe? Is she—is she alive?"

Lamia swallowed and Eirene stiffened.

Lamia had to be careful now. She would not let Leandros use Phoebe, use Eirene, as tools. Not again. She looked away from Eirene and fixed her gaze on her father. "Will you let them go?" she asked him coldly. "Truly, this time?"

He understood her immediately. "Come home with me, my sweet girl, and I will never lay a hand on them again. I swear it. Just come home, where you belong."

"Try to follow her, try to stop them, and I'll escape again," she told him. "And when you catch me, I will *fight*. But if you let them go, I won't. I'll be good. I'll cry when you need me to. Just let them go." She was lying, but that didn't matter. Her father had always underestimated her.

Her father tilted his head and watched her silently for a moment. Then he nodded.

Lamia felt her shoulders sag in relief and Eirene let out a soft gasp, squeezing her eyes shut.

"Where is she?" asked Eirene, her eyes still closed, her hands clasped as if in prayer.

"She's farther down," Lamia told Eirene. "She's fine; she's safe. Keep going and you'll find her."

Eirene put a hand to her mouth, opening her eyes at last. "Thank you." But she didn't move.

"Go and get her," said Lamia.

"I trust you," said Eirene. "If you say she's safe, I believe you." She turned to Leandros. "But I can't say the same for you, so I'm staying right here."

"Lamia is coming with me," said Lamia's father with a sneer. "She doesn't need your flimsy protection."

Eirene still did not move. "You're her father. She shouldn't need protection from you."

Lamia's father let out an incredulous laugh, clutching at his chest as if this were the funniest thing he had ever heard.

The high ringing sound tugged at something inside Lamia, pulled at it again and again until it *snapped*. "Why are you laughing?"

Her father turned back to her, still amused. "What was that, Lamia?"

"Why are you *laughing*?" she repeated. "You hurt me. Me, your child. You . . . you *tortured* me for years and years, and for what? For wealth? For power?"

"To keep you safe." Her father's voice was soothing. "Wealth and power that I could use as a shield, to keep the world from you and you from the world."

Lamia made a noise that was half laugh, half sob. "The only thing I needed to be kept safe from was *you*."

Her father put his hands up. "It is agony to me that I hurt you, my sweet girl. But I had no choice. I needed your power, and your tears were the only way I could get it. I wish there was another way. I wish I'd had another choice."

He made it sound so simple, so logical. But he wasn't telling the truth. The magic wasn't just in her tears; it flowed through her veins. It was part of her. It *was* her. If he'd just *asked* her, she might have helped him. As if responding to her acknowledgment, her power roared in her ears—a cacophony of voices that clamored for her to release them at last. *We are here*, they whispered to her. *We are yours to command.*

"You could have found another way," said Lamia quietly.

"I know, I know." Her father took a step closer. There was no remorse, no *anything* in his voice now but a sort of smug condescension. "And I will, my sweet girl. Just come home with me, and everything will be well." He opened his arms and reached for her.

Before he could enclose her in an embrace, Lamia recoiled. She thrust out a hand and caught him by the wrist, squeezing her fingers tight into his golden flesh.

"You're a liar," she hissed.

He tried to pull away but her grip was like iron. She could feel his tendons working furiously beneath her fingers. She pulled him closer. "You're not just a liar. You're a lie. Your whole life is a farce, a mask you don to conceal what you truly are. And that mask is made of *my magic*. You used me. *You tried to destroy me.*"

"Lamia." He raised his free hand in a gesture of placation. "My Lamia, my sweet little girl—" His eyes slid past her and landed on something beyond her. "Eirene," he said, "she listens to you. You heard her promise. She's mine—"

But Lamia barely heard him. She was beyond placation. She was beyond humanity. "*No*," she snarled. "*I am not yours. None of me is yours.* You lied to me; you manipulated me. You made me a monster. You hurt me and you took my power."

Her whole body was shaking, burning. Where there had once been magic there was now an inferno. Flames danced through her veins with each frantic pulse of her hurt; her blood was made of fire, and it was turning her to ash from the inside out. It *hurt*. She could not keep it in any longer.

She gritted her teeth and forced the words out. "Give. It. Back."

Then Lamia threw her head back and the fire within her burst free.

XLV
FIRE AND ARROWS

Eirene

Eirene had never seen a god, but if she had not known that it was Lamia who stood before her, she might have believed herself in the presence of one now.

Lamia was glowing. Like a star, like the sun, like the most radiant creature there was and ever had been. With every passing moment, she seemed to become more dazzling: her skin pearlescent, her shimmering face tilted back to the sky, and her hair . . . her *hair*. It had come alive, as if she were underwater, and it surrounded her face in a swirling torrent of copper, burning brighter and brighter and brighter until it was like looking into an open flame.

With a yell of effort, Leandros tore himself free from her and stumbled back, almost tripping over himself in his effort to distance himself from his daughter. From the monster he had created. "*Lamia*," he bellowed. "*Stop*."

Lamia swayed where she stood. The light steadied.

"Lamia!" said Leandros again. "I know you're angry, but just *think*. Don't do something you'll regret. Think of what we can accomplish together, what our magic can do. We could have the world in the palm of our hands."

Lamia made a low animal noise.

Eirene recognized it. *Pain.*

She could not explain it, but she knew what was coming.

Lamia made the terrible sound again, her body contorted around it, and then suddenly she was snapping upright again, her eyes flying open, her teeth bared. "*Our* magic?" she howled. "It was never ours. It was never yours. *It's mine.*" As the words tore free from her throat, she thrust her shining hands outward and a beam of light burst free of her skin. Leandros barely had time to raise his arms in a futile attempt to shield himself. The light struck him like a thunderbolt and flung him into the air.

Then it broke him.

His golden hair was burned away in an instant along with the illusion he had so carefully maintained for so many years. He was just like the apricots he'd tricked Eirene into eating: shining golden flesh with a putrid core hidden just below the surface. But Lamia's light destroyed the deception entirely.

Leandros was a living corpse. His skin was like strips of blackened leather; his features seemed to melt from his bones. His nose was gone, and one of his eyes was nothing but a ball of putrid dripping pulp. *His beautiful eyes.* None of it real. The eye that remained was clouded, the blue fogged and flattened. It rolled wildly, looking everywhere but at Lamia and the divine, monstrous power pouring from her in an endless river. His hands were bent into rheumatoid claws, yellowish bones showing where the flesh had worn away entirely. Half his teeth were gone; those that remained were blackened stubs. Eirene could see his heart—an awful wizened thing stuttering behind brittle ribs.

He opened his mouth to speak and his tongue was a revolting slug guarding the entrance to his shattered throat. He made a noise, a cry of anguish and rage. It was not a human sound, nor even an animal one. It was the cry of a Titan, of a giant, of any monster that dared to challenge Olympus, the cry of a broken soldier as he was struck down for eternity by the divine strength of the gods.

Lamia was screaming too. More light blazed from her—not just from her hands, but from her chest and her lips and her eyes—a relentless torrent that was so fierce and bright that Eirene could not watch. She averted her gaze, her vision burning with streaks of white. She squeezed her eyes shut, but the picture seemed to have branded itself in her mind. Lamia, the daughter of an empousa. Her hair blazed, her brass foot was braced against the uneven ground; she was a monster and she was the most beautiful thing Eirene had ever seen.

And Eirene had to stop her. "Lamia," Eirene screamed. "Lamia, you *can't. Stop*."

The light went on, burning red against her closed eyelids. Eirene stepped forward blindly, hands outstretched, searching for Lamia. She wanted Leandros dead, they both did, but it could not be like this. Her reaching fingertips brushed fabric, then sweaty, feverish skin.

Eirene grabbed Lamia, catching her by the arm and shaking her hard, even as the light pouring from Lamia stung her eyes through her closed lids and burned her hands. "Lamia, you have to stop," she bellowed. "You can't kill him. He's your father, Lamia, your blood. The gods will punish you." She gave Lamia's arm another desperate tug. She could smell burning hair—for a moment, she was slammed back into the memory of Lamia's tower room, a flickering brazier, locks of copper hair falling into ash, a glittering fog that sent everything spiraling. She returned to the present just as abruptly, with a surge of pain through her fingertips. She had to let go. She couldn't let go. "*You have to stop*."

At last, at last, the light flickered. The heat subsided. Eirene opened her eyes to narrow slits, peering past her lashes in time to see Lamia stumble, the last of the light sputtering out as her legs gave way. Eirene lunged for her and caught her before she could crumple to the ground.

Beyond her, without anyone to catch him, Leandros fell.

Lamia said something.

Eirene leaned closer. "What is it?"

"Is he dead yet?" croaked Lamia. Her hair was still faintly smoldering, glowing like embers. "Did I kill him?"

Eirene shook her head. "I don't think so." She could hear his ragged breath. Lamia must have pulled back just in time.

"No, no, I killed him. My own father. He's dead, his blood is on my hands, and now the Furies will hunt me until I'm dead too." Despite the horror of her words, her voice was clear and level. Her eyes held a distant, haunted look that Eirene didn't recognize. "How long will it be before they come?"

"He's not dead yet," insisted Eirene. "Your hands are clean. Just let me go and I'll see." She laid her hand over Lamia's, the one that gripped her forearm in a painful vise, and gently pulled at her fingers. "He's alive. I'll see. You can let me go."

Lamia shook her head. "He has to die. He has to."

"I know," said Eirene. "But you cannot do it. Will you—will you let me?"

Lamia blinked. Then she smiled, a little more of the Lamia that Eirene recognized returning to her eyes. "Would you let him live? If I asked you?"

"I . . . probably not," admitted Eirene.

"Good," said Lamia. She let go.

Eirene sprang to her feet. Lamia's father was still alive, but he might not be for long, and Eirene had to make sure the final blow that struck him was not Lamia's.

She ran to Leandros. Or at least, what was left of Leandros.

He had shrunk in on himself—burned and melted and deflated but somehow clinging onto life with the determination he had saved before for ruining everyone else's.

"Hello, Leandros," Eirene breathed.

He made a pitiful gurgling sound as she lowered herself to the sand beside him. He smelled as Eirene imagined a battlefield might—of rot and blood and smoke. His remaining eye rolled horribly as he tried to look at her. There was nothing left now of the sleek smug creature that had once seemed so untouchable, who had smiled at her and been painfully lovely even as he blew Desire into her face. His ruined mouth shaped a word that might have been "please."

"Lamia loved you," Eirene said to him quietly. She drew her knife from her belt and pressed it to his putrid flesh, where she could just make out the pitiful stutter of his heart. "And you hurt her anyway. She spared you before, but you forced her hand. She never wanted it to come to this."

He made another of those helpless sounds.

"All you had to do was love her and you didn't." She leaned in closer, bringing her mouth to a pinkish lump of flesh that might have once been his ear. "But I did. I do."

She drove her knife into his chest.

Leandros died like a smothered lamp: quickly, with a trail of smoke. When Eirene turned back to Lamia, she found her sitting up. The fire had receded entirely from her hair; it fell around her face in a coppery tangle. Eirene left the knife inside Leandros and returned to her.

She knelt before her. "Lamia," she said softly.

Lamia kept her head down. "Is it done?"

Eirene looked over at the smoldering remnants of Leandros. "It's done." She reached out, putting a hand to Lamia's jaw and tilting her chin up. Lamia offered no resistance, but when her eyes lifted to meet Eirene's, they were full of anguish. "It's done," said Eirene again.

Lamia shook her head, pressing her cheek against the curve of Eirene's palm. Her skin still had a faint shine to it, the glowing embers of an extinguished fire. "I loved him," she said. "Despite it all, I did. He was my father. But I'm still glad he's dead."

Anything Eirene could think to say was probably wrong. She could only say what was true, speak aloud the feelings that had unfurled within her like a flower, growing brighter and stronger with each second she spent in Lamia's presence. Yes, she was smeared with ash, her nose was still crooked, she was filthy, her nails were broken and ragged, her skin still clung close to her bones, and she did have that unfortunate habit of biting people and drinking their blood. Eirene still had the holes in her arm. But that did not take away from the fact that Lamia's eyes were huge and shining and framed with wispy lashes and Eirene could not look away from them.

"I love you," she said.

"Eirene," said Lamia gently, "I'm not sure this is the time for that."

Eirene's stomach twisted. "Oh," she said. Had she been wrong about the myrtle, about the token of love? Had she been too presumptuous to think that Lamia might feel the same way she did?

"I love you too, obviously," said Lamia. "I only meant—well, we just murdered my father. And I must look awful."

Eirene laughed: part relief, part joy. "You are more beautiful than the dawn," she said. "And I know which I would rather wake to." Then she tilted Lamia's chin up, leaned in, and kissed her.

XLVI
THE FROTH OF THE WAVES

Lamia

As the euphoria wore off and the last of the magic trickled from Lamia's fingertips in tiny bursts of light, the pain returned. The madcap jump from the cliff top had made its mark; her bones felt strangely brittle and bruises marked the length of her shin. Her throat was still burning, like she'd inhaled hot ash.

But none of it mattered because she was kissing Eirene. Because Eirene was kissing *her*.

Eirene's touch was tender beneath Lamia's jaw, lifting her face, angling her mouth so that they might press together even closer.

Eirene's lips fitted so perfectly between Lamia's that they could have been fashioned for this purpose alone. Was this what Pygmalion had felt the first time he pressed himself to Galatea? Had Eirene's body always been fated to arch into Lamia's, her hair to fall into Lamia's face, her eyelashes to brush Lamia's cheek, and her warm breath to be drawn into Lamia's mouth? Surely the gods, the Fates themselves, had been guiding the two of them together with this moment in mind.

"Lamia?" whispered Eirene against Lamia's mouth, the gentlest question imaginable. She began to pull away. "Is this . . . ?"

Lamia made a sound in the back of her throat, a sound she had not known she was capable of making. "Yes," she hissed, and it was her turn to cup Eirene's face, to pull her as close as she dared and then closer.

Eventually, she had to break away. She'd been forgetting to breathe.

Eirene looked up at her. Her eyes were hazy with desire—not Leandros's awful twisted Desire but something so real that the sight of it sent another wave of heat through Lamia. Eirene's gaze sharpened as she fixed it upon something a little ways down the beach.

"Phoebe," she said, "you could have turned around, at least."

Lamia craned to look over her shoulder at Eirene's sister.

Phoebe looked mortified. "Sorry!" she squeaked. "I was waiting for you to be done so we could go home."

Eirene laughed. The sound was like honey—rich and thick and sweet. Lamia could have lived on that sound alone for a century.

"We can go home," she called, and even though Lamia had no idea what home meant anymore, her heart still leaped at the thought of it. She did not know where they would go or what money they would use or what Eirene's cousin, or indeed the rest of the island, would have to say about it. Home could be anything, anywhere, as long as Eirene was there with her.

As if hearing her thoughts, Eirene turned her attention back to Lamia, her lips curling. The look on her face made Lamia grateful she hadn't stood up yet. Her legs would certainly have given out.

Eirene's dark eyes flashed and the corners of her mouth tilted up. It took all Lamia's self-control not to grab her face and pull her in and kiss her again until they were both breathless and disheveled.

Eirene's next words were just for them. She leaned in to whisper against Lamia's ear. "We can go home . . . ," she said again, "but we certainly aren't done."

EPILOGUE

The house at the end of the village was not a large one, but it seemed to suit its occupants just fine.

They were remarked upon often, the three of them, though they had learned to pay it little mind. People wondered at all sorts of things, after all, though they wondered most often at the tall willowy girl with her long red hair and sun-flushed skin. They said she must have been a nymph, that she must have some kind of magic, for they could not keep their eyes from her and they could not understand it. Not when her nose was crooked and her eyes were an unremarkable brown and, anyway, they were only ever fixed on one thing: the short stocky girl with her square jaw and her bullish stance and the shiny black curls that she never let grow to her shoulders. They said that was the girl who'd found a cure for the strange sickness that had spread among the young wives of the rich men. Gone were the vacant eyes, the bewildered repeated words. She'd not managed to cure their sudden hatred for their husbands, though, and one way or another they all seemed to have returned to the arms of their mothers and their places behind their market stalls.

Then there was the weaver, her infrequent works as beautiful as her face. When they saw her, walking arm in arm with one of her returned friends, they murmured of how the hollows of her body were disappearing with each passing season, her cheeks turning rosy now that she worked only for pleasure, only for the hours she wished.

The townsfolk whispered that they *could* have afforded a far grander residence, but they never seemed to want anything more than what they had. The long low building with its large square windows and neat little garden was theirs and that, it seemed, was enough.

"What a funny house to choose," remarked the baker's girl to her sister one morning, as they strolled by the house, their arms entwined. The sun had not yet risen but there was bread to be shaped and rolled and baked before the rest of the village awoke. "It does not have a single staircase, you know."

She was overheard by the girl with the dark hair—dark eyes, too, and dark brows and a dark humor in the curve of her mouth— and this girl turned to her own companion and laughed. They were standing side by side at the window of the house, heads tilted together and toward the hillside, where the first fingers of light were reaching for the sky. Behind them hung a tapestry—a girl dancing in the shallows of the sea, her arms outstretched and her head tilted back. An enormous spotted cat was curled up beneath the tapestry, her head on her paws, feathers stuck to her mouth. Her tail flicked lazily back and forth. "They think we do not have enough," said the girl at the window, who might have been the girl in the tapestry. "What do you think, Lamia?"

Lamia tucked a coppery strand of hair behind her ear and smiled as she adjusted her grip on the neat olivewood cane in her other hand. Her fingers were stained with ink, dusted with charcoal. Her smile was radiant. "What do I think, Eirene?" She caught

Eirene's hand in her own and brought it to her mouth. A press of lips against the inside of a wrist. An innocent gesture—perhaps. "I think I have everything I want."

Dawn came, a rose unfurling across the skies.

ACKNOWLEDGMENTS

I went into writing *Gentlest of Wild Things* armed with the knowledge that most writers have a terrible time writing their second books, and the naive belief that I would be different. It probably goes without saying that I was wrong; the sophomore slump hit me full force. It is due to the dedication, love, and support of many, *many* people that we finally got here, to the incredibly beautiful, incredibly shiny, incredibly pink book you're holding in your hands now.

Thank you first to my incredible agent, Catherine Cho. There is no one kinder, more measured, more insightful, or more ruthless, and I am so unbelievably lucky to be represented by you. Thank you also to all the coagents representing *Gentlest of Wild Things* in the international markets: Maria Duerig, Marie Arendt, and Annelie Geissler at Mohrbooks; Claire Sabatiegarat, Cristiana Chiumenti, and Elisa Beretta at the Italian Literary Agency; Jeanine Langenberg, Marit Versantvoort, Rik Kleuver, Vera Bank, Paul Sebes, and Lester Hekking at Sebes and Bisseling; Catherine LaPautre at Agence LaPautre; Ania Walczak, Dominika Bojanowska, Beata Glinska, and Agnieszka Zawistowska at ANA Warsaw, Txell Torrent, Mònica Martin, Aida Tarragona, Clara Mateo, and Cristina Auladell at MB Agencia; Amy Marie Spangler at Anatolia Lit; Judit Hermann at ANA Hungary; Jitka Nemeckova at ANA Prague; Andreea Focsaneanu and Simona Kessler at Simona Kessler Agency; Ken Mori at Tuttle Mori; Danny Hong at

Danny Hong Agency; and Gray Tan at Grayhawk Agency.

I have found the best of homes with Electric Monkey. Sarah Levison, you are the most wonderful editor I could have asked for. I love our little lunches and our frantic cover-copy email chains, and I especially love how you can always see right to the heart of a story and help me make it beat even harder. I am so thrilled we'll be working together for many more years. Thank you for everything. Also to Lindsey Heaven, Cally Poplak, Lucy Courteney, Aleena Hasan, Charlotte Cooper, Brogan Furey, Ingrid Gilmore, Emily Sommerfield, Sophie Porteous, Olivia Carson, and everyone else at Electric Monkey who has worked so hard on *Gentlest of Wild Things*, and who always makes me feel so supported, so valued, and just a little bit like a rock star. Thank you especially to Hannah Penny, total hero, for all your work on publicity and events. Thank you to Susila Baybars and Jennie Roman for catching all my typos and very kindly pointing out the turns of phrase I repeatedly misuse. You do Herculean work. Also Rebecca Fortuin, audiobook god, and whichever brilliant actors you end up casting for this one.

Thank you to my *three* editors at HarperTeen this time around. Stephanie Stein, Emilia Rhodes, and Kristin Rens: you are all so brilliant and I am so grateful for all the time and work you put in to *Gentlest of Wild Things*. Thank you also to Jessica Berg, Gwen Morton, Annabelle Sinoff, Trish McGinley, Michael D'Angelo, Taylan Salvati, Patty Rosati and the school and library marketing team, Kerry Moynagh, Kathy Faber, Jen Wygand, and the rest of the sales team. Also, Sophie Schmidt: I miss you.

A huge thank-you to my authenticity reader, Ennis Rook Bashe, for their insight and feedback on the representation of physical disability in *Gentlest of Wild Things*, which strengthened this story and its characters in every aspect. Any remaining errors are my own.

Thank you to the supremely talented Micaela Alcaino for another absolute banger of a cover; to Lolloco for the most beautiful art of Eirene, Lamia, Daphne, and the ram; and to Olivia Adams, Corina Lupp, and Alison Donalty for all their magic on the *Gentlest of Wild Things* interiors and exteriors. I am so lucky to get to work with the best book designers in the biz.

I am unbelievably fortunate to have stumbled into the best of friendships so early in my writing journey. Thank you to my first ever writer friend, Isa Agajanian. I cannot believe it has been five years since we met. I swear that your brilliance grows every day; it is a pleasure and a privilege to watch you soar. Thank you also to Marisa Salvia and Ania Poranek, and the rising tide that is our little critique partner trio. I can't wait to see what we do next. To Zohra Nabi: you are as talented as you are kind and generous, and your insight and brilliance transformed this book. I am so lucky to be your friend. To Grace D. Li: flying across the world is worth it if I get to see you. This book finally came together in your kitchen in Pearland, over boba and wheat tea and more blueberries than is polite to talk about. I am a better writer with you and because of you. Thank you also and always to Rebecca Mix: you and Grace changed my life when you picked me to be your Pitch Wars mentee and I will be grateful forever.

Thank you to all the London writers who have been the kindest and most supportive community for the last four years, especially Bea Fitzgerald, Natasha Hastings, Ella McLeod, Aleema Omotoni, Lizzie Huxley-Jones, Kat Dunn, Kate Dylan, Kika Hatzopoulou, Saara El-Arifi, Tori Bovalino, Samantha Shannon, and Tasha Suri. Also Rebecca Kuang, who is here so often that she might as well be one of us. Thank you to Lyssa Mia Smith, Amélie Wen Zhao, Jamie Pacton, Pascale Lacelle, and Vanessa Len for being the sweetest and most talented friends and for saying such kind things about *Gentlest of Wild Things*.

There are too many other people to thank, so here are the highlights: Lauren, Rosie, George, Juli, Maddy, Annabelle, Gabe, and Clovis; Cherizza, David, Sophie, and Daisy; Amar, Andrew, Emily, Ric, the Rosses, and the Dyers; my PT Mia, who worked very hard to undo the damage I did to myself by writing from my bed curled up like a prawn; Jemma, Kendall, Emma, Jas, Ellie B, Ellie T, Clara, Harveen, Taz, and Alex. Thank you also to Eva Morris, Lara Chammas, and rest of the group at Oxford. I am so glad I never gave up the day job.

My family gave me everything I have and made me everything I am. To mum, dad, Nat, Hel, and Balaj: I could not have picked better people to be obligated to hang out with forever.

And to my fiancé, James: I am happiest when you're with me; I miss you when you're away; I love you all the time.